You Were Made to Be Mine

She realized she was trembling. She curled her hands into his shirt and reflexively clung, and tipped her head against him, careful not to press against his poor sore side. She felt the cold button of his waistcoat and the swift, hard thump of his heart against her cheek.

His arms at once tightened around her and when he pulled in a long slow breath, then released it at length, his body moved against hers, like a tide rolling out again. He'd sighed like a man who had waited a lifetime for precisely this moment.

Here she was enclosed in a man's arms. And yet this one was safety. She knew if she wanted him to let her go, he would.

She never, never wanted him to release her.

He stroked her hair, once, twice, softly. Then stopped abruptly, as he seemed to realize what he was doing. He loosened his arms, until she was held in the circle of them as delicately as an egg. As if she were breakable and precious and he feared hurting her.

Also by Julie Anne Long

After Dark with the Duke
I'm Only Wicked with You
Angel in a Devil's Arms
Lady Derring Takes a Lover

The First Time at Firelight Falls
Dirty Dancing at Devil's Leap
Wild at Whiskey Creek
Hot in Hellcat Canyon

The Legend of Lyon Redmond
It Started with a Scandal
Between the Devil and Ian Eversea
It Happened One Midnight
A Notorious Countess Confesses
How the Marquess Was Won
What I Did for a Duke
I Kissed an Earl
Since the Surrender
Like No Other Lover
The Perils of Pleasure

Julie Anne Long

You Were Made to Be Mine

The Palace of Rogues

AVONBOOKS

An Imprint of HarperCollins*Publishers*

This is a work of fiction. Names, characters, places, and incidents are products of the author's imagination or are used fictitiously and are not to be construed as real. Any resemblance to actual events, locales, organizations, or persons, living or dead, is entirely coincidental.

First Avon Books mass market printing: June 2022

Print Edition ISBN: 978-0-06-304510-1
Digital Edition ISBN: 978-0-06-304418-0

Cover design by Guido Caroti
Cover Illustration by Kirk DouPonce, Fiction-Artist.com
Cover images © iStock/Getty Images; © Shutterstock

FIRST EDITION

22 23 24 25 26 BVGM 10 9 8 7 6 5 4 3 2 1

For JQ, for your extraordinary kindness and generosity.
So grateful to have a champion like you.

Acknowledgments

MY GRATITUDE to my splendid editor, May Chen, and to all the hardworking, talented people at Avon; my stalwart agent, Steve Axelrod, and his amazing staff; and to all the delightful readers who share their love of my books with their friends and fellow romance lovers: what a gift it is to know my words bring you joy. I feel so astonishingly fortunate to have such a lovely cheering section.

Chapter One

Paris, 1820

HAWKES HELD a smoldering cheroot in one hand and the miniature of the Earl of Brundage's missing fiancée in the other.

He saw a pale oval face nimbused in dark curls. Light eyes. Head coyly tipped. She could be any pretty girl anywhere. He'd never once seen a miniature of a homely girl, or, say, of one scowling and shaking her fist, which would have at least made for a change. It could probably be ascribed to the tyranny of commerce—no artist wanted to risk offending a paying customer with accuracy. No one knew better than Hawkes that the biggest lie people tell themselves is that they prefer to know the truth.

"I would like you to do that . . . thing you do so well," Brundage had said when he'd handed it to him.

Hawkes knew the unspoken word was "filthy."

"It was painted when Aurelie was sixteen, I'm told," Brundage said. "She is now twenty-one. She of course looks considerably more mature now. But I fear it's the only one in existence."

"I imagine commissioning larger portraits was not among her remaining family's priorities," Hawkes said absently. The orgy of aristocrat killing known as the

French Revolution had divested the girl's parents—members of the Condé family of the French House of Bourbon—of their fortunes and their heads when she was three years old. She'd been in the care of a guardian since. Somehow she'd wound up engaged to Brundage.

Lucky, lucky girl.

The wedding was meant to be a month from now here in Paris, or so Brundage had just told him. And yet Lady Aurelie, who he'd learned lived a stone's throw away in rented lodgings with her guardian, failed to turn up for Tuesday tea as had been her custom with Brundage and hadn't been seen since. That was four days ago.

Hawkes didn't lift his head from her miniature just yet. The glints in the anteroom in which they sat—glaze on porcelain, gilt on chair legs, the silvered surface of an outlandishly large mirror—were like the stars one sees after a blow to the head. He'd been released from prison less than a week ago. He somehow hadn't fully anticipated the sensory assault of freedom.

He'd received Brundage's message two days ago: "I need your help, and will pay handsomely for it."

Brundage must have weighed all of his options and concluded only Hawkes could do what he needed done. And Hawkes knew that meant Brundage must be desperate, indeed.

The opportunity to witness this desperation was what finally made Hawkes agree to meet him.

The heat thrown off by the huge fire eased the ache in his shoulder. This perversely filled him with a quiet, subterranean fury. That ache was a souvenir of the only time he'd been unable to fight back. Which was the only way anyone had ever gotten the better of him.

He would rather endure another three years in prison than reveal any weakness to the man in front of him. Brundage, he was certain, would love to see evidence of a broken man.

"I was, of course, going to have her sit for a portrait once we were married," Brundage said.

Brundage had always been fond of the words "I" and "my." He liked to own; he liked to lord.

Hawkes looked up, finally. "The mirror is new, isn't it?" he said idly. "I don't remember seeing it in your office or home."

Brundage smiled sympathetically. "I imagine it would seem new to you. I acquired it last year."

"Handsome piece," Hawkes said admiringly. "Must have cost the earth."

Brundage hesitated, as he'd been compelled to do after nearly everything Hawkes had said so far this evening.

"Playing deep again?" Hawkes suggested into the silence with a sympathetic smile, on a bit of a hush, to imply he was jesting.

He wasn't. It had been a secret—from everyone except Hawkes, from whom almost nothing was a secret—that the upright Brundage recklessly wagered staggering amounts, amassing staggering unpaid debts.

Debt which had magically disappeared before the war was over. Another secret Hawkes had learned.

Brundage's smile was small and did not reach his eyes. "I've been fortunate in my investments, thanks to good advice from my accounting firm."

"Well. You always did know how to increase your fortunes," Hawkes agreed warmly.

Which caused another almost infinitesimal silence.

Hawkes had so far spent the evening making casual statements that could be interpreted any number of ways, all of them calculated to unsettle Brundage.

Hawkes was nearly destitute. He'd been obliged to surrender the entirety of his own hard-won fortune to French authorities before he went to prison—it was either that, or face execution by firing squad. After all, "justice" was really another word for commerce, something every man at the mercy of it eventually learns. Brundage himself had skillfully negotiated these terms.

It was, in fact, the generally held view that Hawkes owed Brundage his life.

Alas, Hawkes was unable to buy his way out of prison altogether, and the French rebuffed formal attempts to ransom him. It seemed it wasn't every day they caught a near legendary English spymaster. They wanted to keep him for a few years. Perhaps beat him now and again for his temerity.

Verdun, the prison depot where he was at first taken, had been just barely tolerable, verging on civilized.

Bitche, where he'd been taken after an escape attempt, was a violent, soul-annihilating fortress.

Brundage had proposed to pay him three-quarters of the fortune he'd lost if he found his fiancée.

So he also suspected the immense sum Brundage was offering to pay him to find his fiancée was intended to forever put paid to certain things.

Such as suspicion. Curiosity. Initiative. Memory.

Reflected in that ridiculous mirror in flattering firelight, the two of them looked much the way they had before Hawkes's arrest: the Fifth Earl of Brundage and Mr. Christian Hawkes—*such* a dashing pair. Both so handsome, so brilliant, so competent.

But Hawkes, the son of a merchant, had begun his career in the army blacking the boots of men much like Brundage. He'd swiftly soared to the rank of lieutenant, whereupon he was recruited by the Alien Office in England and charged with tracking down and arresting poisonous little cadres of would-be revolutionaries and recruiting agents and informers, in the process honing some of the filthier tools of his trade—deceit and subterfuge and pantomime, bribery and brutality and blackmail—as well as the more prosaic ones, like managing vast budgets and unpredictable humans. Such were his gifts and triumphs that during the war the home secretary sent him to Switzerland and to Spain, under the guise of serving as chargé d'affaires for the Earl of Brundage, who'd been appointed ambassador to Spain. In actuality, to do what he'd already done in England: establish and oversee a vast mesh of intelligence sources—agents, informers, provocateurs—in support of efforts to quash Bonaparte.

And if initially Brundage occasionally failed to disguise that he viewed Hawkes's work as distasteful, if necessary, and considered him little more than a peasant shellacked in exquisite manners, it was of no consequence to Hawkes. And if Hawkes's patience once or twice frayed to such transparency that Brundage glimpsed how Hawkes saw him—pompous, scarcely adequate at his job, someone to be tolerated, rather than revered—they were both, by nature, diplomats. Their interactions were garnished with civility and humor. Brundage was secure in his supremacy afforded by his ancient title, position, and fine looks.

Until the evening the earl first entered a ballroom alongside Hawkes, and feminine eyes lit on both.

But it was to Hawkes they returned.

And it was on Hawkes they remained.

Things were different between them from then on.

Brundage was nearly invisible when Hawkes was in the room. There was nothing the earl could do about the way Hawkes infiltrated imaginations. His charm was like contraband whiskey: potent, addictive, sometimes scathing, a subversive pleasure. When he laughed, his crystalline blue eyes lit like the sun breaking through clouds. When he was furious, he could freeze a man's gizzards with a single glance. His successes were lauded in newspapers in London. The word "hero" was bandied about. His failures were few, and confidential.

And while Hawkes's morals could fairly be said to be flexible and situational, they were wrapped around an unshakably honorable core. Everything he did was in the name of service to his country.

If he'd been less of a gentleman, or possessed of less hubris, he might have realized before it was too late that Brundage's handsome, noble skin was, in fact, stretched over a core of pure rot.

Brundage was heavier and ruddier now. Hawkes was thinner. His prison pallor emphasized the hard, elegant facets of his face and shadows haunted hollows beneath his cheekbones. His coat fit him just a little too loosely. This, absurdly, maddened him. He'd always been so meticulous about his tailoring.

"Has Lady Aurelie any family still alive? Friends she might be inclined to visit?" he asked.

"Her oldest brother, Louis, died over a decade ago. One brother—Edouard—emigrated to Boston some years back. The Bourbons might be on the throne once again, but she was raised quite apart from any French relatives and as of now they are still strangers to her—

she has only lately lived in Paris. Her guardian is currently on his wedding journey in Spain and planned to return to Paris for our nuptials, as it was assumed we would live here for a time. He was overjoyed at our engagement."

Pleased that he would finally be shed of his duty to his ward, Hawkes thought. From the sound of things. Though he could be commended, of a certainty, for taking in three children.

"And I believe you are already acquainted with her guardian, Hawkes. Jacques Le Clerc. He was the chargé d'affaires for the Spanish ambassador."

"Yes. Of course. I remember Le Clerc. I in fact attended a few assemblies at his residence in Spain when I worked for the Home Office."

Odd to think of the missing girl being somewhere present while he was there, charming guests, mining for secrets. A pity he couldn't go back in time to warn her about Brundage.

"Does Lady Aurelie have any distinctive mannerisms or distinguishing physical characteristics not evident in this miniature?" Her likeness was still cupped in the palm of his hand. "Freckles, a limp, a hump, dimples, crooked or missing teeth? Is she a great strapping lass, a wee thing?"

Brundage eyed him sardonically. "She has all of her teeth, and they are the proverbial pearls. She has, er, lovely brown hair and blue eyes. Not like . . . yours." He made the word "yours" sound vaguely disturbing. "A darker blue. Lots of . . ." he cleared his throat ". . . fetching black lashes."

Hawkes had produced a little pencil and a scrap of paper from inside his coat. ". . . not . . . like . . . mine . . ." he murmured, as he wrote.

"And she's not a slip of a girl—her head reaches

to about here." Brundage laid the blade of his hand against his throat, just beneath his handsome square chin, which gleamed like that vast mirror from a fresh shave.

Hawkes bent his head over his foolscap. "So that means she'll reach to about . . . here," Hawkes said, absently, applying the blade of his own hand against his collarbone, and pretended to take a note, ". . . on me."

He was savoring being a bastard the way he was savoring the cheroot. More than all of the other things that Brundage resented about Hawkes—which was everything—his two inches of superior height probably chafed the most.

Suddenly Brundage leaned so abruptly forward Hawkes held his breath. "Do you remember Therese d'Artois?"

Every muscle in Hawkes's body tensed with the effort not to rear backward.

"How can one forget Therese d'Artois?" Hawkes mimicked Brundage's confiding hush.

"Aurelie's mouth. Reminds me of hers. It . . . rather inflames a man's imagination."

"Ah." Hawkes's smile was small and taut.

He did not want to imagine any part of Brundage inflamed.

Therese d'Artois had been a courtesan living in Spain. Brundage had tried and failed to maneuver her into his bed. She'd invited Hawkes into hers a few times, and only a dead man would decline that invitation.

He supposed Therese might still be a courtesan. Only three years had passed.

Prison played hell with time, if one let it: telescoped it, froze it, dissolved the boundaries between moments until they pooled like hot candle wax. He'd used the long days and nights in his cell to reconstruct the average day of his life, from the moment he woke, in terms of colors and senses, recalling moments as though they were jewels he'd hoarded. The minute changes of color and light in the sky as the sun rose and then fell, from nacre to that black purple of midnight. The scrape of a perfectly sharp straight razor against his soapy jaw. The trickle of coffee into a fine china cup, the chime of a spoon against its side stirring in the sugar.

The satiny heft of a woman's breasts in his palms, her hot breath gusting in the crook of his neck when he moved in her.

Sounds and sensations and sequences.

He'd tried pain, too, as a means to distract: he remembered every stab of the needle that had driven the ink of his tattoo—a dagger beneath his arm—into his skin.

These things were the counterpoint to another indelible sequence of events that had occurred prior to his arrest. If he'd dwelt upon them in prison, he would have gone mad. But they beat inside him like a second heart. Like ceaseless drums of war.

Ironically, it had begun with glinting objects in Brundage's residence.

The subtle proliferation of things like vases and silver waistcoat buttons. A rumor that Brundage's gambling debts had been repaid. A mysterious charity listed in Brundage's budget books called the Society for the Relief of English Prisoners of War, which swelled and shrank about the same time. General Blackmore's—now the Duke of Valkirk's—stunning, rare defeat at Dos Montañas in Spain. Hawkes had surreptitiously pursued a burgeoning dark suspicion linking all of these things to a conclusion that took even his jaded breath away.

Treason.

Even an earl could be hanged for treason.

Hawkes had been steps away from proving it when he'd been captured.

Brundage was the only other English person who'd known where and with whom Hawkes would be the day he was arrested in Cherbourg.

Which could, of course, be a coincidence.

It wasn't.

But it could be.

Hawkes didn't know what he could prove now, if anything. He wasn't certain he ought to try. Likely Brundage was confident he couldn't prove anything, either. A different man would find it wisest to put it behind him, retire to the seashore, put on some weight, cast about for a boring government job he could sleepwalk through until he died.

And yet.

Like a wolf freed from a trap who knows only to run right back into the forest, here he was again with Brundage.

"Aurelie in fact makes Therese d'Artois seem almost plain," Brundage expounded. He shook his head slowly in wondering reminiscence. "The competition for a mere glance from her, Hawkes, when she walked into a ballroom . . . sometimes nearly came to blows. But . . ." He hiked and let drop one shoulder in feigned humility. "Astonishingly, she saw me and the feeling was mutual. I wanted her in my bed the moment I saw her."

He paused.

Hawkes said nothing.

"You know how it is with some women," Brundage continued, relentlessly. He paused. "I expect after years in prison you'd be in a hurry to get one."

He studied Hawkes, his eyes glinting.

Hawkes regarded him coolly. *Get one.* He made it sound like women were cheroots. Or perhaps that shiny porcelain vase currently winking at him.

Brundage, that rank amateur, was trying to elicit a show of tortured envy from him. He wanted some evidence of the suffering that years of confinement and enforced celibacy had taken.

Hawkes could not oblige him.

He was conscious of no emotion apart from that cold, subterranean fury. He supposed it was possible that survival for the last three years had required such contortions of spirit, such superhuman suppression, that the circulation of spontaneous feeling had been stopped, like a limb that had gone to sleep. He didn't know how or in which order they would return to him.

Or perhaps prison had done to his soul what an invading army does to an enemy village: The crops burnt. The ground salted.

Perhaps that was a mercy.

"Your ash, Brundage," Hawkes said politely. "It's about to fall."

Brundage was typically obsessively tidy.

Brundage roughly tapped his ash into a bowl on the little game table between them. Chinese, from the looks of it. Quite fancy for an ash bowl.

Hawkes's cynicism told him Brundage's distraction wasn't merely due to racking concern for Aurelie. He would not risk involving Hawkes for that reason alone. He was biding his time for the moment of discovery.

"Is there anything else notable about her character that might help someone distinguish Lady Aurelie from any other young, beautiful, sheltered, runaway French noblewoman?" Hawkes asked.

"About her character?" Brundage's brow furrowed, as if the word confused him. He pressed his lips together. "Well, she has considerable charm, if that's what you mean. She has an . . . ah . . . pretty laugh"—he gave his hand an irritable flick, as though the need to describe her thusly embarrassed him—"and graceful manners, because she was exquisitely well-bred, of course. And she has opinions about things, and what woman of twenty-one years has an opinion worth a damn? Or knows her own mind? Nevertheless, I've indulged this perhaps too much, as one does when one is smitten. She's perhaps a bit too clever for her own good, but she seems to revel in male attention, as any pretty girl would, and can be a bit of a . . . a bit of a flirt."

Brundage said this last word tonelessly and turned his gaze toward the fire.

There ensued a peculiarly long silence.

Hawkes noted that a muscle in Brundage's jaw was ticking.

"But I never viewed these as the sorts of flaws marriage and babies wouldn't cure her of," Brundage added tersely.

Hawkes wondered if Lady Aurelie thought she needed "curing."

"I've never heard marriage prescribed as a cure for character flaws," Hawkes said conversationally. "I've always thought it was the best way to discover them."

This surprised a faint smile from Brundage.

Hawkes had, in fact, observed enough marriages over the years to conclude that what people liked to call "love" was in truth just like justice: It was for sale. It was the name given to a transaction between a man and a woman, each of whom had something to gain. He wasn't certain he believed in it.

"In short," Brundage said, "marriage would be the best thing for Aurelie. I've long suspected an impulse to flightiness in her curbed only by the presence of her guardian. Unfortunately, it looks as though my suspicions have been borne out. You know how dramatic young women can be."

"Of course," Hawkes said.

He didn't. But Hawkes knew how most people could be. Which meant he knew the words Brundage used to describe his fiancée revealed more about his own character than Aurelie's.

And Hawkes thought he knew Brundage's character very well indeed.

Hawkes had always addressed young women like Lady Aurelie with the careful solicitousness with which he might restore a fallen baby bird to its nest. He wielded his charisma with a certain tender mercy when he danced with them, and he was flattered and amused by their blushes. But as the war bore on and his career engulfed him, the more they seemed like a different species from a different land, one which spoke a language he could no longer speak, or perhaps was no longer entitled to speak. He supposed he might call that language Innocence.

When opportunity and lust aligned, he found himself in the beds of women whose morals were as labyrinthine as his own had become in the name of duty. Like Therese d'Artois.

Hawkes realized he'd been holding the miniature of Aurelie so long it had pressed a little ridge into his palm.

He gently placed it down on the table between them.

Brundage flicked a dispassionate glance at it. But he didn't take it up. It was as if he were punishing her for being gone. "I suppose you may take that with you." He gestured to the miniature vaguely with his chin. "If you agree to help me find her."

Hawkes felt himself go rigid.

Lady Aurelie Capet might well be flighty and willful and shallow. But she was still bloody young and nearly entirely alone in the world.

Hawkes thought of his sister, married, only a little older than Aurelie, living in Scotland, and to whom he'd just written to tell her he was, at last, free. And his mother, who had died while he was in prison. He would never see her again.

It seemed to him that someone ought to give a damn about the only miniature ever made of Lady Aurelie Capet.

He took a moment to contemplate the sheer sport of refusing to help, just for the pleasure of watching Brundage's expression change. Of the mad, delicious righteousness of refusing the man's money.

But his hand was already reaching out. He closed it around the miniature and dragged it slowly back across the table.

He hesitated.

Then he decisively slipped it into his pocket.

"I will find her," Hawkes said evenly. "For fifteen percent more than the fee we earlier discussed."

Brundage became alertly rigid. "Ten percent more. Half payable now, half upon completion of your assignment."

"Done. In addition, I will require a sufficient budget in support of all aspects of the investigation, to be negotiated and agreed upon before I leave this evening, as well as at least fifty pounds in ready cash." Bribery and blackmail and coercion and the like, if the search came to that, did not come cheap. "I will also need a general letter of introduction signed by you stipulating that I should be assisted with any inquiries on your behalf. Should I need to speak to someone who can't be persuaded with a bottle of gin."

Brundage winced. "Very well."

There was no one Hawkes couldn't persuade to speak to him. He had something else in mind for the letter of introduction.

Hawkes flashed a smile. "And perhaps you would be gracious enough to recommend a competent firm I can employ to assist me with my financial affairs, now that I will once again actually have financial affairs. One that will assist me in making investment decisions as clever as yours."

Brundage returned his smile indulgently. "Harrigan & Sons in London manages mine."

Three years ago, Brundage's man of affairs had been a Mr. Markley. Hawkes had utterly disarmed him into letting him have a look at Brundage's personal and embassy account books "as he greatly admired the earl, and wished to make sure he was doing his own correctly."

It was a rare instance of overplaying his hand. He sensed his compliment had been conveyed to Brundage, because the earl liked compliments as much as he liked shiny things.

And he had a feeling Mr. Markley had been sacked *right* about the time Hawkes was being arrested.

They studied each other.

"Well, that's settled then," Brundage said with a little smile. "If anyone can find her it's you, Hawkes. After all, she's not Cafard."

Hawkes offered him a smile and a slow nod, acknowledging the dig. Cafard—French for cockroach—was the name the Alien Office had assigned to a destructive scourge of a French spy because he excelled at disappearing into cracks, and he remained one of Hawkes's few rankling failures. The only thing Hawkes thought he knew about the man was that his real name was Florian Vasseur. But he was uncertain even of this.

"I am probably the only man who can find her," he said calmly.

Brundage went rigid.

But they both knew this was the only reason he'd ever send for Hawkes.

The silence elongated and so did Brundage's ash. He finally, awkwardly, stabbed out his cheroot completely, as if it, like Lady Aurelie, had displeased him, too.

Hawkes leaned back to savor his. He liked a veil of smoke, on the whole. Especially during conversations like this one. But his mind was moving swiftly now.

"Who was the last person to see or speak to Lady Aurelie?"

"Her lady's maid, Madame Aubert. She claims to know nothing about Aurelie's whereabouts and refused to speak. She's lying, of course. The woman was of course summarily dealt with."

Hawkes said nothing. Brundage's title and wealth meant he was accustomed to demanding things and getting them at once, a bit like a tyrannical infant. He'd never needed to learn *strategy*. It was the only way to get something you wanted if you had no money or power. And formulating strategy meant understanding that every person, from thieves to earls, was a delicate puzzle.

"I will of course speak to her," he said.

Brundage nodded curtly.

"I'm afraid I also need to ask what you might construe as a somewhat delicate question regarding Lady Aurelie's other relationships."

Brundage's eyes flared, and then he gave a nod of comprehension. "Ah, yes. I believe I know what you're about to ask. No. I'm unaware of any other men in Aurelie's life. She's been so sheltered, you see, I don't understand how she could have possibly met anyone her guardian didn't intend for her to meet."

"Sounds a bit like prison," Hawkes said brightly.

Brundage opened his mouth. Then closed it again.

Hawkes continued briskly, "Assuming she has not been kidnapped, do you have any notions about why she might have wanted to leave? It may be material in discovering where she might have gone."

Brundage went abruptly quiet.

Hawkes felt that prickle of portent at the back of his neck that meant he was closing in on a truth.

Brundage looked toward the mirror, then abruptly turned away, as if the sight of his own face disconcerted him.

"We did have a . . . disagreement . . . about a month ago, as we prepared to take dinner together. I would characterize it as a lovers' quarrel. She is willful, as I said. I regretted what transpired. Later I gave her a fine piece of jewelry and she graciously accepted it along with my apologies. We exchanged tender words. Three weeks later she, and the jewelry, were gone."

Hawkes noted with interest the recurrence of the tiny tic of the muscle in Brundage's jaw.

He might indeed be worried about Aurelie. He was, at the very least, worried, in general.

But Brundage was also definitely more *enraged* that his fiancée had disappeared than worried.

"What sort of jewelry did you give her? It might help determine where she would be likely to go. Would it finance passage to China, to England, to America, to—"

"It's an emerald. Set between two diamonds, on a gold chain. And yes, to any and all of those, if sold to someone scrupulous. I should very much like to retrieve it. They were family jewels."

He regarded Brundage for a moment through smoke. Now he had it.

"Whose family jewels?" he asked almost lazily.

Brundage stared at him.

And then he made a stunned sound. A sort of shorter, bitterer cousin to a laugh. "Ah, Hawkes. Well done. Not mine. Or, not *yet* mine. I borrowed the necklace from a French family with an eye toward possibly purchasing it for Aurelie. I had not yet decided whether I should, so I have not yet paid for it. They lost nearly everything in the first revolution and have desperate need of the money. I suppose they thought if they left it with me, I would find myself unable to part with it. I thought to do them a favor, you see."

"Of course," Hawkes said gently. "Like the favor you did for me when you saved my life."

Brundage nodded once, humbly. He paused. "You see, there is talk of my being appointed the ambassador to France."

"Ah," Hawkes said. "But the powers that be are disinclined to appoint a man whose fiancée has gone missing, and an accusation of a stolen necklace would be a scandal of both domestic and international proportions should the news become widely known?"

"It seems unlike you to state the obvious, Hawkes." Brundage had clearly made an effort to sound amused. He succeeded in sounding mostly testy.

Hawkes offered him a placating smile. Because of course that's why he'd said it aloud: for the pleasure of making Brundage testy.

This was why Brundage was so thoroughly distracted. And why he'd decided to risk contacting Hawkes. He was in *quite* a bind.

"And does Lady Aurelie have any money of her own with which to flee? To your knowledge, did she still possess the necklace the last time you saw her?"

"She has been given an allowance by her guardian, and it is my understanding—from him—that all of her spending is accounted for. He has also set aside settlement money for when we marry, but she of course does not currently have access to it. I do not know how or where she could possibly get more money. And yes, the last time I saw her, she was wearing the necklace. And all seemed well between us."

Well, it clearly wasn't.

Hawkes perversely admired Lady Aurelie for convincing Brundage otherwise. For nearly four weeks since that argument, from the sound of things.

He wondered why she'd waited precisely that long.

"Hawkes . . ." Brundage paused at length. "I know these details I have to offer do not quite add up to a person. Perhaps I do not seem sufficiently distressed. But I am indeed desperate to find her. My heart is, in fact . . . breaking." He grimaced self-deprecatingly.

Hawkes had once seen Brundage slap a footman

to the floor for apparently pouring the wrong type of brandy. He'd done it with the same casual, swift grace with which he'd lit Hawkes's cheroot tonight.

"That's terrible news, indeed," Hawkes said gravely. "About your heart."

Brundage regarded him intently.

Then decided to slowly incline his head.

Hawkes exhaled a cloud of smoke. "Ah, I missed these cheroots, Brundage," he said lazily. "You always did have the best tobacco, for which I was always grateful. You always did have the best taste in everything, in fact, and I can imagine the loss of such a lovely girl must prey upon you greatly. I look forward to once again taking up all of my favorite vices presently. After I find your exceptional fiancée."

He could see the words work their magic on Brundage, who was reluctant to be charmed, but willing to be flattered. It was the sort of thing Hawkes had said when he ingratiated himself into the inner circle of French diplomats in Cherbourg, winning their trust and friendship, gathering intelligence which he'd deftly delivered to the English military.

He'd eventually fled in the night, coldly triumphant. Leaving behind humiliated and ruined men. A hero to his country. A traitor in another.

But if Lady Aurelie could be found, Hawkes would find her.

He would start by, oh, saying a word to a certain man he knew who frequented a certain pub where the hack drivers liked to gather, and like a flame touched to a fuse, this would travel swiftly throughout the hack drivers, the drunks and dock workers, the clerks and lady's maids and servants and costermongers, the patriots and ne'er-do-wells and opportunists who noticed everything and said nothing except to each other.

And to him.

Forty minutes later, Hawkes took himself back down the stairs of Brundage's rented townhouse, his pockets freshly stuffed with loose English currency and Brundage's letter of introduction.

Exhaustion tugged at his limbs. He was probably about a dozen excellent meals and good night's sleep away from feeling anything like his old self again. But he paused a moment in the marble-floored foyer, his jaw slowly set. This was precisely the sort of home he'd saved a lifetime to buy. A dream that had been wrenched from him when he was arrested.

"If you'll forgive the presumption, Mr. Hawkes, I was sorry to hear about what happened to you, and it's good to see you looking well."

Hawkes spun toward the voice.

In the sitting room adjacent, a strapping young footman was wielding a feather duster and watching him.

Hawkes hesitated. And then he took two slow, cautious steps toward the man and lowered his voice. "I'm afraid I'm at a disadvantage, Mr. . . ."

"Pike, sir. Benjamin Pike. I haven't forgotten the kind thing you did for me, Mr. Hawkes."

Hawkes stared at him, and then he recalled: he'd last seen the man's gray eyes burning with anger and mortification. Because what Hawkes had done was help Pike to his feet after Brundage had casually slapped him to the floor several years go.

"Think nothing of it," Hawkes said shortly. "No man should do that to another man."

Hawkes pivoted to leave.

"Thank you for saying so, sir," Pike said politely. "But I did make a mistake that night. I made a mistake about what I put into the decanter."

Pike's inflection hadn't changed. But his gaze was fixed rather intently on Hawkes, and he'd enunciated each word slowly and meaningfully. "I was new to my position, sir, and did not yet know an important difference."

Hawkes went still, frowning faintly.

And then epiphany was on him like a falcon on a hare.

He lowered his voice and said swiftly, "It wasn't brandy, was it? It was cognac."

He recalled now that Brundage had first taken a sip of that brandy before batting it out of Pike's hands.

Before Hawkes could taste it.

Holy Mother of God.

During the war, cognac amounted to something like liquid treason. The only way a man could get it was by smuggling.

Or by accepting it as a nice . . . French . . . bribe.

Pike turned and resumed dusting. The feathers flicked over the frame surrounding a painting of one of Brundage's ancestors. Across the noble head, and black eyes. Across his nostrils.

"My brother died at Dos Montañas, sir." Pike measured these words out through clamped teeth. It was almost a hiss.

There had been a rumor circulating in British government circles about General Blackmore's loss at Dos Montañas from the very beginning—someone with foreknowledge of British troop movements had sold them out to the French. And those with foreknowledge were very few in number, and included Hawkes and Brundage.

Mr. Pike had clearly been seething for the last three years while in the employ of Brundage, because he had very specific suspicions of his own.

Hawkes admired a man who could hold a grudge so efficiently, then adroitly seize the opportunity for revenge when it came upon him.

He was taking an enormous risk by confiding in Hawkes. But he knew Hawkes by reputation.

Hawkes slipped his hand in his coat pocket and by rubbing two fingers against them freed a pound note from the roll there, palmed it and slipped it into the urn below the portrait, rotating his hand just a little so Pike could see it.

"I'm terribly sorry about your brother, Mr. Pike," he said sincerely and swiftly. "If you do not respond to the following question, I will assume the answer is affirmative. Did you inadvertently put contraband French cognac in the decanter to serve to Brundage's guest? If so, do you know how he obtained it?"

Pike finished freeing the ancestor of dust and applied himself to the porcelain urn below it. Shiny things. How Brundage loved them.

Pike's features were tense now. He swallowed.

At last he said politely, "Sir, if you'd like to purchase a beautiful urn like this one you ought to pay a visit to Mr. Roland Guthrie's Antiquities just off Bond Street in London. I was sent there three times to retrieve objects like this"—he flicked the duster over the urn—"and then sent to return them. I saw no money change hands. The last time was about four years ago. During one of my visits, he gifted me with a libation."

Hawkes took this in, and felt a theory coalescing. And if he was right . . . it was the piece of the treason puzzle he'd been missing.

Ah, Lady Aurelie. Hawkes said a silent thank-you

to the wayward girl for inadvertently leading him here tonight.

Hawkes shot a glance over his shoulder at the stairs. But there was no sign of Brundage.

"Pike, did you happen to overhear or witness any sort of altercation between the earl and his fiancée about a month ago? Would have been on a Tuesday."

Pike gave his head a subtle shake. "But the first Tuesday of the month is the staff day off, sir."

Mr. Pike dipped the duster into the urn, slid his hand down it and retrieved the pound note with admirable dexterity.

It was always so much easier to deal with clever, bribable men.

"My thanks, Pike," Hawkes said. "Until we meet again."

Chapter Two

"I'M BEGINNING to think I ought to call Mr. Barnabus Tweedy out, given how thoroughly he's replaced me in my wife's affections."

Lucien Durand, Viscount Bolt, murmured this with mock severity to his wife from one pillow over. His lips were inches from hers. It was just past dawn, and The Grand Palace on the Thames was rustling into life for the day.

"Only temporarily," Angelique reassured him on a purr, dragging her bare toes down his furry calf. "But don't worry. You're a close second."

Two rooms over, a still-shirtless Captain Tristan Hardy kissed his yawning wife on the top of her head as she sat down at her little dressing table to pin up her hair. "You were awake thinking about Mr. Tweedy all night, weren't you? I don't think you were this excited before our wedding."

"Well, I *was* married once before I met you," Delilah told him with mock gravity. "But this is the first time I've hired the footman of my dreams."

For Angelique and Delilah, the proprietresses of The Grand Palace on the Thames, were going to propose to Mr. Barnabus Tweedy and were almost certain he would accept.

The competition for good servants was fierce and bloody in London, and the enticements The Grand

Palace on the Thames had to offer—an adequate salary, lots of work (much of it hard), an environment of unsurpassed congeniality, excellent food and plenty of it, an epithet jar in the sitting room, and comfortable accommodation in a building situated in a neighborhood in which one was only moderately more likely to be stabbed than in other neighborhoods—meant they struggled to compete. Delilah and Angelique liked to think The Grand Palace on the Thames was elevating the tone of the docks in general, especially since they had at last managed to bribe the local drunk men into urinating on other buildings instead. Helga's scones had done the trick.

The hope they clung to was that the perfect footman would fall in love with the whole notion of The Grand Palace on the Thames once he had a chance to meet them, and would be willing to forego a little more salary or cache for the pure delight of working there.

So far one candidate had stolen a spoon, and Captain Hardy had been compelled to chase him down the street, seize it from him, and whack him with it. Another promising candidate had casually and deliberately dragged his hand right across Angelique's bottom as he departed his interview, as though he'd weighed the job and the bottom and had decided the second was the opportunity he simply could not pass up. Helga, the cook, had driven him out of the house with a rolling pin. There was one who showed up reeking of gin, another who was clearly lying about ever having been a footman because he just wanted a cup of tea and a chat, and others who were merely thick or uncouth.

And while Captain Hardy and Lord Bolt were willing to help with the sort of work a footman would normally do, they had their own work with their ship, and Triton Group, their import and export endeavor. And besides, they were not at all the sort of men who were meant to be at the beck and call of their wives. Or at the beck and call of anyone, really.

Angelique and Delilah had faced challenge after challenge, but so far nothing had been insurmountable when it came to The Grand Palace on the Thames. But the longer the footman search continued, the more likely it seemed that their unbroken streak of indomitability was coming to an end.

And then . . .

Mr. Tweedy had come to call.

His head was a strong, plain box shape, his eyes were brown and twinkly, his smile revealed complete rows of teeth, and his hands were the size of spades. An oxen would envy his shoulders, which were joined to his head by a massive neck. Delilah and Angelique had begun to reflexively assess every man they saw by whether he could reach high places in order to dust them, or polish the windows, or insert candles into sconces, and the top of Mr. Tweedy's head (brown hair cropped to bristle length) nearly brushed the door frame. He'd be able to run errands and return carrying heavy things, and perhaps thump an intruder in the jaw with a fist should the need arise. Perhaps he'd even take up a hammer and nails on occasion, all work that had so far fallen to their beleaguered husbands, or to their previous American guest Mr. Hugh Cassidy, who'd craved hard, physical work the way a big healthy dog needs a good gambol in a park.

On the whole, Mr. Tweedy seemed unlikely to haunt the dreams of the housemaids. Then again, the housemaids, Dot included, all possessed fecund imaginations, fertilized by the gossip columns Dot read aloud in the kitchen and the horrid novels they sometimes read aloud in the sitting room at night. Angelique had come upon them taking turns practicing swooning onto the pink settee in the reception room when they were supposed to be dusting.

And while Angelique and Delilah had fallen in love with Mr. Tweedy straightaway, they were no fools. They asked the pertinent questions.

"Why do you find the need to leave your current position, Mr. Tweedy?"

For a moment, he'd sat in dignified silence. His eyebrows seemed to suggest he was wrestling with a great inner torment.

They began to worry.

He began haltingly. "You see, I do not like to gossip and I would never *dream* of gossiping about you or your place of business . . . so very gauche, don't you think? I am usually the soul of discretion. So I share this with great reluctance and I beg *your* discretion . . ."

"We understand. Of course." They were on tenterhooks.

He sighed. "I confess I am in search of a more peaceful and . . . well, civilized place in which to work. You may be surprised to learn that the homes of earls and viscounts are not necessarily . . ." He closed his eyes, then opened them. He lowered his voice and leaned forward to confide in a whisper, "Dear lord, the *debauchery* . . ."

They'd tried not to look too interested.

"I am not averse to merriment, of course. But my employer's gatherings feature a good deal of . . ." He cleared his throat. ". . . *shrieking* and . . . well, hooting . . . and laughing . . . females. This sound carries to the top of the house, such that the servants struggle to get a good night's sleep, which makes it more difficult to do a fine job, which is all I ever want to do in the world."

They aimed limpidly supportive gazes at him.

"It is difficult to know what my employer requires of us when he is frequently indisposed due to . . . ah, the importunate imbibing of . . . spirits."

The word "importunate" sent delicious tingles down their spines. Mr. Tweedy not only knew four-syllable words, he had earlier demonstrated that he could write and spell them.

"But I think I decided to seek a new position in earnest when I found a . . . if you'll pardon my frankness . . ." He cleared his throat, then sighed. ". . . silk stocking . . . dangling from the chandelier."

He blushed pink.

Bless his heart.

Delilah and Angelique acknowledged this confession with the moment of scandalized silence he clearly felt it deserved.

"We are not averse to merriment, either, Mr. Tweedy, but only crystals hang from our chandeliers," Delilah assured him.

"Mainly because our aim isn't very good," Angelique added.

They all laughed merrily. Mr. Tweedy included, thankfully.

"I am in search of a mature and sensible employer who has his hand firmly on the tiller. And I do like the notion of a variety of guests! And musical evenings—my goodness, what a thrilling idea. And the sea air is so bracing here," he said wistfully.

Mr. Tweedy was clearly prepared to fall in love with The Grand Palace on the Thames, too, given just a little encouragement.

"If it's civility you crave, we've an epithet jar in the sitting room. Good manners are gently enforced and we find that our guests and staff appreciate knowing we will always do our utmost to maintain a safe and peaceful home. We love laughter, but we loathe chaos," Delilah told him.

They purposely did not mention their tenant Mr. Delacorte, who had nearly worn a path between his favorite chess table in the sitting room and the epithet jar. Mr. Delacorte was best experienced personally to appreciate, and was, diplomatically speaking, a bit of an acquired taste.

"And your list of rules!" Mr. Tweedy sighed happily. "So clever. So very *right*. Why, they ought to be framed."

The frame-worthy rules of which Mr. Tweedy approved, printed on little cards and handed to every guest and left on the desks in all the rooms, were:

All guests will eat dinner together at least four times per week.

All guests must gather in the drawing room after dinner for at least an hour at least four times per week. We feel it fosters a sense of friendship and the warm, familial, congenial atmosphere we strive to create here at The Grand Palace on the Thames.

All guests should be quietly respectful and courteous of other guests at all times, though spirited discourse is welcome.

Guests may entertain other guests in the drawing room.

Curfew is at 11:00 p.m. The front door will be securely locked then. You will need to wait until morning to be admitted if you miss curfew.

If the proprietresses collectively decide that a transgression or series of transgressions warrants your eviction from The Grand Palace on the Thames, you will find your belongings neatly packed and placed near the front door. You will not be refunded the balance of your rent.

A new one had been recently added:

Gentlemen may smoke in the Smoking Room only.

Mr. Delacorte had made this mistake only once, but they could imagine it being made again, and thought it wisest to get ahead of the problem.

"They really are so exquisitely well considered, your rules," he said.

"We're pleased that you think so. And oh, what a marvelous idea, Mr. Tweedy. We can hang them in each room, perhaps, stitched on a sampler," Angelique added dreamily. "We do, in fact, always welcome suggestions from our staff."

"I so long to be listened to," he said wistfully.

"It's all anybody ever wants, truly," Delilah said warmly. She did not go so far as to place a companionable hand on his arm, but the moment seemed to call for it.

Mr. Tweedy had informed them that he was obliged to meet with two other potential employers—and one was a marquess, he added, with becoming modesty—but he had agreed to return a week hence for a tour of the premises and to meet the entire staff. They lied and told him they needed to speak to their other candidates, too, because they might be in love, but they were also women of business.

Today was the day he'd be returning for the second interview. And unless he arrived drunk or pinched a bottom or a spoon, they were going to offer him the job.

Not only that, but in a week's time they were expecting Mr. Bellingham, a vicar who had learned of The Grand Palace on the Thames from his parishioners, Mr. and Mrs. Farraday, who were among the boardinghouse's very first guests. They'd extolled the charms of the place to him. Mr. Bellingham's two letters of inquiry to them brimmed with such wit and charming little bits of vicarish philosophy and anecdotes about an intelligent chicken named Eleanor that Delilah and Angelique had actually read them aloud to the other guests in the sitting room at night. Everyone who lived at the boardinghouse felt they were already fond of Mr. Bellingham. They quite looked forward to his arrival.

Mr. Delacorte was prepared to stoically tolerate a vicar. After all, he'd tolerated a duke and an earl, and this had been no mean feat. He liked to think that these sorts of guests were opportunities to further refine his character, a task roughly akin to tumbling a lump of coal into a diamond, and the sort of task which under different circumstances would take epochs to complete. He maintained the ladies at The Grand Palace on the Thames were knocking the rough edges from him.

"The Duke of Valkirk turned out to be a good sort, after all," Mr. Delacorte allowed. "And his wedding was great fun! I still sing the song Miss Wylde wrote about the chap with the stick up 'is bum when I shave. I miss them."

Mr. Delacorte was a sentimental soul. He missed everyone after they left. He was not only fond of Captain Hardy and Lord Bolt—he was now their business partner. He was soon to be godfather to Mr. Hugh Cassidy's child. But no one yet had been able to replace American Mr. Cassidy in his affections. Like Mr. Delacorte, Mr. Cassidy was thrifty and not a debaucher, and was game for an evening of singing bawdy songs in a pub, donkey races, or cheering on men who gleefully pursued greased pigs.

On the whole, as a result, the present atmosphere at The Grand Palace on the Thames was as ebullient and hopeful as the first day of spring.

"Good morning," Delilah whispered to Angelique, when they had met in the little sitting room at the top of the stairs. Here was where they began and ended each day—with a little conversation and a review of the day's business. "Happy New Footman Day, hopefully. You look smashing."

Delilah and Angelique had felt so flush with success that they'd ordered a new day dress each, their first new dresses in a very long time. Delilah in silk the color of bronze, Angelique in deep goldish green.

"Thank you. As do you," Angelique said. "Surely puffed sleeves are the thing that will convince Mr. Tweedy that there's no place he'd rather work in London."

Delilah stifled a laugh. She reached for her apron to cover the fine new dress.

"Mrs. Hardy! Mrs. Durand!"

They both gave a start and whirled to find Dot thundering up the stairs, her face alight with portent.

"We've a lady in the reception room. And by lady I do mean a lady. As in I'll eat my cap if she hasn't a title. *But* . . . she *says* she's a missus. A Mrs. Gallagher."

"I imagine Helga could do something to make your cap palatable, if it comes to that, Dot." Angelique reached out and with one finger righted Dot's, which was listing. "Palatable means edible," she clarified for Dot.

"Pal-a-ta-bull," Dot repeated. She was many things: a collector of words, the former worst lady's maid in the world, a dweller in the clouds, a lover of horrid novels, a dropper of tea trays, unswervingly good and loyal, and a continual source of bemusement, amusement, and exasperation. They could not do without her.

And she most definitely knew the distinction between ladies and . . . not ladies.

"Hmm. As you know, I was once married to an earl, Dot," Delilah said. "Perhaps it's like that?"

"Do you suppose she married someone like Captain Hardy, too?" Dot wondered.

"Well, given that there's only one Captain Hardy . . ." Delilah said. *And he's all mine*, were her happy unspoken words. Although she was kind enough to wish that kind of love for everyone.

"It's just a way of standing, like, and speaking, like," Dot explained. "She looks very young and pretty and her clothes—half-mourning, from the looks of things—are quite good and her complexion is ever so fine." Dot rubbed the back of her hand against her own cheek. "But she's . . ." She paused dramatically and put her hand up to her mouth and whispered, "*. . . alone*."

"Ah, *intriguing*. No companion or lady's maid?" Angelique asked.

"She brought a trunk with her, but no maid."

"Hmm," Delilah mused, dubiously. "Well, widows may now and again travel alone. Look at Mrs. Pariseau."

Mrs. Pariseau was one of the first permanent guests of The Grand Palace on the Thames, a dashing widow of middle years blessed with a wicked sense of humor and a (sometimes disconcertingly) open-minded intelligence, and striking white stripes in her dark hair. When she wasn't enjoying the company at The Grand Palace on the Thames, she gallivanted about London with her many friends, enjoying her late husband's money.

"Mrs. Gallagher downstairs looks a bit like . . . well, I always imagine dice get very dizzy when they're rolled, and she looks a bit like that."

Delilah and Angelique exchanged a swift glance.

"You *always* imagine this, Dot?" Delilah ventured. Glimpses into the deep inner workings of Dot's mind could be disorienting.

Dot hesitated.

"When I think about dice," she clarified, finally, somewhat cagily.

Delilah and Angelique regarded her in bemused silence.

"It's just she looks as though she's had a few jostles, you know, the way dice are jostled when they're rolled," Dot insisted. "And now she's come to a stop and is trying to get her breath and she looks relieved but perhaps a bit dizzy."

In all fairness, put this way, Delilah and Angelique could at once picture this, and this made it a good description, indeed. If anyone knew about jostling, it was Dot. The list of things she'd inadvertently dropped or jostled was long and varied, and the tea tray was at the top of it.

"Will you go and speak to her, please?" She clasped her hands in entreaty. "She seems so nice. I told her we are very exclusive and that you would need to chat with her first."

"Exclusive" was one of Dot's favorite words. She loved to see the expressions on the guests change accordingly.

"Of course. We'll go down and see her. Will you bring in tea, please? And perhaps see if Helga can spare a few scones. Tea is the ultimate restorative."

Dot gave a delighted little hop and went to do just that. Bringing in tea and answering the door to the surprise of new guests were her favorite things.

Chapter Three

WHILE ANGELIQUE and Delilah discussed her, their potential new guest paced before the hearth in the reception room, whispering, "How do you do? My name is Mrs. Mary Gallagher. How do you *do*? I'm Mrs. Mary Gallagher. How *do* you do? My name is Mrs. Mary Gallagher."

During the passage from Calais to Dover, a woman named Mary Gallagher had told Aurelie a witty story about haggling over the price of beef with a butcher. Despite everything, she'd been fascinated. She'd never before had such a conversation. Her life was not meant to intersect with the lives of women like Mary Gallagher, who knew how to do things like haggle. Aurelie had instead learned to conjugate sentences in five languages, embroider, paint, and play pianoforte, and had never questioned that these were the precise accomplishments needed to prepare a gently bred girl for marriage.

Now they almost seemed a ruse perpetuated to prevent gently bred women from learning how to shoot to kill.

It had been one month and three days since her confidence in such assumptions had been blasted to smithereens. And assumptions were like roads cut through a thicket—how did one travel through life if one could not assume from certain observations that a man was a gentleman, or a woman was a lady, or that a person was good or bad? How would one know what to say or do or be? How ironic that she'd been obliged to plunge blindly into the world the very moment she'd been made brutally aware that she knew almost nothing about it.

Through the dirty window of the hired hack, she'd scanned the faces on the London street as though she'd never seen humans before, fully appreciating for the first time now that every person likely contained an unfathomable universe.

And that included her.

A trunk filled with someone else's clothes, an emerald necklace, and a small sheaf of letters: these constituted her plans and her entire hope for the future. But she was learning new things about herself all the time. For instance, somehow she'd known how to alchemize terror and shame and rage into cold, methodical determination.

She'd slept very little for more than a month. Her nerves felt stretched taut as pianoforte wires and her entire being seemed to vibrate at a single urgent pitch that drowned out every thought, feeling, or impulse unrelated to escape.

She'd borrowed Mary Gallagher's name because it struck her as strong and plain, the sort of name countless women shared. She liked to think that if Mary Gallagher had known the reason, she would not have minded. More than anything at the moment, Aurelie wanted to be one of indistinguishable thousands. Like just another blade of grass in a meadow. Invisibility, for the moment, was safety.

After driving over every bump and rut in London, the garrulous hack driver had put her down in front of a little building set like a pearl amongst the coal smut–begrimed structures of the docks. The sea air whipped her hood from her head and stung her cheeks and eyes. She liked it. Above, modest gargoyles presided over the roofline; below, a wrought-iron fence surrounded what appeared to be a tiny park. The freshly painted sign danced in the sea breeze gently on chains which miraculously did not creak.

It was called The Grand Palace on the Thames. She liked the aspirational name of the place. When she'd peered closely at the sign outside, she could see the word "rogues" very faintly visible on the sign, and she rather liked that, too: The building wanted to be something other than what it once was. So did she.

A maid with wide blue eyes and an air of general mystification had asked her to wait, and everything in this pretty little reception room seemed gently blurred around the edges from wear, like a watercolor painting or a rose just past peak bloom.

She whirled and her heart gave a lurch when she heard the sound of slippers clicking on marble. She'd been told a certain Mrs. Hardy and a Mrs. Durand were to be consulted before she could be given a room.

The two smiling, elegant ladies brought into the room with them such a palpable sense of peace and unflappable competence that the invisible belt that had been pulled taut beneath her ribs for days now loosened just a notch.

"How do you do. I am Mrs. Hardy," the dark-haired lady said at once.

Aurelie never used to search faces for kindness; it had been assumed. A layer of precaution now lay between her and every interaction, and this was new, too.

She thought she found genuine kindness in Mrs. Hardy's soft, dark eyes.

"And I am Mrs. Durand."

The golden-haired lady seemed kind, too. Her dress was a clever shade of green with a hint of a bronze sheen and it made her hazel eyes glow. They were a harmonious pair, Mrs. Durand and Mrs. Hardy.

They all exchanged graceful curtsies.

"How do you do? I am Mrs. Mary Gallagher," she told them with what she thought was warm conviction. She had been telling lies for days—to people at inns, to people on the passage over. It was getting alarmingly easier.

"I hope I am not interrupting your day. Your maid, she is . . . a bit astonished, I think, to see me?" She flared her fingers before her eyes to illustrate Dot's expression.

The two ladies smiled at her. "Oh, don't mind Dot," Mrs. Hardy said. "That's her usual expression. The world in general amazes her. I suspect she was merely pleased to discover a potential charming new guest."

Aurelie's cheeks went warm with pleasure. She did, however, take note of the word "potential."

By God, she would win them over. She wanted to stay here.

Mainly, she just wanted to be alone in a room as soon as possible.

"Would you like to sit down, Mrs. Gallagher?"

"Oh! Yes, thank you."

She lowered herself to the edge of the pink settee, folded her hands tightly in her lap, aligned her feet, pressed her knees together, compacting herself as tightly as the springs in the pleasantly bouncy cushion. She could not seem to commit to leaning her back against it yet. She wondered if the rest of her life she would be braced to bolt. She could feel her heart kicking away behind her bodice, like a trapped hare.

All three ladies studied each other for a moment, each wearing a mildly pleased, expectant expression.

"This is a very pretty room." It was only good sense to begin with a compliment.

"We're so happy to hear you like it. The king once sat where you're sitting," Mrs. Durand said pleasantly.

"Oh, my," she said, politely. Wondering if this could possibly be true. She was absurdly tempted to peer beneath her bottom.

And it felt a bit like a riposte. A hint that she was going to have to bring all of her best charm and flattery to bear to deserve to stay where the king of England had once chosen to perch.

"Dot informed me that your establishment is exclusive, which is lovely to hear. One feels so much more at home in an exclusive establishment, don't you think? But Dot said you would like to interview me. If you ask me any questions about Latin verbs, I fear I will disgrace myself and you will cast me out. I hope there is archery instead. I once won a little trophy."

Mrs. Durand and Mrs. Hardy laughed delightedly, and with some surprise.

And suddenly the air was aswarm with sparkly assumptions: they now knew they were all "ladies." Which meant they'd all experienced—or been subjected to—the same education and amusements and possessed similar senses of humor about them. Latin and archery and embroidery and watercolors and so forth.

At once they knew they shared a common language. At once they were more inclined to trust each other.

Aurelie was just a little cynical about this now.

Aurelie wondered what would happen if she asked if Mrs. Hardy or Mrs. Durand knew how to shoot a gun. She entertained a wild impulse to ask them: Do either of you know how dangerous the world, in fact, is? How unexpected and capricious? She earnestly wanted to know.

"Oh, Latin!" Mrs. Hardy exclaimed. "*Why* did they afflict us with it in the schoolroom? And why must we continue afflicting students with it?"

"I don't know why we didn't think of putting our guests through a series of trials, like Hercules," Mrs. Durand added. "Certainly, staying at The Grand Palace on the Thames is worth the effort. Although if there is an eating contest, I fear our guest Mr. Delacorte would win every time."

"Oh, *eating*!" Aurelie said enthusiastically. And a bit inanely.

She was very tired.

Mrs. Hardy and Mrs. Durand regarded her with little smiles.

She was jabbed suddenly with a little ice pick of alarm: something was moving on the periphery of her vision. Her field of vision in general had seemed to expand since she'd fled. She wondered if this enhanced sense was the sort a squirrel or rabbit or some other prey animal might possess. The legacy of danger.

It turned out to be merely Dot. She was taking the slow gliding steps a courtier might make when carrying a queen's train, bearing a tea tray in her hands.

She looked as somber and absorbed as a priest swinging a censer.

Aurelie watched her progress, fascinated now.

Mrs. Hardy and Mrs. Durand watched Dot, too. Each of their brows sported faint puzzled furrows.

When Dot arrived at last, she slowly, slowly, very slowly lowered the tray.

Peculiarly Mrs. Hardy and Mrs. Durand seemed to be holding their breaths.

When the tray finally touched the table without a clink Dot leaped back and gave a delighted little clap.

And Aurelie gave a start. She glanced uncertainly at Mrs. Hardy and Mrs. Durand. Ought she to applaud? Was this an English tea ceremony she'd somehow neglected to learn?

"Well done, Dot," Mrs. Hardy approved, without batting an eye. With alacrity and no other comment, she supplied Aurelie with a scone on a little plate. "Mrs. Gallagher, would you like to pour?"

"Thank you, I shall."

She realized at once she shouldn't have offered to do it. Dot had managed to lower the tea tray without a rattle. But when Aurelie lifted the teapot, she noted to her astonishment that her hands were visibly trembling.

The ladies of the house surely noticed.

"Well, we will not be asking you to clean the Augean stables," said Mrs. Durand when she took up her cup. She said this with clearly full confidence that Aurelie, as an educated lady, knew what the Augean stables were, because such were the nature of assumptions. "It's merely that we consider the guests who stay with us for any length of time as sort of family. It's important to us that the atmosphere remain congenial, warm and lively and safe, so we like to have a little conversation with everyone who walks through our doors. It's our way of ascertaining that any new guests will be happy here and that our current guests continue to peacefully enjoy their stay."

Said pleasantly. And it seemed quite reasonable.

But it also sounded a *bit* like a challenge.

And among the new things that Aurelie was learning about herself was that she was more stubborn than she realized, and challenges only made her very badly want to win.

"So you are saying you are very careful not to admit rogues," she said lightly.

There ensued an interesting, minute little pause.

"We would *never* wittingly admit a rogue," Mrs. Durand said vehemently.

"Have you cast anyone into the street for being found wanting?" She was teasing a little.

"Why, yes," Mrs. Hardy said pleasantly. "Why? Have you uproar in mind, Mrs. Gallagher?"

"I have a long nap and a splash in a wash basin in mind. Perhaps uproar a little later, when I am refreshed."

Fortunately, they laughed.

Her tension eased just a little more. Not enough to compel her to touch her back to the settee, but still. What a pleasure it was to feel a little more like herself. To laugh and tease and charm, the things that others had seemed to value about her, all of the things she had once valued about herself, too.

And then they had been turned into weapons against her.

"Have you had a long journey, Mrs. Gallagher?" Mrs. Durand asked gently.

Hell's teeth. Aurelie had not quite thought this part of her story through.

"Perhaps not so long," she said carefully, "but I think all of my bones and teeth were loosened by the carriage ride across London."

They clucked sympathetically. "Perhaps a tiny shot of brandy will set you right."

Aurelie was quiet. Now she was a little concerned.

She wanted very much to be liked. Was this a test of her willingness to commit debauchery?

"I have tasted champagne but once, and I liked it," she said carefully, "but I have not tasted it again. I enjoy ratafia. I have tasted sherry. But I have not tasted brandy. Back in Ireland, my husband, Thomas, used to say that only men ought to drink it, as it would put hair on my chest."

Mrs. Hardy and Mrs. Durand laughed again.

Her brother Edouard was the one who had, in fact, said this. She knew it must simply be an expression, but she hadn't thought to dispute it. Men seemed constitutionally able to drink and eat things that didn't seem meant for eating or drinking.

"Brandy is a very pretty color," she enthused, "much like the color of your dress, Mrs. Hardy. If you would like to give me a brandy, I shall try it," she added bravely.

They simply smiled very kindly at her. "We do not require your martyrdom, Mrs. Gallagher," Mrs. Hardy said firmly. "We do not intend to lead you down the path of iniquity. Tea first, I should think, and perhaps a wee bit of sherry later. We can work you up to brandy one evening. That was a jest! We spend our evenings playing spillikins and reading aloud from horrid novels and playing pianoforte. Do you play?"

"Oh yes, of course," she assured them, for what lady did not play pianoforte?

"May we ask how you came to find us?" Mrs. Durand asked. "We are not precisely on the beaten path."

"Oh, I asked my hack driver to take me to a very quiet and very beautiful and genteel place to stay and I must say that his judgment appears to have been flawless," she flattered shamelessly. "I've some business to see to in London, and I shall need a respectable place to stay until I secure passage to Boston. I am lately a widow and I now feel the need to be with family, and my brother is there. He is . . . he is all I really have left."

She hadn't quite put it that way before, and as the stark truth of this suddenly settled in, her voice trailed.

Her heart lurched as if it had foundered on rocks.

She *was* alone apart from someone she hadn't seen in six years. But then, she had mostly been alone.

She did not suppose she had ever counted her guardian, Uncle Jacques, as hers, or *of* her. He'd been shelter, like a roof, and not much warmer or loving than that. She did not think he would truly miss her should she disappear, though he might feel a bit of guilt. She did have other distant relatives, who didn't know her at all.

"We are so sorry for the loss of your husband," Mrs. Hardy said gently.

They were both watching her with such sympathetic eyes that tears nearly started up in hers.

"We both know what it is like to lose someone and to feel utterly alone suddenly. How frightening and strange it is. The world looks very different, doesn't it?" Mrs. Durand said.

"Yes." She almost whispered it. She seized upon those words. "It is a little frightening. And strange. Thank you for understanding."

Her throat was thick.

These words *were* true. She was frightened. And it was strange. And the world did indeed look entirely different now than it had a month ago.

There was much relief in admitting this aloud, even though it was not for the reasons they assumed. Losses of loved ones to war and illness were the sort of shared experiences that bound humans together.

There was a sort of nobility to these kinds of sacrifices and griefs; everyone understood them. But she could not imagine saying aloud the sordid and singular reason she was here. Especially not in a soft, gentle pink room like this one.

"Mrs. Hardy and Mrs. Durand . . . may I ask a question? And I hope it is not a presumption. Please do not hesitate to tell me if it is. I do not wish to seem as if I am testing you, as well."

The proprietresses laughed. Somewhat cautiously, she perceived.

"Of course," Mrs. Durand said.

"How did two ladies such as yourselves come to be running a fine boardinghouse such as this?"

She'd surprised them. Mrs. Durand and Mrs. Hardy exchanged a glance. Some sort of silent discussion seemed to take place.

It was Mrs. Hardy who finally spoke.

"A few years ago, our lives took a turn we could not have predicted. And for a time, things seemed very precarious and uncertain and we were frightened indeed. But as a result of these unpredictable events, we became dear friends. We decided to open a boardinghouse so that we could have the kind of home of which we'd always dreamed, surrounded by people we enjoy. And it's a pleasure to make people feel safe and welcome and wanted, because we learned this is all nearly everybody really wants, really."

"Oh," Aurelie breathed. It was the nicest answer she could imagine.

There was a little silence. And then they exchanged another of those glances.

"We'll just leave you a moment to finish your tea and have a look at our rules, Mrs. Gallagher, while we have a little chat. We won't be more than a minute or so."

"WELL," ANGELIQUE BEGAN, once they had crossed the foyer to the sitting room, where their hushed discussions about guests typically occurred.

"She seems *darling* . . ." Delilah continued cautiously.

". . . but if she's 'Mrs. Gallagher, the widow of Thomas from Ireland,' then Dot is Queen Charlotte."

"Precisely," Delilah agreed.

"She sits the way Gordon does when he's very uncertain about something. Limbs tucked in, tail wrapped tightly around his toes." Gordon was the fat striped cat who kept all the rodents at The Grand Palace on the Thames on the hop. "My impulse is, in fact, to gather her up like a kitten and put her in a basket. And yet Dot is right. There's something regal about her. And it isn't arrogance, per se. Just an air. She is mature for her age, and yet also rather young, I think."

"She seems very French," Angelique said firmly.

It was one of those intangible things. A singular sort of grace. The shrug of her shoulders? Her choice of words. A veneer of urbanity? The flutter of her hands. It was charming, and it wasn't English.

"Perhaps she's like Lucien, and she's lived many places, and absorbed a little of the accent from each place, and fell in love with Mr. Gallagher in Ireland. Just like she said. It's possible. Just look at all the improbable things that have happened in our lives, too," Delilah added.

"Mmm. How old do you think she is?"

"Twenty? If that."

"Very young to be a penniless widow, poor thing, if that is the case. At least the two of us were a trifle more jaded by the time we found ourselves destitute," Angelique said.

If they tried, both could conjure that dizzying terror of those days after the collapse of their old way of life.

They preferred to marvel at the beauty of the one they'd created from its ruins.

"Perhaps it's just nerves and being in a new place. Perhaps she's simply trying to make a good impression. A good night's sleep, a hearty meal, and a little kindness can go a long way to settling nerves."

They looked across at Mrs. Gallagher, who had not yet leaned back against the settee. Her posture was flawless, as only the posture of a girl trained by a governess to walk with a book on her head could be.

It was Angelique who reluctantly gave voice to what they were both thinking.

"Do you think she might be trouble?"

They were both remembering the last time they gave the benefit of the doubt to the pair of women who were among their very first guests. They had wound up with a foyer teeming with grim-faced soldiers and had made some startling discoveries about some of the hidden features of their house. In the end—which had been torturous and dramatic and shocking and beautiful—Delilah had acquired a husband.

Admittedly, there were easier ways for a woman to get a husband.

Delilah would do it all again a thousand times for Tristan.

They'd learned a good deal since those early days of The Grand Palace on the Thames. Delilah had shed some of her naivete, and Angelique had shed some of her cynicism, and somewhere between them they'd arrived at a magical formula for contentment and success here at The Grand Palace on the Thames, even if it wasn't always entirely peaceful.

And they'd *both* managed to find the world's most perfect (for them) husbands. That made every day easier.

"I think she is too young and too well-bred to be the sort of trouble that will lead to a house full of soldiers," Angelique posited. "And, well . . . we've no one occupying the suites at present. We could always use a new paying guest."

"We could indeed use a paying guest," Delilah agreed.

"I like our luck lately, Delilah. Mr. Bellingham will be arriving soon, too, and if Mr. Tweedy accepts the position, so will he. Won't it be festive?"

They both gave contented sighs.

"It's settled then. Let's go tell Mrs. Gallagher the news," Delilah said happily.

Chapter Four

"THANK YOU for agreeing to speak with me, Madame Aubert. I know this must be a terribly concerning time for you. Time is of the essence, so I shall not keep you long."

Lady Aurelie Capet's lady's maid, slim and spare as a ruler and chic in russet silk, merely nodded once, warily. She probably wasn't accustomed to a gentleman like Hawkes thanking her for anything, let alone asking to speak to her privately.

It was the day after Hawkes had agreed to help Brundage, and Hawkes sat opposite Madame Aubert in the sitting room of the suites she had shared with Lady Aurelie in her guardian's home in Paris.

Her hands were clasped tightly in her lap, and her hair was twisted into a knot as smooth and gleaming as a doorknob, dead center on the top of her head. This knot was pierced through with a little copper pin.

He noted she'd applied powder and rouge with a somewhat heavy hand, which seemed at odds with her understated elegance.

"I've naught else to do, with Lady Aurelie away." She unlinked her hands for a moment to gesture fatalistically, then folded them back up again.

Hawkes had spent the first few hours of the morning enjoying various seemingly casual conversations with the other servants in the household, each one so smoothly orchestrated that they never sensed they were being steered into useful revelations. He'd then spent another few minutes with Lady Aurelie's guardian's bookkeeper to confirm, among other things, that every last pence of Aurelie's allowance had been accounted for. So if she'd run away, she'd had assistance.

"I'm given to understand that you were the last person to see Lady Aurelie."

Madame Aubert regarded him for a moment silently, her mouth a stubborn line, her eyes implacable. "You are in the employ of Lord Brundage, Mr. Hawkes, I presume. Which means he is paying you to find her."

"He has asked me to find his fiancée before any harm comes to her. He is greatly worried about her welfare," he said easily.

Her chin went up. "You may ask your questions, Mr. Hawkes, but I can tell you no more than I told your employer, Lord Brundage. Which is that I know nothing about where she went or why she went. You can do what you will, but I will cast myself in the river before I say more."

He took this in solemnly.

"This will seem a presumption," he said slowly, "and I apologize if I transgress, Madame Aubert. But the world is a cruel and capricious and often ugly place, and lovely women such as yourself are what make life worth living. I find the notion of you casting yourself into the river distressing. It would diminish the beauty of the world."

Her eyes widened as she listened to this, and then she cast them ceiling-ward and shook her head, clearly fighting a smile. "Oh good heavens. You are incorrigible, Mr. Hawkes."

He'd always appreciated that French women viewed flirtation as an art.

"I am devastated that you see right through me, Madame Aubert."

She lost her battle with the smile, and it was lovely.

He smiled back at her.

He watched everything about her soften just a little.

He'd leaned forward, his hands clasped, ostensibly confidingly, but in truth because he thought he'd seen a dark mark on her cheek below her left eye.

This is what she'd attempted to cover with powder and rouge.

What had Brundage said?

She'd been dealt with "summarily."

He felt a pinprick of ice in his gut.

"I was a soldier, Madame Aubert, and your kind of loyalty is precious and valuable. I admire you greatly. Lady Aurelie is fortunate to have you in her employ."

She hesitated. "Thank you," she said, with dignity.

"You must be terribly concerned about her," he said very gently.

He waited.

Her eyes began to brim.

"She is a *very* dear person." She said this forcefully, but her voice cracked with emotion. She straightened her spine. "She is thoughtful and kind—not at all spoiled. She is not a fanciful or reckless girl. She has not been made to feel a burden, but she knows that she has been *tended* to as a duty, rather than loved. I suspect she hoped to find something of a real family with Lord Brundage. She *could* be hopeful despite the events of her life. The loss of her parents. The loss of her oldest brother. That is the kind of person she is."

It was a rather different picture of her than Brundage had provided.

"So you're saying something serious indeed compelled her to leave."

Her eyes flared in alarm. "I did not say that!"

He let it lie. He didn't press.

Because they both knew it was precisely what she'd meant.

"It's terribly difficult to sleep when you're worried about someone," Hawkes said, thoughtfully. "I remember how my mother scarcely slept in the week after my father's death. She is an elegant woman—you remind me a little of how she was when she was younger."

A ghost of a smile here from Madame Aubert.

"She was a strong person, my mother, and she never liked anyone to worry over her. She didn't want people to be concerned when they saw her pale complexion, so she actually—and she *never* did this normally, mind—wore a little rouge and powder." He smiled slightly. "It covered freckles she didn't like, too."

"Oh, yes, I understand," Madame Aubert said warmly. "Nor do *I* normally wear . . ."

She trailed off. She pressed her lips closed.

They regarded each other for a tense moment.

Madame Aubert was intelligent. She had a sense of him now.

And she knew precisely what he'd noticed.

His story about his mother, of course, was entirely apocryphal.

"I am not so graceful," she said carefully. "I passed too swiftly through a doorway and I bumped my cheek."

"Yes. Doorways can be so perilous," he said gravely.

She didn't smile at that.

Now she was frightened.

He was thoughtful a moment. He'd thought there was nothing left in the world that could possibly send a tremor through the bedrock his soul seemed to have become. He'd witnessed Brundage striking a strapping footman, and now he knew why. But the possibility that Brundage would stoop so cravenly low as to strike a small woman, a servant, simply because she displeased him, unsettled him deeply.

Surely Brundage would never dare lift a hand to Lady Aurelie?

For a moment the stiletto point of his concentration wavered.

It wasn't his business to ask Madame Aubert outright about what happened to her. It had naught to do with what he'd been paid to do. She wouldn't tell him the truth, anyway, because Brundage had no doubt succeeded in terrifying her, and he worked for Brundage.

He reminded himself that his mission was to find a girl, and quickly.

"Lord Brundage informs me that he and Lady Aurelie had a bit of an altercation about a month ago. Did you witness this or overhear it?"

Madame Aubert pressed her lips together in thought.

Finally she said, her voice trembling a little, "I did not witness an altercation."

That answer was a thing of beauty from the standpoint of his profession, in that it was like a lid locked over a chest stuffed full of information. He admired it, and it irritated him. "But you knew about it or heard *about* this disagreement?" he pressed.

He waited unblinkingly until, with obvious reluctance, she dipped her chin in a nod.

Madame Aubert's eyes on him were fixed, and almost pleading. She wanted him to stop this line of questioning.

And then he thought he knew why: she was suffering guilt.

He lowered his voice. "Is Tuesday your day off?"

The same day off Brundage's servants were given.

So Lady Aurelie had been alone with Brundage.

That sense of unease plucked at him again. He changed tactics.

Gently, he said, "I do not wish to alarm you, Madame Aubert—and I don't personally believe it—but I have been made aware of some concerns about . . . how do I put this delicately . . . the nature of your character."

"My *character*?" she repeated. Stunned.

"I have heard a rumor—probably scurrilous—that you may, in fact, be selling your clothing and Lady Aurelie's clothing. The popular theory is that you have gambling debts to settle. It has been noted that your wardrobe has changed in the past few weeks. Specifically, you have not been seen in clothing you normally wear. It has also been suggested that in order to settle your debts you may have caused some harm to Lady Aurelie in order to steal from her."

And then violent color rushed into her cheeks and then out again, until the rouge stood out in red patches against stark white.

Her mouth dropped as she struggled for air. For words.

"I would never . . . upon my life . . . I swear upon my mother's grave . . . *hurt* Lady Aurelie?" she stammered, clearly genuinely horrified. "Sacred Mother. Gambling debts! I have never gambled in my life."

He had, of course, wished to scare the devil out of her. It was the best way to breach ironclad loyalty.

He said nothing.

Her slim shoulders moved with her swift, noisy breaths. Her eyes were huge, hunted, and furious.

And then he witnessed, in the gradual slackening

of her features, a calm that came with a certain kind of surrender.

He waited patiently.

"She is *not* a stupid or impulsive girl, Mr. Hawkes." It sounded like the beginning of a narrative. "She is clever and thoughtful."

"So you *do* know for certain that she left of her own accord."

She hesitated again. She was suffering greatly. He admired her fortitude, but it didn't mean he was going to give her any quarter.

"If you do not reply directly, I will assume the answer is 'yes.' And let me remind you that the longer you delay in sharing information with me, the more danger she could be in. The world can be an inhospitable place for a young woman alone, Madame Aubert."

She gave a short, hard laugh. "Oh, yes, better that men should protect them," she said bitterly.

He said nothing. Primarily because he wasn't certain what to say, which was a rare occurrence for a mind accustomed to swiftly finding an angle and exploiting it.

She would not answer the questions this statement raised; of that he was certain.

The answers were not germane to his goal, which was to quickly find Aurelie. And yet he could feel them as a sort of tightening, a pressure, in his chest.

"Oh! I have *here*," he said lightly, offhandedly, pretending to suddenly remember, reaching into his coat pocket, "a list of all dresses and cloaks Lady Aurelie ordered from her modiste over the past two years. Color and style and fabric and trim. Hats and furbelows and whatnot. Would you be so kind as to show me where they are kept, so I can ascertain which dresses she took with her? It will make her easier to locate, you see, when we inevitably fish her body from the Thames after she's been murdered for her jewelry."

She froze. She took them from him as if he'd extended a dead fish.

She stared at them, her head lowered. For a good long time.

He could see the pulse beating in her throat.

And then she swallowed.

"None of them are missing, isn't that so?" he said softly. "Which would certainly look incriminating for you. After all, a dead girl wouldn't need to take clothing with her to heaven. I believe they provide you with a comfortable robe once you arrive at the Pearly Gates. But I've a list of yours, too. For instance, I have it on good authority that your beloved blue cloak seems to have disappeared as you now only wear a brown one."

For this was what Hawkes had spent part of the morning learning from servants.

Madame Aubert slowly lifted her head. Hunted. Furious. Frightened.

"Here is what I think," he said kindly. "You sold some of your clothing to help her finance her journey, and gave her the rest so that she would not be identified by her clothes. She didn't take her own clothing because she didn't want to be recognized, and she wanted to blend in as a more working-class sort of woman. If you do not deny this vehemently, I will assume your silence means 'yes.' And if you answer 'no,' I will, because I am thorough, set about verifying that you are telling the truth and I have ways of learning what I need to know. Do you doubt me?"

He waited.

The silence stretched. A cloud drifted past the sun, and the light in the room went gray. The kind of light that made inexpertly applied rouge on her cheeks seem downright garish.

"I sold them," she whispered. "I sold them to a modiste. And I gave Aurelie the money. And I gave her the rest of the clothes she took."

It was what he'd come to discover. It was time to be brisk.

"To your knowledge, did she sell any jewelry before she departed?"

"There was not a moment save one when I was not with her in public before she departed, and in none of these moments did she sell any jewelry. She was not in possession of any that I am aware of, apart from the emerald necklace Brundage gave to her. I cannot speak for what she has done with it since I last saw her."

"What was the 'save one'?"

She paused. And then she said thickly, "The night she and Brundage had an altercation. It was my day off, you see." Her eyes had begun to gleam again. She gave a little toss. She wasn't about to cry in front of him.

"She went to see him alone?"

He thought perhaps he might have put a little too much emphasis on the last word.

Regardless, Madame Aubert loyally didn't answer this question.

She stared at him, lips pressed together.

Nothing he could say, no amount of charm, would convince her that he would transfer his allegiance to her from Brundage.

"Do you think Lady Aurelie's brother in America would welcome a visit with her?"

Another of those silences fell, as she struggled to honor what was likely a promise to Aurelie. To find a way to answer his question without answering it.

"Would you not welcome a visit from your sister, Mr. Hawkes?" she said ironically. Finally.

"I would, at that." He flashed a smile.

She blinked as though he'd just flung a shooting star at her.

"Would you say she is close to her brother Edouard?"

"They correspond regularly. She is delighted to receive his letters. I'm given to understand that it's as warm as a relationship can be when siblings are separated by an ocean."

Lady Aurelie was going to try to visit her brother in Boston; Hawkes was nearly certain of it.

"Madame Aubert, I am curious about something. I'm given to understand a month elapsed between Aurelie's argument with Lord Brundage and her departure. Was she engaged in preparation to leave this entire time?"

She paused. She gave him a strange look, examining his face almost incredulously. And then her expression went closed.

"It was the soonest she felt she could leave, Mr. Hawkes," she said simply.

He took this in wordlessly. The oddly specific yet vague way in which she'd phrased this troubled him. It was another carefully deliberated answer, he was certain. And all at once the tension between what he wanted to know and what was actually necessary to know made his head feel tight.

He told himself to focus on his mission and became brisk.

"Why don't you save us some time and tell me which clothing she took with her?"

She took a steadying breath, then released it in a surrendering sigh. "A mauve half-mourning dress. A fine blue cloak with a lined hood. A green wool walking dress . . ."

And as she continued to list them, he swiftly took notes on a scrap of paper with the little pencil he kept in his pocket.

When she was done, she sat expressionlessly silent, drained. Her thoughts seemed turned inward.

He sat with her a moment, pondering what to say next.

He leaned toward her and said quietly, with conviction, "Madame Aubert, you have my word of honor that I will only tell my employer that I have reason to believe that Aurelie set out to see her brother in Boston. He will never hear your name from my lips. And my word of honor is all I have left in the world, so I don't give it lightly. I think you have a sense of me now, and so any assumptions you may make about what I would do to protect the integrity that I have would likely be correct."

He smiled again, this time somewhat crookedly.

She searched his face with a certain wonderment. Her cheeks flushed burgundy once more.

And then he stood and peeled off pound notes and he laid them on the table next to her, one after another. Her eyes went larger and larger. It would be enough to tide her over until she found another position. Or until Aurelie returned, should that day arrive.

He had the sense that she didn't believe it would.

"I thank you very much for your time, Madame Aubert. You have been immeasurably helpful."

He stood and took his hat between his hands. He took two steps toward the door. Then paused to look back at her, considering what to say.

Suddenly self-conscious with his eyes on her, she turned her bruised cheek away from him.

"I believe that you are as sensible as you claim Lady Aurelie is, if not more so. And that you will make a wise decision about what to do now."

He said this in all seriousness. The implication was that she ought to take herself where Brundage couldn't find her.

She returned her gaze to him. Her expression mingled cynicism and admiration.

"I think in some ways you're more frightening than your employer, Mr. Hawkes."

"Oh, now you're just flirting with *me*, Madame Aubert," he said, and restored his hat to his head and departed.

Chapter Five

AURELIE'S SLEEP was like a candle snuffed: sudden and black.

When she opened her eyes again, she wasn't certain whether twenty hours had passed or just a few. The light pouring through the little window scarcely seemed changed. She sat up abruptly.

A quick inspection told her the shadows in the room were a little longer now. She'd taken note of where they fell across the floor when she arrived, as though they were furnishings like the braided rug and the soft blue knitted coverlet and the blossoms in a vase. Probably because her senses were still so amplified and abuzz everything seemed delineated in significance. Requiring assessment as a threat.

The strangeness was heightened by the fact that the fabric of her dress felt foreign against her skin. For a disorienting instant, she felt outside of her body, looking down. She was wearing what amounted to a disguise. The fit was close but not perfect, and yet somehow this very fact was comforting: it was a reminder that someone had cared enough to help her. That someone cared at all. Someone had believed her urgency and distress without asking for details.

She was a bit chilly from lying still. She sprang up from the bed and seized the poker and stirred the fire. When new flames leaped forth, she felt like a conjurer.

Then wearing Madame Aubert's clothes, she did what used to be Madame Aubert's job, and unpacked her trunk and hung her borrowed dresses in the little wardrobe.

Once upright, she cautiously admitted to herself that she felt better than she had in weeks, courtesy of the very good tea, scones, kindness, and sudden nap, not to mention being behind a locked door on the third floor of a building far away from Paris. The little mirror on the wall—just the size of her face—was large enough to reveal she had lavender circles beneath her eyes.

The quiet nearly rang after days of clattering wheels and rushing water and milling crowds chattering in dozens of accents. It amazed her, it filled her with absolute steely amazement, that she had done it.

It was ironic to find bliss in the blessed soft, dim aloneness. She'd never before craved being alone any more than a fish would crave the water in which it lived. It was a fact of her days. She'd thought loneliness would finally end when she married Brundage.

Louis had been killed in an uprising. He'd remembered their parents well, and perhaps that was why he'd never stopped being angry, and never seemed to stop fighting. And Edouard had emigrated to Boston, where no one was currently trying to kill French people.

She'd been so often alone. Her upbringing and education had been entrusted to a cadre of governesses and dancing masters and pianoforte teachers and the like, all of whom had been patient and amusing in turns, but they had been paid to be with her. And while she'd met pleasant girls among the daughters of other embassy officials in dancing or archery lessons, and now and again had them for tea, it had always been difficult to deepen the acquaintances into friendships when her uncle's work required them to relocate from Spain to Switzerland to Belgium before they finally settled again in Spain.

So she'd had no true sense of herself as seen through anyone else's eyes—Am I pretty? Am I likable?—until she was finally of age to attend embassy assemblies and balls. She'd blossomed in the realization that others not only liked her, but actually seemed to delight in her company—especially men. She had, indeed, caused a bit of an uproar. She had always taken such care to be quiet and dutiful, and the discovery that she was considered both charming and beautiful went to her head like bolted champagne.

But the sophisticated attentions of the handsome, dashing, older, very important English ambassador—an earl, no less—enthralled her. And once his courtship was earnestly underway, she'd known, with relief, how the rest of her life would unfurl. It would be very like it had always been, only much, much better, and surrounded by family she could call her own.

Her complacency now seemed criminally foolish. Why had she assumed her life would go according to plan? After all, her parents had not expected to be murdered by a guillotine. Her brother Louis had not expected to die in an uprising. How had she not seen the necessity of identifying an escape route, just in case?

Given a choice, would people bother to be born if they knew what fates awaited them?

And she was reminded again of a man she'd seen only twice in Spain, but had never forgotten. When she was still too young to attend the balls held at her guardian's house she would sometimes sneak out onto the landing, and, in a feat of acrobatic craning, peer down from the stairwell through the ballroom doorway and imagine she was one of the ladies twirling past. And there he'd been, framed in the doorway: a charismatic glow at the center of a small crowd of radiant feminine faces, all raptly turned up to his. Aurelie had stopped breathing, as if in so doing she could stop time, and forever experience that piercing delight of coming upon that particular man and that moment. She carried that memory about like the emerald and diamond necklace now sewn into her bodice.

Years later she'd read in the newspaper that this man had gone to prison for espionage. She had always found it impossible to imagine that glowing man in a cell. Likely he'd never dreamed that was the fate that awaited him.

Part of Aurelie's own fate was sewn into her bodice.

The other half hinged upon one of the letters her brother had sent to her. Time was of the essence. She retrieved them from her trunk now.

Dear LiLi,

All of Edouard's letters began this way. He had called her that since she could remember. All of her letters to him began "Dear Dodo," which wasn't quite as nice but it had never stopped being funny to her—it was the best she could do with his name when she was two years old. He tolerated it, with the stipulation that she never slip up and call him that in front of pretty women, or his friends.

If you need assistance with anything when you are in London, please do send a message on to my dear friend Mr. Erasmus

Monroe. I have written to tell him you will be visiting London soon as a grand married lady complete with a titled husband and townhouse on St. James Square. He owes a favor (something to do with gambling—do not scold me! I won!) and he has informed me that he'll gladly do one for you, instead. Just bring this letter to him. Your husband (it feels so strange to write that, my darling idiot sister) probably lolls about with the king or some such, but Mr. Monroe knows where to buy the best ices. The Strand, which is quite an exciting area and probably not one a lady ought to visit alone, which I know will merely serve to intrigue you.

He had included an address to Mr. Erasmus Monroe's home in this famous place, The Strand.

"Your husband." How proud she had been to read those words in her brother's hand. What a thrill it had been to whisper them out loud to herself, rehearsing various inflections and cadences. Both words equally cherished—"My," because someone would belong to her and she to them, at last, and "husband," because the man she was engaged to was an *earl*, and she would be a countess, and this nourished her Bourbon pride. She'd liked to imagine her parents would have approved. She could never know for certain. Unlike her brothers, she had no specific memories of them; she knew them only as a feeling as distinct as weather. It was as though their love had ignited a little hearth inside her, which burned low and eternally. Throughout her more desolately lonely days she had turned to this warmth to remind herself that she had been loved.

She had nothing of her parents' legacy apart from the mother-of-pearl comb her mother had tucked into her hair the very day her parents had been arrested and taken away.

She had looked forward to being a wife, with everything—*everything*—that entailed. And she *knew* what that entailed, because she'd found books not meant for young ladies to read in her guardian's library, and she'd read them, and had blushed, and was beset by a surely unseemly but titillating restlessness.

"Oh, Aurelie, I must have you. Please say you'll be my wife!"

So somber, so gallant, so torturously restrained, Brundage's proposal, muttered against her hair as he'd pulled her into his arms in a corner of a ballroom, near a fern. Surely Byron himself had never said anything so passionate, she'd thought at the time. *I must have you!* She could feel the thrilling, unnerving truth of this vibrating in his body. She'd said, "Yes, please, thank you," and . . . he'd kissed her. She could feel her body respond to this in startlingly specific ways, quite separate from her emotions, which had careened between fear and exhilaration and uncertainty, and were so overwhelming they were nearly inebriating. Odd to think that her body harbored heretofore unsuspected knowledge and needs that only a man could awake.

Brundage had not been humbly grateful for her acceptance, which she would have liked. Or bashful, or speechless, or joyous. He had seemed triumphant. She saw that now. As though she were a prize he had won. As though her acquiescence was proof of his supremacy. And at the time, the notion of this had thrilled her. It conferred value upon her, too.

She ought to have understood. Prizes are objects, after all. Like vases or spittoons.

One could do the unimaginable to an object.

Despite the now healthily leaping fire, she shivered.

She could not imagine Brundage finding her here, in this little room, in this little place. She also knew too well he did not like to be thwarted.

She didn't think there was any question he would try to find her.

And all at once, urgency was upon her, and her breath came as shallowly and swiftly as though even now she was cornered. She yanked the chair out from the little writing desk and scrabbled for one of the sheets of foolscap.

The quill trembled a little in her hand as she wrote.

Dear Mr. Monroe,

My dear brother Edouard Capet has spoken of you in the highest, most affectionate terms and thinks the world of your character. I am his sister, and I am presently in London. Edouard suggested that I make your acquaintance, as you know many useful things, among them where to find the nicest ices, very important indeed! I sincerely hoped you would be able to provide me with some advice regarding the disposition of some of my personal property in London. I intend to sail for America to see Edouard as soon as possible, so the matter is of some urgency. I would like to call upon you this week. If you would kindly reply to my message by addressing it to "Mrs. Mary Gallagher" at The Grand Palace on the Thames, I should be much obliged. I will explain the name when we meet.

Yours Sincerely,
Aurelie, Lady Capet

She hoped she'd struck the right note of charm, respect, and familiarity, and that Mr. Erasmus Monroe was a clever man. If Edouard had indeed written to him the news of her engagement, words like "America" and "urgency," not to mention the sudden startling introduction of a "Mrs. Mary Gallagher," would alarm, or at least intrigue him. Perhaps he was kind and protective, like Edouard.

Faith was a *decision* one made, she knew, in the absence of absolute knowledge. And she'd decided to put her faith in her brother's judgment, and her brother's friend. She could not afford to do otherwise.

And she prayed Mr. Monroe would help her to sell the necklace, and then help her to find someone trustworthy and respectable with whom she could travel. She was not naive enough to believe that the world abounded with sturdy and congenial Mary Gallaghers, or to think for a moment she ought to go alone.

If she posted the letter first thing in the morning, it ought to reach Mr. Monroe later in the day.

Her entire future depended upon selling that necklace for passage. Thanks to Madame Aubert's generosity, she had enough money for perhaps a month's worth of lodging and perhaps small necessities.

And then she'd have . . .

She'd have nothing.

Black spots scudded before her vision.

She covered her eyes briefly with her cold hands. Then she filled her lungs with a long steadying breath and sighed and pulled her hands away again, as if to admonish herself for the impulse to hide from her reality for even a second.

One never knew. She could just as easily be on the precipice of triumph as disaster.

Still, it was difficult to escape the bitter irony then that she might indeed be useless for anything beyond being a wife for a man like Brundage.

And at that she would have been superb.

No matter what, no matter how foolish or futile it might prove to be, no matter where or how she might end up, she was determined to claim her life for herself. She owed it to her parents, who had not been able to escape their fates.

She sprinkled sand and sealed the letter with a press of wax and a whispered prayer and prepared to go down to dinner.

Chapter Six

OUT OF the corner of Aurelie's eye, the fork held by a man named Mr. Delacorte flashed as it rose and fell again and again with the rhythmic speed of the second hand on a clock. It had taken a minute or two to become accustomed to it. Now she found it almost soothing.

Apart from posting her letter to Mr. Erasmus Monroe, she'd kept to her room for two days as the rules allowed it, resting, gathering nerve to face the other guests, savoring the quiet and safety. She'd written another letter to her brother Edouard to pass the time. Mrs. Hardy had loaned her a book by a Mr. Miles Redmond, which she'd said might be enthralling or sleep inducing. Aurelie welcomed either outcome, and it turned out to be a bit of both. But she could hear the cheerful voices on the stairwell, and the maids were so lively and pleasant when they came in to tend to her fires and to bring her tea, that she began to crave company. So down she went.

Aurelie had never had dinners quite like this one: in a small warm room, surrounded by hungry, cheerful strangers and the sound of chewing and the slosh of gravy. In her uncle's residences—she'd never quite thought of them as her own—she was used to hearing her own footsteps echo as she moved through rooms furnished with Chippendale furniture and framed portraits of wigged and ruffed dignitaries. She'd often dined at glossy tables as long as lifeboats with just the silver candlesticks and the to-ing and fro-ing servants for company. And she'd attended formal dinners when she was older, which were very like balls, only seated, choreographed, and orderly, with servants at everyone's elbow.

Here, the food was passed from hand to hand, and often across the table. Occasionally the potatoes nearly collided with the peas midair, to general chuckles. Fascinatingly, it seemed the general mood was particularly ebullient in part because someone named Mr. Tweedy had accepted a job as a footman. And this was a novelty, too: the notion that a footman, something as ubiquitous as furniture in what she'd come to think of as her previous life, could be a prized acquisition.

Mr. Delacorte had the right of it, she discovered when she got her fork up to her mouth. The fish stew was *delicious* and she hadn't had a good full meal in days. She was certain she would welcome the temporary stupor of being quite full, and set about doing just that.

An actual viscount (Mrs. Durand's husband, Lord Bolt, slyly witty) and a captain (Mrs. Hardy's husband, dryly witty) made for handsome bookends on either side of the dinner table.

"I'm a widow, too, my dear," said Mrs. Pariseau, gently. She had dark, dancing eyes and dazzling white stripes in her dark hair. "It gets better."

All had been gracious and welcoming, lending credence to Mrs. Hardy's and Mrs. Durand's interview practices: Not a cretin or rogue in evidence. Nobody fixed her in their sights and began asking probing questions. The men did not ogle. They were all clearly gentlemen, even Mr. Delacorte. And contrary to how she'd thought she might feel amidst strangers, something in her eased, rather than knotted more tightly. She felt suddenly as if she had just a little more air to breathe. Like a bird reintroduced to the sky from a cage, perhaps. She was not fundamentally made to be alone.

She was grateful for their kindness and solicitousness, even if she still felt she'd come by it somewhat fraudulently. It meant she could take refuge in silence, if she wished, and just observe.

She surreptitiously noted how Captain Hardy sought Mrs. Hardy's eyes from time to time, and how Lord Bolt sought Mrs. Durand's. With merry warmth, or a sort of wondering stillness. As if every moment could be improved by reminding themselves of each other's existence. As if the fact of each other still amazed them.

She realized she'd not ever truly witnessed marriages in their humble domestic form. This cozy intimacy, this silent language, this clear regard and comfort and familiarity, made her heart contract with yearning and something . . . very like shame. Because she simply . . . she simply hadn't realized what a marriage ought to look like. She could not have even guessed.

From their first introduction, Brundage had spoken to her as one adult to another, respectfully and attentively, while his eyes did breathtakingly adult things—fixed upon her mouth a gaze so intent it burned, or dipped swiftly to the swell of her décolletage, only to return to her face, dazed. She had not known whether it was fear or desire which took away her breath when he did this—she'd thought perhaps they were merely the two sides of a coin? She knew so little of such things between men and women.

He'd courted her with exhilarating charm and intensity and intention. If she spoke to or laughed with or even mentioned another man at an assembly, he would refuse to speak to her for the rest of the night. She was moved and thrilled by his suffering and jealousy—it was her first ever taste of her own sensual power and the intoxicating responsibility that came with it.

Now and again, she'd test him to reassure herself of his regard—teasing him with a glance at him over her shoulder as she waltzed by in the arms of another man, or laughing merrily with a crowd of admirers, just so she could later flirt and charm and soothe him out of his glowers and silences.

She had never been so noticed. She had never been so wanted. She had never felt so womanly.

She had never been an *obsession*.

And this made her feel like a heroine in a story.

And she'd thought: Surely such things added up to love?

She'd once watched as a spider wrapped a fly round and round in gossamer-sticky silk and wondered—at what point does the fly realize they can no longer move?

With Brundage, it had happened in silky increments, just like that.

Heat flooded into her cheeks.

She stared down at her delicious fish stew. Suddenly she couldn't eat another bite.

After dinner everyone collected in the cozy sitting room opposite the reception room in which she had been interviewed. None of the furniture quite matched in size or color or provenance, but the glow of the fire and the lamps scattered about cast everything in the room, including its occupants, in a flattering light, so that the result was a sort of picturesque harmony. A pianoforte at one end of the room somehow managed to look poised and alert, as though it hoped someone would come along to play it.

Mr. Delacorte and Lord Bolt faced each other across a chessboard, Captain Hardy had a book and a table to himself, and the ladies embarked on a discussion of whether to play spillikins or perhaps whist while one of them read aloud.

Aurelie still felt cautious, but undaunted. Pulled between the desire for anonymity and the pleasure of being a part of something, of being both wanted and expected by everyone here.

Thankfully, nothing specific seemed required of her apart from her presence, which was novel and lovely, too. Everyone seemed to have taken for granted that she belonged.

"Oh!" Mrs. Pariseau exclaimed suddenly. "Mrs. Durand, you ought to read to Mrs. Gallagher the part of Mr. Bellingham's letter about how Eleanor the chicken can play noughts-and-crosses," Mrs. Pariseau urged.

"Noughts-and-crosses?" Aurelie was astonished. "But she hasn't any fingers!"

When everyone laughed, she blushed with pleasure. It hadn't quite ceased feeling new and delightful, the notion that people might like her or find her amusing.

But she was conscious now of a hesitancy that preceded anything she said. A tension in the pit of her stomach, a bracing, that followed in the wake of laughter she'd inspired. Brundage had at first seemed to revel in her charm. He'd claimed to love her laugh.

And then came the night she'd laughed at something his footman had said about the weather.

Aurelie took a steadying breath.

"With her beak, if you can believe it, Mrs. Gallagher," Mrs. Pariseau told her. She mimicked pecking, complete with flapping arms.

Aurelie, and everyone else, laughed.

"I wonder if she can play chess that way," Delacorte mused. "I wonder if she would take as long to make a move as Lord Bolt here."

"You know you can't intimidate me, Delacorte," Bolt said absently. "But your efforts amuse me, so carry on."

Mr. Delacorte was the resident chess champion, but Bolt won with respectable frequency.

"All three of us are due at White's for drinks with the chaps from Lloyd's in an hour, so I'd be obliged if you'd lose faster, Bolt," Captain Hardy contributed.

Mr. Delacorte grinned. Lord Bolt shot Hardy a wry glance.

"Do you play chess, Mrs. Gallagher?" Dot asked her.

"Oh, yes. In fact, very well, indeed." She smiled across at Mr. Delacorte.

He said nothing, but blushed a rather adorable shade of pale strawberry.

Angelique cleared her throat.

"Let's see . . . I've found the part of Mr. Bellingham's letter, Mrs. Gallagher . . . Mr. Bellingham writes, '. . . and one day I drew a grid of noughts-and-crosses, just for fun, in the dust in the yard of the vicarage. And I aver Eleanor pecked so decisively at a square, I drew a cross there for her. Then I drew a naught in another square. We carried on like this until she won the game!' "

Everyone laughed again.

"If only Bolt had as much of a chance at winning as Eleanor . . ." Mr. Delacorte mused.

Aurelie and everyone else stifled smiles.

"What do you suppose Mr. Bellingham looks like?" Dot asked.

"I think he has a little beard," Mrs. Pariseau postulated.

Everyone turned to her in bemused silence.

"It just seems a beardy name, Mr. Bellingham does," Mrs. Pariseau expounded placidly.

"Interesting! Beards are not very fashionable at the moment," Delilah remarked. "Perhaps we ought to lay a little wager. If Mr. Bellingham has a beard . . ." she prompted.

Aurelie was uncertain about betting. Mild alarm must have registered in her expression.

"Poor Mrs. Gallagher, first we try to foist a brandy on her, and now the talk of gambling. She's going to think we're a den of iniquity. You needn't worry, Mrs. Gallagher! We promise our wagers are always very benign."

"If Mr. Bellingham has a beard . . . then we will read aloud from a book of Mr. Miles Redmond's stories of the South Seas this week instead of *The Ghost in the Attic*," suggested Mrs. Pariseau.

Who promptly exchanged a challenging little glare with Dot.

"Mrs. Gallagher, do you like ghosts?" Dot asked her suddenly. With the faintest, startling hint of belligerence. Not directed *at* her, necessarily, Aurelie sensed.

This was clearly an important, possibly even controversial, question, as everyone had gone silent and was studying her curiously.

And this was what it would be like to be in a family, she supposed. She wanted to say the right thing, but she also wanted to be herself, and she wanted to laugh, and she wanted them to approve of her, and for a moment all of the conflicting wants muted her.

"Well, I am tempted to say no. But I . . . have not yet met one, so I should not like to risk impugning them by offering an opinion."

Everyone laughed, and she was relieved and quite pleased again.

"'Impugn' means insult," Angelique told Dot quietly.

"Thank you," Dot whispered.

"You seem like the sort of person who would like a story about ghosts, and it's *ever* so good of a story," Dot flattered. "I find something new to like about it every time I hear it."

"Mrs. Gallagher strikes me as a *sensible* lady, and she wouldn't go into the attic if she knew a frightening ghost lived in it," Mrs. Pariseau said.

Aurelie rather liked both of their interpretations of her character, frankly. She wasn't certain either of them was entirely true.

"Doesn't someone have to die in order for there to be a ghost?" Aurelie asked. "What if it's someone you once knew? Would it still be scary?"

She'd clearly just lobbed a philosophical grenade of some sort. Everyone's head pivoted toward her. Dot looked stricken, as though this simply had never occurred to her, Mrs. Pariseau's eyes gleamed with fascinated approval at her contribution, and Captain Hardy and Lord Bolt seemed both amused and intrigued.

"I imagine it depends on who it was, and how they feel about being vaporous," Lord Bolt mused.

"I'm not certain ghosts are vapor, Lord Bolt," Mrs. Pariseau reflected. "Perhaps it would feel more like cobwebs if a ghost brushes by you."

Dot's face reflected pure horror. Her jaw swung open. She had clearly not thought about the actual composition of a ghost.

"Why do you suppose you like the story so much, Dot?" Aurelie ventured.

Dot had obviously not deeply considered this, either, and bit her lip. "She's ever so brave to go in the attic when she won't know what she'll find. She doesn't know if it's dangerous or not but she *needs* to know, or she'll never have any peace."

"Perhaps we don't mind being a little frightened by a book when we know we are in no real danger," Aurelie suggested hesitantly. "Perhaps it's a way to remind ourselves that we are safe. And that way we appreciate our safety a little more."

She noticed, because she was now almost painfully attuned to nuances, the swift little glance Delilah and Angelique exchanged. When their eyes returned to her, they seemed to have gone softer with sympathy, and *maybe* a hint of conjecture. Even a sort of knowing. It made her feel briefly unmasked.

She ducked her gaze.

But she had another question, and perhaps it was safe to ask it under cover of the literally spirited discussion.

"If the heroine of the story is confronted by something scary and must run away, and her only choice is to flee into the attic, which may or may not also be scary . . . is she still brave?"

She was touched by how everyone seemed to take the question seriously.

Mrs. Pariseau was gazing upon her with approving interest. "It's quite a choice, isn't it? Not everyone has the nerve to even run from something scary. Some would just give up straightaway, I should think. So I think one would have to be brave. Or perhaps optimistic, or possessed of faith."

It was a very good answer. She *was* possessed of faith. Even if she hadn't yet heard from Mr. Erasmus Monroe.

"I think *you're* ever so brave to go on a journey across the ocean by yourself, Mrs. Gallagher," Dot flattered. "Which is why I think you would like this story. It's a story about a *brave* woman who goes into the attic."

Not a stupid *woman,* were Dot's unspoken words.

It was well played. Mrs. Pariseau cast her eyes heavenward and sighed.

"Does it have a happy ending?" Aurelie ventured. Suddenly she was curious to hear how other terrifying stories ended.

"I don't think I ought to tell you how the story ends," Dot said, craftily. "Because that's the best part."

Aurelie suddenly, fervently hoped this was true.

"I think we should read aloud from *The Ghost in the Attic* while we can, because Bellingham will probably want to read sermons aloud or some such," Mr. Delacorte said grimly. "And make little declarations and moral pronouncements and whatnot."

"I suppose it could go either way," Mrs. Pariseau said. "He seems amusing. And I should think vicars have seen and heard a good deal of humanity and are the recipients of all manner of confidences, and that little surprises them."

"Well, he's never met Delacorte," Lord Bolt said idly.

Aurelie's head shot up worriedly. But Mr. Delacorte snorted in delight, looking positively radiantly pleased to be teased.

"At any rate, we'll find out tomorrow," Angelique said with relish. "Mr. Bellingham expects to arrive just a few hours after Mr. Tweedy. And Mr. Tweedy will be here first thing in the morning."

The notion that other people did indeed carry about burdens they could never share with anyone but a vicar, or perhaps a priest, made her feel briefly less alone. She wondered if it would show on Mr. Bellingham's face—the secrets he carried about.

She touched a hand to her cheek, then dropped it immediately.

She wondered if it showed on her own.

Chapter Seven

"Berwick! You're not dead yet, more's the pity, you scurvy bastard."

Berwick squinted through the smoke of the Goat's Head pub and his broad, seamed face lit up with a blend of delight, surprise, and wicked speculation when he saw Hawkes approaching.

"Well, well. A pox on ye, Hawkes. I was lookin' forward to spittin' on yer grave, I was. Them Frenchies missed an opportunity when they didna shoot ye. Ye're not quite lookin' in the pink, are ye, sir?"

Affectionate greetings out of the way, in one fluid motion, Hawkes yanked a chair out, sat down, and thunked the bottle of gin in the center of the table.

All eyes nearest them in the pub went to the sound. They knew precisely what it was, and most of the men in there dangerously hungered for it.

Hawkes counted on it.

Seven years ago, Berwick had tried to rob Hawkes in an alley, and found himself up against a wall, the point of Hawkes's knife glinting at his throat, instead. They'd swiftly come to an understanding whereby Hawkes agreed not to send him to the gallows if Berwick fed him useful information. They'd ultimately forged a sort of alliance. And after a fashion, a friendship.

Berwick became a hack driver after that failed robbery. It was, in fact, Berwick who had driven the man suspected of being Cafard to his own wedding in Norfolk and, showing admirable initiative, had lingered to read the church register, where of all bloody things, Cafard had signed the name Florian Vasseur. And Hawkes had only pointed out Cafard to Berwick once before.

Truthfully, Hawkes *wasn't* quite feeling in the pink. He'd slept badly for days, unaccustomed to decent beds and beset by fitful dreams. But the morning had begun with a triumph: Mr. Harrigan of Harrigan & Sons had scrambled to answer Hawkes's questions when he'd stopped into their offices and produced the letter of introduction from the Earl of Brundage. Did an important personage such as the earl truly entrust Harrigan & Sons to keep all of his account books, present and past, both personal and for the embassy? By way of reply, Mr. Harrigan gestured proudly to the earl's books, neatly labeled by year, arrayed on the shelf behind him. And would they be so kind as to give a former prisoner of war the address of a particular charity listed in one of those books so he could write to them and thank them for their efforts to supplement the meager prison rations?

Of a certainty, for Mr. Hawkes, war hero and friend of the Earl of Brundage, they would.

Thusly Hawkes learned that the funds submitted to the Society for the Relief of English Prisoners of War had been collected by a purveyor of fine antiquities in Bond Street by the name of Roland Guthrie.

The same bloody place Pike the footman had mentioned.

"And then I presume the funds were submitted to Lloyd's Patriotic Fund, sir," Harrigan told him. "Like all the other collections taken up in shops and coffee houses to help our prisoners. Because it's no longer on the books after the war."

When Hawkes departed (like a wraith, five minutes and a few seconds later), Harrigan & Sons were the proud keepers of all of Brundage's account books . . . save two.

He'd feigned a coughing fit and tucked them into his coat when Mr. Harrigan went to fetch a glass of water. So he was, after a fashion, a thief—even if the ends justified the means.

Which he supposed gave him something more in common with Berwick, whose hand was creeping across the table toward the bottle of gin.

Hawkes's arm shot out and swept it out of his reach. "I have a few questions."

"And 'ere I thought we be celebratin' our reunion," Berwick said with great bitterness. "Not an ounce of sentiment in ye, Hawkes."

"I'm looking for a woman."

"Git yer own woman. That is not me line o' work," he said pompously.

"A very pretty, obviously well-bred woman," Hawkes continued patiently. "She's about your height. Would have departed in prime murder and robbery hours of the morning two days ago in a hack from somewhere near the docks, deposited by a mail coach. Perhaps spoke in a slight but noticeable French accent."

Hawkes had told Brundage only that he'd learned Aurelie had likely gone to London, and that he'd be taking a room at the Stevens and questioning his sources in pubs frequented by hack drivers, a notion which made Brundage just barely suppress a shudder. Brundage said he would make the crossing to Dover a day or so after Hawkes; they fixed a date to meet a week hence at Brundage's townhouse in St. James Square.

Time was on Hawkes's side: bad weather had delayed Lady Aurelie's Channel crossing from Calais to Dover for six days. Innkeepers and hack drivers and dock workers remembered a genteel young woman traveling unaccompanied. And from Dover she'd allegedly boarded a mail coach.

But his own crossing was uneventful, and took the usual six hours.

All of this meant she'd arrived in London only about two days ahead of him.

She'd been deposited by the mail coach near the docks in London and was allegedly promptly whisked away in a hack. Which is when her trail went cold.

Assuming she'd been unbothered or unrobbed until now, Hawkes knew enough about the world not to have faith in her luck holding. Urgency dogged his heels.

"Oh, pretty French piece? Aye, she indeed left in an 'ack," Berwick said at once, nonchalantly. He maneuvered a bit of what was likely meat pie from between his teeth with a fingernail and then brushed his fingers on his waistcoat.

Hawkes didn't blink. But he felt that familiar tingling along his scalp that presaged a truth. Berwick knew everybody in his current particular stratum of society—the drivers, the watchmen, the costermongers, the shop clerks—and he *heard* about all the other strata—the lords and ladies, the prostitutes and thieves—and he *loved* to talk.

Hawkes made a rude scoffing noise. "Come now. Do you expect me to believe you? Who told you this?"

There was nothing like a little scorn to spur on a stubborn man.

"Davie Plunkett, that's 'oo told me," Berwick said indignantly. "'e said he picked up a fine piece what tipped him *large*. And by that I dinna mean she fucked 'im, I mean she gave him a nice little bit of extra jingle."

"Thank you *indeed* for the clarification," Hawkes said dryly.

"DAVIE!" Berwick bellowed across the pub. He beckoned with great scoops of his hand.

A man swiveled his head around, then scraped his chair back from a table and maneuvered through the crowd. Davie proved to be a small man well insulated with fat, a practical sop to the chilly career of hack driving. His tiny eyes were bright and shrewd. A surprisingly dashing knitted scarf was wound around his neck.

"The girl what you saw in the wee hours," Berwick commanded. "Tell our friend Hawkes 'ere about 'er."

He brightened. "Oh, aye. Was a wee gift to a lonely man at that time o' the mornin'."

"What was she wearing?" Hawkes asked.

"Wore a hood up over her head at first, ye see. Her cloak was blue, I think. Like a queen would wear. Soft and flowing, like." He traced the air eloquently with his hands. "She was no light skirt, and I knows me light skirts, if ye takes my meaning." He winked. "Then a wind came up like it does, ye see, and her hood blew away from her face—what do I sees? I sees just a glimpse of a face like an angel, and I thinks to meself, what if she *is* an angel and this is a test of me immortal soul?" he said earnestly.

"As any man understandably would," Hawkes said amiably.

"Gave me pause, I tell you. And so I took 'er to an inn by the East India docks, because I knew 'twas out of the way, like. Used to be a brothel. Called summat to do wi' rogues? Must be a decade on since 'twas called that."

He bellowed over his shoulder. "What was that place called where a bloke could get a girl to do the Vicar's Wheelbarrow wiv 'im for harf a crown once upon a time?" He called over his shoulder to a general drunken approbation and hoots.

Hawkes didn't ask for a description of the Vicar's Wheelbarrow, but he could very well imagine what it entailed and who played the part of the wheelbarrow.

"The Palace of Rogues, Davie," a grizzled fellow by the fire bellowed. This was followed by a low rumbly chorus of prurient reminiscence.

"That's the one! Ye take the Barking Road. Then just before them livery stables, ye can cut right through 'em—there's a narrow street between, like—makes a bit of a"—he traced a Z shape in the air—"you'll come out abut a wee street called Lovat or Lovely or summat like that. That's where it is. Shiny and white and respectable on the outside now. They likes to call it a *grand* palace, methinks." He shook his head. "Anyhow, I thought an angel belonged at a Grand Palace."

Triumph and relief burned through the layers of Hawkes's weariness: if she had, in fact, made it to an inn, she was still safe.

Hawkes wasn't about to fish out his gold timepiece in this particular pub, but the watch had cried ten o'clock before he set foot in the place.

He pushed the bottle of gin over to Berwick, stealthily produced two shillings for the two men, which they snapped up, and pushed away from the table with a "My thanks, gentlemen."

But first thing tomorrow morning he'd go in search of an angel at the former Palace of Rogues.

TWELFTH NIGHT AND Saint Nicholas Day were nothing compared to the breathless anticipation of the night before Mr. Tweedy Day.

Angelique and Delilah greeted each other at the top of the stairs, yawning but filled with the joy of the day. They'd both tiptoed about getting dressed to allow their husbands to sleep a little longer: Captain Hardy and Lord Bolt had come home (by curfew, of course) mildly foxed from having brandy after brandy pressed upon them at White's, toppled straight into their beds, snuggled up to their wives, and commenced snoring.

The two women could faintly hear Mr. Delacorte, who had gone with them, still snoring, two floors down. ("Try to think of it as the house purring," Delilah had once suggested to Captain Hardy, who had, upon his original arrival, been installed in the room below Delacorte.)

On the second floor landing they were delighted to encounter Mrs. Pariseau and Mrs. Gallagher, both dressed and reasonably bright-eyed and clearly ready for breakfast.

"Good morning, Mrs. Pariseau, Mrs. Gallagher. We hope you slept well," Mrs. Durand said.

They were pleased to see that Mrs. Gallagher, pretty in a mauve dress, looked a little more rested each day.

"I did indeed, thank you," Mrs. Gallagher told her. "I'm hoping the mail I've been expecting will arrive today," she told them.

"Perhaps Mr. Tweedy will bring it up to you when it does," Mrs. Hardy said with giddy relish.

"Ohhh, *perhaps*!" Mrs. Pariseau enthused. "All of the little tasks we can hand off to a footman!"

Together they clambered down the stairs.

"Well, look at this!" Angelique exclaimed when they arrived in the foyer.

New footman fever seemed to have infected the maids with fervor. Maggie and Rose were sweeping the black-and-white marble and dusting the buttocks of the cherubs that frolicked on the carved banister, respectively. Dot was in the reception room, installing and fluffing fresh flowers in the vase. All the fires were leaping healthily. The chandelier crystals sprinkled a few rainbows over this idyllic scene.

And Helga had even come up from the kitchen, where the work she loved never ended, to complete the greeting party. Her golden hair was neatly braided and pinned up on her head and her round cheeks scrubbed to rosiness.

"I thought we could take a little morning tea first, then lay out a nice breakfast to get thoroughly acquainted," she told them. "And I wanted Mr. Bellingham to finally taste my scones as soon as possible."

Mr. Bellingham had mentioned his enthusiasm for scones in one of his letters. The Farradays had exulted about Helga's to him.

"Oh, splendid idea, Helga, thank you!" Delilah told her.

They all turned at the sound of Mr. Delacorte's familiar footfall on the stairs. He paused, yawning broadly. He was still a bit bleary-eyed, but fully dressed. He gave his bottom a surreptitious little scratch.

"Did we wake you, Mr. Delacorte?" Angelique asked apologetically.

"Oh, I think perhaps, but no trouble at all. It's a big day, ain't it? I didn't want to miss it, either."

They smiled at him.

Helga said, "We've coffee made, Mr. Delacorte, if the maids haven't yet brought yours up to your—"

WHUMP.

They all gave a start and whirled as something hit the front door.

In unified motionless silence, they stared at the door. Nonplussed.

"I've never heard a knock quite like that," Dot ventured quietly.

"I . . . don't think that was a knock, per se," Angelique replied, cautiously.

"It sounded a bit like a bag of flour thrown at the door," Helga mused.

And Helga would know what a thrown bag of flour sounded like.

"Perhaps a large bird crashed into it," Dot suggested.

"How very colorful, Dot," Delilah said a little tensely. They could do without surprises today.

Everyone continued to eye the door warily.

"Well, we wouldn't want to leave either Mr. Bellingham or Mr. Tweedy waiting, would we, just in case this heralds their arrival?" Angelique said brightly. "Best have a look, Dot."

So Dot took the liberty of opening the peep hatch. "Funny, but I don't *see* anyone . . . or anything . . ." she reported. "I suppose I'll just have a look outside."

Before Angelique or Delilah could issue any sort of message of caution Dot pulled open the door.

And in staggered a man.

Everyone gasped and leaped backward.

A glance told them it wasn't Mr. Tweedy: the cravat, the fine coat, the boots as shiny as the marble floors—this was a capital "G" gentleman.

He seemed to struggle to remain upright, but he lost his battle with gravity.

He dropped hard to his knees, and they gasped again.

His hat bounced off and skittered across the foyer.

He attempted to right himself. He collapsed, and flopped over onto his back, his arms and legs splayed, head lolling.

Which is when they all saw a great red spreading stain on his clean white shirt.

For a tick of absolute silence, they stared down at him, mouths agape in horror.

Then Dot threw back her head.

And there emerged from her throat a scream so ear shattering and operatic and blood freezing that Rose shrieked and crumpled into her first actual swoon in an unromantic thud on the marble. Maggie saw the perfect opportunity to also shriek and feign a swoon, and dropped with more deliberation next to Rose on the foyer.

The foyer was now littered with bodies.

"Mr. Bellingham! *Someone killed the vicar!* SOMEONE KILLED *MR. BELLINGHAM!*" Dot shrieked, sounding both absolutely indignant and horrified.

That's when the ground began to vibrate beneath them.

Everyone gasped and moaned in terror again.

AURELIE'S HEART LURCHED like a banged gong.

The whole building trembled, and then a low rumble became audible, and the rumble swiftly swelled into a deafening thundering that surely heralded

Armageddon and Aurelie found herself instinctively reaching out for Delilah's hand as Delilah was reaching out for her, because if this was the end of the world it seemed, somehow, important to be touching another human. At one end of the foyer, Helga and Mrs. Pariseau leaped into each other's arms; at the other, Angelique continued to muffle Dot.

But it was just the sound of Captain Hardy and Lord Bolt taking three flights of stairs at a run.

"DELILAH!" The word was a primal roar. The bare-chest blur that was Captain Hardy skipped the last four steps, hurdled the banister, and landed in the foyer, pistol in hand, and Lucien, trouserless, shirttails sailing like wings, soared after him, and that's when Maggie, conveniently already on the floor, fainted in earnest.

"I'm here! Tristan! We're here!" Delilah steered them to the bloody man.

Bolt, long shirt whipping about his legs and barely protecting his modesty, whirled like a mad compass until he saw Angelique.

Aurelie would never forget the look on his face then.

And then he and Captain Hardy dropped to their knees next to the man in the foyer.

Dot took a long, long breath and began anew. *"SOMEONE KILLED MR. BELLINGMMPH—"*

Angelique clapped her hand over Dot's mouth and walked her backward toward the parlor.

Captain Hardy pressed his fingers against the man's pulse. "He's alive. Can you tell us your name please, sir?"

There was a brief lull while everyone held their breath, and waited, and prayed.

"I'm going to *kill* that bastard," the man muttered viciously.

Two complete seconds of absolutely shocked silence dropped like an anvil.

"Knife wound, looks like," Lucien told Captain Hardy grimly. He'd swiftly, gently gotten the man's shirt up. "A slash, not a puncture. Ugly, but it could be worse. I think."

Aurelie looked down at Mr. Bellingham's face, then regretted it, because she felt as though she'd committed a violation. His eyes were half-closed, his bronze lashes stark against pale sharp cheekbones, his hat jarred from his head, his hair mussed. His throat tipped back and exposed. His clothes were a gentleman's well-tended clothes and for some reason his shiny boots moved and upset her unbearably. All the humble things people do every day, caring for their boots and such, suddenly seemed almost silly, like acts of pure faith, when dignity and life could be stripped in seconds.

His utter vulnerability filled her with such an inexplicable and nearly intolerable rage her heart ricocheted about her chest like a trapped animal.

Before she realized she was even moving, she was across the foyer crouching next to Lord Bolt, her handkerchief in hand. She pressed it into Lord Bolt's hand.

"Thank you," Bolt said curtly.

Until that moment she hadn't known she was the kind of person who would run toward a bleeding man rather than shrink away.

Bolt swiftly folded it and pressed her handkerchief against the wound.

It was quickly scarlet.

Her head went light with fear. She briefly closed her eyes and mouthed one word, half prayer, half oath, and she stood back quickly to allow Captain Hardy and Lord Bolt to take charge of him.

"Delacorte, we'll need your help to get him into a room. We need to get them out of here," Lucien ordered tersely. He jerked his head in the direction of the prone maids.

After a few seconds worth of milling about in indecision, Helga and Mrs. Pariseau gamely but gently seized the maids' ankles, hoisted their legs, and like horses hitched to plows, undertook to drag them very gently across the smooth, spotless marble foyer.

Just as Mr. Tweedy cheerfully stepped through the ajar door.

He was wearing a happy smile.

(Delilah would remember this later, and it comforted her a little. He'd been so happy to come to them!)

He attempted to fling his arms up over his eyes, but it was too late. His vision was at once filled with Maggie's stockinged calves all the way up to her garters, two half-naked men brandishing pistols crouching over another half-naked man bleeding beneath the chandelier, while Mrs. Durand seemed to be smothering a bulging-eyed, shrieking Dot with one hand in the reception room.

He quickly backed out and closed the door behind him, turned, swiftly departed the way he came.

They never saw him again.

(To his credit, while he did have a few confusing dreams about it as the years went by, he never spoke of it to another human.

He was, indeed, the soul of discretion.)

Chapter Eight

THE WOMEN currently residing under the roof of the house had gathered in the kitchen, as though it were the keep of a castle under siege. They all felt a little like they'd been drained of blood, too. Their hearts and nerves (and vocal cords, in the case of Dot, the recipient of many a sidelong baleful glare) had taken some punishment. Copious amounts of tea would be required to restore them to anything like equilibrium. They'd all gotten two cups down so far.

Bolt and Hardy, both seasoned fighters, familiar with getting and inflicting wounds and then doing something about them, had determined that the gash was a bit long but it wasn't horrifically deep. All of the man's nearby organs seemed to remain whole and safely inside his body. He was as lucky as a man who'd been stabbed could be.

Lucien had bravely volunteered to sew up the man. Because, as he said, "I've done it before. My stitches are a thing of beauty."

The ladies had been told that Mr. Bellingham had been in and out of consciousness and shockingly silent and stoic, apart from hissed-in breaths and a white-knuckled clench around the block of wood they'd given him to grip. It was as though he'd known precisely how to get sewn up.

But he seemed unable to say another complete word after his first startling ones.

Visiting that kind of horrible pain on another man even as a life-saving measure took a toll. After he'd finished, a white-faced Lucien had gone outside to the little park named for his mother to be alone for a moment and take deep breaths. There he waited for Mr. Delacorte and an apothecary; Mr. Delacorte had run up the road to fetch him, as he knew which of the remedies in his case cured or alleviated various ailments but he wasn't always certain which doses to administer now, and he didn't want to go and poison a man who seemed to have survived, so far, being stabbed.

"It was the sort of thing Mr. Tweedy could have done," Delilah said wistfully.

"Fetch the apothecary for stabbed men who topple through doorways?" Angelique mused.

"Precisely."

They'd both seen Mr. Tweedy back out of the building. Mostly they'd seen the whites of his eyes, which had been bulging like billiard balls.

It seemed an ill-omened day indeed.

"Perhaps puffed sleeves weren't the way to go after all," Angelique reflected.

Delilah attempted a laugh but it became a sigh.

They were both, in fact, genuinely a bit glum and a bit reeling.

An earl and his family had resided comfortably with them for some weeks. So had a duke. And not just any duke—the Duke of *Valkirk*. The *king* had visited. No one had stabbed any of them. They supposed anyone could be assaulted anywhere at any time in London. And yet they could not help but feel responsible.

But dear Mr. Bellingham . . . on the threshold of their own building . . .

The work of The Grand Palace on the Thames house continued while all of this with poor Mr. Bellingham was being sorted out. Peeling (apples and potatoes and onions), rolling, kneading, cleaning. The maids, revived, soothed and set upright, were soberly finishing up the dusting and scrubbing blood droplets from the foyer.

But everyone in the kitchen, easily distracted, kept starting and stopping their tasks to stare into space.

Aurelie sat quietly at the table, listening to the work going on about her. Though she had been provided some instruction regarding decisions involved in running an aristocratic household, she had not been trained to cook, of course, and so this room fascinated her, too. She was pleased to be among the women, but she suspected everyone present would assume that someone named Mrs. Gallagher would know how to cook, and she worried that the conversation would turn to recipes and such things.

"I find it soothing to fold apples into tarts," Delilah said to her. "When I am full of thoughts."

And so that was what Aurelie was doing, following Delilah's example. She'd been given some apples and dough. She was, indeed, full of thoughts. Of the poor fallen man, and of two men all but soaring through the air at the sound of terror and trouble, and of how everyone had reached for each other and helped.

"If Mr. Tweedy is so fainthearted," Aurelie ventured, "perhaps he is not the right sort of person to work here after all?"

Delilah and Angelique looked at her with surprise. Then they both slowly smiled.

"I think you have the right of it, Mrs. Gallagher.

Why, Helga here was brave enough to chase someone out with a rolling . . ."

They stopped, probably when they freshly realized they were speaking to a guest, who had been assured in her own interview that they didn't let rogues get in the door.

"I think you can ask someone if they are brave and they might *think* they are brave," Aurelie reflected. "And perhaps Mr. Tweedy looked as though he ought to be brave. But one never knows until one is tested."

She was learning what she was made of. She wondered if it was perhaps steelier stuff than was strictly thought ladylike, although she wasn't certain she wasn't still a little blessedly numb from the lingering shock of her recent life events.

Her life had been pocked with violence since she was born, but today's shock and terror had been met at once with an explosion of love and breathtaking competence.

Men could do such terrible harm.

And yet it was clear they could love so powerfully well.

She was glad she now knew.

And if she weakened at all, self-pity could set in that the sort of man she'd nearly married was the first kind.

On his way out the door, the apothecary, Mr. Waxworth, had stopped in to report that Mr. Bellingham was alive, if unconscious. And that he'd been dosed with laudanum and a remedy from the Orient meant to ease fevers, then slathered with Saint-John's-wort ointment and properly bandaged.

"And have you any Saint-John's-wort salve for wounds to care for him after today? Some comfrey salve, perhaps? Some linen for bandages?"

"Of course!" Helga said, almost but not quite bristling. "What kind of house would we be if we did not? I've me own recipes. Why, just have a look." She gestured grandly to her shelf of herbs and the apothecary made appropriately appreciative noises.

"Splendid. But I think he was unwell before he was assaulted, poor sod. He has a fever. He ought to be looked in on at intervals today and I think he ought to be watched and tended throughout the night. It could be a near thing."

A stricken silence followed. As the thing that he could be near was obviously death.

"I will look after him tonight," Aurelie said at once, before she realized she was even forming the words.

She suddenly couldn't bear the idea of him being alone in the dark. Perhaps awakening frightened and bandaged in pain in a strange place, with no memory of what happened to him, where no one would hear him call out for help. Her heart balled into a tight fist at the notion.

She realized everyone in the kitchen regarded her with a sort of cautious, gentle sympathy.

Perhaps imagining her caring for her fictional dead husband, Thomas.

She again felt a bit of a bounder for absorbing the unearned sympathy.

"Mrs. Gallagher . . . while that is tremendously kind and so brave of you to offer, we do not want you to think you've any obligation at all," Mrs. Hardy said gently. "You are our guest, and he is *our* responsibility. As you suggested, we are all rather stalwart."

"It is no trouble," she said firmly. "You have already done so much for him. I want to help. I know how to do it. I will do it." She sounded a bit queenly, she realized. Perhaps more so than a Mary Gallagher might.

As though she were someone unused to being countermanded.

But what she said wasn't precisely a lie. When she was younger, she had once been gravely ill. She had been tended by a nurse throughout the day and night; a doctor had been called in. She remembered the cool cloths on her head and the mustard plasters and the gentle voices. She supposed there had been kindness and tolerance in her life but so little of anything that felt like tenderness and real care and she wanted an opportunity to give it.

It seemed this, somehow, was the secret to survival. The point of anything.

She'd said it so unequivocally that everyone was silent in the face of her conviction.

"Very well," Mrs. Durand said. "Thank you, Mrs. Gallagher. The rest of us will look in on him throughout the day."

"You can lay damp cloths on his forehead and chest, Mrs. Gallagher, if he seems warm. Refresh them at intervals," Mr. Waxworth told her.

She had not considered that she would be draping cloths on a slightly or possibly completely bare man. But certainly, it was something she could do.

"Willow bark," Helga said suddenly. She leaped up to shake some out of the jar as she measured it. "Mr. Bellingham will want it for pain when he can drink a tisane."

So far everyone was speaking as though Mr. Bellingham was going to live. But they'd all known someone who had died from an infection and it was a whistling-in-the-graveyard sort of bravado.

Suddenly they all looked up in surprise.

Captain Hardy had appeared in the kitchen doorway.

He was fully dressed and shaved now. They stared

at him, absurdly nonplussed, as if a bear had wandered in. It wasn't as though he wasn't welcome there. It was just that no one could recall him, or Lord Bolt, ever before making an appearance in the kitchen during working hours. (Though he had, on occasion, sneaked in very late at night for a slice of cheese.) It was so patently a female domain, the way his ship was a male domain.

He didn't say a word. He took two steps toward Delilah, gently lifted her hand from where it rested on a potato she'd just peeled. Threaded his fingers through it.

Then tugged and led her away, wordlessly.

"Tristan . . . ?" she said. She cast a wide-eyed wondering look over her shoulder at the ladies.

He didn't turn around.

So she allowed him to lead her, as she would follow him anywhere. Up the stairs they went, and into the foyer, into the pink reception room, where he finally released her hand.

He closed the door.

"Tristan, what on—"

He drew her into his arms. Tucked his face in her neck. Then his arms tightened.

"I just . . ." he murmured against her hair. "I just needed to . . . when I saw all those bodies on the floor . . . when I heard the screaming . . ."

She understood.

She held him tightly, too.

"I know," she whispered. "I'm sorry. I love you, too," she soothed. "It's all right. You are my heart."

She would never forget the way he'd roared her name. In fury and terror and pure love.

His arms tightened on her. She fancied she could

feel his heart beat against hers, but they were one and the same now, so it was difficult to know.

A LITTLE LATER, just before dinner and while Mr. Bellingham lay in the throes of laudanum sleep, Captain Hardy and Lord Bolt went through his coat to see if they could determine definitively whether this was, in fact, poor Mr. Bellingham. Since no one else had yet arrived, the assumption seemed, unfortunately, a safe one.

The first thing they found was a gun.

"What on earth is a vicar doing with a W.A. Jones with a saw-handled butt? It's like mine," Lucien marveled.

And it was a beauty. It looked startlingly polished and well used, as though the butt of it snuggled into the man's palm all the time. It wasn't an idle target shooting sort of pistol. It was the sort one could use to kill highway robbers and the like.

It was loaded with powder and shot, too.

They set it aside.

"Pity the poor sod couldn't get it out in time. Look in his boots. I have a hunch," Captain Hardy said dryly.

They'd gotten his boots off. In them they found a boot pistol and a beautiful sheathed knife so sharp and sturdy it could have skinned a deer. Or skewered a vicar.

"And what vices do you suppose our vicar has that require that much money?" Captain Hardy displayed the thick wad of English paper notes and a jingle purse of coins.

A further search revealed a fine gold pocket watch with a simple fob and what appeared to be a hotel room key.

Lucien frowned faintly. "Quite a watch for a vicar to possess. If it was an heirloom, you'd think it would have been engraved."

But they found no initials on it. Nor on the handkerchief they found. It looked new.

"So somebody tried to kill him but it wasn't for his money. Or his watch," Hardy mused.

"Perhaps he's been dispatched by his friends in the country to buy gifts from London," Lucien suggested. "That's common enough. Hence the money."

"That makes sense, I suppose. And perhaps his attacker didn't get an opportunity to loot his pockets after he stabbed him. Someone came upon him, or our friend Bellingham got away. Or maybe he had yet another knife up his sleeve and somewhere nearby there's a dead man lying about with a vicar's knife in him."

"No trunk," Lucien said. "Unless it was stolen during the initial chaos. Christ, poor bastard, if that's the case. That's what I call a bad day. Good cheroots, though." He sniffed them. "A man's entitled to his pleasures. And this doesn't quite look like a letter of introduction, but if it was . . ."

He produced half a sheet of foolscap which was mostly covered in blood and entirely illegible.

"Maybe this is a more worldly type of vicar. I like a man who knows what's waiting for him in London and is prepared for any eventuality," Bolt mused. "Which found him."

Like the ladies, they took to heart that he'd been assaulted practically on their doorstep and this made them quietly furious.

Hardy grunted.

If one was a country native and a vicar, London was

often their version of Gomorrah. But every man in the country knew how to shoot.

Hardy continued his tour of the man's pockets. "There's something in the lining."

After some determined maneuvering he retrieved a miniature of a girl, or young woman.

She had dark hair and blue eyes.

"She's pretty," he said absently.

Bolt looked over his shoulder at it. "His sweetheart, perhaps? Did Mr. Bellingham mention whether he was married?"

"I don't think his letters mention a wife."

Hardy turned it over, but nothing was written on the back.

They suddenly both felt as though they were rummaging around in the man's heart.

Hardy put the miniature back in his coat pocket. The guns and knife and money they took for safekeeping.

THAT EVENING, *EVERYONE* in the sitting room felt like tumbled dice.

When they spoke, it was in short, dazed sentences or fragments of sentences. Everyone was still pale and spent and a little bit mussed. The men did not go to smoke and swear and break wind in the smoking room after dinner. They wanted to be where they could see the women.

"If Mr. Bellingham dies, do you think he'll haunt The Grand Palace on the Thames?" Dot asked.

"Perhaps," Angelique mused sadly, as Delilah hurriedly said, "Of course not, Dot. Don't be silly. And he's not going to die."

"But it is a nice place to spend eternity," Mr. Delacorte

maintained stoutly. "In fact, I might just decide to do that!"

"We'd be happy to have you for an eternity," Delilah said warmly.

"Are *you* going to die, Mr. Delacorte?" Dot's voice had gone up a quavering octave. Probably as much out of fondness for Mr. Delacorte as fear of another ghost.

"Not for decades," Mr. Delacorte assured her.

"And Mr. Bellingham is *not* going to die," said Mrs. Pariseau sagely. "He's a big strong country-bred man and they last for ages."

Of course, no one knew this for certain, but they liked her confidence. Mrs. Pariseau always seemed to know a lot about many different kinds of things.

"No doubt he'd confine himself to the attic, since he hasn't paid for the room, if he does become a ghost," Angelique mused.

"I don't know why a ghost would only want to live in an attic when there are so many comfortable rooms here and you could just float from one to the next," Lucien said somberly.

Captain Hardy bit his lip against an inappropriate laugh.

Delilah shot Angelique and Lucien a reproachful glance.

Dot made a tiny whimpering sound.

Mrs. Gallagher was upstairs with him now. He was still sleeping, lightly, it seemed, and fitfully.

Delilah and Angelique had provided her with fresh clean cloths and pitchers of water and a basin in which to dip them.

She'd pronounced herself quite prepared, and then she'd firmly closed the door.

"She's a sturdy girl, for all that she looks a bit ethereal," Mrs. Pariseau mused aloud. "Mrs. Gallagher is. I think she will get on just fine tonight. Once you've lost someone, you don't forget it. It toughens your hide a bit, if it doesn't end you."

Everyone in the room had lost someone at some time, and knew the truth of this, and fell silent.

A long silence ensued while they somberly contemplated mortality, and the fragile nature thereof. Everyone had a way of coping with chaos which was often an exaggeration of their best or worst qualities. This meant that Angelique and Lucien, who already had a tendency to mordancy, found refuge in it, and Delilah was kinder, and Captain Hardy was even quieter.

Another long somber hush ensued, punctuated only by the crackle of the fire and the click of knitting needles that Delilah had taken up and an occasional rustle of a page turned, but not read.

"He's very handsome," Dot said quietly.

"Dot!" Delilah admonished, astonished.

But he was.

Long limbed, broad shouldered, a face fashioned of the sort of precise magical ratios that stamp themselves on a woman's memory. Not to mention stir her senses.

Quite a surprise for a country vicar. It wasn't how they'd pictured Mr. Bellingham. But why couldn't cozy, charming people also be gorgeous?

And frankly, they'd all noticed, every last woman there and likely the men, too, and what did that say for their characters, or their immortal souls? Surely a possibly dying man ought to be exempt from ogling and judgment.

But what this also meant was that they were fully alive and whole, if they could still appreciate beauty, and that was another thing for which they were all grateful.

ANGELIQUE HAD LOOKED in again on Mrs. Gallagher before climbing into bed with Lucien.

Her husband was lying so quietly she thought he might already be asleep, so she slipped under the coverlet stealthily and scooted over until her bottom was pressed against him. It warmed her up nicely.

"I've seen a number of people die. I never expected to, in my wild youth, witness this. But I have. And I have also killed. I killed a pirate. As you know."

Angelique turned to her clearly awake husband in some surprise. "I remember when we used to talk about things like . . . oh, how you thought my bottom was shaped like a peach . . . in bed."

Lucien gave a short laugh and turned to her. She'd been planning to read a bit, and she hadn't yet doused the lamp and he was cast half in amber, like a delicious pagan statue.

And he was looking at her as if he was seeing her for the first time. His expression was so . . . fierce. So oddly intent.

In truth, they had discussed nearly the entirety of the world in meandering low murmurs in bed. They enjoyed each other's company immensely.

"Lucien . . ." she said softly, as she traced his lips with her fingertip. "Tell me what's troubling you."

"I haven't told you when I knew for certain I was in love with you. And I want to tell you now."

"All right," she said gently. Cautiously.

"It was the evening we were all playacting pirates. When I first met Hardy. Do you remember?"

"Mr. Delacorte will never let us forget it. He keeps begging us to do it again."

Normally Lucien would have laughed. He didn't. "There was a moment when you fell to the floor and pretended to be dead. I think Dot ran you through with a pretend sword to cause this. And Angelique . . ." He gave a soft, humorless laugh. "I swear my world stopped. My heart stopped. I *knew* it wasn't real, but . . ." He smiled ruefully. "At the time, I was *none* too pleased to realize I was at your mercy of such a thing. At your mercy. But that's when I knew I loved you."

Her eyes were beginning to sting with tears.

"And today . . . today was so much worse than that," he said. His voice frayed. "I knew at once how selfish I truly am. How fragile. There was a man bleeding on the floor and all I cared about in that moment was you. Because if anything happened to you . . ."

She brushed her knuckle against her eyes; he'd gone swimmy with tears. This weeping at the slightest provocation lately appalled and amazed her. It was such a luxury for someone who had, of necessity, so carefully disguised her emotions for so much of her life in order to survive. Who had, of necessity, been whoever a man needed her to be. Lucien needed only for her to be herself.

"Thank you for loving me," she said. "I would tell you the moment I knew I loved you but it's like trying to find the very beginning of the sky."

He smiled at her, then his smile faded. "I didn't know it would be like this," he said pensively.

"Terrifying?"

". . . and shaped like a peach," he murmured, as his hand slid down to said peach and pulled her up against him. They were alive, and they were going to use their bodies to celebrate it.

Chapter Nine

Mrs. Hardy and Mrs. Durand had looked in on her before going to bed, reassuring themselves that she'd been provided with everything she needed, and that she remained certain of her mission.

Aurelie had quietly soothed their concerns and thanked them.

And now she was alone with Mr. Bellingham.

The room was dark apart from lanterns flanking the bed. Both were turned down low.

He seemed to have flung off a coverlet; it was heaped near his hip. Mr. Bellingham was bare to the waist, and the lamps tinted his torso gold. He still wore trousers, but they were unbuttoned, already loose, and they'd been folded at the waist and pulled down a little lower, away from his wound. One of his arms was bent at the elbow, his loosely curled fist near his cheek, and his face was turned toward it. The other arm rested at his side, palm up. His head was tipped; his profile, cleanly, elegantly articulated against the white pillow. His lashes shivered against his cheeks. He was sleeping.

A wide, thick bandage had been wound neatly and carefully round him, and it remained white, which was a relief. His wound had been stitched well. He wasn't losing blood.

She didn't know the histories of everyone now sleeping under the roof of The Grand Palace on the

Thames. But no one had been there to protect Mr. Bellingham when he'd been attacked, and in this she felt a kinship with him. She wanted very much to be with someone who understood precisely what that was like to be attacked without the ability to defend. To be stripped of one's pride and humanity. To have no choice but to endure it.

Caring for him was a defiance, of sorts. Almost a radical act. It was a declaration to herself of who she was and who she always meant to be, no matter what had been done to her: she would do no harm. She would always be kind. She would *not* be afraid. She could not be broken.

It was violence inverted.

But paintings and statues in all their detailed bareness had not quite prepared her for the breathing flesh of the beautiful, battered man on the bed. Her breath stilled in her lungs; she could feel in her every cell a surge, a bracing, as if withstanding a burst of music. His earthy, foreign male beauty stunned at first. Then unnerved. And enthralled.

So hard, his forearms and his shoulders, the taut bulging slopes of them. His chest, carved in sections of muscles, furred lightly in curling dark hair, rose and fell with his breath. The furred hollow of his armpit. The dark coins of his nipples.

His torso with a faint sheen of sweat.

He looked built for, and capable of, violence.

Perhaps strength was a better word.

But his face was sweet in repose.

She gathered her nerve and laid her hand on his fine forehead.

He was still unnervingly hot. She left her palm there, as if she could cool him with just the force of her will. With a simple touch.

How odd the instinct had been to reach for and touch another human in a moment of terror. She hadn't known she would do that; there had never been anyone there for her. She supposed instinctive hope lingered in every human, regardless of how life had shaped them: that someone would be there for them when needed.

She didn't think she'd ever forget how Captain Hardy had come for Mrs. Hardy today.

He stirred a little, his legs shifting. He turned his head slightly.

"Aurelie," he murmured.

She froze. Her heart leaped into her throat in terror.

Gingerly, very, very slowly lifted her hand from his forehead.

She stared, mouth parted in shock, her breath coming short.

His eyes remained closed.

No: she must have heard it wrong. Surely he'd said something like "Emily." If he'd indeed said a name at all. Although an Emily hadn't been mentioned in his letter. Perhaps he'd been attempting to call for Eleanor the chicken. Who would surely miss him if he died.

For some reason it was this that made the tears start up. She pushed them roughly away. What use were they to her? What did they solve?

It must be that she ached to hear her name spoken aloud at all in this place. Where everyone was so kind, the kind of place she thought she might happily stay forever, if only she thought it was safe to remain motionless. If only she could afford to.

She wondered if she'd ever be able to safely claim her name or herself again. Or if she'd only find true safety by inventing a new person to slip into like the clothes she'd borrowed.

Or, more specifically, like armor.

She needed to get to her brother. To someone who knew her, before she lost herself completely.

She said to Mr. Bellingham softly, "I'm here. I'm here."

It seemed to settle him. But his breath still came swiftly between parted lips and his eyelids shuddered in the throes of dreams that looked anything but peaceful.

After today, she knew now she yearned to hear her own name invoked with love and terror and fury, like the trumpets that shattered a wall in the biblical story. Like Captain Hardy sailing over the banister.

He seemed such a quiet man, Captain Hardy. Dignified and taciturn. But this violence had stripped him bare before the world, too, as bare as Mr. Bellingham. Both literally and figuratively. His heart—and his torso—had been on display for all, when he'd called for his wife.

She would never forget the expression on Captain Hardy's face when he'd come for Mrs. Hardy today in the kitchen. He'd fixed on his true north, and he'd taken her hand and led her away and she'd gone. *You are all I need,* it seemed to say.

To be so loved.

Her throat felt thick again.

She had been so terribly wrong about Brundage. She hadn't loved him, nor had she been loved at all. She might never have realized this if things had gone differently.

She wondered if the person Mr. Bellingham called for—Emily? Lorelei?—was a comfort to him. For wasn't that what people did? She'd had no one to call out for one month and five days ago. And perhaps that was why she'd been nearly silent throughout. Some perverse pride would not allow her to scream again with the full knowledge that no one would come for her, hand outstretched to lead her away.

This, too, was why she wanted to stay with Mr. Bellingham: so that no matter who he called for, he would not go without an answer. She could think of no more hollow feeling.

She dipped the cloths in the basin of water, folded them, and then gently pressed them to his chest. And she only felt a little guilt as her hand lingered lightly, there against his skin, feeling, with wonder, the thump of his heart. It seemed properly steady. She allowed her palm to spread. And this was an indulgence: to feel his skin.

Shockingly soft over muscle that felt like rock.

This is our bargain, Mr. Bellingham, she thought. *I will tend you, and you will enlighten me. You will reveal the mystery of men to me. You will help ease a fear.*

His chest expanded and fell in a sigh. And her hand, like a ship in a sea, rose and fell along with it. So odd, so thrilling, to feel his life surging against her hand. Like she'd captured a beast.

But the bones of his hips seemed very sharp. His belly a bit too concave. He was beautifully built but thinner than he ought to be.

Even so, she knew he was stronger than she was.

Every man was likely stronger than she was. She fought back that surge of despair.

She wrung the cloth and dipped it in the basin to wet again. Then wrung it to lay across his forehead.

He was still warm.

For a time, she sat with him in silence.

And suddenly his breathing became rough.

And all at once his sleep was bedeviled. She reared back with a gasp, as he kicked out. He fought with the light coverlet and threw it from his body. "No!" he muttered. "Son of . . ."

And just this motion looked personal and so skillful, an act of orchestrated violence that made her step back and catch her breath. Her heart thundered, awed and frightened, as she watched him. She willed herself to calm.

He might have been reliving today's battle.

Or some other battle he had lost or won.

He lay still in a moment, breathing hard. Muttering to himself.

"I am here," she said softly. "There's naught to be afraid of. I will not let them hurt you."

He huffed out a breath and flung his arms up over his head. His chest heaved with his breathing. And there to her shock she saw a beautiful, simple tattoo of a dagger beneath his arm, alongside his rib cage.

She stared, stunned. Why on earth had he done it—allowed himself to be so deliberately marked?

Her impulse was to trace the contours of this secret thing with her fingers, and this shocked her, too.

And then he shifted again, and the fight in him eased.

She leaned back, and then sat down. From her chair she saw that he was breathing more quietly.

As if she could will him to peace, she breathed right along with the rise and fall of his chest. And it slowed, at last, to the peaceful cadences of deep sleep.

She moved the chair a little away from him, so as not to disturb him.

"Mr. Bellingham, I hope you do not mind. I should like to tell you a few things I have never told anyone. When I was four years old, I took the boiled sweets meant for guests and I blamed my oldest brother, who was given three swats with a switch. I did not know they would switch him! I know you are not a priest but surely a man of God . . . perhaps you understand. I have a thousand memories of my brother, but this one—it lingers. I would take a thousand switches for him if only he were here."

She listened to the music of his deep, steady breathing. Her own eyelids began to grow heavy.

"Is it a sin to say I sometimes used to wish I had died in his place?" she whispered. "But then that is visiting more suffering on him, no—my death? And alleviating mine? And also, I am not certain it is true. He would not want that of me. He would want me to avenge him. And also, I'm afraid that I am glad I'm alive. Even despite . . . even if I am not . . . am not as I once was."

She had once taken such joy in her facility with words. Now, thanks to Brundage, there was something in her experience she could not ever imagine saying aloud.

Running had not been an act of fear, she told herself. It was an act of self-preservation. She owed it to everyone in her family who had been unable to escape their fates.

". . . I'm not . . . worthy . . ." he muttered.

At least that's what it sounded like. Her heart clenched. She stared at him, stunned.

Had she heard him correctly?

What torments haunted a vicar? Did he worry about the souls of his parishioners? Did he think he could not possibly be worthy of such confidences? Of such responsibilities?

"I am here," she said softly.

Whoever he wanted her to be in this moment, whoever he needed, she would be.

He exhaled again, as if in relief.

She swallowed. And her heart began to speed.

"Mr. Bellingham. I have not told a soul this. I cannot bring myself to say what happened aloud to anyone, and perhaps I never shall, so I shall whisper it. I think perhaps Madame Aubert surmised, but I did not say anything aloud to her. And it is as though it happened to someone else while I watched. In some ways I feel as though I am still outside of myself, and I think that this is a mercy. I will tell you that I stared at his throat while it happened. I would not look him in the eye. Because then he would know he had gotten the better of me and I would not give that bastard the pleasure. I heard you say that word today, Mr. Bellingham, and this is the first time I've tried it out, and thank you. I like it. I think it will be useful. I stared at that bastard's throat. I screamed once but I soon knew there was no use. No one would come. And so, then I made not a sound. I would not give him the pleasure of my fear, because that is what he wanted. He wanted me to be afraid. He wanted to *best* me. I would not look him in the eye while he did it. And I did not weep. I did not weep."

Her breath shuddered now. Her throat was thick.

Brundage deserved her rage, not her tears. But they came, and poured quietly. She dashed them away.

"And then I smoothed out my skirts and left the room without a word. All my life I have heard that my mother went to the guillotine with the same dignity."

She had told him this story she could not imagine ever telling again, yet it had seemed necessary to hear it in her own voice.

And almost as if her story had released him, too, it was suddenly clear that Mr. Bellingham's fever had broken. She refreshed the water in the basin from the pitcher, and gently, gently stroked the perspiration away from his brow.

"Mama," he murmured.

Her heart jolted again.

"Yes, sleep, my sweet," she whispered. "You will feel better in the morning."

She wondered how many times *she'd* said that word in her sleep when she was small. For a mother long lost. Into a dark room, with no one to hear her.

And fatigue was a weight on her, but a sort of peaceful release, like a fever breaking, and she kept her eyes open and she watched him.

Chapter Ten

CONSCIOUSNESS SEEPED in a bit the way a high tide gradually fills a dark cave.

It began with an awareness of a burning itch below his ribs. Perhaps the fires of hell already getting to work licking at him for eternity.

But tenderly cradling his head was a cloud.

No. It was a pillow.

Why would he be given a pillow in hell?

He fought to the surface, but tendrils of memory snagged him in the shallows of consciousness. Screaming. There had been so much screaming of glass-shattering caliber. The treble of women's voices, the bass voices of men speaking in clipped military cadences. He knew those kinds of voices. Who were they? Were they real? Were they fever fragments, fashioned of his own memories, the way dreams were?

Then later . . . oh, there had been a voice of such tenderness and beauty, and it had sifted down over his senses through the nasty vise of the fever, penetrating a sleep teeming with shadows and terrifying images, and the voice had buoyed him like feather down. Perhaps he had overheard angels haggling over his mortal soul. But he could have sworn a woman had spoken of boiled sweets, and staring at throats, and a bastard. She had not screamed. That's what she'd said. He remembered some of her sentences clearly.

Perhaps *he* was the bastard? It seemed a reasonable assumption.

He'd certainly been called one more than once.

He'd thought, but could not have said, please keep talking. Say anything at all. I'll stay alive just to hear you speak.

He decided to inventory the rest of his body. Something cool and soft supported his back.

Which was bare.

How *much* of him was bare?

And how had he gotten that way . . . ?

And . . . *who* had gotten him that way?

He moved his toes and shifted his legs. He was still wearing trousers, but they'd been pulled down to his hips. He wished he was naked, because the sheet beneath his back was smooth and cool and he realized it had been so long, so long, since he'd allowed himself to merely savor comfort.

He lifted his left arm, touched his fingers to it, testing to see whether he was still corporeal. His flesh sank beneath his fingertips. He was clammy, but he was made of flesh and bone, of a certainty.

And then he slid his hand down to his ribs and found the bandage.

His eyes snapped open as memory returned as a whole, in a rush.

The alley. The one between the livery stables and Lovell Street. By the docks. He'd followed the information given to him by the hack driver, and he'd walked down the narrow zigzagging street alongside the livery stables adjacent to Lovell Street.

Some bastard had lunged, stabbed, and vanished like smoke.

In fucking daylight, he'd done this.

If Hawkes hadn't been fast—he should have been faster—if he didn't have eyes in the back of his head as well as everywhere else, if he hadn't twisted his body just so in time, the would-be assassin would have emerged with Hawkes's liver on the tip of his knife and Hawkes would be a corpse in an alley.

He must have been followed from the Stevens Hotel.

But why?

His instinct told him that had naught to do with Lady Aurelie Capet, and everything to do with his visit to Harrigan. Brundage must already be in London, and he must have heard somehow that Hawkes had been to visit Harrigan. Perhaps he knew the account books were missing.

They were, at this moment, locked in his chest at the Stevens Hotel.

One of the books—reflecting Brundage's embassy budget—showed the ebb and flow of money into the mysterious charity. The other book included Brundage's meticulous records of personal purchases and payments—debts and creditors paid in concert with the ebb and flow of that charity's balance, and shiny objects purchased, and the like. Including, as Pike the footman had told him, three vases from Guthrie's Antiquities ranging in cost from three pounds to five pounds fifty, purchased in 1812 and 1813. An ambassador's finances were always the subject of some scrutiny, particularly during a war. Brundage would have needed to disguise any unorthodox influxes of money.

Together those budget books were damning. But it wasn't the whole story. He still didn't know to whom, specifically, Brundage had sold secrets.

Brundage must have realized that Hawkes was now on the trail of the whole story.

And he'd likely reweighed his options and decided that between being shot by a firing squad—or at best, imprisoned for the rest of his days—for treason, and losing a fiancée and a valuable necklace, he preferred the second. Hawkes had to go.

Why else? What were the odds it was a whimsical stabbing?

He'd find out once he got a look in his pockets to see if his money, guns, and watch were gone.

Christ. He couldn't yet think clearly.

It was infuriating.

He remembered staggering, careening against walls, stumbling as far as that thick red door of the inn. He had no sense of the distance. He only remembered falling through it.

Apparently, he hadn't wanted to die alone.

He hoped he hadn't left a trail of blood leading right up to the inn, because that would certainly be useful when it came to finding him and stabbing him for keeps next time.

Was Lady Aurelie even here?

Urgency surged through him again. He shoved himself upright and swung his legs over the side of the bed.

Oh, God. That was a mistake.

He sucked in a breath and gripped the edge of the bed with both hands.

The room spun grotesquely and his stomach heaved.

He closed his eyes and let the room do a circuit or two before he attempted to open them again and breathed hard breaths through the nausea. He had a suspicion he'd been dosed with laudanum or something like it.

Bloody hell, he was weak. He must have been well drugged.

And, well, he was ill. Clearly. Or had been. Apart from being stabbed.

He could and would not complain. Someone or several someones had clearly administered to him and he was alive because of that.

He breathed. Deeply, held it, released it. Air, he'd learned, was also medicine.

And he needed water. To begin to clear the laudanum or whatever it was from his blood and the furry feeling from his mouth. He hefted the pitcher he found on the little table near his bed; it was nearly empty.

He turned his head to find that a bar of sunlight slanted through a slit in the blue curtains hung at the window. It traced a bright path across the floor, slanting across the wardrobe, terminating at the door. Not one speck of dust danced in that beam.

On the whole, he felt as though he'd been beaten like a horseshoe on an anvil, but somehow that still impressed him.

Gratitude roared through him like sunlight through that window. Fucking hell, but at least he was free and alive.

Perhaps he just couldn't be killed.

The room smelled improbably of spring. He located the culprits: a little froth of blossoms stuffed into a vase on a modest writing desk, a few feet away from his nose. The chair in front of the desk was draped with what looked like his shirt, which was probably suitable only for use as a surrender flag.

A fire burned cheerfully and the hearth was spotless.

Next to the hearth stood his boots. If his—hosts? Captors? Rescuers?—were going to rob him while he was helpless, surely they wouldn't have given him flowers, or left his boots? A pair made by Hoby could finance a good long debauch, if their tastes ran to that.

When the room stopped spinning he noticed a little heap of clean white linen torn into strips piled on the writing table.

There *must* have been bloody ones. They'd been taken away.

He'd a packet of cheroots and a flint in his coat pocket. A good smoke would go a long way into jolting him into full consciousness, too.

Barefoot, bare chested, head feeling odd, like a lead bubble, he managed to move, one foot in front of the other, like a man trapped in treacle, across the spotless floor. His first stop was the curtains and he whipped them open. His arms worked just fine.

He exhaled gustily. Never, never would he take for granted sunlight again.

He got the window open and a gust of sea air obligingly whipped through and made the shirt flutter. He lifted it to examine the carnage.

Which was, surprisingly, difficult to find. He studied it, wonderingly.

Some great effort had been made to get the blood out. Some magical elixir—he knew housekeepers and butlers often had proprietary recipes for that sort of thing, passed down through generations—

must have been employed. Only a faint tinge of pink remained around the perimeter of what appeared to have been a jagged cut, sewn so neatly, with the tiniest of fine stitches, it was scarcely detectable.

He huffed out a stunned breath. A wayward sort of warmth surged through him.

He didn't know why this so moved him. It seemed a long time since he'd been thoughtfully *tended*.

He held on to his shirt for a moment as though it were a talisman. He didn't know of what.

But it was women who thought of these kinds of things. Who provided life's little grace notes.

He found his coat and overcoat in the wardrobe. Both, he saw with amazement, seemed to have been brushed.

He plunged a hand at once into the inside pocket and his gut went cold.

He'd suspected as much.

His gun was gone.

Bloody. Fucking. Hell.

He swiftly shoved his hand into the side pockets.

His great wad of bills and purse of coins were missing, too.

He'd been left the cheroots and the flint. In place of his wad of money something else rustled.

He pulled it out and discovered it was a little message.

Dear Sir,

We took possession of your money and your weapons in order to ensure their safety and yours while you were indisposed. In the happy event you regain consciousness and health, we will return them to you. We did take the liberty of using a little of your money to pay the apothecary for his services.

Regards,
Mrs. Angelique Durand

Mrs. Delilah Hardy

Proprietresses, The Grand Palace on the Thames

Such a polite way to tell him he'd been disarmed and was now at their mercy.

Hawkes was grimly amused by the pretty handwriting and the exquisite politeness. He begrudgingly respected their reasoning. He suspected even the most honest maid might have had to wrestle with her conscience if she'd encountered a fist-sized clip of British currency and a loaded gun.

Perhaps they didn't realize he felt nearly as undressed without his gun as without his shirt.

He maneuvered his fingers deeply into the pocket, into the lining useful for small secret things, and his fingers found the shape of Aurelie's miniature. Perhaps they hadn't found it.

He searched his boots and his suspicions were confirmed. No gun. No knife.

But he'd known that would be the case. The dustless room and nearly bloodless shirt were clues that Mrs. Durand and Mrs. Hardy did not do things by halves.

His trunk was still at the Stevens. He hadn't much in it, apart from toiletries. And, of course, the account books he'd taken from Harrigan's.

Christ, but he needed to sit down again.

He took the shirt with him and lowered his sorry, battered body to the bed. The water in the basin was clean.

He was just about to shake out his shirt so he could drop it over his head when something glinted in his peripheral vision. He pivoted sharply.

The doorknob was slowly turning.

He realized he'd already subconsciously scanned the room for weapons when he at once seized the lantern as the best likely projectile. He could hurl it or bludgeon with it.

His breath suspended, his every muscle locked and cocked like a loaded pistol, he watched that doorknob complete its revolution and the door open soundlessly, because of course the doors wouldn't creak at The Grand Palace on the Thames.

A young woman slipped into the room and gently, slowly closed the door. He noted slim shoulders. A long neck.

The way her dress poured in a lyrical line from her shoulders to waist to sweetly flaring hips instantly communicated something primal to his groin.

Her brown hair shifted to dark gold when she turned into that beam of sun.

And saw him.

She froze. Her hand flew up to cover her heart.

"*Oh! Mon di*—you are awake. I am so sorry!"

His breath left him as though he'd been punched.

He slowly, slowly lowered the lamp. He loosened, but didn't relinquish, his hold on it. It seemed important to touch something ordinary to anchor him to earth.

Wonder crescendoed into a strange sort of unspecific fury—very like he'd been captured against his will. Then receded gently again into wonder.

He'd been blessed by the sight of beautiful women before, but could not recall ever before experiencing what amounted to sensual panic. As if he would be imperiled somehow if he didn't *do* something about her at once.

That jolt he felt was like a key turning in a lock. He instinctively knew he'd already been fundamentally altered somehow.

His muscles remained tensed, absorbing her impact as if she were a rogue wave. He took a surreptitious breath.

He supposed he could blame laudanum or fever for the strange sensation. And he would have, if he'd been more cowardly, and less brutally honest with himself.

That this should happen while he was pale, ill, half-naked, sticky with sweat, and hadn't made love to a woman in three years . . . well, he was just going to do what he did so well, and that was brazen it out.

He had no sense of how much time had passed while they regarded each other in apparent amazement.

"It pains me *greatly* to hear that you're sorry I am awake," he said gravely.

Her smile was swift and small and illuminated her entire face. It lasted mere seconds. Her faint accompanying blush made him restless.

But the woman seemed to have been shocked mute. Her fingers were curled into her skirt, as if she, too, needed to hold on to something lest she be borne away. Her eyes were blue. Blue like that rogue wave slapping the devil out of him. Blue like the color of the sky just after sunset, right before darkness takes over. He knew these blues. He'd counted them to himself while he was in his cell, so he wouldn't forget the most beautiful things in life.

Lavender shadows of sleeplessness curved beneath them.

"If you'll indulge me in what may sound like a mad question, madam . . . are you real? Or are you perhaps an attendant in a sort of surprisingly pleasant waiting room for the afterlife, where I await judgment?"

She had a dimple. That dimple all but speared his heart.

"I am real, sir," she assured him. "But downstairs there is a sitting room if you would like to sit in one. And an epithet jar which will judge you if you curse in company. The charge to curse is one pence. But there is a room to smoke in, I'm given to understand, and you may curse there."

He listened to this in bemusement, bizarrely enchanted.

"I shall look forward to it," he said somberly.

She smiled again, slowly, wryly, knowing she was being humored.

He frowned a little when she did it, as if to punish himself and her for enjoying her smile more than he wanted his next breath.

"May I ask how you feel, sir?" she asked shyly. Her hands were folded before her now.

"Like an anvil has been dropped upon me from a great height. But I probably feel better than I smell."

"Oh! You do not smell very ba . . ."

There was no way for her to finish that sentence that didn't imply she'd sniffed him.

He shook his head reproachfully. "And I thought *this* hurt." He pointed to his bandage.

She smiled again, somewhat crookedly, eyes crinkling at the corners. But didn't apologize.

Which was when he decided he liked her. But somehow he'd known he did and would.

The silence that fell was as textured as music.

The palms of his hands hummed as though they could feel the shape of her face cradled in them.

It was shaped a bit like a heart.

There was scarcely a dip in the center of her top lip, otherwise it would have been a heart, too. Her mouth was the same pale pink shade as those petals bursting from the vase, and it looked as plush as the pillow he'd discovered beneath his head this morning.

And then, as if from a nasty wound, reality seeped in.

What was it Brundage said?

Aurelie's mouth had *inflamed* him. She had a mouth like Therese d'Artois.

Hawkes went rigid. Wary now.

Perhaps he *was* still dreaming.

Because why the bloody hell would Lady Aurelie Capet feel free to waltz into the room in which he'd apparently been carted after he'd been stabbed?

She didn't look very much like her miniature. Nevertheless.

He was momentarily breathless with what felt like resentment. Almost despair. He wanted more than anything just to abide in awe for a little while longer, because his life had contained so little of grace.

But this woman was wearing a mauve dress.

The color of half-mourning.

A blue-eyed, brown-haired woman in a mauve dress with a beautiful mouth, a faint French accent, wearing a dress no doubt borrowed from her lady's maid.

He was beset by a fleeting surge of helpless primitive, possessive fury at the possibility that Brundage had in any way touched *this* woman.

Or could lay claim to this woman.

Or worse than either of those . . . harmed this woman.

Cold rationality, his longtime companion, asserted its seniority.

The other possibilities could be swiftly eliminated. She couldn't be a housemaid here to poke up the fires or empty the chamber pots. Not in that dress. She wore no cap and no apron. And he'd warrant her hands were as soft as her skin looked.

If he took a few steps toward her, he'd learn whether she would reach to about his collarbone in height. It seemed wiser to remain at a distance. If he knew how *she* smelled, he suspected it would work on his senses like a dose of opium.

All right, then. An innocent, sheltered girl, or so he'd been told. Gently bred. She had opinions. A bit prone to flirting and flightiness. He had about two seconds to decide what to say to her next.

And where once such a thing had been as instinctive as breathing, he'd never before had to do it with this awe playing havoc with his equilibrium. He cursed the need to do it, but that was no reason not to do it.

"If you'll indulge me in another question, madam. You walked in as though you belong here . . . I seem to have lost a day or two of memory while I was indisposed. We haven't . . . that is . . . did we . . ." He tipped his head toward the bed. "I haven't gone and seduced you, have I?"

Chapter Eleven

AURELIE'S BREATH left her in a shocked gust and heat rushed her face.

She went still.

Surely . . . *surely* vicars didn't say that sort of thing in casual conversation?

Although . . . she conceded that he had a point. She had indeed walked into the room as if she belonged there. And as if *he* belonged to her. And who did that apart from a woman accustomed to waltzing in and out of the bedrooms of strange men?

"A pity," he muttered, abstractedly, mildly amused. Clearly her scarlet complexion had answered the question for him. "Forgive me," he added firmly, as an afterthought.

He didn't sound contrite.

Something was very amiss. Her impulse was to turn around and swiftly leave the room.

She would perhaps begin with the benefit of the doubt, given that this was the beloved Mr. Bellingham.

She cleared her throat. "Mr. Bellingham, sir, my name is Mrs. Gallagher. I . . . looked after you last night. You were very ill indeed, so it is perhaps understandable you do not remember my presence. Your fever broke very early this morning. As you seemed to be sleeping peacefully, I stepped out briefly, and returned expecting to still find you sleeping. I am sorry to intrude. Shall I go?"

His extraordinary face registered gathering bemusement as he listened to this. "A pleasure to meet you, Mrs. Gallagher. Don't go. Who the devil is Mr. Bellingham?"

She worriedly studied him. ". . . you are, sir?"

"I assure you I am not."

He sounded unnervingly convinced of this.

She cleared her throat. "Sir . . ." she began carefully, "perhaps you are still a bit . . . confused from your fever? The liberty was taken to give you some laudanum, too. I will bring some fresh water or some coffee to you and perhaps you will be able to think more clearly. And I think I ought to tell you that you might not want to say . . ." she lowered her voice and whispered, "'who the devil'—in the sitting room. You will be obliged to put a pence in the jar."

He took a breath, and it sounded suspiciously as though he were siphoning patience from the very air.

"Mrs. Gallagher . . . I am at a number of disadvantages. You seem to believe my name is Mr. Bellingham, and I feel obliged to inform you that this is not the case. Though it sounds as though you're fond of Mr. Bellingham, which makes him an enviable man, indeed. And I am most decidedly not a vicar."

She was speechless.

"But . . . then . . ." Her voice was faint.

She was horrified.

But *then* last night she'd shared a few of her darkest secrets with a man she'd assumed was accustomed to hearing them. A man who, she'd thought, was a sort of conduit to God by virtue of his profession—the dear, benign Mr. Bellingham, with the intelligent chicken.

She'd touched this man's bare skin with her hand and soothed him, and soothed herself in so doing. They had both gained from the evening.

Did this man in front of her—whoever he might be—deserve that care less than a vicar?

Had he heard anything she'd said?

Had he *understood* her?

Did it matter?

Surely not. He'd been sleeping.

She was furious to realize she'd been a victim of her own assumptions again. Or perhaps, more accurately, her instincts.

Because she had no idea how she'd move through life assuming every human was something other than who they appeared. Trust was freedom, she understood now. It was a luxury. Without it, life was a cell. No emotion could ever get through unfettered and it seemed a hellish way to live.

Did she want to live that way? Could she? Was her every action to be a choice now? Her throat felt tight.

She knew there was no ocean vast enough to free herself from that.

And now she understood she ought to have known from her first look at him that he was nothing so benign as a country vicar. This man's character seemed to animate his entire person with a sort of complex intensity. It was in his gestures. It blazed in his eyes, which were a dazzling crystalline blue, like fast water dashed over rocks. They never left her face when he spoke. She was being thoroughly *seen* for the first time in her life, as both a person and a woman. Brundage had never looked at her this way.

No one had ever looked at her this way.

In this instant of epiphany, she understood that this mattered a good deal.

If she had known the difference sooner, perhaps she never would have needed to flee across the Channel and then across the ocean to escape the consequences of not knowing.

The man's expression shifted and gentled as he studied her.

"Forgive me," he said swiftly, humbly. "I fear my manners are a casualty of my awkward circumstances. It's just that you are unexpected, Mrs. Gallagher. It was very kind of you to look after me. It seems I am in your debt. Thank you very much."

She nodded slowly, once.

He studied her again. A faint frown shadowed his brow.

"Why did you do it?" he asked almost shortly. Then he smiled faintly. "Did you draw the short straw?"

"I didn't want you to call out in the night and find no one there. I didn't want you to die alone, if you were going to die."

She hadn't meant to be quite so blunt, but she was still reeling from the revelation.

He went still.

He eyed her somewhat warily. She sensed she'd thoroughly surprised him.

In the silent moments that followed, she thought he was assessing—perhaps reassessing—her, too, and his expression was inscrutable.

His eyes felt far too penetrating, as though whetted by a lifetime of peering into consciences. Or perhaps her soul was far too raw, and from now on gazes as direct as his would now feel like fingernails dragged across it.

She cleared her throat. "Sir, if you are not Mr. Bellingham, then . . ."

He hesitated a moment.

"My name is Mr. Hawkes."

She let this information settle in.

It seemed portentous, somehow. Of a certainty the name fit him better than "Bellingham" did. She supposed it was a common enough English name. But she'd known of two others—one was her brother's fencing master for a time.

The other Mr. Hawkes was the man she'd seen in the ballroom so many years ago, surrounded by rapt women, glowing beneath the chandelier.

But that Mr. Hawkes was in a French prison. And this Mr. Hawkes was thin, and covered in a bristly beard. He didn't radiate.

"It was no trouble to look after you, Mr. Hawkes," she said quietly.

"Nonsense," he said firmly. "I expect it was harrowing and unpleasant at times for you, and it was valiant and generous of you to do it. I should like to say again, thank you very much, indeed."

She liked his version of her, and she liked this directness.

She ventured a smile again.

A moment later he asked, "How much of me *have* you seen?"

It was increasingly clear that he was incorrigibility filigreed with exquisite manners. And he flirted in such a cleverly adept, subtle way she could feel it, little by little, winding about her like a spell. Or sneaking under a door, like a mist.

"Why, sir? Do you care about propriety or do you wish to catch up on all the blushing you were unable to do when you were ill?" She said it acerbically.

He smiled slowly at this in what appeared to be absolute approbation.

"Blushing," he repeated, bemused, as if she'd said

something quaint. "Refresh my memory, Mrs. Gallagher. Is that the thing people capable of shame do? Not that I've anything to be ashamed of," Mr. Hawkes added, a moment later, wryly, mostly to himself. But very much for her benefit. The corner of his mouth tipped up.

She was silent. If he was referring to how he looked half-dressed, she would have to agree, and she wasn't about to do that out loud.

"Are you disappointed I'm not a vicar?" he asked more quietly. It sounded as though he genuinely wanted to know.

She shrugged with one shoulder. "Men are seldom who women want them to be."

He gave a low, impressed whistle. "That worldly, are you?" he said on a hush, all gentle mockery.

How odd that, having nursed him to health, she suddenly felt she'd like to throw something at his head.

"I do not know what you happen to be, if not a vicar," she added. "Perhaps I will be less disappointed."

"I'm a gentleman," he said brightly.

Apparently, her face reflected skepticism.

"And perhaps I'm someone who may one day do you a good turn, as well. Mrs. Gallagher."

This sounded sincere, if also suspect.

He began to, at last, pull his shirt down over his head.

She turned her head slightly. Transforming from half-naked to clothed seemed more intimate, somehow, than the reverse. It was far too late to do the proper thing, like turn her back or stare at the ceiling or, better yet, leave the room and leave him to it. It seemed ridiculous to pretend virginal modesty. She had, after all, counted the sections on his abdomen. (Six.)

He seemed so unaffected by the fact that he had an audience while he dressed that she was instantly certain he'd done it in front of women any number of times, and for the third or fourth time since she'd formally met Mr. Hawkes, her temperature and probably her color changed.

But it was difficult not to feel proprietary about this man, given that she'd watched over him in the night. She suffered now as his face went determinedly blank and so taut her every muscle tensed in sympathy. Enduring pain with stoicism simply seemed like something he knew how to do, like pulling on his boots or shaving his face.

His hands trembled a little.

Mr. Hawkes was exhausted and either stubborn or foolish or both.

Or simply male.

She'd seen him at what was likely his weakest. Men were dangerous when they felt weak, she thought. Like wounded animals. But there was a difference between a man feeling weak and being weak, and she thought she knew it now, watching Mr. Hawkes.

"I should think, Mr. Hawkes, that someone ought to have a look at your wound and perhaps change your dressing. I shall tell the others the happy news of your survival. Perhaps you should . . . begin your day with some broth? Some coffee or tea?"

"I want to smoke," he said abruptly.

Then he surreptitiously took a breath and released it, as if recovering from the effort to put on his shirt.

He glanced toward the wardrobe thoughtfully. He seemed to mull something over.

"Mrs. Gallagher, would you be so kind as to hand my coat to me? I shouldn't normally ask you to do it, but my dignity might not survive the way I suspect I would move across the room in front of you, and my already bruised vanity demands that I appear as virile as possible."

It sounded facile. But there was something—not defeated, but definitely thwarted—about the set of his shoulders and the tension about his eyes now. She sensed this was someone accustomed to marshaling panache to get through untenable situations, and when confronted with a choice between either death or asking for help he would really have to think about it.

And he'd asked her for help, and oddly, this felt like something a strong man would do.

Wordlessly she fetched his coat and gently handed it to him.

He retrieved a packet of cheroots from the pocket.

"It's against the rules to smoke in the rooms," she said stiffly.

He went still. "Ah. I fear I've not been apprised of these rules."

"They're printed on a little card."

"A little card you say? I must see it at once lest I be tempted to break another rule."

She fetched it from the desk and silently handed it to him.

He took it from her gently; his eyes lingered on her face before they dropped slowly to study the card. And she felt that everywhere in her body, in the shortness of her breath, a heat between her legs, as surely as if he'd drawn a finger down her spine.

It was one of the most strangely sensual moments of her life.

She couldn't speak.

The onslaught of things she felt in this man's presence confused her. They were as distinct as they were untrustworthy. And they were nothing, nothing like anything she'd ever felt for or with Brundage, even when he'd kissed her. Even when, at first, she hadn't hated his kisses.

For the first time since she'd fled, she felt something other than determined and frightened.

She felt fiercely *glad.*

This was the other gift Mr. Hawkes had given her unwittingly.

"And Mr. Gallagher?" he said idly, as he perused the card of rules. "Is he also a guest at this inn?"

He looked up swiftly.

"I am a widow." She'd said those words aloud a half dozen or so times now but suddenly they echoed woodenly in her ears. This had a bit to do with that penetrating gaze of his.

"I see," he said gravely. "I am very sorry for your loss."

She inclined her head graciously. "Thank you. It has been some time since my husband, Thomas, passed away. I am not long out of mourning."

"Yes. I can see that. Mauve, I believe women are calling that color this year."

"It's unusual for men to know the names for colors unless they pay the modiste's bills. Is Mrs. Hawkes very stylish, then?"

"There is . . ." he said, quite slowly and deliberately, and paused to light the cheroot anyway, clearly just for the pleasure of witnessing her reaction, ". . . no Mrs. Hawkes."

He regarded her coolly and drew in a lungful of smoke. He closed his eyes in ecstasy.

She studied him. She did not one bit like the upward leap her heart gave when he delivered that bit of news.

"Do you do what you want to do simply because you're a man, Mr. Hawkes?" She waved a hand in the general direction of the cheroot, and managed to wave the smoke away, too.

"Oh, most definitely not," he said easily. "That is, that's not the only reason I do what I want to do, typically."

"All the other gentlemen here obey the rules, and one is a viscount."

Too late she heard how she sounded: like a prim little girl.

The corners of his eyes crinkled in amusement, most of it at her expense. "You don't say. Imagine my luck at collapsing on the doorstep of an actual viscount. And everyone knows they *love* rules. May I ask what this one is styled?"

"His name is Lord Bolt."

His eyes flared in surprise. Then he gave a sudden short, shocked laugh. "Come now. You *can't* be serious. Bolt? Lord Bolt? He's alive, is he?"

She bristled. "But I am indeed telling the truth! The last time I saw him he was alive but you can likely attest to how quickly men can transform from living to dead."

"Very well," he said more gently. "I promise I was not laughing at you, Mrs. Gallagher. Forgive me if you feel as though your honesty has been called into question. That's an unpleasant feeling, indeed, isn't it? Why, just a few moments ago someone tried to tell me my name was Mr. Bellingham and implied I was a looby."

She opened her mouth and an arid squeak emerged. "I . . ."

He smiled beatifically at her.

Her lips, like a snake charmed from a basket, turned up.

His charm was sophisticated and quicksilver but undershot with a devastating sort of gentleness, a deference, that suggested he was protecting her from something. Perhaps the full force of his personality, which he had not yet unleashed. But she wanted to move toward the gentleness. She could feel it working away at the bones of her knees, weakening them.

This was the truly dangerous bit, she realized. This was the thing that exerted a sort of tidal pull.

The nature of tides, however, was that one could never quite predict if they were the sort that would lap gently at your toes or pull you right out to sea.

"In all seriousness, I do appreciate the points you are making," he said seriously. "I shall regretfully obey the rules, if only to remain in your good graces, Mrs. Gallagher."

"You ought to follow them because the people here are very kind and very concerned about you, and will likely still feel that way even if you aren't a vicar. Lord Bolt stitched you. Helga cleaned your shirt. And Mr. Delacorte gave you some medicine from his case and it helped to break your fever and to treat your wound."

And now she sounded like a scolding governess. Well, so be it. She spoke the truth.

"I look forward to meeting everyone, especially this Mr. Delacorte. He sounds a useful fellow, if he carries medicines about in a case."

She considered this. "He is a surprising fellow."

"Rather like me, I expect." Gently mocking her again, yet in a way that included her in the joke.

She couldn't help it: she smiled at him again, more fully.

She was surprised when he angled his head slightly away, as though he'd just caught a sunbeam in the eyes.

She wondered what he would do if she said aloud all of the ways in which he had surprised her. *You've a tattoo of a dagger beneath your arm, Mr. Hawkes, and a fluffy nest of hair in your armpit, and I have never seen such a thing, and another fine trail of it vanishes into your trousers. I saw all of this when you fought your enemies in your sleep. You are shaped in beautiful sections, like the jewel Brundage gave to me. Your skin is soft over hard, hard muscle and you are too lean. When you are asleep, your face is a Renaissance painter's dream. You look the way your mother must have seen you when she looked in on you at night when you were a little boy. And now, awake, you look like you've never been innocent in your life.*

She wondered if she looked different now, too. Did her face now reveal that she was no longer innocent, hint at the life she'd led, the things that had happened to her?

Was she a different person in her sleep? Why did it all fall away then, she wondered, and why did we carry it about when we were awake?

She *knew* she could disarm this man with words. He had his assumptions, too. And his vulnerabilities.

She sensed that one of them was now her.

There was a lovely, breathless power in this. And a responsibility.

"What brings you to this charming inn near the docks, Mrs. Gallagher? Are you perhaps in the midst of a journey?"

"Yes," she said shortly. Warily.

He spent a moment in silent perusal of her.

"May I ask to where on this globe of ours you are journeying?" he said politely.

"I am going to live with my brother . . . who needs me."

She hadn't said this part aloud before, and she

liked the sound of this. She wanted to be necessary to someone, and she thought it safer to tell one man that another cared about her and needed her and expected her.

He took this in wordlessly.

He paused to tap an ash on the little saucer on the table next to him. "I should think Bolt of all people would appreciate a little rule breaking," he said half to himself again.

"I could not say," she found herself saying primly. "I have not known him long. He is married to Mrs. Angelique Durand."

He smiled slightly even at this. As though she were a source of continuous quiet delight, like a fawn.

"Oh, yes. Mrs. Durand. I've heard of her," he said ironically.

"Yes. And Mrs. Hardy, our other proprietress, is married to Captain Hardy."

"Captain Hardy, did you say?"

While his words were all but uninflected and his face betrayed nothing, the quality of his interest had sharpened so intensely she could feel it.

"Yes. They have been all that is good and proper and I feel safe and welcome here. I expect you will, too. I will go and tell Mrs. Hardy and Mrs. Durand and everyone who helped you up the stairs you lived through the night, so that they may rejoice, too. But I passed the interview for admittance, Mr. Hawkes, and you have not yet had yours."

It was both a dare and a bit of a tease.

He tipped his head thoughtfully. "An interview is the price for the pleasure of staying here?"

"A rather exacting interview."

"Splendid . . ." he paused to exhale an elegant ribbon of smoke ". . . as I always make an excellent impression."

His smile this time was crooked, wicked, and self-deprecating.

He had more confidence than any human she'd ever met. Part of it was because he was male, another part of it was because he was gorgeous, and the rest was clearly born of something she could not possibly guess at. Because by rights being stabbed would have given most men pause. He behaved as though surviving getting stabbed was something he simply knew how to do, the way he knew how to get his shirt on.

But he was too sure of her, and too sure of his charm, and she thought he deserved to get a sense of her, too.

She pivoted and made for the door, then paused. "You called for your mama last night," she said softly.

She held his shocked gaze for a moment, then she arched a single eyebrow and gracefully backed from the room and closed the door.

Chapter Twelve

HAWKES REMAINED frozen, staring at the closed door.

And after a moment he gave a soft, stunned laugh.

If they'd been fencing, that was the moment she'd flipped the épée right out of his hand.

He was frankly winded. By both her precise, gentle piss-taking, which he loved and deserved, and the implication of what he'd apparently muttered last night.

As it turned out, he could be hurt. And there *were* people he'd loved, and that's what he'd called out for at his weakest.

He missed his bloody mother and she'd died while he was in prison.

Odd how Mrs. Gallagher witnessed more of his wounds just last night than any other human had in the last several decades.

Brundage had used many of the right words to describe her. She was beautiful and charming and she had wit. She seemed clever. But never from what Brundage had said would he have conjured the woman in his room this morning, any more than the word "blue" could fully conjure the sky.

Why had he done it—given her his real name? He'd a mere heartbeat's worth of time to consider and he'd decided it worth watching to see whether her face betrayed suspicion. Or if at any time she'd heard of Mr. Hawkes in association with Brundage.

It remained possible she would have heard of a certain Christian Hawkes somehow, despite the fact that he'd been in prison when Brundage had courted and won her. But Englishmen named Hawkes were hardly scarce, and he certainly wasn't related to all of them.

There had been no pleasure in disconcerting her into scarlet blushes, but it had been revealing, which had been the point. There had, however, been great pleasure in experiencing how she'd refused to let him get away with it. For all she looked like the very personification of a blossom, she struck him as bracingly pragmatic. He hadn't detected a single flighty or capricious thing about her. But a single encounter couldn't possibly be conclusive.

Many, many others seemed required.

Madame Aubert, she of the rouged cheeks that failed to disguise that dark mark—he suspected she had the right of it. Mrs. Gallagher was kind. It seemed a kindness without motive, something innate, and Hawkes was unused to this, too. And this realization made him feel old and jaded.

If this did indeed prove to be an accurate depiction of her character, it meant something serious indeed had made her run away.

And if Lady Aurelie Capet was indeed this same girl who had rested her cool, gentle hand on his forehead last night, then her soft, soothing words, the ones that had sounded to his feverish mind like fragments of dreams, could possibly be the kinds of confidences one might share with a vicar. The sort of person accustomed to hearing such things.

Because she'd said, *I would not look him in the eye.*

He tensed. What the bloody hell did that mean?

Was he even remembering the words correctly?

He flung his arm across his eyes and took a deep breath to steady his mind so he could coolly contemplate his circumstances.

But whatever they'd given him for pain had begun to wear off, and no clear thoughts could get past the poisonous fury that uncoiled in him like a snake at the very notion of Brundage ever touching that woman. Whether it was to kiss her or otherwise. Whether he was engaged to her or not.

Had she . . . cared for him? This, too, seemed intolerable.

If she had, why would she run?

If she wasn't the flighty and foolish sort, she must have had nowhere to turn for help.

And this, too, made him feel a little desperate.

None of this speculation had anything to do with the agreement he'd made to find a girl who'd fled with a necklace. He was blackly amused that he'd walked out of prison and right into a different kind of crucible.

Although it was now clear that prison had only delayed a reckoning a long time coming with Brundage.

And while there remained a slim possibility that his had been a whimsical stabbing, he would be his usual vigilant self when he left the premises. Brundage might be a diplomat and as such accustomed to schooling his features, but Hawkes suspected he might twitch a brow if a man he believed to be dead came calling. Hawkes intended to keep his appointment. Well armed, of course.

Mrs. Gallagher—who he was nearly one hundred percent certain was, in fact, Lady Aurelie Capet—had the right of it: he ought to be in bed. He ought to lie still. He knew now that the only thing that would restore him to rights was rest. And a lot of food. And probably a few more salves and potions.

But for fuck's sake.

He generally found self-pity defeating and draining. But weakness made him furious and enforced stillness made him irritable and he suspected he was going to be a perfectly horrible patient if compelled to be one for long. He was restless for his guns to be returned. He lay back for a moment, and the cool, comfortable bed was too blissful. He mistrusted bliss. He knew irritability, too, that he could not swiftly surrender to trusting the things he had once trusted and taken for granted. Comfort and shelter and quiet.

He felt not so much winded so much as worn, like a boot. Feeling his age, which was not yet forty, and the passage of time. And oddly, a new disorienting emptiness that could only be wrought by a sudden profound absence.

He realized that this was merely the contrast between how he'd felt when Mrs. Gallagher was in the room.

And how the room felt when she wasn't in it.

IT WAS JUST a few hours past dawn at The Grand Palace on the Thames, and Mrs. Gallagher had not yet appeared downstairs to report on the state of Mr. Bellingham.

The possibility of the day beginning with more bad news was a miasma over the breakfast table at The Grand Palace on the Thames. It curbed conversation but not appetites. The stack of fried bread disappeared as rapidly as if locusts had been set loose upon it. The coffee was poured and poured again. Everyone, even those who occasionally liked a good lie-in, like Mrs. Pariseau, was up early and seemed to feel more comfortable together, just like last night in the sitting room. As though they were each a plank in a life raft and stronger together.

One by one they pushed away from the table and dispersed, Captain Hardy and Lord Bolt and Mr. Delacorte off to a meeting with a potential investor that could not be postponed, Mrs. Pariseau out to see a friend. Delilah and Angelique and Dot waved all of them off.

"I think we ought to go up and see how Mr. Bellingham and Mrs. Gallagher fared during the night," Delilah said. Angelique concurred.

They were just moving across the foyer to the stairs—Angelique and Delilah to go up to the rooms, Dot to go down to the kitchen, when a very benign, ordinary rap sounded at the door.

They all froze like deer before wolves.

It had once been such a sound of rejoicing, or at least delicious anticipation.

"It was a proper knock this time," Dot said, cautiously. "Not a sort of 'whump.'"

"Have a look, Dot," Delilah encouraged firmly. One needed to face one's fears, after all.

Dot took a deep breath and very carefully, very slowly, opened the little peep hatch.

"Good morning!" a man said delightedly at once.

Dot gave a little start.

It seemed fairly clear that he hadn't been stabbed.

Dot peered out at him.

She turned and addressed Delilah. "His spectacles are glinting," she whispered. "I can't see his eyes."

This sounded rather chilling when delivered in a whisper.

"You must be Dot," the man said more loudly. Still determinedly cheerful.

"I *am* Dot," she said, surprised, suddenly, and so pleased to be known she opened the door before Delilah or Angelique could issue any warnings or advice.

There stood a rangy man in a greatcoat, clutching a hat. His dark hair was mowed to no-nonsense length. His spectacles and smile were equally sparkling. A trunk and an air of happy expectation accompanied him.

"I'm so terribly sorry that I'm a day later than I expected to be! A horse on our carriage threw a shoe, you see, and we were compelled to stay in an inn on the road. My *heavens*, the haunch they served was threadbare. I think the poor thing was killed two years ago and they've been picking at it ever since. I'm looking forward to the wonder of Helga's cooking."

They all stared at him in utter astonishment.

His smile faltered just a very little. It was an indomitable thing, his smile.

"Mr. . . . Bellingham?" Delilah guessed dazedly.

And this, of course, was the moment Mrs. Gallagher appeared on the stairs.

She paused in her descent, noticing the tableau comprised of motionless people and a man clutching a hat.

At once, the attention of everyone in the room was aggressively tugged between Mrs. Gallagher and the man in the spectacles as though they were all strapped to a Catherine wheel.

AURELIE UNDERSTOOD AT once what was happening.

"I just spoke with *Mr. Hawkes,* who is awake and well," she said loudly, slowly, and pointedly from the stairs.

It took about two seconds for Angelique and Delilah to crack the code.

"But . . ." Dot was puzzled. "If Mr. Bellingham was stab—"

Angelique gently but firmly closed her hand around Dot's arm and gave a quelling and affectionate squeeze. "Mr. Bellingham, we are overjoyed you arrived safely!"

Mr. Bellingham bowed. "Oh, I am, too! What a pleasure it is to finally arrive at The Grand Palace on the Thames. And oh my, you described the chandelier so well. Isn't she a *beauty*?" He gazed upward, happily. "You must be Mrs. Hardy, and you're Mrs. Durand, and you're of course Dot, and I have not had the pleasure of meeting the lady on the stairs yet."

It was like hearing themselves recited as celebrities, and it was, admittedly, irresistible.

"Oh, we were just a *little* concerned, Mr. Bellingham," Angelique told him gaily. "But please do not think of apologizing—we are all too familiar with life and its vicissitudes and we are quite resilient." She aimed a swift glance at Aurelie. "It is *delightful* to meet you at last. You'll want some tea, of course, and we've scones and apple tarts. Dot, take Mr. Bellingham's coat, and we'll have your things brought up to your room. Why don't you have a seat in our reception room."

"Oh, that sounds splendid. Madam, I do not yet know your name, but I expect we'll come to know each other over a game of spillikins or some such pleasant pastime in the sitting room I've heard so much about."

It was pleasantly, not oozily, said, and Aurelie liked him at once.

"I am Mrs. Mary Gallagher, sir. A pleasure to meet you, Mr. Bellingham." She curtsied, and he bowed.

He looked like a Mr. Bellingham. His smile was charming and one of his eyes skewed just a little more toward his nose than it ought, which lent him an air of conspiratorial delight.

She liked to think she would have tended him as gently last night, but she could not be certain.

Nevertheless, somehow she found she could not regret her choice.

After gingerly swiping himself with some water and the rags, Hawkes had gotten into the rest of his clothes, slowly and painfully, because being dressed made him feel more like himself. He had cause to be pleased they were all a little loose, this time, because it made the whole wretched process easier. There wasn't a mirror in the room, which was both a shame and probably a mercy.

He dragged the back of his hand across his whiskery jaw, ruefully. He probably looked like bloody hell. His vanity twinged. He'd been so known for his elegance.

And then came inevitable rustles, murmurs, the shuffling of feet.

All of which heralded the anticipated knock sounding at the door.

He tossed back half a tin cup of the remaining water in the pitcher and swiped the back of his hand across his mouth. One needed to not be parched in order to charm.

"The door is unlocked," he called.

It opened to reveal what appeared to be a small, handsome mob. He smelled coffee. A maid was among them, and she was holding a tray laden with what looked like scones, and he gave thanks that his stomach didn't make an audible noise.

"Please, don't stand on ceremony," Hawkes said pleasantly. "I am at home to guests. Do come in."

And they did, smiling cautiously.

And then he understood at once and yet too late that the legacy of prison was such that he had lost his comfort with facing a crowd of people, all pointed at him. And him in a corner.

Several to hold him, several to beat him a little: that had been the rhythm of things there.

He'd never known when it would happen.

And his mind knew better. Even now, it was diligently rationalizing away the problem.

His body, his faithful servant, simply did not. The memory was stored, and it did what it always did when it sensed danger, and everything in him flexed and primed to defend and his breath was short.

He took a surreptitious breath, and reasoned his pulse to slow.

And then, gradually, like a bit of feather on a breeze, Mrs. Gallagher detached from the crowd and drifted over to have a look out the window as if admiring the view, before wordlessly and decorously sitting down in the chair next to the window, nearer to him than to everyone else.

She'd sensed his unease. He was nearly certain of it.

At this realization his tension evolved into a different kind of tension. He did not think he'd ever before had a protector. It was an extraordinarily gracious thing to do.

But she didn't look at him. She'd at least spared him that.

How had she known?

The rest of the crowd eased into the room, too, perhaps encouraged by her casualness and smiling comfort with him, and spread out a bit, until it all looked more like a salon and less like an ambush.

The maid, a fair-haired girl in a cap with eyes the

size of guineas settled the tray down on the little desk. Heavenly.

He assessed the rest of them swiftly. A golden-haired woman and a brown-haired woman, both lovely—those would be Mrs. Hardy and Mrs. Durand. They looked like the sort of ladies who would employ beautiful penmanship to compose and then stuff gently unyielding messages in the pocket of a man's coat. Two of the men appeared to be the sort who commanded respect because they were accustomed to it—military, former or current, if Hawkes had to guess. Their aspects were simply distinctly different from those of hothouse-bred London gentlemen. They hovered rather protectively near the women. The one with the black hair and unusual green eyes was likely the infamous Bolt. And if it was—well, no one knew better than Hawkes how quickly life could change. Incarcerations, reincarnations—none of it was out of the realm of the possible.

The man with a gaze like flint must be the famous (to some) Captain Hardy.

A third, shorter, very sturdy man who resembled an egg on legs and sported a tuft of dark hair on top wore a fine, plain suit that fitted him splendidly. He exuded a general air of bonhomie and satisfaction with life.

For his part, Hawkes was certain he was wearing his most benignly welcoming expression. He knew how it *felt* on his face; he could don it like a mask, when circumstances made it difficult to do it sincerely. It was no different in his line of work than a soldier's uniform.

A few seconds elapsed during which nobody seemed to know precisely what to say. A diplomat at heart, he decided to take matters in hand.

"I fear I have already inadvertently taken advantage of your hospitality here at The Grand Palace on the Thames, and I cannot thank you enough for what you have done for me. And if you'll forgive my unfortunate choice of words, I would do murder for a whiskey, if your hospitality extends to such."

This was met with a brief and fascinated silence.

Then swift smiles.

Perhaps because he had the kind of accent that, like rare orchids and fine liquor, could only be a product of cultivation and good breeding. Impossible to fake.

"Well, whiskey, and possibly a mirror, since your fixed stares suggest my appearance inspires some horror, or at the very least astonishment. Or were you all still under the impression that I was Mr. Bellingham?"

"You could do with a shave," the egg-shaped man critiqued. "I'll lend you my soap and brush and razor," he added kindly. "Mrs. Gallagher told us who you are."

"Thank you, sir. You're a true gent. I suspect you're the man with the case of remedies. Mr. Delacorte."

"I am he," Mr. Delacorte said proudly, and bowed. "A pleasure to meet you, Mr. Hawkes. I import 'em from India and the Orient. Pills and teas and powders and ground-up animal bits and bobs. Sell them up and down the coast to surgeons and apothecaries. Most of 'em work a treat and some of the others are good if you like a hallucination or two, which, mind you, I don't, but I won't judge. Anything you need next time you're stabbed, or shot, or aching of head or limp of—"

"*Thank* you, Mr. Delacorte," interjected the dark-haired woman swiftly.

"A pleasure, Mr. Delacorte," Hawkes said. "I do hope I can someday repay your generosity. And may I never have need of that last remedy you mentioned," he said smoothly.

A lot of little smiles were swiftly suppressed here, which boded well, given that he was likely going to stay for a while and that was the sort of thing he often said.

"Perhaps you've a footman who would be willing to run out and fetch a few things for me from my previous location?" he suggested to Mrs. Durand and Mrs. Hardy.

This suggestion was met with a puzzling, awkward, and decidedly glum little silence. He let it lie for now.

"Bolt sewed you up," Mr. Delacorte, who had likely been a champion silence breaker his entire life, said. He gestured with his thumb to Bolt, who bowed in turn.

"My thanks, sir," Hawkes said humbly to Lucien. "You must be the viscount. I haven't had a chance to inspect your handiwork, but given that my insides remain inside and the bleeding has . . ."

It just wasn't done. A gentleman didn't discuss gore in front of ladies. Regardless of whether they were the ones who'd cleaned his blood from the marble foyer. He wasn't going to do it.

Bolt said easily, "I should thank *you* for the opportunity to practice that skill. I considered stitching 'bless our home' on you, but ran out of room."

Hawkes laughed.

And this was how they knew they spoke a common language, that of manly men being men, and pretending that nothing ever hurt and that stitching up a human was child's play and so forth.

The rest of the introductions followed apace, accompanied by bowing and curtsying. His guesses about who everyone might be proved correct. And the maid was named Dot.

"You're the screamer," he guessed.

"Yes, sir," she said shyly.

"Impressive. I'll never forget that sound," he told her sincerely. "You ought to lead cavalries. We could save the money we'd normally spend on trumpets."

She flushed scarlet in pleasure. "Thank you," she whispered.

"I do have a burning question. Is Mr. Bellingham real, or is he a figment of Mrs. Gallagher's imagination?"

He said it specifically because he knew it would either make Mrs. Gallagher smile or get her lovely eyes to crackle and either of those things would be as bracing as that cup of coffee.

She met his swift sidelong glance with a wry sidelong glance of her own.

Her hands were folded together protectively in her lap, and he realized she had kept them folded for much of their conversation, earlier, too. As if she wanted to occupy as little space as possible.

Suspicion shivved him.

As if she were perpetually braced to bolt if necessary.

Just like he'd been a moment ago.

And the possible reasons why she was like this swarmed in his brain like biting gnats.

"I let him in the door a few minutes ago," Dot volunteered happily. "Mr. Bellingham."

"Well, I'm certainly pleased for your sakes that the beloved vicar has arrived safely. Perhaps I'll be given an opportunity to ingratiate myself to you, as well. I've been carefully studying your rules, so I'll be prepared if there is a test." He gestured with the card.

Clearly the right thing to say.

Now everyone was smiling at him.

Well, Bolt and Hardy were smiling, but he knew it was the conditional sort of smiling men did in order not to alarm women. They hadn't decided yet what sort of man he was, and this was fair. Clever and thorough as Mrs. Durand and Mrs. Hardy might be, he sensed it was the men he needed to persuade of his suitability, given that he'd arrived bleeding and bristling with weapons, and that was going to be a slightly tricky conversation.

"I should say I hope there will not be dancing of evenings. Although if properly blackmailed, I might be persuaded to sing."

Everyone laughed at this, too.

The ingratiating was underway.

"Assuming you pass the interview," Mrs. Gallagher said pleasantly.

He shot her another sidelong glance.

"We all did dance once," Mr. Delacorte said wistfully. "We even waltzed."

"It will happen one day again, Mr. Delacorte," Mrs. Hardy reassured him.

Hawkes noticed the swift, amused look she exchanged with Mrs. Durand.

"Do you remember what happened, Mr. Hawkes?" Hardy asked shortly. "If it's not too difficult to recount, that is?"

He'd been watching Hawkes with unabashed unblinking assessment.

"There's a tobacconist next to an apothecary who stocks a blend I enjoy—I'm in London overnight on a bit of business and your establishment was recommended to me. I strolled over to have a look at the livery stables adjacent and considered stopping into the little pub next door when I was accosted. Clearly, the blighter mistook me for someone who needed stabbing. I dodged or I think he would have ended me."

"Oh! *Terrifying!*" Dot breathed, her hands to her cheeks.

He shrugged with one shoulder and lifted an insouciant hand.

(Dot found this thrilling. She would repeat this story and imitate that little hand gesture for maids in the kitchen the moment she got an opportunity.)

"I confess I felt a little unwell some days before it happened and hoped I merely needed a good sleep, and it seems I've had a bit of a fever. Admittedly, I feel considerably better this morning, if, alas, not absolutely in top form. Again, I cannot thank all of you enough for your extraordinarily kind efforts on my behalf. And please do not allow my depleted condition to dissuade you from extracting payment."

As Mrs. Hardy and Mrs. Durand smiled at him, he tensed when he caught a minute movement out of the corner of his eye—Captain Hardy was reaching into his coat like a man reaching for a gun.

Hardy's hand emerged holding a flask.

Hawkes wondered if either Hardy or Bolt had his guns tucked into their coats, too, ready to return them. "Have anything else interesting in your pockets, Captain Hardy?"

Hardy smiled pleasantly. "Would you mind if Bolt and I spoke privately with Mr. Hawkes?" Captain Hardy gestured with the flask. "I think we can make at least one of his dreams come true and his coffee more interesting."

"Of course," Mrs. Hardy said. "We look forward to coming to know you, Mr. Hawkes—and to having a little conversation. We'll have someone look in on you at intervals to see if you need assistance with anything."

"I look forward to it, too. And please extend my warmest regards to whoever managed to get the blood out of my shirt. I feel more myself and it is much appreciated."

They left prepared to like their new guest very much, Mrs. Gallagher bringing up the rear, sending him one unreadable yet strengthening glance from those eyes of hers.

Chapter Thirteen

"HARDY," HAWKES said immediately, when the door closed. "I recall hearing during the war about the exploits of a Hardy who was a blockade captain. Put the fear of God in smugglers." He poured a cup of coffee for himself and held it out to Hardy. "Supposedly impressed the devil out of the king."

"At your service." Captain Hardy tipped a splash of whiskey into Hawkes's cup.

And then with smooth alacrity, he produced from his coat Hawkes's two guns, knife, and money and laid them on the desk next to Hawkes.

Hawkes exhaled and picked them up and gave all of it a count and a swift, proper little inspection, as any man would when reunited with his guns and money. The guns were still loaded. He locked them and reinstalled them in their hiding places while Bolt and Hardy watched, wordlessly.

"The only other Hawkes I'm aware of was a diplomat critical in the establishment of the intelligence community during the war and imprisoned by the French for espionage," Hardy said.

Hawkes smiled faintly. His successes had been reported in the newspapers. So had his arrest.

And then, presumably, he'd been all but forgotten.

"I was released about a fortnight ago."

He had the pleasure of watching two sets of eyebrows shoot up.

"Cheers," he added, and bolted the coffee. Oh, that was it, he thought, blissfully. That was what was missing from his blood. Coffee. The whiskey did its job of blunting pain and nerves.

"It's an interesting pleasure and honor to meet you, sir," Hardy said.

"Call me Hawkes."

Hawkes turned to Bolt. "You're really Bolt? Viscount Bolt, son of Brexford, wild as bloody hell, who allegedly drowned in the Thames, and so forth? That Bolt?"

"I was scooped out of the Thames by a Dutch ship headed to the Orient. My next decade was rather . . . full," Bolt said laconically. "Most importantly, I learned how to sew up a human in that decade. I'm now blissfully . . . 'domesticated,' I suppose is the word. Married for life. Hardy and I and Mr. Delacorte are in an import and export partnership called the Triton Group. Met with some associates from Lloyd's last night at White's, otherwise we would have been up much earlier. And dressed," he added dryly.

Hawkes went on alert at the mention of Lloyd's, the originators of the Patriotic Fund—the fund which collected and disbursed smaller funds to prisoners of war. They were insurers; they likely underwrote the Triton Group's cargoes.

"Ah. Interesting. Bolt *and* Hardy," Hawkes mused. "Imagine that. Honestly, I'm not convinced I'm not still foxed on whatever magic powders I was administered last night."

Hardy took a swig of the whiskey, which was quite

sociable of him, given that it was just after breakfast for him. He passed the flask to Bolt, who did the same, lest a man need to drink alone.

A little silence fell.

"If there's anything a diplomat appreciates it's a delicate situation in which one must carefully choose how much to share with his hosts," Hawkes began.

"How much of the real reason you were here by the docks, in other words," Hardy said.

Hawkes gave a short, somewhat humorless laugh. "I am," he said with care, "on an assignment. I fear I am not at liberty to say more than that. I am not convinced my assignment is related to the reason I was attacked. Neither am I convinced it was not. I would appreciate it if I could have your word as gentlemen that you will not repeat what I have just told you, or reveal my identity to anyone as anything other than Mr. Hawkes, a gentleman—which, in truth, is all I truly am at present. As this is all I am comfortable divulging at the moment, I hope it will suffice."

He'd said it in a way that managed to be elegantly polite and respectful and absolutely nonnegotiable.

He waited. Patiently.

Hardy gave a short nod. "Do you think your presence at The Grand Palace on the Thames will put anyone else here in harm's way?"

And that was the crux of this little meeting.

"Certainly not with the two of you here," he said. A trifle glibly. But dryly.

They offered him patient smiles.

"In all seriousness, I don't think anyone attempting to murder me would get past the phalanx of people at your door and the stringent interview process. I do not expect to abide here long, but I'm grateful for the shelter and I would sincerely rather die than allow any harm to come to anyone here."

"That sounds fair."

Hawkes grinned at Hardy's dryness.

"I do have some things at the Stevens I rather urgently need, and for certain reasons I don't think it will be safe for me to fetch them."

Eyebrows went up again.

Hardy said, after a moment, "We'll get them for you. They know me there."

"Again, my sincerest thanks."

Bolt gestured with his chin toward the bed. "Rest, Hawkes. No need to be a hero for either of us. Come down this evening if you feel ready to be social."

Mr. Hawkes caused another astonished little silence when he appeared in the sitting room that night. It was like they'd gotten yet another new guest.

He'd shaved. He'd had a proper wash, in water heated and brought up in a basin by a maid.

He was as hard and polished and gleaming as a guinea. He looked both a little bit dangerous and refined, like a ceremonial knife.

His smile, self-deprecating, a little wry, as if he knew precisely what everyone was thinking, made all the feminine hearts skip.

Angelique and Delilah had spoken to him a little more at length that afternoon, gently admonished him about smoking in the rooms, and departed pleased with their new guest.

Aurelie had spent part of the afternoon sleeping to recover from her night with Mr. Hawkes, but she was at once certain there could, in fact, never be a recovery from Mr. Hawkes.

It was odd to know that she was, after a fashion, a keeper of this polished man's secrets. None of these people knew he had a tattoo of a dagger beneath his arm. Or had thrashed invisible enemies, or called for his mama. Admittedly a few of the people here had the extreme good fortune to know what his torso looked like beneath his clothes.

And she knew other secrets, too: something or someone had once cornered Mr. Hawkes and he'd been unable to fight back. She wasn't certain it was just because he'd been stabbed. She'd seen at once his tension and stillness and shortness of breath.

She supposed he was, whether he realized it or not, a keeper of her secrets as well.

They were bound, in a sense. And she felt it. Because at once the room seemed better for his presence in it, as though all it had been missing was him.

"I took the rules of your establishment to heart, you see, and I am here for the familial environment and spirited discourse," he told them, solemnly.

"And we are *grateful,* Mr. Hawkes," Mrs. Pariseau breathed. She was eyeing Mr. Hawkes as if he were indeed a lost guinea she was prepared to brawl over should another person attempt to grab him first.

Angelique and Delilah shot her startled glances.

Mrs. Pariseau could perhaps be forgiven. Everyone had been given a little sherry by way of celebrating Mr. Bellingham's arrival and Mr. Hawkes's survival, and nearly everyone in the room was some small degree of tipsy.

Mrs. Hardy poured a sherry for Mr. Hawkes and handed it to him, and said, "Mr. Hawkes, I should like to introduce you to one of our cherished guests, Mrs. Pariseau."

Mrs. Pariseau leaped to her feet to curtsy.

"Indeed, it is a pleasure to meet you, Mrs. Pariseau," Hawkes said. "I would bow, but the part of me that bends has been sewn nearly motionless."

"Oh, stay as you are, Mr. Hawkes, right where we can admire you from top to toe. I can curtsy twice to make up for it," Mrs. Pariseau said. She did just that.

They both laughed, merrily.

Aurelie was shocked when a veritable lightning bolt of jealousy pierced her.

Mr. Hawkes seemed not at all nonplussed. He must be very used to the Mrs. Pariseaus of the world.

For heaven's sake. She had no claim on this man and Mrs. Pariseau was certainly not about to do anything untoward.

Was she?

He hadn't even looked her way yet.

But then she realized that he had been drifting ever closer to her from the moment he'd entered the room. Her heart gave a little jolt of anticipation.

Hawkes toasted the room at large and sipped at his sherry. He did not yet sit.

Aurelie imagined the getting up and getting down was painful and she felt her stomach muscles contract a little in involuntary sympathy.

And finally, he looked directly at her, as though he'd been mustering nerve to do it, or saving a pleasure for last.

"Mrs. Gallagher." He nodded to Aurelie. He'd lowered his voice just for her. "A pleasure to see you once again. Why, I was just reminiscing about our first meeting."

She perversely wished it was impossible to smile, because she did not want to seem so easily charmed. She mistrusted a man who had such power; she didn't want to be at a man's mercy ever again.

When she smiled, something solemn and intent briefly flickered across his face, as though she'd just handed a delicate gift to him. Something he wasn't certain he deserved.

And that was how he took her breath away, yet again.

There was an unvarnished honesty to the way he regarded her. He could not help the intensity of his gaze, she supposed, any more than the sun could calibrate its own heat. She knew he very much admired her womanly charms, and the way in which he made this apparent did not make her feel cornered. There remained a sort of bemused tenderness in the way he addressed her.

It seemed clear that he was, to some degree, at her mercy, too. He either wanted her to know it, or he did not know how to disguise it. And oddly, she felt protective of this.

In a few days' worth of time, she had come to understand too clearly the difference between what she thought she should feel and what she did indeed feel. She hadn't suspected that her body would tell her the truth about everything, *everything,* until she'd encountered Mr. Hawkes.

"Rest suits you, Mr. Hawkes," she said softly. She could not flirt with the trumpet-blast confidence of Mrs. Pariseau, but she did know how to do it. "But ought you to be downstairs so soon?"

"Perhaps not. But I know you'd miss me if I left now, Mrs. Gallagher," he said pleasantly. "And I couldn't countenance visiting that sort of suffering upon you, after all you've done for me."

She pressed her lips together but it was futile, and she smiled again and she gave her head a little shake.

"Mr. Hawkes, you have not yet met our latest cherished guest, Mr. Bellingham," Mrs. Hardy said.

"Mr. Bellingham." Mr. Hawkes turned to face him. "It is indeed a pleasure to meet you. I have heard so much about you."

Mr. Bellingham seemed shyly dazzled by Mr. Hawkes, too.

"A pleasure to meet you, too, sir." Mr. Bellingham shot to his feet and bowed. "And I'm so terribly sorry to hear of your troubles. But if one must be assaulted, you couldn't have chosen a finer establishment in which to convalesce. Why, just look about you!" he said expansively, gesturing.

Mr. Hawkes did, as though taking Mr. Bellingham's suggestion to heart, and with evident pleasure. "You're so right. I've seldom seen a lovelier room."

His impulse, Aurelie had noticed today, was to make people like him by finding the things they liked about themselves and celebrating them. He'd sensed at once the ladies were so proud of the home they'd made for everyone. It was a lovely quality.

Or perhaps, viewed more cynically, it was a skill.

Nonetheless, it was difficult not to like it. And she, like everyone in the room at that moment, had turned her face up to him to smile.

Suddenly she was assailed with a disorienting, peculiar déjà vu. Of watching that other Mr. Hawkes from her vantage point at the top of the stairs so many years ago, and those smiling faces aimed up at him.

But surely he could not be the same man?

"What brings you to London, Mr. Bellingham, if I am not being tedious in asking a question everyone already knows the answer to?" Hawkes asked.

"No trouble at all to tell you, Mr. Hawkes. It seems I've inherited a property from a great-aunt—a charming little place in Sussex called Starling Cottage. I've just been to see it and to have it tidied a bit and prepared for guests, but it still needs a few repairs and the like—I've a back door all but hanging from the hinges, you see—a good tug would take it right off. Some thatch missing from the roof. A stuck window or two. And I'm here in London to see to a few lingering details about the inheritance and to see old friends. I've left my parishioners in my curate's good hands. I know he'll shine in my absence."

"Lord Bolt has a little property in Derbyshire, and it needs a little attention of that sort, too," Mrs. Durand said. "One day we'll spend some time there."

"Oh, imagine a little country inn, like this one!" Mrs. Pariseau said, happily. "Perhaps we can all go and stay with you there one day!"

Lord Bolt shot Angelique an eloquent, darkly amused, hunted look.

"There can only ever be one inn like this one," Delilah said at once, both mistily and diplomatically.

"I never thought I'd own a place and the vicarage suits me down to my toes, but it is a blessing I never anticipated." Mr. Bellingham beamed at this. "Oh, you ought to see it. The cottage is tucked in a little bend right where a stream widens, and it's lined with hawthorns so it's easy to miss as you drive right by, and there are big old apple trees dropping apples all about in a great meadow. But it's near the town of Baggleston and the mail coach goes right through midday Wednesdays and Fridays, so it's civilized, too. There's a pub, and a little bookshop, even a fine little notions shop where one can buy or sell anything you can imagine."

A simple life on the outskirts of civilization: it sounded exotic and blissful to Aurelie, who was accustomed to moving through echoing rooms or promenading, well chaperoned, through manicured parks.

"I grew up in the country, Mr. Bellingham," Mr. Hawkes said, "and I understand your joy. I'm in London on business as well, and while my stay here wasn't precisely on my itinerary, I find I cannot resent it."

A roomful of smiles were aimed at him again. Aurelie suspected this happened to him a good deal.

Mr. Hawkes turned to her. "Mrs. Gallagher, you mentioned you were going to visit your brother. Has he a country cottage as well?"

Aurelie hesitated, but she'd already told everyone in the room what her plans were. Surely it was silly now to equivocate. "He is in America, Mr. Hawkes, in Boston. I hope to sail there from Dover, after I conclude my business in London. I do not think Boston is considered the country anymore."

"And you're doing this alone, Mrs. Gallagher?"

Was it her conscience, or were his eyes particularly searching?

She didn't care for the reminder that the notion of a woman doing anything alone was inadvisable.

"I should like to find a suitable traveling companion while in London," she said. Which was true. She'd hoped Mr. Erasmus Monroe could recommend or help her to find one.

"Have you ever before crossed an ocean? Or perhaps the Channel?"

She noted the word "an." As if he'd gone and crossed all of them. As if they were all different, requiring different skills and expectations, and while she was hardly ignorant of geography, this nuanced possibility had simply never occurred to her. The Atlantic Ocean was merely the great expanse between where she was and where she needed to be and she would do whatever she needed to do in order to close it. She had no illusions about it being easy, or pleasant, or comfortable. She simply did not want to think about any of these things, because it made that belt of tension tighten around her ribs again.

"This will be my first ocean crossing," she said. "I am very much looking forward to it."

This was not, in its essence, untrue.

She sensed that Mr. Hawkes was now tempted to say a number of things, and was perhaps merely deciding which one to say first.

Her heartbeat accelerated and her palms went a trifle damp.

"If you find it a challenge to get passage from Dover when your business here in London is concluded, Mrs. Gallagher, I took a packet to Boston from Falmouth some years ago, when I was just out of university," Mr. Bellingham told them. "A few days journey from here on the mail coach. It was a gift from my uncle, the trip. I enjoyed my visit very much and Americans are the most bracingly interesting sort of people. I suspect you'll be happy there, Mrs. Gallagher."

It was a very kind thing to say, and it felt a little like a benediction, coming from an *actual* vicar. "Thank you, Mr. Bellingham. My brother is indeed happy there."

"Is this your first trip to the city of London, Mrs. Gallagher?" Mr. Hawkes asked pleasantly. "I shouldn't like to presume, but you sound as though you may hail from France, and every person I've met in life to date named 'Gallagher' has been Irish."

She was aware, suddenly, of a room full of bright, friendly, interested eyes upon her. Damn him. She had so far dodged more searching questions, for which she was grateful. She hadn't much practice with lying and she didn't know whether she'd be able to keep track of a fictitious cast of characters once she began inventing them.

"Oh, yes, my dear late husband, Thomas, was Irish," she said.

Then cast her eyes down to her lap.

She had done this, rather guiltily, several times before and it seemed to end whatever line of questioning was underway.

A little respectful sympathetic silence ensued.

When she finally looked up again she found Mr. Hawkes regarding her with the faintest of frowns. And then his expression shifted into pensiveness again.

She looked away, and back down at her folded hands. Her face was hot.

And there was a little lull in the room.

"I've been waiting for an opportunity to muster the courage to mention something. It's something a little embarrassing, I fear," Mr. Bellingham said suddenly.

"The smoking room is where we go to do embarrassing things, Mr. Bellingham," Mr. Delacorte told him crisply, as though giving a guided tour of a museum. He moved his knight on the chessboard.

"Thank you, Mr. Delacorte," Mr. Bellingham said graciously. "I shall take that under advisement. This is more after the fashion of . . . well, it's about a . . . well a . . . predilection I have. Or rather, a pastime I might have in mind. Harmless I think, but I wondered if . . . if anyone shared it?"

Most of the expressions in the room were now decidedly wary.

"It's just a little something I began to enjoy in the country, and I've heard of it occurring in London, too."

(Secretly, both Delilah and Angelique fervently, fervently hoped this embarrassing thing wasn't the Vicar's Wheelbarrow. They still now and again needed to turn men away at the door who came looking for it.)

Mr. Bellingham cleared his throat. "I don't suppose

there's any hope of persuading any of you to . . . well . . . go with me to a . . ." he lowered his voice self-consciously ". . . donkey race?"

Mr. Delacorte sat bolt upright.

Then went as rigid as a statue.

His face blanked.

He rose slowly, slowly to his feet, hands braced against the table.

Then sat down again.

Then shot again to his feet.

He opened his mouth. No sound emerged.

Everyone in the room witnessed history being made: Mr. Delacorte was too excited to speak.

"Bellingham . . ." he finally managed, in a voice hoarse with emotion. "I fecking . . ." He closed his eyes, and then swore again softly. "I fecking *love* donkey races."

"Oh, truly, Mr. Delacorte?" Mr. Bellingham was delighted and relieved. "Do you mean it? It's just so funny! I mean—the jockeys trying to cling to them! Their little hindquarters are so droll when they run, don't you think?"

"So are Lord Bolt's, when he runs," Mrs. Pariseau murmured.

Nearly every head in the room whipped toward her in shock.

Mrs. Pariseau widened her eyes innocently at them. "Oh, come now, I'd only got a *tiny* glimpse of his hindquarters when he flew over the balcony in only his shirt. I could not *help* but see. Should I put a pence as penance in the jar?" she said contritely. "I think I shall. I have never before made a visit to the jar and I should feel very daring if I did."

"Don't let us stop you, Mrs. Pariseau," Mrs. Hardy said sweetly. And quellingly.

The contents of the epithet jar often bought the morning newspapers, thanks to Mr. Delacorte.

It looked like the jar was going to get a lot of traffic tonight.

"I think Maggie may have gotten a bit of a look at his frontquarters," Delacorte said frankly. "Which is why she fainted."

Lord Bolt slowly raised his head from the chessboard and stared purely astounded daggers at Delacorte.

"Lucien . . . are you *blushing*?" Angelique murmured, peering closely at her husband.

It was possible history was being made for the second time tonight.

She was torn between defending him and enjoying it, because it was admittedly bloody funny, and she'd had a little sherry, too.

At the table behind Lord Bolt, Captain Hardy's eyes had practically vanished with stifled mirth.

"I wonder if hindquarters ought to be a jar word," Lord Bolt said tautly. "Also 'frontquarters.'"

"Indeed. Look what you've done to poor Mr. Bellingham, you two," Mrs. Hardy said reproachfully.

Mr. Bellingham had gone the shade of a tomato.

Aurelie was, in truth, blushing, too, though she very much wanted to laugh. It was easier to laugh now that Hawkes was alive.

She surreptitiously watched him to see if he was enjoying himself, and it seemed very clear that he was, and he was decidedly *not* blushing. She was pleased, because she frankly loved this room, and this kind of discourse. She could imagine days upon days just like this. Every one a little different, and yet reassuringly the same.

"We are usually more civilized, Mr. Bellingham. Our *sincerest* apologies," Angelique said earnestly. "We've had a very exciting few days and everyone is feeling their oats, it seems."

"Oh, it's only a blush," Mr. Bellingham said easily. "I shan't perish from it. Perhaps I ought to have a little more of the sherry, too, just to catch up with everyone else."

Mr. Delacorte stared at Bellingham and his happy smile took on a bemused, somewhat pensive quality, as though he just couldn't *believe* his luck. He was likely imagining dragging Bellingham to a variety of pubs and getting him happily drunk enough to sing bawdy pub songs.

Mrs. Pariseau got up and put her penance pence in the jar and Mr. Delacorte paid three pence for all of his "feckings," as well, and they returned, each happily enough, to their chairs.

"Lord Bolt sailed through the air over the banister in just his shirt to help rescue Mr. Hawkes," Dot explained helpfully to Mr. Bellingham, just in case he wasn't tired of picturing it.

"Oh," Mr. Bellingham said, politely, with a somewhat wobbly smile. He had not been apprised of all the dramatic details of Mr. Hawkes's arrival.

"We were all there. In fact, Mrs. Gallagher was one of the first by his side," Lord Bolt added gallantly.

Mr. Hawkes turned sharply to regard her with such wondering solemnity that Aurelie nearly clapped her hand over her jolting heart. As if to disguise the fact that just like that, he'd set it aglow.

She found she could not speak. Her own cheeks were likely turning shades of red.

"It's funny, ain't it," Mr. Delacorte mused. "It's obvious Bolt puts his shirt on first, but Hardy puts his pants on first. I guess we all do it differently. I like to do shirt, then pants. The Duke of Valkirk said he had a series of servants lift him on pulleys to lower him into his pants, lest he be unduly abraded. Ha! He was a very amusing fellow. I miss him."

Aurelie gave a start.

Because Mr. Hawkes had gone as still as an arrow striking its mark.

"Valkirk?" Hawkes said nearly sharply. "Valkirk was a guest here?"

"He stayed with us for some weeks and left with a wife," Delacorte said. "He was splendid, and she was splendid, too. Everyone seems to leave here with a wife," he added. Somewhat wistfully.

"Good man, Valkirk," Captain Hardy said. He was looking at Mr. Hawkes, somewhat meaningfully.

"The finest," Hawkes said shortly.

But Aurelie noticed, because it seemed she noticed everything now, that sharpened, concentrated quality of Hawkes's attention at the mention of the famous General Blackmore, now the Duke of Valkirk.

Everyone—everyone in Europe, and probably the world over—knew who the Duke of Valkirk was. Valorous Valkirk, they called him now.

It did indeed seem remarkable that he'd come to stay at this little place. Perhaps that accounted for Mr. Hawkes's reaction.

"What about you, Bellingham?" Mr. Delacorte said, while Bolt considered his next move. "Do you put your shirt on first or your pants—"

"Mrs. Gallagher," Mrs. Hardy said brightly. "Would you be so kind as to favor us with something pretty on the pianoforte? And perhaps Mr. Delacorte would like to sing?"

"Mr. Delacorte would *love* to sing," Delacorte said delightedly.

Chapter Fourteen

DELACORTE WAS almost at once in full, fine voice while Mrs. Gallagher played the pianoforte.

But before the singing got underway in earnest, Captain Hardy and Bolt retreated to the smoking room adjacent to the sitting room, and Hawkes went with them because not only had he been curious about it since Mrs. Gallagher mentioned it, he wanted to get Hardy and Bolt alone for a few questions. Mr. Bellingham had charmingly demurred when invited along. He wanted a turn at singing.

The room had clearly been furnished by women who understood men, Hawkes thought approvingly. They'd created a refuge for male visitors and residents of The Grand Palace on the Thames to be quietly disgusting or profane if they so chose. It was decorated in shades of brown, spread with a lush carpet in a stain-hiding pattern of brown and cream and hung with long dark brown velvet curtains. The chairs were vast, worn, and comfortable and the little table, upon which a man could hoist his booted feet, had seen better days.

Hawkes lowered himself carefully into the chair, and was given a glass of brandy by Hardy and a lit cheroot by Bolt, and he sighed.

As they all quietly, reflectively enjoyed that first inhale, Hawkes thought of Mrs. Gallagher—Aurelie—preparing to go to Boston, apparently alone. It was about as far as someone could run. It was hardly a frivolous undertaking for someone who had never taken an ocean voyage. They were expensive and could be perilous, and either she wasn't aware of this or had decided the risk was necessary, and his money was on the latter.

It was a fairly desperate act of someone who could not get far enough away, fast enough. It made him restless.

Although, from a professional perspective, he appreciated the invention of a dead husband. It was the sort of thing one could wield skillfully as a shield.

He hadn't much faith in her ability to continue that ruse, however. No one knew better than he that successful deception required a certain innate talent for it and years of practice, and she had neither.

She must be very certain that Brundage would look for her.

And she must be terribly determined not to be found.

What was he going to do now that he was nearly one hundred percent certain he had found her?

He was due to meet with Brundage tomorrow. Hell's teeth.

"You're acquainted with Valkirk, then, Hardy?" he asked.

"We've become friendly. He loaned us his box at the opera, as it so happens. And he stayed here, then married one of our guests, as Delacorte said. An opera singer."

Hawkes smiled wryly. "Well, felicitations to him. God knows he's earned some happiness."

"You've met Valkirk, Hawkes?" Hardy asked.

He was quiet for a moment, considering how to begin. "Yes. I've had the honor of speaking with him a few times. The last time, in fact, was in Spain the night before the battle of Dos Montañas. We attended the same assembly."

Everyone in the room went somber. Dos Montañas was fairly widely known as a startling disaster for the general who almost never lost a battle.

"I'll never forget his expression when word arrived that French troops had amassed ahead of his planned advance. As if they were anticipating it. And no one should put that expression on the general's face. I took it personally, though it had naught to do with me." Hawkes added this last rather pointedly.

"What do you think happened?" This was Hardy.

Hawkes was silent for some time, deciding how much he ought to tell the two men. But he knew Hardy had conducted his own investigations in order to root out smugglers. He likely possessed a similar set of skills and a similarly cynical view of the caprices of men.

"When one is in the habit of gathering intelligence, one recognizes the hallmarks of a breach," he finally said, carefully.

He likely wasn't telling them anything they didn't already know.

"You think the French had foreknowledge of Blackmore's troop movements and were prepared."

Since he hadn't said it aloud—Hardy had—Hawkes merely remained silent and returned Hardy's gaze with a speaking one.

"I should say I found it disturbing," he finally, said shortly. "And it has never stopped being disturbing."

"I thought so, too, at the time," Hardy said.

They smoked in silence.

"Are either of you personally acquainted with the Earl of Brundage?" Hawkes asked casually after a moment.

Though both Bolt and Hardy sensed it was not a casual question.

"Brundage. I recall him playing alarmingly deep," Bolt said. "There were whispers that he was in the habit of it, in fact. And given that I, too, played alarmingly deep once upon a time, if his habits made an impression on me, that's saying something. In White's last night, we heard a rumor that he was in the running to become the ambassador to France. I always found him to be a sort of prig possessed of a certain oily charm, but then everyone was a prig compared to me when I was younger."

"Astute assessment," Hawkes said shortly. "Although, I am perhaps a trifle prejudiced." He paused. "Bolt . . . you're a member of White's?"

"For better or worse."

"And the two of you have a relationship with Lloyd's?"

"The Triton Group—me, Hardy, and Delacorte—does. They underwrite our ship," Bolt confirmed.

Hawkes inhaled smoke, exhaled it at leisure. "Did the meeting with Lloyd's go well?"

"It was civil, and we all parted drunk and fond of each other."

Hawkes smiled faintly. He mulled for a moment how to say what he wanted to say, and whether he should. He finally decided the opportunity presented was pure serendipity. And perhaps yet another example of destiny.

"I should be obliged if you could ask your friend from Lloyd's a question, and I fear it's of a rather urgent nature. And it's whether a charity called the Society for the Relief of English Prisoners of War ever turned over the funds it collected to Lloyd's Patriotic Fund for the prisoner of war relief fund."

Both men looked at him sharply.

"That's quite a specific question, Hawkes," Bolt said, carefully.

"It is, indeed."

"Where did you see this charity?" This was Bolt asking.

Hawkes studied him.

"You can trust him," Hardy said simply, finally.

"It was in Brundage's budget before the war."

A taut, wordless interlude.

"It strikes me as unusual," Bolt proceeded carefully, "for an ambassador to sponsor such a charity. White's collected funds for war prisoners, which were transferred to Lloyd's. Twining's took up a collection."

"You don't think it's a real charity." This was Hardy, who'd sussed out the run of things.

"I shall just say that the time frame during which it appeared in the books gave me pause. As did the way its balance grew and shrank."

The two other men, who were intelligent and also, in their way, probably crafty, were silently drawing conclusions about what this meant.

"And who oversaw Brundage's budget?"

"Brundage," Hawkes said shortly.

"Do you think Brundage . . ." Bolt stopped.

No one wanted to ask that question aloud.

"If you could ask the question of your associate at Lloyd's, I would be appreciative," was all Hawkes said. "Perhaps I'll join the singing now. I find myself lured like a sailor to a siren at the sound of Mrs. Gallagher's pianoforte playing."

Back in his room, Hawkes lit the lamp and kept it low, then moved to the window to inspect the view, beyond which thin black spires of ships pierced a pewter sky layered in mist.

He slid open the window briefly and hung out his head so the wind could give him a good bracing slap.

Tomorrow morning, he intended to pay a visit to a certain antiquities dealer by the name of Guthrie. Unless he discovered Mrs. Gallagher had simultaneous other plans, in which case, wherever she went, he would follow.

Pain and weariness were beginning to assert themselves through the pleasant haze of brandy and the evening's bonhomie. He ought to lay his wounded self back on the bed and rest, decide upon a course of action. Have a proper night's sleep, if he could.

But the thought of Mrs. Gallagher sent restlessness rippling across his nerves.

And as though it was a pleasant drug of the sort Mr. Delacorte might carry about in his case, his thoughts returned to the moment earlier in the evening when Mrs. Hardy was playing pianoforte and everyone had gathered around her to sing, and he'd found himself standing and signing alongside Mrs. Gallagher. Somewhere mid-song their eyes met, then held perhaps longer than was proper. Her singing faltered, and a flush spilled into her cheeks. But before she dropped her eyes, her lips had curved in a little smile that was as sensual as a hand brushed across his cock.

He relived that moment second by second now for the fresh surge of pure, primal masculine satisfaction.

Because he'd done that to her—caused that flush, that smile, that head-duck. As if his presence was simply too potent to bear.

But the truth was more humbling: in the moment, her smile had all but clubbed him senseless for a beat or two. Rendered incapable of speech or thought, never mind singing. He'd watched, mesmerized, balanced on the razor-fine line between fascination and something almost like anger, the quickening rise and fall of her bodice. Because in that moment it had irrationally seemed a crime against nature, worse than treason, not to touch her when mere inches separated them.

He imagined how her expression would change if she knew why he was really here.

And he closed his eyes and swore softly aloud.

He understood the dance and delicacies of diplomacy, but he'd never been able to indulge in the luxury of a formal courtship. Its intricacies and graces, its etiquette and implications. Its vulnerabilities and uncertainties. He wasn't even certain he knew how to do it.

From the time he'd bought his first commission he'd been caught up in a spiral of ambition and reward. Fueled by success and admiration. Exhilarated, intoxicated, by danger and challenge. Until his work comprised a sort of whirlpool from which he couldn't escape. It had only stopped when he'd been imprisoned.

In prison, remaining present had been a form of survival, and longing to be elsewhere was a form of torture. He'd been unable to imagine what might be next for him; moreover, he'd refused to do it. He wasn't a fantasist by nature.

But he seemed powerless against the one that crept in now, as stealthily as a London mist: evening after evening like the one he'd just had. Meandering, congenial, familial, warm, homely. Loud singing, fine playing, amusing company. All in a room containing a woman who made him feel as though he were not subject to the laws of time when she was near. As though he was weightless and entirely new. That nothing was of consequence apart from the fact that he was alive and so was she, at the same time. He was the world's most brutally pragmatic man, but it felt as though he finally understood what the word "destiny" meant. And destiny, ironically, felt not like a misty fantasy but like a cold hard fact:

She was meant for him. And that was why he was here.

But bloody hell. Why now? Why like this?

In frustration, he abruptly turned away from the window.

Then froze, heart lurching.

Something was under his bed.

And it was moving.

Breath held, heart hammering, he inched toward it. Then craned his head to peer beneath.

For God's sake. It was just a scrap of dark cloth trapped against the wall next to the bed leg, set in motion by that vigorous breeze he'd let in. He might never have seen it at all if he hadn't opened a window, and he supposed The Grand Palace on the Thames's maids could be forgiven for missing it. And as it ruffled in the breeze, he noted it had a white corner.

He realized he was looking at a once-white bloody rag.

He angled his foot behind the bed leg and dragged it out with the toe of his boot.

As no doubt it was his own blood and he wasn't squeamish on the whole, he retrieved the fireplace poker and slid it beneath so he wouldn't have to bend to pick it up.

Its delicate weight revealed it was a handkerchief, not a rag.

Soaked in blood.

Someone had likely pressed it to his wound as a

reflex before bandaging him. Captain Hardy, or Lord Bolt, most likely.

It was sobering to see. He stared at it a moment, thoughtfully.

He ought to buy the owner a new one for their trouble, regardless.

As he plucked it from the poker his fingertips brushed the raised silk thread of embroidery. Initials or a design of some sort were stitched into it. He brought it over to the lamp to read.

He exhaled, stunned.

Aurelie, Lady Capet

He wasn't certain why he was so moved to see her entire name. Likely, in fact, stitched with her own hands.

But his throat felt strangely tight.

Had she been right next to him when he fell into the foyer? How else had her handkerchief become soaked in blood?

She'd disguised herself in her maid's clothes, but she'd forgotten about handkerchiefs. She'd told everyone at The Grand Palace on the Thames she was going to visit her brother in Boston, which was where her brother Edouard allegedly did, in fact, live.

And her impulse to help him had revealed her definitively to him. He held the proof of that in his hands.

Hawkes knew he would never have forgotten about details like the handkerchief. That was how corrupt *his* soul was, he thought darkly amused. He made a thorough job of being a liar when he was obliged to be one.

And he felt again a simmering fury that something had altered her life so completely that she'd felt the need to learn how to lie. It was a skill that took years to perfect, he could have told her. And then you wear your lies and your disguises around like a carapace, and it hinders your soul from expanding and your heart from feeling until life strips you down to your essence. Until you're humbled completely.

It had been only a few days, all told, since that meeting with Brundage in Paris, but it already felt another man entirely had made that gentleman's agreement to find the earl's fiancée.

And to think he had once felt invincible. Impossible to believe now he'd been so deluded. He'd once felt he had the might of the British Army behind him. The whole of England itself. He'd felt arrogant and righteous and gifted and brilliant and charmed.

And he'd still been taken down by the banality that was Brundage.

Now Hawkes was just a rather battered man who was alive because "justice" was for people who could buy it. And he'd felt utterly alone in his icy fury and speculation until he'd revealed a little of his suspicion to Hardy and Bolt.

What had Aurelie said?

I didn't want you to call out in the night and find no one there. I didn't want you to die alone, if you were going to die.

God. She must have felt—must now feel—entirely alone, too.

He suddenly realized his breathing had gone shallow. As though he ought to have been able to protect her from whatever had made her run.

He dragged the tip of his finger softly over that word. "Aurelie." As if in so doing he could soothe away her fears. Undo harm done.

His fortunes were currently staked on revealing her whereabouts to Brundage.

So what now was he going to do?

But he thought he already knew.

He recalled sitting across from Brundage and holding that miniature of her so tightly it had pressed a groove into his palm. As if his future was already imprinted upon him. As if he'd known even then.

Chapter Fifteen

THE LAST thing Aurelie had expected when she'd fled across the Channel was waking up with a sherry head and her ears still ringing from a certain Mr. Delacorte's fine, if unsurprisingly loud, baritone.

The evening had been odd and splendid, and the more pleasant it became the more guilty she felt for lying to these people, which only redoubled both her determination to leave and her regret that she must. The sooner she did, the less time she needed to spend pickling in her own conscience.

And leaving meant she would likely never see Mr. Hawkes again—except in her memories, where that other Mr. Hawkes lived as a remote glow.

This seemed like an unbearably unfair price to pay.

After having what was apparently a good smoke with Captain Hardy and Lord Bolt in the correct room for that sort of thing, he'd returned to sing two songs in a lovely baritone, and he'd turned the pages of the music for her, gallantly, when it was her turn to play. And in those moments of absorption and pleasure and the spiky intoxication of his nearness she had forgotten everything her life had become.

Such that when the weight of it returned and settled back into place her circumstances seemed much more oppressive. And as the numbing protection of fear and fury began to fade, her flight from Paris began to seem more and more mad and frightening than brave and determined.

Best not to mull upon it, she thought. Best to simply do as she'd been doing: step by step. Best to keep moving.

She took a pleasant breakfast with the very earliest risers, the proprietresses of the house, and Dot—while everyone else was sleeping off the sherry, or apparently taking breakfast in their rooms.

And then everyone scattered to the day's activities.

She had no day's activities, unless she took herself directly to the address on The Strand.

Because no message had arrived from Mr. Erasmus Monroe. She'd asked Dot about it twice just today—once after breakfast, once just before noon—and felt she could not ask her three times without seeming like an absolute looby.

Perhaps her own message somehow hadn't yet reached him?

But the longer she waited to hear from him the longer she would remain at The Grand Palace on the Thames, and the more money she would spend, which would cost more money. And sooner rather than later she would have no money left at all.

And surely Mr. Monroe would forgive Edouard's sister for taking a liberty?

She could say, perhaps, that she was in The Strand for an errand, and had impulsively decided to see whether Mr. Monroe was at home. She was supposed to be a widow, and surely widows could roam about untethered to chaperones?

She sat for a moment with this notion, mistrusting her own instincts, wondering whether desperation had taken her reason hostage. It just seemed imperative to do *something*, rather than to merely sit with her thoughts, which would torment her regardless of whether she applied them to worrying about the future or allowed them to flood with Mr. Hawkes, the way a room could fill with sunlight if you so much as parted a curtain.

And so to The Strand she went.

ON HIS FIRST walk to The Grand Palace on the Thames from the Stevens Hotel, before he'd been set upon by a would-be assassin, Hawkes had taken swift note of who the neighborhood characters were. The ones who saw everything. Who loitered in alleys and peered out windows from attic rooms. The costermongers, the merchants, the prostitutes.

So the next morning, shortly after the maids were in to poke up his fire, he was out doing the necessary work of espionage.

A bottle of gin and a conversation bought him two garrulous friends who were leaning against a nearby building and whom, he discovered, were quite fond of Mrs. Durand and Mrs. Hardy, because they had been given scones in exchange for not leaning on The Grand Palace on the Thames. One of them had even recently been invited inside the Annex to hear a soprano sing. Or so they told Hawkes.

Hawkes briskly hailed hack after hack for a swift little conversation during which he handed drivers coins and promised more if he was discreetly alerted to the comings and goings of a certain pretty young woman wearing a blue cloak.

And he'd thought he'd wind up deploring the dearth of bribable servants at The Grand Palace on the Thames. But he soon found that he seemed to have already paid Dot in flattery when they were first introduced.

Because he learned within fifteen minutes of the

event that Mrs. Gallagher had been taken to an address on The Strand. One of the hack drivers he'd paid earlier had asked for him at the door of The Grand Palace on the Thames, and Dot had raced to tell him straightaway.

One of the drivers he'd earlier bribed was, in fact, waiting for him, face alight with the anticipated thrill of a chase. He took Hawkes swiftly to that lively part of London.

Once in The Strand, Hawkes thumped the ceiling of the hack to be let down about five houses away from the address to which the driver had taken Mrs. Gallagher. Which put him conveniently across from a row of shops, cheese and confectioners and books and tea, all things he very much enjoyed.

He purchased a newspaper at the Andrew Millar bookshop, and then nonchalantly strolled past the address, which turned out to be a small, unprepossessing townhouse in need of a coat of paint.

He slowed when he heard the unmistakable cadences of an argument—a woman's voice, adamant, distraught, a man's voice, insinuating, strident.

Closer now, he could see that the front door was open and a man, young, hard faced, hatless and cravatless, nearly tall enough to fill the doorframe, stood with one foot inside the house and the other outside.

Suddenly Mrs. Gallagher—it was unmistakably she, as his first ever sight of her had been from behind and the view was branded on his memory—backed away from the man swiftly, and continued walking backward, as though she was afraid to let the man out of her sight until she'd joined the crowds on the street once again.

Hawkes froze when the young man took two long steps after her.

The man came to an abrupt halt when he noticed Hawkes standing rigidly, staring death into his eyes.

He immediately turned about on his heel and vanished into the townhouse, slamming the door behind him.

Mrs. Gallagher finally whirled about, dashing her fingers against her eyes.

Oh God. She was weeping.

The realization felt like a knife slashed through him all over again.

For an instant he couldn't breathe.

She nearly collided with him.

"Mrs. Gallagher?"

She reared back in shock, her face tipped up.

She swiftly turned her head, clearly embarrassed by her brimming eyes. "Good morning, Mr. Hawkes. My apologies. I did not see you."

Something like a surfeit of emotion stopped his words.

Mutely, he found a handkerchief for her in his pocket and handed it gently over.

For an instant, they stood there, a private little island on the teeming, noisy street.

"Thank you," she said quietly.

They stood together wordlessly as she applied the handkerchief to her eyes. She kept her head down.

"Mrs. Gallagher," he said gently, "I should be pleased if you'd allow me to buy you a cup of tea."

She slowly looked up at him. Her eyes were still pink about the edges but some of the spirit returned to them. "Ought you to be gallivanting, Mr. Hawkes? How will you ever heal properly?"

"Well, I certainly shouldn't be gallivanting, so it's a very good thing I'm merely strolling. I shall go raving mad if kept inside. Dot will need to throw raw meat through the door of my room."

She smiled at that.

She completed two eye dabs with his handkerchief then handed it back to him resolutely, as if she'd decided to never shed another tear in her life.

"Why don't you keep it," he said.

She drew it between her fingers, her head down, contemplating this.

And then she gently installed it into the pocket of her lady's maid's pelisse and looked up at him again.

"I should like a cup of tea, thank you, Mr. Hawkes."

IN THE GENTEEL quiet of Twining's, they might have been any pair of spouses resting from a bout of shopping.

He learned that she put in one spoon of sugar and no cream, and he stored this fact as if it was found treasure. He took his tea with neither.

Soothing as a babbling brook, the sound of tea gurgling from pots around them. The ring of spoons in china. The low murmur of patrons. They bathed in the sounds, for a time.

"Something has upset you, Mrs. Gallagher," he began gently. "Perhaps you would feel better if you shared it."

She was quiet for some time. Perhaps composing a story.

She took a breath, and sighed it out. "I do not know quite how to begin. You see, my brother . . ."

"Forgive me for interrupting. What is your brother's name?" he asked patiently.

"Edouard," she said.

And then she immediately went still and her eyes

flared in alarm. As if she wished she could unsay the words.

He merely nodded. "I've a younger sister named Diana. Your brother Edouard . . ." he prompted.

"He told me that if I should ever need help, I should pay a visit to his dear friend Mr. Monroe, who lives in London and owes him a favor and would happily help me—Edouard told him all about me. I wrote to Mr. Monroe once I arrived at The Grand Palace on the Thames, but he did not respond immediately. So I . . . well, I took it upon myself to visit him on my own. I thought it wouldn't be untoward, as I am a widow and he is my brother's friend, after all. But it seems . . ." She cleared her throat. "It seems Mr. Monroe has moved away. He no longer lives in the house. This is not my brother's fault, mind," she said hurriedly. "He would have told me, if he could."

"Of course."

"And the man who was present in the home construed my presence . . . ah, rather differently, and I found it difficult to persuade him otherwise. He received and read my message, as well, and tried to coax me into the house and I am . . ." She cleared her throat. "I am so terribly embarrassed." Her voice was hoarse. "And gravely disappointed."

He took this in, thoughtfully. "Do you want me to call him out?"

She laughed, startled. She took a breath. "Yes. Rather."

"That's the spirit, Mrs. Gallagher."

"Perhaps after your stitches have healed, in case he's wily."

He smiled. "I'll add it to my schedule of events."

She laughed again, and he calculated that there

wasn't much he wouldn't do to hear that sound, over and over.

"I *do* know it was inadvisable to go there alone, Mr. Hawkes . . . It's just that it . . . the matter is rather urgent. And I'd hoped he could . . . I'm afraid I needed a favor." Her voice went nearly inaudible on the last word.

"Name it."

Too late he heard how he sounded: low and ardent and fiercely, deadly earnest.

Her lips parted as if he'd snatched the breath right from her.

He rued it at once. He could not recall ever using that tone before in his life, and yet he hadn't been able to stop it. This was who he was, apparently, stripped entirely of anything ulterior. He wanted to help her. He needed to help her.

He was afraid he'd frightened her instead.

But instead, her eyes traveled thoughtfully over his features, and as they did, they gradually went hazy and amazed, as if she was trying to ascertain the source of her own thrall. When they settled speculatively on his mouth his body jolted.

Nearly three *years* since he'd had a woman. But he now understood the difference between appetite and desire. And desire of this sort—that felt as though it might rip the top right from his head, that surged through him at the very thought of covering her body with his own—seemed entangled with how he felt about her. Lust might be the larger part of how he felt. He didn't know. It was base and he wanted her. It was merely fact. He wanted to feel *her* lips crushed against his, her nipples chafing against his chest. He wanted to feel her thighs against his palms when he eased them apart so he could lower his head to touch his tongue to the velvety wetness between.

Her innate sensuality would draw any man. What revolting thing had Brundage said? *I needed her in my bed from the moment I met her.*

But it was everything else about her—the indefinable and definable qualities—that made her feel like *his.*

He'd enjoyed friendships and flirtations and passionate liaisons. But never had a woman affected him as though she were the weather. As though he could feel her in his bones, like an ache, and on his skin, like sunshine or a breeze.

His life had contained nearly equal parts glitter and grit. But it was clear to him now how shockingly barren it had been in many ways.

And how different it was when one truly *wanted.* And one truly cared.

"That is very kind of you, Mr. Hawkes," she said gently. "But I do not want to trouble you with the matter."

He nodded once. Shortly. A little subdued.

The quality of the silence that followed was different. Shimmering. Taut. It was as though an intent had been revealed, and was under consideration.

"Which part of your encounter with that man has upset you the most? His mistaking you for a lightskirt or the missing Mr. Monroe?"

The question seemed to surprise her.

"I may only choose one?"

"Yes."

"Well, perhaps I should be otherwise, but I am not so delicate as all of that, Mr. Hawkes. I withstood the shock of learning you were not a vicar, after all. I'd hoped he could . . . advise me on a matter of the passage across the sea to my brother."

"It is very important that you leave at once? You can't linger in London for a time?"

"My brother expects me, you see, and he shall worry if I don't arrive when I told him that I would. I should like a new beginning as soon as possible." She took a breath and looked him steadily in the eye. "And to be frank, I cannot afford to linger in London."

"Well, nobody can, really."

She smiled at that.

"You cannot begin again in England?" he pressed.

It was a moment before she spoke.

"I feel as though I cannot have a new beginning on the whole of this continent."

She nearly whispered it. Carefully. As though she was ashamed of this, or he would think she was mad for saying such a thing.

"Is there a memory you're trying to outrun, Mrs. Gallagher? I've terrible news for you. They do not confine themselves to continents. They tag along wherever you go."

She snorted softly. "You are a sage, and yet you are not so very much older than I am."

"I can't imagine why you would need to flatter me, so I'll assume you believe that, for some strange reason. I've a decade on you at least, I'd warrant. I am old and hardened. Perhaps you need spectacles like Mr. Bellingham."

She laughed.

"My memory is going at my advanced age, and I've forgotten if it's rude to ask a woman her age."

"Yes, it's rude, and it's twenty-one."

Which is what Brundage had told him.

"I am thirty-five. If I'm remembering correctly."

"Good heavens, you *are* old. Shall I raise my voice so you can hear me speak?"

He smiled at her. "My hearing is still recovering

from Dot's impressive screaming, so, in answer to your question, yes."

She laughed again and this was better. Everything was better when she laughed.

She sipped her tea.

"I've no illusions about memories vanishing like this"—she flicked her fingers in the air—"when one crosses an ocean." She lifted her eyes to him again. "But do you think a place can be . . . too saturated . . . with events and associations, and so it is of no use to you anymore? As if it could not possibly hold new ones, or anything good at all?"

He nodded thoughtfully. "Saturated," he repeated. "Like a handkerchief soaked in blood?"

He witnessed these words entering her. And detonating.

Her face blanked in shock as the realization of what he must have found: a handkerchief embroidered with her name.

"I suppose so," she said a moment later, in attempted insouciance.

But her voice was hoarse.

He idly stirred his tea and sat with the words she'd said. He knew her history: the murder of her parents, the death of her brother.

But it was Brundage who'd made her *bolt*. And, with, from what it seemed, the most tenuous of escape plans in place.

"I am distressed that life has been so unkind to you that you must leave an entire continent behind." His voice was gruff.

"That is kind of you to say, Mr. Hawkes."

"You do keep saying that," he said somewhat amused, but also somewhat impatiently. "In truth, I do not know if I am a kind man. And Mrs. Gallagher, you would be surprised at how difficult I am to distress."

Something fierce and beautiful, a sort of yearning, suffused her face then. It was just as swiftly gone. "I am not certain anything about you would surprise me," she said softly.

She sipped her tea.

"He must have been a remarkable man, your husband," he ventured.

She eyed him warily. "Why do you say that?"

"He convinced you to spend the rest of your life with him."

She shook her head with a little smile. "Oh, not very subtle, Mr. Hawkes. Now you are flirting. It is amusing but I feel I ought to point out that you are very bold."

"Boldness comes with age, and the knowledge that I've one foot in the grave, I suppose."

There was another silence. Aurelie wanted so badly to speak of Brundage, to outline his character, to hear Mr. Hawkes's thoughts on the matter.

"I do not know if he was remarkable. I thought . . . I thought he was charming and handsome and good."

He took this in, thoughtfully. "And was he?"

Aurelie exhaled slowly. He was deucedly clever. It was exhilarating and unnerving.

"He is two of those things," she said. Somewhat thickly.

He didn't say anything.

"Was," she added hurriedly. She stared down at her tea.

She was absolutely certain he'd noticed her little mistake with verb tenses.

He seemed to make it his business to notice things.

"Why have you not married, Mr. Hawkes? It seems

the thing a man ought to do when he is old and wise, as you are."

His head went back briefly in surprise. He studied her, pensively.

At any rate, he seemed to be considering her question.

He said slowly, "I was never certain I was the sort of man who could be a good husband."

She'd lied, apparently, when she'd said he couldn't surprise her. "This matters to you?"

"Oughtn't it?" Now *he* sounded surprised.

"I didn't know that men worry about such things. The world is generally arranged to suit them."

"I suppose it is. And we do muck it up."

She twisted her mouth, ruefully. "What sort of things do you think make a man a good husband?"

He leaned back in his chair and looked at her almost accusingly, faintly impressed and amused. As if this was a question he'd never before been required to answer aloud.

And he didn't, for at least a moment or two.

"I suppose I always thought that the least of a husband's duties was to protect his wife and children from . . . everything," he began, almost hesitantly. "To the extent that this is possible. Ugliness. Danger. Deprivation. To provide a life of comfort and safety. And to be present for all important things—the good moments, the hard ones, the raising of children. My own father was that sort, until he died when we were still young. And my profession required me to travel a good deal. I was brought into contact with many people, some of whom were . . . not possessed of fine characters, but with whom it was necessary to work. It was occasionally my duty to see . . . and do . . . unpleasant things."

It was quite an oblique and fascinating answer.

He clearly had not revealed the whole of the truth of his life. Perhaps he could not. But what he had said amounted to a breath-stealing vow: what he wanted was to honor and protect. He hadn't mentioned love, that potent grenade of a word, but it seemed to her the very definition of love: *Being* there, no matter what.

"Unpleasant people." She recalled the shocking, competent violence with which he'd fought his blankets. The startling discovery of a knife tattooed beneath his arm. The way he'd tensed when the residents of The Grand Palace on the Thames had filed into his room. As though he was someone who expected attacks.

She was almost afraid to ask.

But she at last did. "What is the nature of your work?"

His hesitation was brief.

"I was a soldier. And then I worked for the crown," he said shortly.

The swift way he'd said it called to mind someone deciding to gamble on an uncertain hand of cards. His expression was unreadable. A gambler's game face.

And she noticed he'd said *worked*. Past tense.

She was beset by a vague sense of unreality. It was becoming increasingly difficult to reject the possibility that the man in front of her was also the glowing, dashing, urbane man she'd seen long ago in a ballroom. The one who had gone to prison for espionage.

The similarities surely could not all be ascribed to coincidence.

Could they?

But why—and how—did he come to be here?

Surely that could be a coincidence, too.

The more she considered it, the less likely it seemed to Aurelie that Mr. Hawkes's appearance in front of that house on The Strand at the precise moment she was leaving it was a coincidence.

And yet, why couldn't it be? She wanted it to be serendipity. She wanted evidence to fuel her desperate hope that life was kind more often than it was not. She wanted to believe that lovely things could happen with the startling suddenness of violence.

She could not ask him to expound without revealing who she was, or how she knew who he might be.

And if he had worked in the diplomatic corps, it was entirely possible he'd known Brundage.

She could not believe his presence at The Grand Palace on the Thames was related to Brundage in any way. They were two astonishingly different men.

"If it is any comfort to you, Mr. Hawkes . . . I am not certain I would be—I was—a good wife. I was brought up mostly alone and raised to do things I have lately learned were not particularly practical. I never learned to haggle, to cook, and that sort of thing."

"To *haggle*?" He was amused.

She nodded. "There were servants. I learned languages and pianoforte and stitching of pillows and how to dance and play music and so forth. But I am only meant to be one kind of wife, I think. I fear I shall disappoint a man who needs someone more useful. I was very hopeful. I meant to try very hard to be a good wife, at any rate. I intended to do my very best."

He took this in thoughtfully.

"But then your husband died."

Suddenly, she could not agree to that. Or even nod. She let the words ring.

She was not certain she could continue to lie to him.

Her tea was growing cold but she sipped it anyway. She lowered it carefully to the saucer again.

"I should like to say something you may construe as bold, Mr. Hawkes."

"I will in all probability survive it," he said easily.

She said, somewhat hesitantly, "I saw the knife beneath your arm."

He frowned faintly, briefly, then his face cleared. "My tattoo?"

She nodded. "It struck me as unusual for a gentleman. Although perhaps every gentleman has one, for all I know. You see, I have not seen under many . . . bare arms."

And all at once between them was the memory of darkness and bare skin and vulnerability.

She seemed to have stolen his breath. He said nothing.

"Did it hurt very much?" she whispered.

"Yes," he said simply. With a ghost of a smile.

"Why do you have it?"

He was quiet for a time.

He was not a fidgeter, Mr. Hawkes.

"I wanted to know how much pain I could endure," he said slowly. "I thought it would be useful to know. I wanted to learn about endurance, because I was in a situation in which I could do nothing but endure. And I wanted to be distracted from another painful circumstance. And . . . I wanted a reminder of what I'd survived."

She was shocked and mesmerized by this precise list.

He had clearly deliberated over it. The unapologetic, bald honesty left her breathless.

It was now clear that they were, little by little, delicately revealing things to each other. Feeling about the periphery of trust.

Or maybe it was more that they were coming into

focus to each other. As though each of them was a sun, burning away each other's obscuring mists.

"Did it work?" she whispered.

It was not a remedy she would have even conceived of. But she saw the brilliance in isolating a moment of pain as art. To externalize it.

When he went still, she realized he understood she was asking this question on her own behalf.

It was a moment before he spoke.

His words seemed carefully chosen.

"Yes, it worked. For a time, it did. But no one thing works forever. And it's forever we have to contend with, Mrs. Gallagher. It is an evolving thing."

Was there a different quality to the way he'd said her name? Had it sounded a little ironic?

But so gentle.

He was like that knife inked onto his body. All implacable, dangerous, bright edges. But vulnerable beneath, she thought.

She stared at his remarkable face, and imagined again tracing the contours of that tattoo with her finger.

The space between them suddenly seemed as hot and dense as flesh. For a mad instant it seemed unbearable that there should be any distance between them at all. Heat flared in her limbs and robbed her of breath.

Desire was complicated, but it was unequivocal, she understood now. It was not something that could be rationalized into being. The way she had done with Brundage.

Mr. Hawkes had a good deal more experience with not blinking than she did. She didn't mind. His eyes fascinated her. They both revealed and obscured his moods.

"Passage across the sea comes dear," he commented almost idly. "A packet crossing costs fifty pounds or more."

"Yes," she said shortly. When she heard the sum, her stomach tensed again.

She was afraid of the onslaught of inadvisable, anarchic things she felt in his presence. One of those things was happy. Such a simple thing seemed destined to be strangled like a flower among the weeds of her life. She'd told him her brother's name because she'd forgotten to lie, and that was foolish. She was too tired, and he was too charming, and she was obviously not good at subterfuge and she didn't like to be reminded of this.

She ducked her head and studied the remaining leaves of her tea, which revealed nothing to her.

And for a time neither of them spoke.

Finally, she took a steadying breath and looked up again.

"Thank you, Mr. Hawkes. I am grateful to you for the tea and sympathy. My mood is much improved. If you would be so kind as to help me into a carriage, I should like to return to The Grand Palace on the Thames now. I have interrupted your errands long enough."

He understood people, Mr. Hawkes did. He seemed to, at least. And while he hesitated, and she sensed he was still full of questions and concerns, all he politely said was, "It would be my honor."

Chapter Sixteen

HAWKES WANTED badly to sit for a time alone and bask in the aftermath of being with Aurelie, the way one would linger after watching an astonishingly perfect sunset. He wanted to sort through her words for meaning that might have escaped him.

But time was critical. So after he assisted Mrs. Gallagher into a hack, he directed his separate hack to Guthrie's Antiquities off Bond Street.

He finally found it—a very small shop, with a small elegant sign hanging on chains over the door, featuring only three objects in the window—vases of varying sizes and dubious provenance. It didn't appear as though a good deal of effort had been made to intrigue passersby. Perhaps their custom was all by referral.

Or perhaps it was a front for nefarious activities.

A little bell hung from the door handle jingled when he entered. Inside it was sparsely furnished with objects, arranged on shelves, which had all been dusted. He possessed some sense and knowledge of antiquities. Some of the things displayed *were*, in fact, decent pieces.

"Good morning," he said admiringly to the young woman behind the counter.

She gave a start. Then straightened from her bored slump to bosom-jutting posture when she got a look at him.

She gawked. He wasn't certain whether she was

admiring his person or was marveling at the very fact that anyone had entered at all. She was young and charming: springy red hair scraped back from a face sprinkled with freckles, the kind of blue eyes that featured little yellow suns in the middle.

She blushed when she saw him, which was a good sign. It was so much more difficult to extract information from the jaded.

"I'm looking for a gift for a very—*very*—discerning friend whom I should like to impress, and your establishment has been recommended to me."

"Well, you've come to the right place," she said brightly. As though she'd memorized a script.

"I can also see that the proprietor was *indeed* discerning when he hired his help."

He'd also done the right thing. Her blush deepened and she tucked an escaped strand of hair behind one fetching ear.

"My friend is the Earl of Brundage."

"Oh, the earl is an esteemed customer," she said at once.

"I should think so!" Hawkes expostulated. "I wondered if you had a record of his purchases. I imagined you would, given the scarcity and value of the objects you purvey here. I should be horrified, you see, to duplicate the kind of spectacular acquisitions he's already made."

"Oh, yes, that would be shocking," she said dutifully.

"And I know he's purchased a few beautiful things from you."

"Indeed, he has," she said.

"So you've met him."

She hesitated. "I've been informed that he is a devoted customer."

It wasn't quite an answer. He let it lie for now.

"I'm prepared to spend a *great* deal of money. I've got simply bags of it, all waiting to be spent frivolously." He gave a merry shout of laughter.

She laughed, too. It was then, judging from her expression, that she fell in love with him.

"Of course, sir. I'll just have a look." She reached beneath the counter and retrieved a large book, which sent up a small cloud of dust when she hurled it onto the counter and flipped it open, ruffling the pages, which weren't precisely crowded with notations. "We do not often sell vases or urns of the caliber the earl seems to prefer, so his transactions are easy to find and rather leap out," she told him. "There are four, it seems. Yes, the Earl of Brundage he purchased one case February of 1812, and returned it a week after. Then again in 1813. It cost . . ." She gulped here, and nearly stammered the words. "Two hundred fifty pounds."

"Two hundred fifty pounds for a vase," Hawkes marveled, craning his head to look at the entries. "Good heavens. Is that all?"

Miss Wallace regarded him with dumbstruck wonder.

It was a ridiculous price for a vase. And it wasn't at all what Brundage had recorded for the value of it in his account books.

So *this* was how payments were funneled to Brundage. But from whom?

"The earl is indeed a very particular man," Hawkes mused, "so I wonder . . . are you perhaps an expert in porcelain?"

"Oh, I fear I am still learning."

Hawkes took pains to appear crestfallen. "And you *haven't* had the pleasure of the earl's acquaintance, by any chance?"

She hesitated, then shook her head slowly.

He paused.

"Do you get lonely and bored in here with just the vases and whatnot for company?"

She blushed again. "We have very few customers, sir. And they all seem to want to speak to the owner," she said wistfully. "I hear the girls what take this job never last long in it."

They were probably cycled in and out of the job, was Hawkes's guess.

He thought quickly. Brundage had actually likely paid a pittance if anything at all for the objets d'art, recorded the purchases in his accounts, and then returned them to this shop in exchange for full—or greatly exaggerated—cash value. The ensuing proceeds he'd then hidden in the invented charity—hopefully Hardy or Bolt would be able to get an answer from their friends at Lloyd's about that—and from this charity Brundage had likely paid his debts and bought silver buttons for his coat and the like.

And he'd probably done it this way because the finances of an ambassador were always under some scrutiny; the acceptance of nearly any kind of gift would be, if not suspect, at the very least noted, given the sensitive nature of the information he was privy to and the demands of diplomacy. New acquisitions would be noted, too. Brundage would have needed to hide *any* unorthodox influx of money, and he'd decided a virtuous charity would be just the thing.

He imagined the cognac that Pike had fetched back had merely been a gift to seal some sort of bargain made. The kind of gift only a French national could provide.

Judging by these purchase dates—someone—perhaps the proprietor of this shop—had made a deposit on any information Brundage had promised to provide. And later, Brundage had delivered spectacularly.

All told, Hawkes estimated that Brundage had been paid about five hundred pounds by the time he'd likely, somehow, delivered information about troop movements that led to the defeat at Dos Montañas in late 1814.

Hawkes had been arrested shortly after that.

He considered whether he ought to try to steal this account book now—asking the bored young lady to make some tea, absconding with it when she retreated to the back of the shop, that sort of thing.

But he didn't want to alarm the proprietor. He sensed Mr. Guthrie, whoever he might be, would disappear once he got wind of a missing account book. And Guthrie was key to the whole thing.

That led Hawkes to his remaining critical question.

"Is Mr. Guthrie in this morning, Miss Wallace? I should like very much to discuss my potential acquisition with him in detail."

"Oh, no, sir. There's no Mr. Guthrie, sir. That's just the sign on the shop, you see. The owner is in Paris, at present, but he's expected in London by Wednesday next. He owns a shop in Paris, as well, and it seems he is always searching for new antiquities."

Hawkes resisted the temptation to point out that antiquities, by their very nature, could not be new.

His heart picked up an extra beat, and his old friend, portent, prickled at the back of his neck. "What is the owner's name, if I may ask?"

"Mr. Florian Vasseur, sir."

Her French accent wasn't very good, but the slow smile Hawkes gave her then, she later confided to her sister when she told her about it, "fair made me want to drop me knickers then and there."

THE IRONY. THE sweet, sweet irony that both Brundage's and Vasseur's—Cafard's—downfalls would come at the hands of women. Because Hawkes was only here because of Aurelie, and Vasseur apparently possessed a sentimental streak—or a fear of God—that had caused him to write his own name in the church register when he was married. Berwick, bless his grimy soul, had been *right*.

Hawkes immediately tracked Berwick down near Piccadilly and gave him five pounds to watch Guthrie's Antiquities in the event Monsieur Vasseur made an appearance before the projected forthcoming Wednesday, and gave Berwick dispensation to hire another person he trusted to help, provided he didn't share any details beyond the description of the man. It was the best Hawkes could do, given that he currently had no authority at the Alien Office. The case he was building was so sensitive and incendiary he would need to carefully consider whom outside of Hardy and Bolt he could trust, and ironically, Berwick was at the top of the list.

He'd promised Miss Wallace of Guthrie's Antiquities he'd return on Wednesday next.

And then, because he wasn't a complete idiot, he returned to The Grand Palace on the Thames to rest for at time. Impatiently, but determinedly. If one could lie still impatiently but determinedly.

First, on the pretense that he wished to borrow a book from her, he asked Dot whether Mrs. Gallagher was in. Dot told him that she was, indeed.

Hawkes finally gave himself permission to rest.

First, he unwound his bandage, salved his neatly

stitched wound, and bandaged himself again. Slowly, carefully, and painfully.

He rubbed at his shoulder, which twinged him. He tamped back his frustration by clamping his teeth together. He didn't want to be the sort of man forever obliged to drink to drown pain or to take medicine for it to get through a day, and that meant he needed to be more responsible and actually behave as though he was injured.

Most importantly, he would need to be sharp and nimble and fully alert for his meeting with Brundage in a few hours.

He would need every ounce of his self-control not to lean over and squeeze the man's throat between his hands.

Because not only was the bastard a traitor, he was more and more certain that Brundage had gravely harmed Aurelie in some way. And he'd probably done it because he'd known full well she had no one to turn to. In other words, like treason, he'd done it because he'd thought he'd get away with it.

It was so clear the struggle to maintain her secret was little by little wearing Aurelie down. He sensed her yearning for someone in whom to confide.

But if she'd known Hawkes had been paid by the earl to find her, she would consider him just as much a traitor as he considered Brundage.

It was a *bastard* of a predicament.

Hawkes lowered himself to the bed and stretched out along the length of it, surrendering his head to the splendid pillow, and set his thoughts loose on his predicament.

I suspect she hoped to find something of a real family with Lord Brundage. That was how her lady's maid had put it. She'd been raised by a guardian who was frequently away. One brother was dead, the other across the ocean. With some grave discomfort to himself, he could well imagine the joy she must have taken in her engagement. Her face lighting the moment she'd said yes to his proposal. The hopes she must have had for the future.

She had meant to be a good wife, she'd said. She would have done her best.

And he felt again a tightness in his throat and a pressure in his chest as though something were slowly crushing it. It was how he imagined she must have felt the moment her illusions had been brutally shattered.

Because of a certainty, they had been.

He laid an arm over his eyes and drew in a long, slow breath.

He'd never before articulated aloud his thoughts about being married. He realized he felt, in fact, a little raw and unsettled in the wake doing it. But he'd told Aurelie the truth, a truth that amounted to a revelation even to him even as his words emerged. He found that he hadn't a taste for lying to her. He didn't want to maneuver her; he didn't want her to be a *strategy*. When he was with her, all he wanted was to experience the lightness of being only his truest self. When was the last time he'd felt that way? Was he even capable of it anymore?

He now understood that marriage was a frontier about which he knew nothing at all, his previous cynical assumptions about it notwithstanding. It felt like a lifetime since he'd undertaken anything at which he wasn't, through practice, aggressively competent.

He realized he hadn't thought about it because no other woman had ever before felt like "forever" to him.

He wanted to fix everything for Aurelie, and that meant, once and for all, settling old business with Brundage.

Then he could tell her the truth. Only then.

He absently ran his fingers beneath his arm, over the tattoo of the dagger. Imagining her eyes upon it. Remembering her questions about it. As though she sought solutions to her own pain.

What hurt or frightened Aurelie so badly that she presently could find no surcease from it?

He thought of proud Madame Aubert, her rouge failing to disguise her bruise, and to something she'd said that troubled him still. What had she said? Aurelie had waited four weeks to leave Paris.

Why that long?

Why, *specifically*, that long? Channel crossings from Calais to Dover occurred every day, weather permitting.

It was the soonest she felt she could leave, Mr. Hawkes.

A corrosive, ugly suspicion was suddenly metallic in his throat.

He realized the droplet of suspicion had been born the moment Madame Aubert had said those words. The horror of it had merely taken this long to sink in fully.

Like blood soaking a fine silk handkerchief.

AURELIE HAD BEGUN to worry that the single-minded determination that had propelled her across the Channel was actually nothing more than a very energizing terror, of the sort which mice use to flee cats.

And which stops being useful when there is nowhere left to run.

She'd careened between hope and mortification and gratitude today, but the net result was that she felt as though she were in a maze, rather than moving forward. She had no idea what to do now that she'd discovered Mr. Erasmus Monroe had apparently moved away. It felt horribly like any thread connecting her to her brother had been snapped, even though she knew it wasn't the case. Edouard was still in Boston. Probably even now worrying about her.

She could almost feel the doubt and uncertainty sucking at her ankles, like quicksand that Mr. Miles Redmond wrote about in his book about the South Seas.

And yet.

For the rest of the afternoon, Aurelie was uncomfortably suspended between a vague sense of unease and a probably ill-advised, breathless joy that Mr. Hawkes had actually followed her because he could not get her out of his mind any more than she could get him out of hers.

Today, he'd been precisely what she'd needed at the precise moment she'd needed it. He'd also been an anodyne of sorts. The attraction, the flirtation, the intimacy, the intrigue: it had been, for a few moments, as good as—and dangerous as—laudanum in making her forget her turmoil.

But he could be only that, and nothing more: a respite.

Couldn't he?

He seemed an unnecessary complication in a life that had contained so little of complication until one month ago. Not even *The Ghost in the Attic* would have dared introduce such a twist in the plot as the appearance of Mr. Hawkes.

She could ask him if he'd ever attended a ball in Vienna. Or whether he was a diplomat.

Or . . . a spy.

How did one ask another person if he or she was involved in espionage, without sounding mad? How did one slip it into conversation in the sitting room? Perhaps a natural segue could be found between the stealth of ghosts and the stealth of spies?

But if Mr. Hawkes told her the full truth about himself—if this was indeed his truth—what sort of truths would she owe to him?

She simply didn't know what to do now. Her pride recoiled from asking Mrs. Hardy or Mrs. Durand if they knew where she could sell a piece of jewelry. She didn't want them to worry whether she'd be able to afford to stay here. There seemed something so craven and desperate about begging for their help. She wondered if pride would eventually be one of the things she'd need to jettison.

Mrs. Hardy had loaned her the first volume of Mr. Miles Redmond's series of books on the South Seas, and she stretched out on her little bed with it.

She woke up when she dropped the book on her face. She hadn't realized she'd dozed. Immediately after there was a tap at the door.

"Mrs. Gallagher, a message has arrived for you."

Dot seemed delighted to be imparting the news. She'd even brought it up on a little tray. "It's from a Mr. Erasmus Monroe."

Aurelie snatched her reaching hand back and stared at it as if it might bite her.

"Are you certain it's from Mr. Erasmus Monroe?" she asked Dot.

Dot nodded vigorously.

"Did you happen to speak to who brought it, Dot?"

"A boy, who scampered right off."

Well, then.

How on earth would Mr. Erasmus Monroe, if this was indeed a message from the real Mr. Erasmus Monroe, know she was here? Unless . . .

Her brow furrowed as she entertained a possibility, which was threatening to evolve into an ill-advised hope.

Aurelie gingerly reached for the message and broke the seal. Her hands were trembling again.

Dear Mrs. Gallagher,

I'm terribly sorry to have missed you when you called at my previous residence. Your message has found its way to me at my place of business, and I understand the current tenant of my property was a perfect ass when you called upon him (forgive my use of the word, but I feel he deserves it!). I would be delighted to apologize to you in person and talk with you of our dear Edouard. If you would like to call upon me at seven o'clock in the evening at my very respectable place of business, a printing shop called Turnbull & Sons, near Hyde Park (near a bookseller, which I think you'll agree is a clever location for a printer), I should be delighted to make your acquaintance. I am an investor there, you see, and work there to learn about the business. Perhaps your brother has told you about it? I will welcome you as one welcomes a princess and I should be honored to offer any advice. My direction is below.

Yours Sincerely,
Mr. Erasmus Monroe

She stared at those sprightly words, so full of character, and stubbornly kept her heart on a short leash. It wanted to leap, but she didn't dare allow it. But how seductive it sounded: "our dear Edouard." "Our." Three people who were connected to and belonged to each other. The use of it implied she was not alone in the world. She belonged to someone and they belonged to her.

It *could* be a ruse. It was *probably* a ruse, she told herself. But . . . to what end? It was just that the letter writer sounded *just* like someone her brother might indeed esteem, and surely if they were to meet in a public place, and in such a busy location, during the social hours when decent people were still out and about making calls and driving about in open carriages, she could remove herself quickly if she felt unsafe. Surely whoever had sent this note couldn't kidnap her in front of a crowd.

She wanted it so desperately to be true. She wanted this perhaps too-familiar-but-lively voice to be a link to her brother and then a bridge to her new life. She wanted to watch someone else's face light up as they spoke of someone she loved.

And though it might be—probably *was*—foolish . . . she already knew she was going to go.

Could she afford to take the chance to keep missing him, if it was Mr. Erasmus Monroe? She could endure another disappointment. And she knew she could extricate herself quickly if they were meeting in public with people milling about.

Dot was still waiting as patiently as a potted plant.

"It seems I have an engagement this evening, Dot," she began hesitantly, "so I'll take a light meal in my room instead of joining everyone for dinner. I'll be home before curfew, of course."

"Oh, an *engagement*!" Dot was pleased for her. "How lovely! Very good, Mrs. Gallagher. I'll make certain everyone knows."

As IT TURNED out, Dot quite literally if inadvertently did this.

Hawkes was washing his face in preparation for his encounter with Brundage when he heard a knock on his door.

He patted himself dry and peered out the peephole to discover Dot.

He opened it.

"Mr. Hawkes, will you be down for dinner this evening?"

"Well, let me think, Dot. Will everyone be present at dinner?"

"Oh, everyone, I believe, except for Mrs. Gallagher, who has an engagement for seven in the evening."

Oh, *did* she now? thought Hawkes.

"What a coincidence, Dot. I'm so glad you mentioned it, because as it turns out, you helped me recall that I have an engagement this evening, too. As delightful as it is to enjoy everyone's company and Helga's cooking, I shall take dinner out."

"An engagement! Oh, how lovely!" Dot was always willing to rejoice in the good fortunes of others.

Chapter Seventeen

HE WAS fairly certain he'd been followed from the Stevens Hotel to his stabbing location, because he'd told Brundage that's where he'd be staying. Brundage had likely provided a helpful description of him to his would-be assassin.

He had at no point since then gotten the sense that anyone realized he'd staggered all the way to The Grand Palace on the Thames. His assailant had likely left him for dead, confident he'd gotten the job done.

But Hawkes nevertheless made his way to Brundage's St. James townhouse circuitously, which was the way he intended to leave it, as well. No sense making it easy for someone to track and kill him, should someone take the notion to try again.

He asked his hack driver to stop a hundred feet or so away from Brundage's townhouse. He swiftly walked the final distance, maneuvering between the pedestrians and equestrians of St. James Square. He hadn't been followed.

He rang the bell.

To his surprise, Mr. Pike, the footman, opened the door.

Mr. Pike's face lit. "Mr. Hawkes. Pleasant to see you again, sir."

"Good day, Pike," he told the footman. "Likewise. You traveled with the earl from Paris, did you?"

"Yes, sir. He's spent so little time in London during the war that he didn't see cause to keep the London house fully staffed."

He suspected Brundage couldn't quite afford to keep the house fully staffed when no one lived in it.

"What can I do for you, Mr. Hawkes?"

"The earl is expecting me," Hawkes said firmly.

Pike hesitated. "Forgive me, sir, he is in . . . but I fear I wasn't informed you would be coming today, and he normally leaves instructions with the staff regarding the reception of guests."

It wasn't definitive proof, of course, that the earl was confident that Hawkes had been successfully murdered. Forgetfulness beset all men from time to time. But Hawkes knew full well the Earl of Brundage was usually scrupulously organized.

Poor Pike looked uncertain. Determined to do a good job for a man he loathed, determined to help a man he liked and admired, and quite uncertain about what Hawkes might have in mind today.

"No need to stand on ceremony, Pike," Hawkes said lightly. "I expect he has a good deal on his mind. I promise I shan't be long. I'll just go on up with you, as I know he'll want to speak with me straightaway."

Perhaps he saw something in Hawkes's face that indicated he was going to go up whether Pike thought it wise or not. Intelligent fellow that he was, he opted not to argue.

"Very well, sir." Pike stepped aside so Hawkes could enter.

And so up the staircase they went, to a vast room.

"Mr. Hawkes is here to see you, sir." And then Mr. Pike melted away.

Brundage frowned and swiveled his head toward the door. "What the devil? Pike, did you say . . ."

He froze when he saw Hawkes.

They regarded each other in silence from across a handsome study. Lots of shiny wood and turned legs in here, Hawkes noted. Curtains like heavy velvet waterfalls. A fine globe on a stand. Behind Brundage, gold-embossed titles twinkled from a wall of leather-bound books with uncreased spines. Pristine from being unread.

"Hawkes," Brundage said finally, brightly. Sounding a trifle more tinselly than usual. "Good of you to come."

"Of course," Hawkes said pleasantly. "Nothing short of prison or a violent assault would prevent me from keeping my word. Or of course, death. Death would keep me from it, too."

At least two seconds elapsed before Brundage spoke.

"I appreciate your attention to duty," he said politely. His voice betrayed just a hint of strain.

"I am nothing if not dutiful. I'm a great believer in duty. To one's country. To one's agreements. I wouldn't miss our meeting for the world," Hawkes said sincerely.

Brundage cleared his throat. "Sit down. Care for a drink?" He turned to where his decanter—likely filled by Pike—rested, on a little tray alongside snifters, within arm's reach of where he sat at the desk.

Hawkes took the chair before him. "Gracious of you to offer, thank you. Have you any cognac?"

Brundage's hand stilled for a moment on the decanter.

"I fear I must decline the drink this time, Brundage. And I won't keep you long, as I'm sure you'd like me to return to the important work I'm doing. I wanted to tell you that I've acquired some intelligence regarding

Lady Aurelie's location that I feel is worth pursuing, and as I'm in the process of verifying it, I do not yet feel it appropriate to share details. Likely you've learned over the years that sometimes the information you receive can be misleading. Or downright inaccurate."

It was, of course, a reference to his own failed assassination.

Hawkes could just imagine the run of Brundage's thoughts. Was he considering the possibility that Hawkes had discovered nothing incriminating in the books he'd "borrowed" from Harrigan's? Was he realizing there really was no way to ask Hawkes about it without incriminating himself, or at the very least, inspiring unwelcome curiosity?

"I should think the amount I'm paying you entitles me to some details about the results of your questioning and your search," Brundage said finally. Politely, seasoned with just a dash of pompousness.

"I'm given to understand that she is sound, if this is a matter of concern to you," Hawkes said ironically. Given that Brundage hadn't asked after her health. "And while I respect that you believe that, we negotiated no such thing, and I regret that I cannot accommodate you," Hawkes managed to say with elegant sincerity. "And yes, you are indeed paying me appropriately, for which I am grateful. One of the first things I learned when I worked for the Alien Office was to budget very well for any service, no matter how unsavory, you wanted completed to your satisfaction. Although I imagine it's frustrating to believe you've been cheated out of something you've paid to have done."

The last words emerged almost silkily.

And suddenly, the very air in the room might as well have been boiling water.

They stared at each other.

Neither one of them blinked.

Brundage was perhaps beginning to realize just how coldly, dangerously furious Hawkes was.

"I've a few more questions, which might assist me with my assignment," Hawkes said finally, mildly, into the silence.

Brundage nodded once, shortly. Mutely.

"Assuming I'm able to locate her, what do you then intend to do?"

"What do you mean, what do I intend to do?" Brundage said tautly.

"I mean, do you intend to capture her in a net? Press gang her to the altar?" He smiled a little, tightly, to convey he was jesting. He wasn't. "How do you intend to proceed once I inform you whether or not I've indeed located her?"

"I intend to talk to her. Surely she'll understand that returning is the best thing in her circumstances. Her guardian need never know she ran away. We'll forget it ever happened, and call it jitters. She's all but alone in the world and surely there are no better options for her. She will be a *countess.* Tell her she has my heart, now and always."

Every one of those words felt like a boulder layered on Hawkes's chest, pressing the breath from him. Revulsion crawled over the back of his scalp, and he felt something cold and primal that was almost fear. Of the sort one felt when confronted with a simple evil.

Was it true? Did Brundage think he loved Aurelie?

And yet, it wasn't as though Hawkes was any expert on love. He only knew that when one loved, one cherished. One protected.

"Noted, thank you. My next question. What if

I should discover that she doesn't want to return to you?"

Brundage went still. His eyes flared.

And then Hawkes watched as suspicion evolved into realization, which evolved into a dark spasm of rage, before Brundage got control of his features.

"Where is she, Hawkes?" He said this slowly. Coldly.

"Allow me to reiterate I'm not yet at liberty to disclose what I may or may not know."

"Where. The bloody hell. *Is. She. Hawkes*?"

"I'd like to refer you to my previous sentence. And I would ask that you please modulate your tone when addressing me."

Brundage eyed him in seething amazement. "You know where she is."

And Hawkes was silent, because he knew silence was the thing that would madden Brundage the most and in lieu of placing his own hands around the man's neck and squeezing, maddening him would have to do.

"I have another question, a somewhat philosophical one. If you could save only one life—hers, or yours—which would you value more?"

Brundage was beginning to fully realize that Hawkes had arrived today to toy with him.

"I don't think I need to dignify that with an answer."

Hawkes smiled knowingly.

The little muscle in Brundage's jaw was ticking.

"Does she have the necklace?" he demanded swiftly.

Hawkes considered this. "If you could have one and not the other, which would you choose? The woman or the necklace?"

Brundage's brows dove. "What the bloody hell kind of question is that? They are both. *Mine*."

Hawkes smiled pityingly. "I think you may need to review the definition of the word 'mine.'"

Brundage lunged forward and his hand shot out.

Hawkes caught it with the speed of a striking snake before Brundage could connect with his jaw.

Deftly, efficiently, he made a vise of his own fist and swiftly bent Brundage's wrist back just shy of making what Hawkes knew would be a hideous snapping noise.

Brundage's eyes widened in shock when he couldn't tug his hand away.

"Come now," Hawkes said almost tenderly. "Did you really think you would get the better of me? I'm not a woman who is much smaller than you, after all. And I've so much more experience than you with this filthy business. You can scream, but I will have broken your wrist by the time someone thinks to come running. And if you scream, or try this nonsense again, that's precisely what I'll do."

Brundage's eyes were now slits. His complexion had gone faintly green. His noble brow gleamed with sweat.

Hawkes altered his tone to hypnotically soothing. "I appreciate you are under enormous stress, given that a man of your stature must daily bear so many important responsibilities. You're confronting a challenge, but all challenges come to an end, eventually. Rest assured that matters are progressing as they ought, and that it's always best to handle such things with finesse and delicacy."

He uncurled his fingers.

Then gently released Brundage.

Brundage slowly, slowly returned his hand to lie flat on his desk. He circled his wrist with his other hand.

And Hawkes could see in the other man the temptation to succumb to his charm. To the substance of the words. To the flattery. The battle within him was reflected in his features. He wanted to hear what he wanted to hear, and yet he knew, he *knew* the truth of things. He could not order reality to be anything other than what it was. The only thing left to him was rage.

Hawkes regarded him fixedly. His own fury simmered in his veins.

"Losing a woman like Aurelie would madden any man. I understand completely." He said this almost on a purr.

Brundage's face blanked as if he'd taken a blow to the head.

And then cold fury bordering on panic suffused it.

"So *help* me God if you touch her, I will see you dead, Hawkes."

Said the man who had in all likelihood done far, far worse than just touch Aurelie.

Hawkes nodded sympathetically; his brow furrowed quizzically. "But how will you manage that? You apparently didn't even budget for a proper assassin on your first go. *Although* . . . I suppose you could create a new charity and solicit donations for it, and pay the assassin out of that."

He probably shouldn't have said that, but it was worth it for Brundage's reaction.

For the first time, naked fear flashed across the earl's face.

"Never fear, Brundage. I'm a gentleman. Touching another man's woman would be tantamount to treason, as far as I'm concerned. And I've very strong feelings about treason."

"You are *nothing*," Brundage said coldly. "You are

no one. And it's about time you learned your place, Hawkes."

Hawkes nodded with polite disinterest. "I'll keep you apprised of my findings. I'll see myself out."

HE WAS FURIOUS at himself. He'd overestimated his ability to keep his rage at Brundage leashed. As he finally returned to The Grand Palace on the Thames, he could still feel rage fizzing like a chemical in his blood.

He was uncertain whether he'd been rash. He was *never* rash.

As luck would have it, Captain Hardy was leaving as Hawkes was crossing the foyer for the stairs.

He eyed him askance. "You should rest, Hawkes."

Hawkes almost smiled. "I look that good, do I?"

Hardy didn't answer that. "I wanted to let you know Bolt spoke privately to our man at Lloyd's and stressed the urgency of your inquiry. No monies from a charity of that name have ever been transferred to them. They have no record at all of the Society for the Relief of English Prisoners of War."

Hawkes took this in and slowly nodded with a hard little smile. "Thank you very much indeed, Hardy."

"If there's anything else we can do to be of assistance, please don't hesitate to ask."

Chapter Eighteen

A COSTERMONGER'S CART had overturned in the street, so the hack driver put Aurelie down a good fifty feet or some from the direction she'd given him for Turnbull & Sons. It wasn't an auspicious beginning to the meeting. And perhaps she ought to have taken the blocked road as an omen.

She disembarked, and made a concerted effort not to gaze into the faces of passersby as she strode past them.

Nevertheless, she could sense the heads turning to look at her. She might be a fake widow, but she supposed she was not yet stately enough or briskly no-nonsense enough, like Mrs. Pariseau, to confidently march unaccompanied down a crowded street without inviting speculation. She was a fast walker, and fortunately her destination was easy to find, because *Turnbull & Sons* was handsomely lettered across a large window.

Aurelie paused before it, beset with a fresh wave of indecision about whether to enter or to turn around and hail another hack and go back to the safety of The Grand Palace on the Thames.

She had just pivoted a half turn to leave when a man burst out the door of the shop, his face wreathed in a smile. "Mrs. *Gallagher,* I presume?"

She stepped backward in alarm. He was so very *hearty*. It was like taking a hot, brisk wind to the face.

"Mr. Monroe?" she said carefully.

"At your service," he said cheerily. "You resemble him, you know! Edouard! Such an attractive pair, you two are. And I feel as though I know you so well through the things that Edouard has told me that I ought to sweep you up in a hug! I shall refrain and bow instead." Mr. Monroe whisked his hat from his curly head and did just that.

She was fairly certain a gentleman would never presume to sweep a lady into a hug, let alone mention the temptation aloud, but it sounded a bit like something Mr. Delacorte might say, and Mr. Delacorte was a very nice and good person.

She remained silent.

She desperately and swiftly tried to draw a few conclusions from what she could see. She didn't suppose his clothes were fine, but neither were they not fine. His coat was blue and his buttons were brass and his trousers were pressed. His boots were polished, if creased. His face was friendly, and reminded her a bit of a hound's, with brown eyes flanking a pointed nose and deep grooves about his mouth. His smile was very broad.

Aurelie kept her own smile in place, but it felt stiff. "Has my brother told you very much about me, then?"

"Forgive me, Mrs. Gallagher—*wink!*—I do wonder at your alias! But I so hoped you would be so kind as to take a brief walk with me? I should like to buy you the nicest ice in London so we can have a chat, but I've to bring these books to a fellow down the street before his shop closes. He was promised them earlier in the day but we had a bit of trouble with the press."

He gestured with a little bundle under his arm: he was indeed carrying books.

Regardless, he was already walking away from her

at a very brisk pace, threading through the crowd. And this struck her as ungentlemanly, indeed.

Her choice was to hover there in front of the shop, board the nearest hack, or to chase him, something no lady would ever likely do.

Her rapid internal coin toss decided it. She found herself walking alongside him, struggling to match his speed.

"What is it you would like to sell?" he asked cheerily. "I surmised that 'dispose of personal property' was a fancy way of saying 'sell something,' am I right? I've many friends among the merchants here and I can probably help easily with anything you need to convert into good English currency."

"I don't know if I should . . ."

And now she was nearly panting to keep up. His long-legged stride seemed astonishingly rude, even if he had a very good reason to hurry, but his vigorous cheer was so at odds with this she simply could not decide what do to.

"Oh, come now," he said jocularly. "You can tell me. We might even be able to sell it tonight!"

"I've a necklace," she said shortly.

She regretted it at once.

She turned to look behind her. She saw no hacks on the street, and none ahead of her either.

"Is it a very fine one?" He didn't sound unduly interested. "Must be, if it's important to sell it."

That's when she realized two things at once.

They'd come abreast of a little alley, into which he swiftly turned.

And sunset was officially over, the sky was dim, and that alley was filled with shadows.

She came to an abrupt halt and turned back toward the street.

Whereupon he swiveled so that he stood in front of her, herding her into the alley, while his tall, broad self blocked her view of the street. And the street's view of her.

She spun to flee; the shadows only seemed deeper at the other end of the alley. There appeared to be only one way in and one way out.

Mother of God. She was trapped.

"You're not Erasmus Monroe," she hissed.

He laughed, almost ruefully. "My dear friend handed your message over to me, as he knew precisely what I would do with it. Now *you* hand over the necklace—there's a good girl," he said briskly, "and everything else you have in your dainty bag without a fuss. A scream might get the attention of a Charlie, but then it will all come out that you're the kind of woman who goes unattended to an unmarried man's house during the day, and for a stroll with another strange man down this alley, well, I don't think that will go well for you at all. Why don't you do the sensible thing, so I won't have to hurt you."

She was shocked to find that her rage was stronger than fear. It was just that she was really very, very weary of being afraid. For a mad moment she was almost glad she'd been herded into an alley. Because he might very well bloody kill her, and it might partially be her own fault if he did, but she was going to jam a foot in his baubles first. She was going to kick and scream and scratch. She was going to do some damage.

She raised her knee to do that.

"I've not got all evening, Mrs. Gallagher," he said impatiently. His hand reached toward her. "Give it—"

"Choose where you'd like the bullet to end you. Your head or your heart. It's all the same to me."

Like the proverbial ghost who was not there one

minute and there the next, Hawkes had somehow materialized. And he, terrifyingly, had a pistol aimed right at the back of the man's head.

"Holy shite . . ." Not-Mr.-Erasmus-Monroe froze. His face went slack with shock.

And then a shadow detached from the depths of the alley and proved to be another man. Who also appeared to be holding a pistol.

Aurelie sucked in a scream when Hawkes pivoted a half turn and from the sound of things—the sound of things being a loud grunt—landed a boot hard and squarely in the second man's gut, then turned and jammed an elbow down on the other man's back.

They both hit the ground with shocking thuds.

"The good news is that I have two pistols, and both are loaded, both are to hand, and I practiced for *years* how to shoot in the dark," Hawkes said. "I can smell fear and evil, and I aim at that. So neither of you need go to hell alone tonight."

He cocked the gun. "That's the first gun," he said cheerily. "I'll count to three. Run now or it'll be the last time you ever run. One . . . two . . ."

There was a great rustling scramble of limbs, much cursing, and then they tore away.

She peered out from behind Hawkes and in silence they watched the men vanish into the street.

"There's never only one," he said, sounding more irritated than anything else.

He locked his gun, tucked it away.

Then he turned, and without preamble gathered her into his arms.

"Sweet *Christ*," he muttered. One of his hands hovered, then lightly cradled her head.

The other slid from her shoulder blades, gently, gently, and came to a rest on the small of her back. Its journey left a breath-stealing trail of sparks over her skin.

She realized she was trembling. She curled her hands into his shirt and reflexively clung, and tipped her head against him, careful not to press against his poor sore side. She felt the cold button of his waistcoat and the swift, hard thump of his heart against her cheek.

His arms at once tightened around her and when he pulled in a long slow breath, then released it at length, his body moved against hers, like a tide rolling out again. He'd sighed like a man who had waited a lifetime for precisely this moment.

Here she was enclosed in a man's arms. And yet this one was safety. She knew if she wanted him to let her go, he would.

She never, never wanted him to release her.

He stroked her hair, once, twice, softly. Then stopped abruptly, as he seemed to realize what he was doing. He loosened his arms, until she was held in the circle of them as delicately as an egg. As if she were breakable and precious and he feared hurting her.

She uncurled her fingers from his shirt. "That's a very distinctive sound," she said with a sniff. "The sound of a gun being cocked."

"If you're impressed by that, you'd be simply amazed by the sound they make when they fire." His voice was taut.

He took another what felt like a steadying breath. Then lifted his arms and released her and stood back.

His face had gone carefully expressionless.

"I have heard the sound," she said.

He said nothing for a moment. He was looking away from her. She had the strangest sense that he was gathering composure.

Two attacking men hadn't rattled Mr. Hawkes. But she'd felt the rapid thud of his heart against her cheek for a moment, and she knew, with a sort of terror and fierce joy and a painful tenderness, that holding her had indeed done it.

"You're not an ordinary gentleman, are you, Mr. Hawkes?"

"Are there truly any ordinary gentlemen?" he asked rhetorically. Somewhat remotely.

She said nothing.

He turned again and was regarding her thoughtfully. In repose, when he was not attempting to charm, his face was fierce. His very spirit must be terribly fierce.

She was beginning to understand that hers was, too.

"Come with me," he said briskly.

HAWKES TOOK HER hand and stepped out into the street, and she followed him without question. He hailed a hack promptly.

"Drive around Hyde Park until I tell you to do otherwise." He spilled coins into the driver's hand.

He helped Aurelie up into the carriage, closed the door, and locked it.

"All right, then," he said briskly at once. "If you'll pardon the intrusive personal question, Mrs. Gallagher—what the bloody hell are you doing here? Alone? With that man?"

She was silent for a moment. And then she swallowed.

"He sent a message to The Grand Palace on the Thames saying he was Mr. Monroe, and that he was sorry he missed me and I . . ." She paused.

He waited. Hawkes's heart literally felt raw and bruised by her obvious misery.

"I just . . . wanted so much to believe that he was." Her voice was thick.

He said nothing, because he couldn't. He'd gone airless from the need to take her unhappiness away.

"I suspect you have begun to think I am rash and foolish, Mr. Hawkes," she said into the silence. "An . . . an adventuress."

The word sounded quaint and so very specific and it made him smile, despite himself.

"One rarely has call to use that word. Thank you for reminding me of its existence."

"It is the right one in this circumstance, no?"

"Well . . ." He sighed heavily. "Here is the thing, Mrs. Gallagher. Rash implies you've been impulsive, and I think you've been very deliberate about doing things that, coincidentally, put you in harm's way. And you're clearly not a fool, so I'm a little puzzled by your choices. I would be honored if you'd care to confide in me. Because if something harms you—"

He stopped abruptly.

He looked away again, out the window toward the rapidly darkening street. He didn't want to frighten an already frightened woman. And the truth of what he was about to say unnerved even him. But he wanted very much to give her only that. And so he said it.

"I have borne a lot in my day," he said quietly. "But I don't think I could bear that."

He slowly turned to face her.

Aurelie's breath left her in a swift little gust. She searched his face, eyes wide, lips parted.

He met her eyes evenly. As though he'd merely uttered an inalienable truth. And yet there was the faintest hint of rueful amazement in his voice. As if this condition was entirely new to him. As if somehow the sight of her could explain it to him.

With reluctance, she turned away again. Her heart was racing.

She wanted to savor the aftermath of those words. The thrill and terror of them.

For a time they were quiet together.

"I am puzzled, too, Mr. Hawkes, that you happen to be in the places where I make those choices," she said quietly.

"And by 'puzzled' you mean 'lucky.' You are lucky that I happen to be in those places where you make those choices."

"It is indeed fortuitous. I am not certain it is a coincidence, however."

There was a beat of silence.

"Coincidences abound in life," he said comfortably.

"Do they? Of course. I have forgotten. You are so wise in the ways of the world. How fortunate I am to benefit from your superior wisdom."

"If you only knew how superior, Mrs. Gallagher."

"It's just . . . surely . . . the entire world cannot want to assault me. It cannot all be like a box of knives."

"Is that your logic? The world is exactly like a box of knives. Especially for lovely young women who rattle around alone in it. Surely you know this." He was incredulous now.

"But not all of it," she insisted, almost desperately. "It can't be. I do not believe it. I cannot believe it. Or why . . . or why live at all?"

Her voice frayed and she heard the despair she'd been holding back push its way through.

He was absolutely silent. Even in the dim light of the carriage, his eyes managed to seem bright as beacons.

"The world is a box of knives," he amended slowly, gently, "and all of those knives are scattered about in a beautiful green meadow between the dandelions."

She rolled her eyes. "Oh, much better."

He laughed shortly. Then sighed.

"Do you know about green meadows, Mr. Hawkes?"

"I grew up surrounded by them," he said shortly, abstractedly, after a little delay. "A thousand years ago."

"In the country, with your mother and father and sister."

He smiled slightly. "Yes."

"I think I should like to live in a place with green meadows," she said, wistfully. "Are they very nice?"

"They are, at this point in my life, very nearly my definition of paradise. A bit like what Mr. Bellingham described. Yes. They are nice."

For a moment neither spoke, and neither bothered to look out the window.

"Mr. Hawkes . . ." she ventured softly, finally. "What happened to you?"

"Well, most recently I was stabbed—"

She shook her head very slowly.

"War, Mrs. Gallagher," he said shortly. His voice was gruff.

"Is that the entire truth?"

He hesitated. "It encompasses the entire truth. The actual truth is like a box of knives."

She didn't press.

He thought he could happily spend the rest of his life circling the city of London with this woman. They could make love, raise children, in the cozy confines of this somewhat fetid hack.

"I have been kept safe for much of my life, Mr. Hawkes. Or what passes for safe for women. But I can tell you something. There is danger in too much safety. In too much shelter. And it seems to me things that appear safe often are not, and things that appear dangerous are often the very things we ought to run toward."

"You have the right of it, Mrs. Gallagher."

They quite clearly meant each other.

"And I know there are dangerous people and dangerous places, Mr. Hawkes. I know there is violence in the world! Do you think I lived sheltered from everything, under a great silver dome of a tureen, like a roast of goose?"

"Definitely not like that," he said. "And now I'm hungry. Damn you to hell anyway, Mrs. Gallagher."

She gave a little shout of laughter then covered her mouth as if loath to disturb the silky, quiet dark of the hack.

They were quiet again.

"You ought to eat more so that your coat will fit you properly once again," she ventured, staring straight ahead.

He went abruptly silent.

"You've got quite the eye for detail," he said almost coldly.

She was unperturbed. "Forgive me if this is a delicate question. Were you ill for a time before you fell through the door of The Grand Palace on the Thames, Mr. Hawkes?"

During the following long silence, he contemplated the number of times he'd been able to tell the purest truths about himself to anyone in recent years. How very much he wanted to tell her everything. The weight of it warred with the lightness of being with her.

"After a fashion," he said gruffly.

"'After a fashion' is the sort of answer that someone gives when they have a secret."

"I suppose you ought to know, Mrs. Gallagher."

Well, then.

They were both silent.

They stared straight ahead as the hack clattered forward into the night.

"It's just . . ." she began, then hesitated. "There are certain errands I must undertake on my own in order to secure enough funds for my journey. I need to sell a valuable item of personal property."

He seemed to absorb this information silently.

"Jewelry." It wasn't a guess. It was a statement.

There was a pause. "Yes."

"You did not think to ask someone to accompany you? I would have gladly done it. Even Dot would have been better than no one."

She hesitated. "I did not feel I ought to trouble anyone else."

He merely studied her, mutely.

"What is it? Do you think I am lying, Mr. Hawkes?"

"No. Nor do I think you are telling the entire truth. I think you do not want anyone to know why you're here, in London, at The Grand Palace on the Thames."

Aurelie couldn't speak for a time.

"Mr. Hawkes, tell me why you followed me, for you did."

He was quiet for so long she knew he was trying to decide what to say. Her heart thudded in anticipation. She craved his secrets, and she feared them a little, too.

"I sense that you are in quite a bit of trouble, Mrs. Gallagher. And I want to help."

He said this so quietly, so very, very gently.

She stared straight ahead, refusing to look at him. She drew in a long, shuddering breath. Her throat was thick now and her eyes began to sting. His mission, it seemed, was to erode her defenses, little by little. He *could* help her, she supposed. But how on earth could she tell him the truth? She didn't think she could bear his pity. Her entire being recoiled from the idea of watching his expression change to something she could not predict when her story spilled from her.

She turned out the window and watched a darkened London go by. She could find no answers in the view.

"Does it hurt now?" she asked softly. "Your wound? From the . . . the exertion?"

"Ah, *exertion,* is that what we're calling what just happened?" He was mordantly amused again. "I like it. Shall take care to call it that the next time it occurs. Yes. It does. A little. But I shall drink some whiskey, and then it won't hurt. The whiskey will help me to sleep, and then, if necessary, I'll do the same thing the following day, and life will go on as it has," he said matter-of-factly.

"You will not. You shall drink a healthful tisane, not whiskey," she said firmly. "With willow bark in it for pain. Helga will make one for you."

He coughed a stunned laugh. "Are you giving me an order?" he said incredulously. "Are you giving Helga an order? Have you *seen* Helga?"

"I watched you nearly die and I daresay I played a role in preventing it. Perhaps you will care to value your life if only because I do. I should be grateful."

He fell quiet.

"I might say the same of you, Mrs. Gallagher. Will you promise me this is the last time you'll head out alone to meet strange men?"

Part of her rebelled at the notion of such a vow demanded of her. The other part of her almost desperately cherished it. That she mattered so much to someone seemed improbable. Almost magical.

"You have my word," she said finally.

A moment later they had reached the livery stable. He thumped the ceiling and the driver came to a halt.

"I will disembark here, and the carriage will bring you to the door of the inn," he told her." It will be unseemly for the two of us to be seen arriving together. But I'll watch from the garden to make sure you are inside safely."

"Very well."

But he didn't move. He was looking at the seat back, his posture rigid. She studied his profile almost hungrily, savoring these last seconds in which they would be alone. He looked etched out of the dark.

"Mrs. Gallagher." He turned to her, resolutely, his voice low and taut. "Forgive me. I might be a selfish bastard, but given how capricious life is, and on the slim chance either of us dies in our sleep tonight—"

Swiftly, softly, his hand was alongside her cheek and his mouth on hers so suddenly she gasped.

Oh, God. His lips lingered against her parted lips long enough to taste the heat and dark richness of him. Just long enough to send something sparkling and molten down through her very core. Just long enough to coax from her a soft, low, broken moan of pure longing.

It was, shockingly, the sound of relief.

He ended the kiss and ducked his head.

Took two short sharp breaths.

And then pushed the door open, climbed out, touched his hat to her and shut the door.

And the carriage lurched away.

Chapter Nineteen

SHE CLOSED her eyes and touched her fingertips to her lips.

There was a pressure behind her eyes, and then the tears began. For the beauty of it. For the brutal frustration. For the gorgeous terror she felt. For how precarious her life was now.

He'd left every cell of her aflame and hungry.

And . . . the way he'd ducked his head to recover from that kiss. As if the very essence of her had gone to his head like whiskey.

Thanks to Hawkes, she now possessed a collection of moments, each more precious than an emerald: the long, slow breath he'd released when she was in his arms today, as if he'd been waiting a lifetime to hold her. The drum of his heart against her cheek. The shockingly competent violence juxtaposed with the knee-buckling tenderness.

And yet, here he was, like a rudder that righted the wildly listing ship that was her life.

But *why*?

There was indeed safety in danger and danger in safety, and he was both. He was so very careful with her.

As if he already knew all about her.

The way she was beginning to think she knew all about him.

THE HACK ROLLED to a halt before the little inn, with its sign on chains and its gargoyles. She understood The Grand Palace on the Thames was merely a way station in her life, but when it came into view, she suddenly fervently wished she could live safely here forever, with evenings and dinners and breakfasts precisely as they were, with Mr. Hawkes bound to appear in the room at some point.

At least she now knew how she wanted her life to feel: the love, the kindness, the safety, the truly excellent food.

As she slid across the seat to disembark, her hand skidded across something small, hard, and round. She jerked her hand back just as the hack driver yanked open the door. The soft light from The Grand Palace on the Thames struck a glint from it, and she saw at once it was a miniature in a frame.

Her heart gave a few painful, hard thumps. As if it had been shoved down a small flight of stairs.

The miniature must have fallen out of Mr. Hawkes's coat pocket.

Of course, it could have been left by a previous passenger.

But Mr. Hawkes noticed everything. He would have found it, surely?

She carefully picked it up and peered down. But she simply couldn't see the image clearly in the weak available light.

An agony of indecision held her fast.

She could give it back to him without looking at it at all. Call his name softly. She knew he would come if she called him. She would hand it over when he appeared, and she never need know what it was.

But he intended to wait out here in the dark and cold until she was safely inside, and God only knew who might be watching from the upstairs windows. And he had the right of it. It mattered what people thought, both of him and of her.

"I've been paid, madam," the driver said to her quietly.

Hawkes had paid him, of course, and the driver needed to move on with his evening, too.

"Thank you. Good night," she said.

She put the miniature in her pocket and went inside.

THE JOURNEY UP the stairs felt interminable with the miniature throbbing in her pocket.

The kiss was one thing. But somehow it was this that had brought her feelings for Mr. Hawkes to an immediate, stiletto-fine point.

She came to a stop when she encountered a smiling Dot on the second-floor landing, heading down the stairs with an empty tray.

"Good evening, Mrs. Gallagher! Would you like me to bring in some tea before you go to sleep?"

"Oh, no thank you, but it is kind of you to ask. But Dot . . ." She paused. "Would you be so kind as to ask Helga to send up a willow bark tisane for Mr. Hawkes? I do not know yet if he is in, but he will need it, don't you think?"

Dot tipped her head and studied her briefly, eyes lit up. She opened her mouth to say something, but apparently decided against it.

"Oh yes. I'll do that straightaway."

"Thank you," she said. As if he were hers. She knew how it sounded and yet she couldn't not do it and at the moment she couldn't quite care.

With every step she climbed her heartbeat accelerated, until it was a thudding hammer in her chest. Her key bumped and scratched away at the hole in her trembling hand; finally, she jammed it in and turned and was inside her room.

Before she closed the door behind her, her heart jolted again as the sound of Mr. Hawkes's cheerful bass voice greeting Dot drifted up to her.

She knew relief that he was safely inside.

He said he hadn't a wife. She believed him. Surely she could not be so very wrong again about a man?

Perhaps it was a portrait of his sister, or a sweetheart, long gone, someone he'd cherished?

And what could she possibly learn from looking down into the portrait of a stranger, anyhow?

Why did it *matter* so very much?

She only knew that it did.

That she wanted to trust him, she wanted to tell him everything, and yet the full truth remained gauzed.

Her breath came swiftly through parted lips as she moved across the room. She turned up the lamp at once.

She drew in a long breath.

Then she retrieved the miniature from her pocket and brought it close to the light.

Then the room tilted and shock sent black spots scudding across her vision as she looked down at her own face.

He shouldn't have kissed her.

Not when she didn't know the truth of him. Not when she was so vulnerable. And not given what he'd begun to believe had happened to her.

But he frankly thought even now that he would have died if he'd waited another moment to kiss her. And as long as he still drew breath the possibility of making love to her existed. As long as he drew breath, he could somehow help her.

The *sound* she'd made.

Lust speared right through him at the memory. He sucked in a hot, unsteady breath.

And the *need* he'd tasted. The sweetness and heat of her mouth.

The places he could have taken that kiss, then and there.

He swore softly and brutally.

He could also feel her uncertainty, all entwined with the desire. Inextricable from it.

It was *this* he would always honor. He wanted her to be certain. He would not coax or persuade or seduce.

And he would not kiss her again until they knew the truth of each other.

He knew she was near a point of breaking. She wanted so very badly to trust him, but her will was surprisingly, gratifyingly indomitable and stubborn. He was paradoxically glad that she was cautious with her trust. It was only sensible.

He just . . . wasn't quite certain what to do next. And his mind had always ticked along methodically. He *always* had a strategy. He only knew it would be best for her to tell him the truth before he revealed his reasons for being here. He would then, carefully, gently, reassure her that his original mission had changed irrevocably.

He lowered himself carefully to the bed and sighed. Whereupon his roiling thoughts and restlessness were interrupted by a knock at the door.

He rose again and peered out the peephole.

He opened the door to behold Dot bearing a little cup on a tray.

"Here is your willow bark tisane," she said.

Which amused him. She said it as though this was unequivocal. As though he'd demanded it.

He took it gently, as if it were her hand. He and Aurelie both were finding grace in caring for each other.

He drank it.

Presently, he did indeed feel better.

AURELIE STARED DOWN at the miniature she had given to Brundage as a gift.

The only one ever painted of her. The one that looked as much like her as it did any dark-haired, blue-eyed girl. In other words, not much like her, really. But she'd been so proud to have a miniature at all, and proud to give it to the man she was meant to marry.

Brundage had promised he'd have a large portrait done of her once they were wed. One that . . . how had he put it? "Did her justice."

And then realizations came at her in a brutal cascade:

The very first night she'd seen him, she'd thought she'd heard Hawkes murmur her name while in the throes of fitful sleep. And she'd assumed she'd misheard him.

But he *had,* in fact, said her name.

Because that's what he had come here to do: find her.

Who better than an expert in espionage to find Brundage's missing fiancée?

And at that realization terror cleaved right through her. For a ghastly instant she was utterly mindless with it. She could find no thoughts in the blackness of her mind.

Hawkes had probably known from the very first sight of her who she was, because he would have had a description of her. And she, in her ignorance, had probably left the kind of trail an expert in espionage could easily follow. He'd probably even spoken to Madame Aubert.

And if that wasn't enough, she'd helpfully provided a handkerchief, soaked in his blood, with her name stitched right onto it. He must have found it.

Perhaps he was merely trying to keep her here until Brundage could be brought to where she was.

And at that notion her limbs went numb.

"Oh God. Oh God. Oh God, please help me. What shall I do?" Her breath sawed painfully.

Reason fought its way through the blank terror.

No. No. She didn't believe it. She didn't believe a man who had saved her, and held her as though she were breakable and precious, and listened attentively to her, even as he surely wanted her the way a man wants a woman . . . would do anything other than *help* her. He was a good man. She felt in her very soul that he was good. Nothing in the world was true at all if Hawkes was not good.

But this meant he must know what Brundage was like. It was clear Hawkes suspected something terrible had happened to her. And he *cared.*

Why would this matter to him at all if he'd merely been charged with finding her? He could tell Brundage immediately where she was.

Perhaps he was merely . . . undecided.

And at that terrible notion caustic doubt and fear made a cauldron of her stomach.

She struggled to steady her breath.

What would Hawkes do if she showed him the miniature?

What would he do if she claimed she had no idea who the woman in the painting was?

She didn't know if she could bear to hear him lie about why he had it.

She didn't know if she could bear to hear the truth.

And worse, far worse, than either of those things . . .

. . . she didn't know if she could bear to leave him.

He needed her. As surely as she'd needed him. She believed this, or was this pure fancy born of a desperation to belong to anyone at all right now?

Tears stung her eyes, which made her furious. She squeezed them closed, as if to blot out a world in which she would need to make still more decisions, now, when she was exhausted. Now, when she'd just been held in his arms and wanted to linger in that feeling.

She knew she simply could not risk it. She could not know Hawkes's motives for certain, and if he was indecisive about telling Brundage . . .

She saw no other solution. Freeing herself forever and definitively from Brundage meant running again.

Tonight, if she could do it.

But where would she go? What were the odds that in all of England there was another such place, with kind people, and safety, and delicious scones? How absurdly lucky she'd been.

How absurdly, foolishly complacent she'd been.

But she was going to leave.

Once she'd made the decision to leave it was like a door swinging open on to clarity. She saw her options.

She knew precisely where she would go and what she would then do.

And she leaped up, gripped her skirts in her hands, and took the stairs as fast as she dared, her hand gliding over the banister that Captain Hardy and Lord Bolt had sailed over in order to get to Hawkes. In order to get to the people they loved.

Thank God. She reached the bottom of the stairs just as Dot was bringing in the lamp and barring the door.

Dot turned to see her and clapped a hand over her heart. "*Cor,* Mrs. Gallagher!" she whispered loudly. "I thought you were a ghost! Did you come down for some tea? Or perhaps a tisane, as well?"

If *only* a tisane could take away her troubles.

Aurelie took a breath to steady her voice. "No, thank you," she said swiftly. "I've a favor to ask, however. Would you mind terribly helping me to bring my trunk down the stairs? We should be able to manage, just the two of us, while it's empty. And then after that . . . would you mind helping me to bring my clothes down to it?"

Dot's pale brows dipped worriedly.

Aurelie silently, fervently prayed.

"I will give you a shilling to help," Aurelie said desperately.

"But, Mrs. Gallagher, if you're bringing your trunk down that means you're . . ."

"I have learned that I need to depart as soon as possible." Aurelie's voice shook, despite her efforts.

Dot looked stricken. And then bit her lip. "Oh, dear. I could fetch Mr. . . ." She paused, realizing that all the misters, everyone sturdier and stronger than the two of them, were in bed, and Mr. Hawkes was in no physical condition to haul a trunk down, and Mrs. Gallagher must have indeed sussed all of that out.

"No, Dot. It must be us and it must be now and you mustn't tell anyone else and we must be quiet." Her voice had grown taut and tears were starting up again. "Please," she whispered.

Dot's eyes went soft with great sympathy, and something fiercer: understanding and resolve.

"Will you help me?" Aurelie said desperately. Her voice cracked.

"I was a lady's maid, Mrs. Gallagher," she told her. "Of course I'll help you. And you keep your money. It is no trouble at all."

Aurelie closed her eyes. "Thank you."

AURELIE DIDN'T DARE wander out alone in the misty dark. Dot kept her company in the little sitting room until dawn tinged the skies dove gray.

And then she went outside to wait in the little park, shivering, listening for the sound of carriage wheels turning over the cobblestones.

Dot had given her a packet of food to take with her and a little flask. "Bread and cheese and scones!" she informed her on a whisper. "And tea!" Then she'd pushed a folded, knitted coverlet into her arms, as well. "We've lots!" she whispered. "And it's chilly in the hack."

Impulsively she hugged her and Dot squeezed her back.

"Godspeed, Mrs. Gallagher," she'd said.

Hack drivers were used to guests coming and going from The Grand Palace on the Thames now, Dot said; they made a point of driving through their little street in case they could acquire a fare.

Aurelie hailed one as the sky turned nacre and offered an extra pence to the driver to fetch her trunk from inside the boardinghouse. He hoisted it easily.

Aurelie looked back one more time, and as the door closed behind him, she caught a glimpse of the chandelier, the marble upon which she'd first seen Mr. Hawkes bleeding and outstretched, and Dot in the foyer, waving goodbye.

Chapter Twenty

DELILAH FROZE on the stairs on her way down at the sight of Dot standing in the foyer at dawn, apparently waving at a strange man departing with a trunk.

"Dot, to whom are you waving? And who was that man?" She peered more closely at Dot. "And did you sleep at all?" Her voice had gone up a half octave. Oh, God. Did *Dot* have a secret life after dark? Anything seemed possible after the week they'd had.

"Mrs. Hardy, please don't be angry, but Mrs. Gallagher needed to leave straightaway and so I helped her to pack and I stayed awake until she could get a hack." She clasped her hands beseechingly.

Delilah froze. "She . . . you . . . what? At *dawn*? Why? What happened? Where is she going?" She heard her voice steadily climbing the scale and she took a breath.

"She didn't say, but oh, Mrs. Hardy . . . she seemed very sad and upset and frightened. And she said that it was urgent and she *had* to leave right away. She seemed a bit how she was when she first arrived, but now more so. And she reminded me much of how it was for us when the Earl of Derring died . . . and you were so frightened, and I was so frightened . . . I just had to help her. Please don't be angry. I'm sorry. I'm just worried about her."

Tears were filling Dot's big blue eyes.

Delilah sped down the rest of the stairs and produced a handkerchief and slung an arm about Dot's shoulders. "Oh, Dot! I'm not angry. I was just very surprised. We've had so many surprises lately. You did a very kind thing because you're a good person, and it's why we appreciate you so very much."

"You do?"

"Of course we do!"

Angelique had appeared on the stairs just then, and was on her way down. She paused, and looked a question down at Delilah, and Delilah cast an eloquent, silent look up at her over Dot's shoulders.

It was beginning to feel like the events of this week might take years off their lives.

"I'm just worried for her, too," Delilah said. "As we naturally worry for people we like and care about."

Mrs. Gallagher was a woman full of secrets, if she'd ever seen one, and the secrets all had jagged edges, she would warrant.

"Everything turned out wonderfully for *us*, didn't it?" Dot brightened. It was difficult to sink her for long. "Do you think she'll be all right?"

Delilah wished she could be certain. There was a nascent indomitable quality about Mrs. Gallagher. Most women come by their strength the hard way, and she was concerned that Mrs. Gallagher was just at the beginning of that particular journey. She could only fervently wish her well.

Angelique joined them.

"I'm afraid Mrs. Gallagher just left without saying goodbye," Delilah told her. "Urgently. And that's all we know about it."

"Oh, dear." Angelique bit her lip. "I wish . . . I wish she'd . . ."

Delilah knew what she meant. They both wished

she had confided in them. Or that they had asked more questions. They'd been so careful of her. Too careful, perhaps.

But she and Delilah realized their instincts had been good about Mrs. Gallagher from the beginning: something was troubling her.

They all jerked, startled, when a swift and aggressive rapping sounded at the door.

"And to think we once yearned for knocks on the door," Angelique murmured to Delilah.

Enlivened by the possibility of yet another surprise on the other side, Dot brightened at once and glided across the foyer to open the peep hatch.

"I need Hawkes!" a man hissed through the opening.

"Sir . . . !" Dot was indignant when people weren't polite.

"Name's Berwick! Tell 'im my name and 'e'll come runnin'. It's urgent. You go and tell 'im now. *Please,* ma'am."

The man sounded frantic.

Dot stared worriedly at him.

Then she turned to Delilah and Angelique, and mouthed, "He's not a gentleman."

And Dot certainly knew her gentlemen from her not-gentlemen.

The look on her face suggested he occupied the extreme end of the "not-gentleman" category.

Quite tense now, Delilah and Angelique both hesitated. It seemed absurd to have a succession of people peer out the peephole at Mr. Berwick to ascertain this fact.

It was inconvenient to lament the absence of a huge footman, but it was certainly felt in that moment.

"Ask him to wait outside while we tell Mr. Hawkes

he's here," Delilah finally said calmly. "And I'll go and wake up Mr. Hawkes. And Captain Hardy."

HAWKES WAS AWAKE even before the maids came in to see to his fire and leave his tea for him. Sleep was fitful; his stitches began to itch when the willow bark tea wore off about three in the morning and then his mind began to itch, too, with thoughts of a woman sleeping (was she sleeping?) a few rooms away.

And as gray light began to fill the room, he decided he might as well get out of bed and poke the fire himself. He did this slowly and a little stiffly, and the stiffness at once reminded him of how he'd spent part of yesterday. He hadn't planned on leaving prison and promptly kicking armed thieves in their torsos. It wasn't really something one could practice, like shooting at Manton's. He'd done his share of roughing up and being roughed earlier in his career for the Alien Office and he knew how to do it, but in prison he'd been unable to fight back, and sometimes it seemed all of the fighting he'd been unable to do and all the anger he'd suppressed remained coiled in him like a spring.

He splashed his face with cold water, then turned to address the fire and stopped abruptly.

Something—a tiny bundle, wrapped in foolscap—was on the floor beneath the door and the room. Someone had tried to push it through.

He crouched, slowly, to attempt to drag it all the way through and succeeded in pushing it all the way out again.

He sighed and opened the door to retrieve it and scooped it up.

It was only about two inches high and wide. There

was something strangely familiar about its heft. The scrap of paper was folded about it snugly and artfully.

He was a few seconds unwrapping it, but he knew before he had it undone.

And then he was struck dumb.

He was holding the miniature of Aurelie.

How the . . .

Bloody, bloody hell. It must have fallen out of his coat pocket in the hack.

His heart jabbed him hard when he noticed the writing on the foolscap.

To remember me by.

Barbed, ironic, tender and heartbroken.

He *knew* she was already gone. He closed his eyes and swore viciously.

He opened his eyes to see Mrs. Hardy standing in the doorway, politely shading her eyes from his bare-torsoed self.

"Good morning to you, too, Mr. Hawkes," she said calmly. "A Mr. Berwick is outside and wishes to speak with you. Urgently."

"THEM REDCOATS CAME into the Goat's Neck looking for you last night, Hawkes. Well, they went into *every* pub askin' about you and a Lady something. But the Goat's Neck is where they found Davie. And I think they might be coming here."

"Why the bloody hell would they go in the Goat's Neck? Or come here?"

Berwick hesitated.

"Damn it, why, Berwick?"

"Davie told 'em before I could stop 'im! He didna see the 'arm. Seems they want to arrest ye, Hawkes.

Summat about kidnapping and stealing jewels. Made you sound right dangerous."

Hawkes was silent, thinking furiously. Christ, he *had* mentioned to Brundage that he'd be starting his search for Aurelie in pubs frequented by hack drivers.

"Not your best day, my friend," Berwick added somewhat wickedly.

Hawkes shot him a baleful look.

"Any sign of Vasseur?"

Berwick shook his head.

"My thanks, Berwick." Hawkes reached into his pocket for a shilling.

Berwick, to his shock, waved his money away.

"Well, I expect if you live through *this,* you'll buy me a couple of pints."

HAWKES, THINKING FURIOUSLY, followed Berwick out the door of the inn, scanning the surroundings for one of the drunk men he'd tipped to keep an eye out for a woman in a blue cloak. And he found him, one building away, predictably enough leaning against a wall.

"Good morning, my friend," he said politely, and proffered the shilling Berwick had declined. The man's eyes bulged. "Did you happen to see a young woman get in a hack this morning, very, very early?"

"Oh, aye. 'eard her tell the bloke t' take 'er to Sussex."

Sussex? Why would she . . . what could be in . . .

And then he knew.

And it had to do with green meadows, and a town with a mail coach, and a place one could pawn a necklace.

HAWKES BOLTED BACK up the stairs and found Captain Hardy heading down, which meant at least one thing was going his way this morning: it was Captain Hardy he wanted to speak to.

"Hardy . . . may I have a word, please?"

Hardy paused. Then took one look into Hawkes's face and wordlessly followed him into Hawkes's room.

Hawkes told him everything.

Without preamble, swiftly and succinctly, filling in the details of what Hardy likely already surmised. About Brundage, and how he'd probably been behind Hawkes's capture years ago, and how he'd likely hired someone to stab Hawkes to death when he realized Hawkes wasn't giving up his investigations. About the antiquities, the contraband cognac, and Vasseur. About what he'd learned since, and about who Mrs. Gallagher really was, and his assignment to find Aurelie, and how she'd been given the necklace, and why he suspected she'd fled Brundage.

And why he thought she'd fled yet again.

He hated admitting this last thing.

Hardy's expression went darker and darker and then finally, coldly inscrutable.

It was a painful narrative to deliver. He didn't know how he could have done anything differently about her, or about Brundage, and he thought he would probably always wonder.

"Brundage is a bloody traitor, Hardy," he concluded, "and I can't let him get away with it. He's trying to stop me from proving it. And I'm sorry, but I've had some intelligence that suggests they'll be coming here to search for me. I wanted to warn you. And I need to go find Aurelie now."

He heard the tautness of urgency in his own voice.

Hardy was silent a moment, studying him, brow only faintly furrowed, and then understanding broke over his face.

"Tell me how you'd like us to help," he said simply.

"It's been some years since I've worked for the Alien Office. I don't know how quickly I can roust someone into listening to me. Can you get word to Valkirk? If anyone can apply a little influence . . . I realize it's a lot to ask. You have my permission to tell him everything, confidentially. Because if they're hunting for me, he could be instrumental in getting the dogs called off. I will leave with you the budget books, and you can show him the entries I've described. I've had a man—a reliable informant and associate, name of Berwick—watching Guthrie's Antiquities. Vasseur will supposedly make an appearance at the antiquities shop about Wednesday, the day after tomorrow. If he is indeed in Paris at the moment, then a lot will depend on whether he has an uneventful Channel crossing. If I haven't returned with Aurelie by Wednesday, someone needs to intercept that bastard."

"We were the reason Valkirk has his new wife, so I suspect he'll do this for us," Hardy said, somewhat dryly. "He's in town for Parliament. I'll send urgent word to him. I'm confident of a reply."

Hawkes blew out a breath. "Thank you. I'm going to try to get out of here before they get here."

BAM BAM BAM BAM.

They froze.

The pounding on that sturdy front door reached them where they stood.

"The sound of a sergeant's fist on a door, if I'm not mistaken," Captain Hardy said evenly.

"Efficient," Hawkes said dryly. "As former military, I'm perversely proud of how quickly they got here. Is there a window I can leap out of?"

"Oh, I've got something better," Hardy said. "Follow me."

Dot, Delilah, Angelique, and Mr. Delacorte, who was up early looking for coffee, as he'd taken Mr. Bellingham out last night to sing songs in a pub and they'd both gotten carried away buying each other pints, remained frozen in indecision following the first round of pounding. Mr. Bellingham was still in bed.

BAM BAM BAM BAM BAM BAM.

Dot cleared her throat. "We've had such a lot of different kinds of knocks, lately," she mused. "I wonder who would knock like—"

"OPEN UP, BY ORDER OF THE CROWN!" a man bellowed.

"Don't open it, Dot," Captain Hardy ordered from the stairs. He was rushing down, Lord Bolt behind him. "Everyone, stand well behind me and Bolt. And don't say a *word*."

They obeyed, forming a little phalanx beneath the chandelier.

And Captain Hardy opened the door.

He didn't so much as twitch a brow at the sight of a half dozen or so red-coated men queued up.

A self-important young man with a long chin at once said, "We are agents of the crown and we've a warrant to search your premises for one Mr. Christian Hawkes."

Hardy studied him quizzically.

"With all due respect, Sergeant . . ." Captain Hardy cocked a brow.

"Pangborne," said the young man.

"Thank you, Pangborne. My name is Captain Tristan Hardy. This is Viscount Bolt."

Sergeant Pangborne went still. As did every soldier behind him. His expression went warier and warier by degrees, as he began to realize that some terrible and strange mistake had been made.

Or that he was about to become embroiled in a controversy he'd truly rather avoid at this point in his career.

Because *everyone* who was a soldier knew who Captain Tristan Hardy was. He was a bloody legend. The blockade captain who'd finally crushed the reign of the murderous Black Rock smuggling gang. Who had been rewarded by the king.

And, well, everyone who read the broadsheets at one time in their lives knew who Viscount Bolt was. He was rather a legend, too.

"Who or what are you looking for and why." Captain Hardy made it sound like an order, not a question.

"Mr. Christian Hawkes is suspected in the abduction of Lord Brundage's fiancée, Lady Aurelie Capet, and in the theft of a . . ." he cleared his throat ". . . the theft of a jewel."

His confident delivery wavered in the face of Captain Hardy's scathing incredulity.

"I have honestly never heard anything more ridiculous in my life," Captain Hardy said in utter contemptuous mystification. Almost a hush. "The only Mr. Christian Hawkes I know who might have some association with Brundage was a chargé d'affaires in Switzerland during the war and an officer of the Home Secretary here in England. He nearly sacrificed his life in perilous service to his country. He was instrumental in laying the foundation of English intelligence and is coincidentally an enormous part of the reason you're still able to wear a red uniform. He is a damned hero. Last I heard he was still a French prisoner of war. It would be my honor to meet him. Yours, too. You couldn't possibly mean *that* Christian Hawkes, could you?"

A long silence ensued, during which no one blinked.

"I . . . suppose so, sir?" the sergeant said miserably.

"Perhaps Brundage is confused, as we recently had another hero staying with us by the name of the Duke of Valkirk. Are you insinuating that Valkirk likes to frequent establishments haunted by criminals?"

The sergeant speedily blanched.

Captain Hardy took pains to seem bored. "We've never heard of a Lady Aurelie Capet. Needless to say, neither she nor Mr. Hawkes is anywhere on these premises. You blaspheme his name and the name of every soldier who has given their lives for their country by suggesting he's a criminal. And you've frightened our wives and our guests, which we simply will not tolerate."

"Captain Hardy, sir . . . Lord Bolt, sir . . . our apologies, sir . . . it's just we have a warrant . . ." He said this weakly.

Bloody hell.

"How the bloody hell did you get a warrant? The king never signed that," Captain Hardy snapped.

"No, sir, but the magis . . ."

He mutely handed the warrant to Captain Hardy to read.

Captain Hardy then handed it to Lucien, and Lucien read it and handed it to Angelique and Delilah. They owned the building, after all. It was *their* business the soldiers wanted to search.

Captain Hardy fixed Delilah with a rueful stare.

There wasn't much they could do about a warrant.

But they could certainly make Brundage look like a bloody fool.

"It's all right," Delilah said serenely, to the sergeant. "Why, you might want to stay here one day, after you see how lovely it is."

Captain Hardy stepped aside. "If you so much as damage a dust particle there will be hell to pay."

And thusly, red-coated soldiers filed into The Grand Palace on the Thames for the second time in its short history. And Delilah and Angelique experienced the dubious pleasure of realizing that their premonition about Mrs. Gallagher, aka Lady Aurelie Capet, was manifesting before their eyes.

They were dutiful. They were good men. They did their jobs, very thoroughly and respectfully. They searched the kitchen and the scullery. Then Delilah, keys jingling as her hands, which trembled only a little, led them upstairs and into every room. She knocked to roust a still-a-little-drunk and bleary-eyed Mr. Bellingham, who would go right back to sleep and wake up thinking he'd dreamed the whole thing.

Mrs. Pariseau was fortunately already dressed when they knocked on her door. She listened, one eyebrow arched, to Mrs. Hardy's explanation. And then, not the least bit nonplussed, she coolly watched the soldiers work.

"Do your mothers know you spend your days rifling through the stockings and undergarments of a woman old enough to be your mother?" she wondered pleasantly, as they peered into her closet and trunk.

They departed her room wearing scarlet blushes.

When Delilah opened the door to Mr. Hawkes's room, the soldiers found it empty of all traces of habitation, and the bed neatly made.

In every room, occupied and unoccupied, soldiers looked in the wardrobes and under the beds and peered in the chimneys and behind doors. They climbed into the spidery attic. They fanned out through the annex, and into the ballroom where lately the Duke of Valkirk's new wife had stolen the hearts of a crowd of people with her voice.

They filed out of the place inside of forty-five minutes.

It was clear from their expressions that there was not one minute bit of evidence suggesting Mr. Christian Hawkes, or Lady Aurelie Capet, or an emerald necklace, had ever visited The Grand Palace on the Thames.

"Our deepest apologies, Captain Hardy, Mrs. Hardy, Lord Bolt. Clearly there has been some miscommunication," Sergeant Pangborne said soberly.

"Duty is duty, Sergeant Pangborne, even when it's stupid," Captain Hardy said pleasantly. "Condolences to the Earl of Brundage on his dementia."

"Come again if you need a place to stay," Angelique called sweetly, as Captain Hardy shut the door in their faces.

IN ABSOLUTE SILENCE and stillness all waited, and listened until even the echo of the soldiers's hoofbeats had faded.

And then:

"He went out the tunnel?" Mr. Delacorte guessed quietly.

"He went out the tunnel," Captain Hardy confirmed, just as quietly.

There was a little silence.

"And Lady Aurelie would be . . ." Delacorte prompted.

"Mrs. Gallagher," Captain Hardy confirmed shortly.

"Lady Aurelie fits her better," Delacorte said cheerily, and with some relief. As if something secretly troubling him had been resolved. "And let me guess. There's no husband Thomas?"

Captain Hardy shook his head slowly.

Mrs. Pariseau had come down the stairs to join them in time to hear this startling bit of news.

They all pondered it.

"It stands to reason no one here is to say a word about this to anyone outside of this building and not present at the moment," Captain Hardy said. "Understood?"

Every head present bobbed up and down.

"I told Hawkes that if it was safe to return the way he departed we'd tie a ribbon to the lamp hook outside. Just to warn all of you, and the maids, that he may reappear in the hallways within a few days. And he won't be a ghost, Dot."

They stood together a moment, everyone quietly reeling yet exhilarated to have gotten away with something.

"Breakfast?" Lord Bolt suggested evenly.

"*Cor*, I love living here!" Delacorte said passionately, under his breath a moment later, as they all filed to the table.

Chapter Twenty-One

THE DOOR at the back of Starling Cottage was indeed loose on its hinges. Just as the sun had dipped low enough to tint the house amber, Aurelie seized the knob and pulled, and the entire door nearly toppled off onto her.

She heaved it up, then propped it back where it was. She sidled into what appeared to be a little kitchen.

She was grateful that Mr. Bellingham apparently wasn't hyperbolic, and that the cottage was indeed rather snugly secluded, if not remote. It was situated on a little rise, and as the hack had rounded the bend, she could see the town of Baggleston nestled in a valley—the smoke rising from chimneys, a church spire, a man on horseback, pleasant houses clustered in the town and scattered about the hills. It looked peaceful. She wondered how much secret turmoil was contained behind the walls of the houses.

It had been nearly half a day's easy journey to Sussex with a hack driver grateful to get out of London for a change, and she'd paid him well. The cottage was just as Mr. Bellingham described—tiny and thatched, tucked back neatly into the bend of a road lined with hawthorns, just past where a gurgling creek widened.

Inside, it was enchanting.

If she stretched her arms, she could very nearly touch the walls. It was the sort of place an elf would be happy to call home. Considerably smaller than any place she'd ever lived, but she instantly saw the appeal of burrows to little animals.

All the cooking would be done on the little hearth, she saw. Heavy curtains of wool hung in the front windows, which closed with shutters, and tammy cloth hung in the windows in the kitchen. To allow in light, she flung them open.

She would need to close them and shutter them soon enough to keep out the cold.

Two little rooms, one with a bed covered in a well-patched quilt, and a fireplace, and all of it, just like Mr. Bellingham had said, looked as though it had benefited from a recent tidying.

A further search revealed two oil lanterns and two candles pressed into holders.

And then she saw three skinny logs stacked next to the hearth.

She stared at them.

Only three.

How had she not considered this?

The house felt snug enough now, but nights would be a different story. And she would be here for at least two nights before the mail coach came through town.

Because that was now her plan: take the mail coach to Falmouth, and from there buy passage on a packet. Tomorrow she would walk into Baggleston, the nearby town, to attempt to sell her necklace at the notions shop Mr. Bellingham had mentioned, and perhaps find the baker and buy more food and inquire about obtaining firewood. If she couldn't find a buyer for the necklace in Baggleston, perhaps she could sell it in Falmouth.

She could not think beyond either of these possibilities. Falmouth was where the road, and her money, would run out.

Suddenly the setting sun was her enemy.

In the main room was a round wood table and a set of four chairs. If she could find an ax she might be able to chop them to bits, but she'd never swung an ax before, and it seemed more probable that she would chop herself to bits, and poor Mr. Bellingham didn't deserve his inherited furniture reduced to kindling.

She maneuvered the logs into the fireplace and found a flint and steel on top of the mantel. She crouched and struck and struck until one of the logs finally caught and she felt like she'd conquered an enemy. It would be quite some time before any actual warmth filled the room. Thank God the chimney and hearth were clean.

She'd asked the hack driver to leave her and her trunk in front of the house. She unpacked it the same way she and Dot had packed it, by emptying it and carrying things in a little at a time. Then she alternately pushed and dragged the emptied trunk into the house. This exercise certainly went a ways toward warming her up.

She shoved the trunk up against the back door and refilled it with her clothes. Just in case anyone else should wander by and take a notion to try to sneak in that way while she was there.

She returned to the outdoors, where apple trees were indeed flinging their bounties on the ground. She found a metal pail next to the hearth and she used it to gather twigs and little branches she could carry that looked dry, which were very few, and apples, which were plentiful.

And during her gathering she stumbled across a well, which felt like a miracle.

After she emptied the pail of twigs and apples, she

filled it halfway up with water, and lugged it with her to the house.

HAWKES LED HIS hired mount, a bay with a white blaze on his forehead, along the road lined with hawthorns. The two of them took it at a leisurely, companionable pace, after taking it at an almost inadvisably breakneck pace intermittently for an hour.

He and the gelding had both enjoyed it for a time.

But he could sense that at least one of the stitches had given way and pain was making itself known.

Nothing ought to surprise him after the last week, but the smuggler's tunnel beneath The Grand Palace on the Thames, reached through a wardrobe in a room on the third floor, raised his eyebrows. It had once been used to move smuggled goods—and prostitutes, well before that, when The Grand Palace on the Thames was The Palace of Rogues. Hardy had been in search of a notorious smuggling gang when he'd arrived at The Grand Palace on the Thames, and they'd discovered it as part of their investigation.

He and Hardy had fetched his trunk, including the budget books. Clutching a borrowed lamp, Hawkes opened the hatch inside the floor of the wardrobe, climbed down the ladder leading into the tunnel, and Hardy had dropped the trunk in after him. He'd fetch it later.

Following Hardy's instructions, Hawkes followed the tunnel, peering upward until he saw the hairline seams of light that indicated the hatch above.

The one that miraculously emerged in a stall in the livery stables.

He'd shoved open the hatch and climbed out into a stall occupied by a horse who seemed fairly sanguine about his emergence, as though it wasn't the first time he'd seen such a thing. Unobserved by the staff, he slipped out of the stable, entered through the front, hired that horse, and while British soldiers roamed the halls of The Grand Palace on the Thames looking for him, he was riding out for Baggleston, in Sussex.

Any pain and weariness he felt vanished as soon he saw the thin trail of smoke from the chimney of the cottage. She'd made it safely.

Either that, or marauders had decided to camp there. His money was on the former.

He paused to let the horse drink his fill from the little stream, and nibble at some of the Sussex grass, while he dipped a handkerchief in the water to drag over his own face and across the back of his neck. He'd stopped along the way to buy some food that could handle jostling, which meant sturdy bread and cheese. He'd filled a flask of water before he departed and he was equipped with a flint and steel.

Anything else he could purchase in the town of Baggleston.

As the sun dropped and the sky went mauve, Hawkes tethered the horse to the little gate outside the house, and quietly, gun at the ready just in case he was wrong, approached.

The door was ajar.

He pushed it lightly and entered.

She was kneeling next to a just-started fire, feeding it twigs she'd likely collected.

He tucked his gun away.

She stood.

She turned and saw him and went utterly still.

Rather like the first morning he'd seen her.

She had run from him. But now that she saw him again, all she felt was relief.

And a quiet, immeasurable joy.

Because she saw the expression on his face and she knew unequivocally that he was there to free her.

"You found me, Mr. Hawkes."

And at first, he seemed unable to speak. He was drinking in the sight of her wonderingly.

"I think I would follow you to the ends of the earth."

He said it gently. Almost wryly.

But he laid those words down like an offering to a queen.

They were a confession.

And a declaration.

They both knew it.

The air in the room had gone velvety, suddenly.

He moved a few more feet into the house. "Do you mind if I close the door?"

"No," she said softly.

He closed it.

They regarded each other from a safe distance.

"I believe I know who you are," she said carefully, finally. "And I believe you know who I am."

"Well, I gathered," he said gently, easily enough. "But I wonder if you will tell me how you know who I am."

She felt her face flushing. But she wanted to give him truths the ways he'd given truths to her.

"I did not realize it at once, you see. And then when I suspected it, I thought surely I was mistaken. You cannot possibly remember me, but I saw you . . . twice. At an embassy ball in Spain. I had never seen anyone so dashing, Mr. Hawkes. You looked so different then, somehow. And yet . . . I see now you are the same, only more so."

"I suppose time and prison change a man. Like what happens to whiskey in a barrel."

"Yes," she said gently. "I imagine so."

For a moment nobody spoke.

"You went to prison for espionage?"

"Yes. The French object to that during wartime."

"You were guilty?"

"Well, naturally. I was Head of English Intelligence. And I was very, very good at my job until I was caught."

"They like to execute people for that sort of thing."

"Yes," he said gently. "But they liked my fortune better in this instance, so that's what they took instead of my life."

She took this in thoughtfully.

"I am . . . so very glad you are not dead," she said. Her voice nearly cracked.

And at this, Hawkes for a moment couldn't speak at all. He thought he would remember those words, in her voice, for the rest of his life.

His eyes burned, too, with a surfeit of emotion he could not precisely identify. But he needed to tell her the whole truth before he went to her. Before he took her in his arms. Just as she needed to unburden herself of hers.

And so he proceeded.

"It was, in fact, Brundage who negotiated for my life."

Neither spoke for a moment. She was watching him carefully.

"So you are actually in his debt," she said evenly. Not bitterly. As though a negotiation of sorts was taking place.

"So he would like me to believe. It is, in fact, a bit more complicated than that."

"You've been sent to find me and bring me back to him. Or bring him to me."

He realized she couldn't bring herself to say his name aloud, and he tensed against a fresh rush of rage at the man who had so frightened her.

He got it under control. Because he always got things under control.

"That was indeed my assignment," he said gently.

"Was." He'd used the world deliberately and he was certain she'd noticed.

"And he is rewarding you for this?" Her breathing had quickened a very little.

"Yes. He is paying me to find you."

There was a long silence.

"And they took your fortune."

He inclined his head slowly.

A heartbeat or two of silence ensued.

"I won't go." She said this almost offhandedly. Experimentally. Gauging his expression. But he could hear the tension in her voice at the very notion.

It was time.

He felt that what he was about to do bordered on cruelty, though it wasn't as though he hadn't undertaken the same strategy before in the name of extracting information. But this time he knew it would feel as though he was pulling the spike from his own flesh.

Or driving a knife in again.

It seemed he'd known from the moment he'd held the painting of the sweet-faced girl in the palm of his hand that he hadn't come to return her to Brundage.

He'd come to free her.

And then to claim her.

"But I've been charged with a duty to find you and return you safely."

"I've not committed a crime. I will not go back." Her breathing had accelerated. Her fingers curled into the palms of her hands.

"He says he misses you and is terribly concerned for your welfare. He says his heart is breaking."

"Lies." Her voice was frayed and furious and horrified. "He *lies*."

He pressed on, gently merciless, hating himself for inflicting the necessary pain, the necessary pressure, to drive her secret to the surface. "He's such a very good match. You'd be the envy of many a young woman. He has all of his limbs and teeth. He's handsome. He's wealthy and powerful and influential. He told me he is in love with you. You will be pampered and protected. You will be secure for the rest of your—"

"I can't go back! You don't know what he—you don't know him—what he—he did. I can't." Her voice broke. "I can't," she said wretchedly. "Oh, please. I cannot. I can't. I can't I can't I can't—"

"Aurelie," he said softly. "Aurelie. Aurelie."

It was first time he'd said her real name aloud.

It sounded like a benediction. A secret they shared.

It cut through the hysteria at once.

She looked up finally, her face stunned, then glowing, then almost beseeching.

She cleared her throat. "Perhaps I ought not to have allowed him to kiss me at all? For I did, you know. I did not hate his kiss the first time, Mr. Hawkes. Does that make me a wanton? I wanted to see what it would be like. But I did not yet want another that evening. For he was in a dark mood, you see, for the day before I had laughed at something the footman said about the weather . . . he was very jealous of my attention. He tried, and I said, 'No, thank you.' And if I had not said this, then perhaps he would not have . . ."

"No," he said firmly at once.

". . . perhaps then he would not have gotten so angry? If I had not denied him? Perhaps I should not have laughed at the footman's jest?"

"Aurelie, no."

"I thought it mattered to him what I thought, or what I did or did not want, you see . . . and so I told him." She gave a little stunned laugh. Full of bewildered bitterness and self-contempt. "I feel so foolish now. When he tried to kiss me anyway . . . I gave his chest just a little push with my fingers. Just a little one." She illustrated this by pushing the air before her now. "I knew I was testing his temper, but I felt very sure of myself and my attractions. Is that not absurd?" She paused. "He did not like being . . . countermanded, I think is the right word."

"Aurelie . . ." He could scarcely breathe. Oh, God. Oh, dear God.

"He was so angry." Her voice was anguished. "He was furious. I wonder . . . perhaps if I were not so proud in general? Perhaps I should have been less adamant?"

"No, Aurelie," he said softly. At least he thought he spoke softly. A roaring sound had started up in his ears. The pounding of his blood.

"You see . . . there was a wall just behind me, and . . . I could *see* in his face the moment he decided to . . . that he wanted to . . ." Her voice was shaking. "Did you know, Mr. Hawkes, one hand was all he needed, to . . ." She touched her wrists. She swallowed. "He could hold them in one hand. Both of my wrists."

Hawkes fought hard not to close his eyes.

But he could see it too clearly: Brundage's hand glinting with a heavy signet ring trapping her slim wrists.

"He held them . . . over . . . over my head."

I stared at his throat. I would not look him in the eye while he did it.

Black spots scudded across his vision.

Her darkest secrets had comforted him in his wretchedness, through his fog of fever. But he supposed, in his way, he'd been her comfort, too.

"It's very surprising to realize, Mr. Hawkes . . . that you cannot move at all."

He honestly hadn't thought there was anything left of him to break.

"He took you against your will."

He said it so she wouldn't have to.

He didn't inflect the words with judgment or horror or astonishment or fury or pity. He managed to deliver them quietly, even as an eviscerating fury at the vicissitudes of fate nearly separated his soul from his body.

He didn't want her to feel obligated to manage his emotions, or to be swayed by them.

Her truth was *hers*. She could feel what she felt. He would be the cliff against which her emotions could wash. He could take it.

It hadn't destroyed her. And he knew that it wouldn't.

"Yes." Her voice was scarcely a whisper.

Her face was pinched and white. Her features pulled taut against suppressed emotions.

And then her chin went up.

But she didn't turn away from him. She was so brave. She searched his face.

Perhaps she saw in his expression he'd gladly do murder for her. Perhaps she saw how he suffered for her.

Whatever it was she seemed to take immediate strength from it.

Color flooded into her cheeks. Her shoulders rose and fell as she drew in a breath.

Together they honored her revelation with silence. And just breathed.

"Aurelie," he said quietly. "Please know that I speak absolute truth. It was in no way your fault. You did *nothing* to deserve it or cause it. I know this isn't a comfort, but there was likely nothing in the moment you could have done to stop it. It was an act of violence committed by a man who is so very good at seeming noble and fine that for a time even I believed he was. He is not. He takes what he wants. And you know that I'm difficult to fool, because I'm an old cynic who trusts no one. It was a hideous crime for which he ought to hang. *Nothing* about it was your fault. Do you understand? Do you believe me?"

He heard the hint of command in his voice. The urgency, though he tried to disguise it. He desperately needed her to believe it. He needed to offer her something of value from his singular store of experience, hard and bloodily won.

And after a moment of studying his face, she nodded slowly.

He closed his eyes briefly. His own breath was still coming short.

"I cannot adequately express how sorry I am that it happened to you."

His military training—his English reserve—usually steadied every word he spoke.

But in the middle of the sentence, his voice nearly broke with grief.

The radiance in her weary face then was a gift to him. "Thank you."

"You can stop running now. You are safe from Brundage now and will be as long as I draw breath," he said abruptly.

He went outside.

He was propelled there almost reflexively.

Because he felt like a feral thing. Not fit to be indoors. He needed to think, and it seemed, suddenly, he required the entire sky and all the air in the world to restore him to anything like equilibrium. He hated himself a little for what he'd just done to get her to tell him.

And right now, she likely hated him a little.

He took two more blind steps out into the night.

He dropped his hand on the neck of the horse he'd hired to get him here, and was answered with a little whicker.

Four weeks. She'd waited four weeks, pretending everything was well between them, because if she'd been with child, she'd have had no choice but to marry him. To be bound to Brundage forever.

He dragged in a long breath of cold air, released it, then partook of another in order to keep from retching.

He felt both poisoned and intoxicated.

He stared up at the impartial beauty of the stars. They winked down with equanimity on the evil and the good all over the world. Where did he fall on that spectrum? He had done his duty to his country; he had ruthlessly used his charm and talent for deceit and subterfuge and quick violence in the name of a country that had almost forsaken him, but which he still loved. And while his conscience had on occasion twinged him during his career, he was proud of every bit of that filthy business. He couldn't begrudge any of it, even if it had led to him being locked up. They'd won that war.

But there had been a cost to him.

What did he deserve now, if anything?

All he knew is that he might not have known how

irrevocably, fatally he was in love with her if not for this pain.

But damn, wasn't he still alive, after all of it? After all he'd endured? All he knew for certain was that his life was his own and he knew now he would fight like a dog in the street for it with anyone who tried to take it from him. Aurelie was clearly just as bloody-minded. She had made a run for it, an act of extraordinary courage and pure raw nerve, in the hopes of finding something better.

And damn, hadn't she almost succeeded?

He was going to make sure she found whatever that was. No matter the cost to him.

And Brundage . . .

Oh, Brundage was going to pay.

AURELIE. TO HEAR her name, on Hawkes's lips. At last, at last. He hadn't howled it. He'd made it sound like the prayer he said every night before he went to sleep. The thing he'd yearned for.

Aurelie watched him go, and she knew from now on, wherever he went, even if it was a mere few feet away, her heart would go with him.

Her entire being seemed to buzz as though she'd been adjacent to an explosion. But she felt oddly weightless. As if a breeze might send her adrift. It was an indication of how much her secret had weighed. She hadn't fully appreciated how much of herself was involved in accommodating it.

She imagined it might shift back in some form for her to address.

What had happened was part of her now.

And she did feel as though she might sleep for a year.

But she didn't feel drained, nor defeated.

Because this man who'd survived stabbings and beatings and that tattoo had gone outside because he could scarcely, in that moment, bear her pain. Her pain was his. She had never meant so much to anyone.

He was deucedly clever and ruthlessly tender and relentless and she knew it had cost him to surface her truth the way he had. He'd been right to do it.

And now she knew of a certainty that just as Hawkes had survived his battle wounds, so would she. She liked thinking of it this way: a wound one picked up in battle. She was the heroine of her own story. She would be the victor.

And she was changed forever, yes. Because of Brundage. But mainly because of Hawkes.

Chapter Twenty-Two

HE RETURNED and stood before her, and they regarded each other wordlessly.

The little cottage seemed filled with a strange, soft peace now.

Then he retrieved a flint from his pocket, one of those things that men always think to carry with them, and moved easily, slowly, to light the lamp, already neatly trimmed. It flared like a firefly, and then he turned it up and suddenly the room glowed.

"I should like to tell you something, Mr. Hawkes. I am not so fragile."

"Oh, I know that."

She smiled a little.

"Lord Brundage is but one man. I know there are likely many millions of men in the world. And my ancestors ruled France. Do you think one mere man could break me?"

"Not a chance."

She smiled again, fully.

Christ. He might be willing to face a firing squad for the pleasure of seeing that smile.

"Other men have been kind to me. Other men have listened to me. I have no illusions about the world being just, for my life is a testament to its caprices. I do not judge the whole of your species by him. I am not prone to hysterics."

"I know that, too."

The word "but" hovered in the air. She seemed reluctant to give voice to her thoughts.

"But now you know," he said, "what men are capable of. And it has reshaped how you see yourself and everything in the world. And how you move in the world."

She exhaled in some combination of surprise and relief. "It's what you know. Because of prison. Because of . . . war."

"Perhaps what I know best," he said quietly.

He eyed the fire critically, wondering how on earth they would stay warm when they had so little good wood. He could be of service to her by making sure she was warm. He wanted very much to do something. Anything.

"I . . . do not always think about it. During my days? I sometimes feel I ought to have been killed by the shame, if I were more of a proper lady. That I ought to marinate in it. That I should not be able to play pianoforte and drink tea and . . . ride in carriages with handsome men."

He turned away from the fire.

"I will not ever presume to tell you how to feel. But I don't suppose you are required to think about it or to feel any one way about it. I suspect that how you think and feel about it will change over time. How you . . . bear it will change."

He wanted to close the distance between them. Hold her like the precious thing she was. He didn't know if this would be for her benefit or for his. She had taken comfort from him once before, but perhaps she might still feel raw in the aftermath of such a confession and not welcome his arms surrounding her. His uncertainty kept him rooted.

"My name is Christian," he said instead.

She smiled slowly. "It is perfect."

Her smile faded. "I suspect there is danger to you if you do not return me to Brundage as you promised, Christian. I think he is a bad man. And not a dangerous man like you are, but bad."

"Bah," he said lightly, dismissively. Though of course she spoke truth. He would have to explain the whole of it to her. But not just yet.

She smiled at him again.

"Dangerous, am I?" he said a second later. *"And* handsome?"

"You ought to lie down, Christian."

She was right.

There was a little settee in the tiny front parlor, and he stretched out on the settee.

She sat opposite him on a chair.

He passed his water flask to her and she drank. She found the packet of food he'd brought with him. Wordlessly, she set some of it out on the table. She handed the cheese and apples to him so he could cut slices with his knife. She passed these back to him assembled with bread. Then he passed the knife to her and she cut the scones and gave him a larger piece.

There was peace and utter satisfaction in being with, and taking care of, each other in this elemental way.

"There is a well," she said offhandedly. "And I found it. I brought in a bucket of water. You see, I am not so useless as I thought."

"Well done. We'll visit it again in the morning. You are not useless in any sense of the word. You are *essential."*

She smiled across at him. Rather wryly. A little wistfully.

She looked away from him, toward the fire. "May I tell you something?"

"You may tell me anything," he said easily.

She seemed to be gathering her thoughts. "I think at first I felt one thing only after . . . after. I felt terribly clear and filled with rage stronger than fear. I imagined killing him. I did not know how I would do this and I think it would not solve a thing, but it is the worst thing I can imagine. I did not have those feelings before and I do not want the stain of those thoughts on my soul. My parents were murdered as was my oldest brother, and here I am, thinking about taking a life."

She said these outrageous things that, judging from her expression, she knew by rights would make most other humans blanch.

But Hawkes merely nodded, thoughtfully, as though they were having a discussion in the sitting room of The Grand Palace on the Thames.

"I know a little about being trapped in a cage with murderous rage, Aurelie. And I soon realized that rage, if I . . . I suppose the word is nurtured it, or attempted to stifle it, would eat me alive. It made me feel weak. Which I *loathe.* And in that way, I was its captive. I think it must be acknowledged. You cannot ignore it. But I tried to . . . make it my servant, I suppose. To use it as fuel for determination. And honor. And . . . service."

The last word he almost said was "love."

It was there in the room with them, that word.

Saying it aloud would require a new kind of untested courage from him. He did not feel free to do it just yet. It would be like introducing yet another new weather system on the heels of the storm that had just broken, and passed.

Regardless, he didn't feel as though he was telling her something she didn't know. It was why she had tended him, a stranger, through the night. She hadn't wanted him to cry out in the dark, alone.

Never again. *Never* again would she ever cry out in need, alone. He would be there, if she wanted him.

She cleared her throat. "Christian . . . I should be obliged if you would keep what I told you a secret. I cannot imagine telling anyone else. Perhaps . . . ever."

"Your confidence is a gift and I would never dream of betraying it. You have my word of honor."

"Thank you." Her voice was graveled. She brushed the back of her hand against her eyes again.

In his chest burned a confluence of emotions. A tenderness and awe he could scarcely bear circulated with a cold, nearly apocalyptic fury. And he was already planning.

Even if she leveled an accusation of rape at Brundage, the only crimes peers could be tried for were murder or treason. If she so much as intimated he'd assaulted her, her character would be shredded and her reputation destroyed, while Brundage's reputation might merely suffer a bit of a taint, if that. This was the brutal truth of their times, and such was the balance of power between men and women.

And Brundage had robbed her of enough already.

So she might not get formal justice.

But Hawkes was bloody well going to avenge her.

It was the prospect of this that brought him a measure of calm, for now.

They spoke of other things. He told her about his sister, and his mother, and the place he'd been raised. He told her what he'd already learned about her from Brundage. She told him about her brothers. Their conversation acquired a rhythm that felt easy and natural;

they took up topics, digressed, returned to them. Their words were undershot with the peaceful pleasure and acceptance with which longtime friends shared things. There was laughter. It was bliss. There would be an endless trove of treasures to discover about each other. This they knew.

Finally, he noticed she was struggling to keep her eyelids aloft.

"Aurelie, you're about to fall asleep sitting up."

"You're about to fall asleep lying down."

This was also true.

With some effort, he got himself upright and moved to close the shutters and the curtain against the night chill.

And he stood there, wondering quite how to say what he needed to say. He needed to give voice to what they were both likely thinking now.

He took a breath and turned, and managed, evenly enough. "Our situation tonight is this: There is no wood cut for a fire beyond what we see here, and what I could gather. I do not think it will keep us sufficiently warm throughout the evening. And to get through this night without suffering or burning furniture I think we will need each other to stay warm. You are brave and resourceful and you've made a decision to live life on your terms. So now you have another decision to make, and that's whether you trust me enough to sleep against me. If not, I will sleep in here on this settee."

Quite a shifting array of subtle emotions moved across her face while he gave this speech. None of them appeared to be dismay, disgust, or fear.

What settled in was that soft inspection. And inscrutability. Perhaps a little amusement.

"Well, I would *have* to be very brave, wouldn't I,

to consider such a thing?" she asked him, brow furrowed.

Taking the piss, in other words.

"*So* brave," he agreed.

She tipped her head. "You will be but a pillow?"

"My original life's ambition was to be but a pillow."

She studied him somberly. "This is of course the sensible solution, Christian."

He couldn't speak at all, because shouting "hosanna!" was inadvisable at the moment and it seemed the only appropriate word.

She rose to her feet elegantly, and shook out her skirts, then went to rummage about in the trunk propped against the back door.

She produced the coverlet Dot had given to her and handed it to him triumphantly.

"See? *Essential*," he told her, impressed.

Rapidly, however, conversation dwindled to nothing.

Perhaps because awareness—or perhaps self-consciousness—was deafening.

He gathered up the other things with which they would cover themselves, and went into the bedroom, where they sat on opposite sides of the bed. There was no awkward discussion of which side either of them preferred. It was as if they knew just how to do this.

And yet he didn't think he had *ever* done this. A woman and a bed equaled mutual ravishment, in his experience. An efficient satisfaction of appetites. No cozy preparations. No homely getting into night clothes.

Behind him, a beautiful woman was unpinning her hair. He glanced over his shoulder in time to watch it spill in a dark wavy tumble down past her shoulder blades. His heart stopped.

He heard her unlaced walking boots land lightly on the floor—*tap! tap!*

It was a ridiculously erotic sound.

He, however, struggled a little to get his boots off. Perhaps in part because his hands were not so steady.

She noticed.

"I will help," she said reasonably. "Do not bend."

He was amused at how little he minded taking orders from her.

The sight of her kneeling before him slipped beneath his control and his animal instincts reared up and he slapped them back with some effort.

She staggered backward with a boot in her arms and they both laughed.

The two of them in stocking feet. Ridiculous, and moving.

He felt somewhat abashed. And strangely new.

He ought not feel so absurdly, simply happy, and awkward, and new given the current circumstances of their lives.

It just seemed the moment contained so many unexpected gifts: Her trust. Her presence. The solitude. Something beautiful glimmering on the far horizon, increasing in brilliance, that they were moving toward together.

He lay back first.

She stood at the foot of the bed and watched him.

"Here is where I thought your head should go," he said gruffly. He tapped his shoulder with his hand.

Something fierce and tender surged in her expression, suppressed quickly. "It will be a fine pillow," she said gravely.

She moved, unhesitatingly, to her side of the bed. Then stretched out, and scooted until her body was up against his, and her head found his shoulder.

The sweet, soft shape of her body alongside his was the kind of hybrid bliss/torture he could never have possibly imagined.

He layered the two of them with the quilt, and the coverlet, and his greatcoat, and her pelisse.

And then once they were submerged in this nest, he gingerly, slowly, looped his arms around her.

He realized his breath was held.

She rested her hands on top of his. Her hands were icy, and he folded his hands over hers.

Her slim wrists that Brundage had held in one fist.

His teeth ground together at the choking wave of fury and pain. If he tensed, she would notice.

He wanted to lay his lips against the pulse beating there.

He frankly, of course, wanted to lay his lips on every part of her.

And he knew how to seduce artfully. He loved women's bodies, their curves and hollows and the soft swells of their hips and breasts. He loved discovering their secrets—the places that made them moan with helpless pleasure when he visited them with his lips or fingers.

And dear God, he was merely made of flesh and blood. It had been three years—three years—since he'd made love to a woman. It remained an inalienable fact that he wanted to ravish her, and he was certain she knew it, and in knowing this she was a lamb lying down with a lion. He'd never dreamed that he could burn so intensely for her and yet find an almost equivalent richness in just being with her, in this moment.

He would frankly much rather die than breach her trust.

He was just so grateful for the opportunity to hold her. Grateful he could provide some sort of comfort and shelter. If prison had taught him anything it was that sanity could only be found in the present moment. He focused on that rise and fall of her rib cage beneath his hands as she breathed.

"Forgive me. I think I cannot engage in spirited discourse. I think I shall fall asleep at once," she murmured.

"Close your eyes," he said softly. "You watched over me when I was ill. I will keep watch tonight, just in . . . case." He hadn't yet told her soldiers might very well be on the lookout for both of them.

"You will stay awake?" she objected to this sleepily.

"Absolutely," he murmured. "I've a positive gift for staying awake."

"Very well. I do not want to hurt you if I lean against you."

"If you do not thrash, we will survive the night nicely."

"I cannot promise anything."

He gave a short laugh.

They both sighed as if finally, finally they had come home.

"You *are* very warm," she murmured.

"Didn't I tell you."

"Mmm," she said.

There was a little silence.

"Will you say things in your voice, please?"

"Will I say things in my *voice*?" He was amused. His voice was graveled with emotion, presently.

"It is low and perhaps a little scratchy, but not in an unpleasant way. A bit like rough silk. Or a purr."

He was charmed airless.

He was helpless against her weapons that weren't weapons.

In a thousand ways, she would be the death of him, even as she'd saved him.

"What things shall I say?" he said evenly. But his voice had gone gruff.

"Mmm . . . do not say anything very interesting, for I shall want to listen hard to it. Perhaps you can tell me a story." Now she was amused, as anyone would be, at the very idea of him inventing a story. "Nothing with a ghost, however."

Had he *ever* told anyone a story? He supposed, in some ways, his whole life had been a story.

What story would he tell if he could? Where would he begin?

"Once upon a time," he began, "there was a headstrong, proud, clever young woman with eyes the color of the sky at that time of day just between sundown and proper nightfall."

That seemed the point, now, of remembering what the sky looked like: so that he could tell this story.

She turned with a start to look at him.

"Shhh, now. Close them." She turned around again. "On the outside, she looked as soft as a petal. But inside this young woman beat the heart of a lion. And here is the thing about lions. Good men feel privileged to be in the presence of their fierce beauty. They will honor it by allowing the lion to be itself. But weak men will try to conquer it with brutality and tricks, or turn it into a trophy. These kinds of men can try, but they can never hope to break that lion's spirit. And this young woman who had a heart of a lion prevailed, because just as these men cannot escape their natures, she cannot escape hers. She will *always* prevail."

He whispered those last words, vehemently.

He could feel her unsteady breath. He wouldn't fish

for a handkerchief or fuss. He reckoned some tears ought to be allowed to flow, and she ought to be able to do it in front of him.

She brushed her hand against her cheek. "And then?" Her voice was husky.

He cleared his throat. "And *then* . . . this woman, like a clever resourceful lion, using her ingenuity, escaped a frightening, brutal cage. And sailed across the sea. She had many adventures, all of them pleasant and interesting. And her life was . . . Her life was very happy."

He was not a whimsical man; the story would not be embellished. If he could he would incant this destiny into being for her, like a sorcerer.

He didn't know if he'd truly ever been a source of comfort for anyone before. Why hadn't he known what an honor it was?

"Did she find love." It was a murmur so sleepy the question wasn't inflected.

He waited until her breath was steady.

"She found love," he told her.

But he thought she was asleep.

Aurelie awoke more than once during the night, less startled than she might think to find herself wrapped in the arms of a man she'd known for mere days and underneath a pile of coats and a borrowed coverlet in a strange cottage. His hands—long elegant fingers, rough palms—formed a little blanket for her own. She savored the feel of his skin against hers. She in fact thought she'd awakened just so she could consign these moments to her sensory memory forever. How he smelled: of smoke and the outdoors, sweat and tobacco, and a sort of singular, alluring, musky, freshly-baked note that was clearly his alone.

Thrilling and foreign and manly. How he felt: safety and danger.

His thigh was hard and hot against hers; his shoulder a nook for her head. She could feel the rise and fall of his breath against her. Her heart felt like a kite. Her body felt like it hummed with currents that he stirred in her as if he were Poseidon himself.

It ought to have felt strange and scandalous and even frightening, but somehow fit her more comfortably and felt more instinctive than the clothes she'd borrowed from her lady's maid.

She was luckier, she supposed, than she deserved to be—that such a man existed, and that he was her protector. The notion that she'd intended to marry someone else who had attacked her seemed like a fragment of a dream she'd once had. At the moment she could not quite call it into focus. That the two men even belonged to the same species seemed preposterous. Granted, she was probably exhausted. Perhaps there was lingering shock. She had no doubt Hawkes spoke truth, from experience: how she felt about everything that had happened to her would evolve over time. But it seemed to her that if one found an island of joy amidst the box of knives one ought to linger there. And so she did, until she drifted to sleep again.

Chapter Twenty-Three

AURELIE AWOKE with a start from a dream of having suddenly been set adrift at sea.

She realized it was because Hawkes had slipped from the bed while she was sleeping. He was like an island and she the castaway who'd been lucky enough to crawl ashore.

And her thigh was suddenly chillier.

Signs that he'd been up and about for at least a few minutes: The fire had been built up. He must have been outside to see to his horse and gather more wood. She thought she smelled tea—had he found some tea, or brought some? He must have brewed it on the little hearth.

Then she noticed his shirt was draped over the back of the little chair and her heart gave a jolt. He was roaming about half-dressed, so it would seem.

But then she heard what sounded like the trickle of water into a basin.

She slipped out of bed.

The air was chilly on the back of her neck where she'd loosened her laces. She pushed her hair from her face and moved, quietly, to peer into the main room.

He was standing before it, trousers loosened and rolled to his waist.

He was pressing a cloth to his face, as though he'd just finished giving it a wash.

And then he unwound his bandage, and he was attempting to clean the edges of the wound with a scrap of cloth.

That's when he saw her. He went still.

Their eyes met and a great rush of emotion crashed over her heart.

She wanted to tell him she loved him. The words wanted to burst from her, like a song.

What if she was wrong? She'd been wrong before. It was just that it seemed the only word that fit this strange, vast peace and rightness with which she now felt surrounded, that odd sense that boundaries had dropped from time. This peace was laced through with spiky, breath-stealing desire and tenderness. It seemed born whole, this feeling. Could she love someone she'd known for so short a time? Her soul must have recognized him years ago, when she stood admiring him from the top of the stairs. She must have known he was hers.

It didn't feel irrational, but it certainly wasn't reasonable.

But reasoning was how she'd decided she loved Brundage.

They regarded each other almost somberly.

"Good morning," he said. He gave her a little smile. His voice was still gravelly from sleep.

It was a long moment before she could speak. "Good morning."

He didn't make a coy lunge for his shirt. The way his torso tapered from shoulders to waist made her head light. She knew he wanted to touch her, and kiss her, and more, and it thrilled and unnerved her. He would not do it unless given permission, because that was the sort of man he was. He loved her, too, after all. She was certain of that, too.

"Hawkes, does it seem unfair to you that I have touched your skin, and you have not touched mine?"

Hawkes's lungs ceased pulling air.

They were both still for a fraught moment.

"You may have noticed that the world does not pivot on fairness," he said finally. His voice was a rasp.

This made her smile. Ruefully.

Good God, but how he liked her. She was just so damned *gallant*.

He took a breath. And of all the things he'd been obligated to endure in his life, her gaze on him now seemed the least fair. The yearning flickering with the uncertainty. The heat and wonder and invitation. Desire that she clearly felt but perhaps did not fully understand because that first experience of it had been brutally stolen from her.

"I will do it," she said matter-of-factly. "I cannot bear to watch your face go very stoic and brave. It will be easier for me."

She already knew him so well. She'd said it because she knew he couldn't bear for her to suffer. She knew that he couldn't deny her a thing.

So he handed the handkerchief to her.

She dipped it in the water. He drew in a breath, and gently, gently she cleaned.

"It is not true that you are an old cynic who trusts no one," she said softly. "You trust me."

Her strokes were feather delicate and so careful.

His throat was tight. He couldn't speak.

And his groin was tightening, too.

"Salve now," she said.

He'd brought it with him, and he'd had the jar out and opened in preparation.

Very gently she applied it. And then with great precision and delicacy wound the bandage around his wound again.

And when she was done, she laid her hands softly, softly, flat against his chest.

His breath stopped.

"Christian," she whispered. "May I touch you like this?"

And slowly, slowly, she slid them upward.

It seemed an eternity before he could answer. The words needed to travel through endless layers of sensation.

"Yes," he said hoarsely.

He stood motionless while with her fingertips, her nails, she traced the gullies between his muscles, slowly, softly, as if he were a rare map she was poring over at the beginning of a quest. She tangled her fingers in copper hair over his chest.

She slid them along the ridge of his collarbone.

"I think perhaps you have long needed someone to be gentle with you, Christian," she whispered.

He'd lost the ability to speak.

How odd that this pleasure should shock his body more than even pain. He had learned to accommodate pain. There was no precedent in his life for what surged through him when this particular woman's fingertips moved over his skin. For the way his every cell came alive with a near frantic demand.

It was a terrifying thing, realizing the power she had over him.

It was a beautiful thing, witnessing her discover the power she had over him.

Watching her reclaim her own power over a man was yet another gift.

But *he* was going to lose his mind.

In no time, his cock was so hard he thought the top of his head might launch like a cannonball.

Slowly, as if the air through which they moved was soft and thick as velvet, his hands rose to cradle her face. He dragged his thumbs along the clean edge of her jaw. Back and forth. Back and forth. Her eyes had gone smoky blue. The man he saw reflected in her big black pupils was utterly in thrall.

He touched his lips to hers, soft as a breath, a tease, dragged them lightly, lightly across that pale pink curve of her bottom lip. Showing her that he knew how much pleasure was hidden in her lips alone.

She sighed. Her eyes shuddered closed.

"Aurelie." His voice was a scraped whisper. "What happened to you . . ." he brushed his lips against hers again, this time more lingeringly ". . . it bears as much resemblance to lovemaking between a man and a woman as the slash on my torso does to what you're doing now. One is violence. One is heaven."

Did he tell her because he wanted her desperately?

Did he tell her because he knew she wanted him, and needed permission?

Did it matter?

"Show me." Her words were scarcely more than an exhale against his lips. "Please show me."

"Aurelie . . ." His voice was shredded with doubt and an absolute agony of want.

"Please show me. I want to feel *you* inside me." Her voice shook with vehemence. "It's you I need. *You*. I want you in—"

She met him fiercely when he crushed her lips beneath his.

He moaned low in his throat. He felt savage; need coursed through him with such violence his limbs nearly shook from the effort to leash it. And he could *taste* her hunger: everything furious and everything loving. The lush silk give of her lips, the sweet, velvety heat of her mouth, the wild joy with which she met him, all nearly brought him to his knees.

And he began to show her.

Like a magician, he turned her knees to smoke, and the room into a whirlpool, and the kiss into a world. She slid her arms around his neck and clung, and as she gave herself up to the hot satin of his mouth, the demand of his lips, the sinewy twine of his tongue around hers—his fingers trailed ribbons of sensation along her throat, up the nape of her neck, the whorls of her ear. Everywhere he touched he awoke pleasure, and like a chorus of wild things, every part of her he touched called to the other parts of her body. She hadn't known that her body contained such hidden treasures of bliss. Pleasure spilled into her veins like a drug.

And the trails his fingers blazed were followed by his lips . . . and tongue . . . and breath.

She turned her head, an absolute weather vane to the pleasure he gave.

"Hawkes," she breathed, wonderingly. It was already too much and not enough, because she already sensed there was more. She wanted more.

"Do you see? We are *made* for pleasure," he whispered into her ear. "To give it and revel in it."

He drew his fingers down. Across the bones at the base of her throat. Into the valley between her breasts.

Then lightly down, dragging his thumbs across her nipples, peaked against her bodice. A shocking bolt of pleasure drove right down through her, snatched the breath from her. She moaned softly.

"If you tell me to stop, I shall stop. If you are afraid, tell me. Tell me anything. Ask me anything."

"Christian . . ." She ducked her head. "I am not afraid. I think . . . I will not want to speak again . . . only feel . . ."

His lips, his tongue, his breath, found the pulse in her throat, and then his voice was in her ear, sending shivers along her entire nerve endings. "I am going to make you feel extraordinary."

She felt faint with lust. She *was* a little afraid. Not of him, but of the enormity of what she felt, which was wild and needful and portentous: It was building and building, hinting at unanticipated glories. It was like contemplating a journey across an ocean. He was the navigator. She was entirely at his mercy.

But then, when she looked into his eyes, she saw that he was at her mercy, too. It made her want to give him anything he wanted. Do anything he wanted.

Gently, he guided her backward, until her knees pressed against the bed and she sat down.

His eyes had gone so dark. It excited her, that darkness. It seemed to promise delicious, devastating mysteries.

Their lips met and clung again and the kiss was so slow, thorough, and inebriating she scarcely noticed that his hands had reached behind her to spread her already loosed laces. He dragged the sleeves of her gown down. Slowly, slowly, so that she could, she supposed, stop him at any time, but that's when she understood how potent a tool of seduction anticipation was. Her breathing was short and rough now.

She would not have stopped him for the world.

"You are so beautiful, Aurelie." Just this whisper against her ear sent a shower of sparks everywhere across her skin.

Her breathing escalated.

And then he filled his hands with her breasts, sliding his palms up over her nipples, then down again to tease them; a whimper of stunned pleasure snagged in her throat and her head fell back.

He eased her backward until she lay flat against the bed, and she closed her eyes as he slid her dress, and then her shift, and then her stockings down the length of her body until, gradually, she was clothed only in air, every swift second of this a caress.

She was completely nude and he was not.

He touched his tongue to her nipple, then drew it into his mouth and sucked, gently.

"Oh God . . ." Breath-stopping pleasure forked through her like lightning. It left in its wake pulsing heat and need everywhere, but most particularly between her legs. She ached for him. *Touch me here,* her body seemed to say. Her body already seemed to know what it wanted.

She combed her fingers down through his hair as he circled her ruched peaks with his tongue. Pleasure was like a spear down through her.

"Christian . . ." she gasped.

It was just the beginning of his journey over the terrain of her. With his fingertips and palms, with his breath and lips and tongue, he made it clear how beautiful he found her shape. His hands followed the dip and swell of her waist to her hips while he left a trail of kisses along the seam of her ribs, to the rise of her belly, to the curls at the crook of her legs.

She was in thrall to it. And now she understood she needed only submit to each new sensation, some of them subtle, some shocking, all of them glorious. She'd no idea such wonders could be hers. She sighed, arching beneath his hands.

When he parted her thighs gently and placed slow kisses on their vulnerable insides, she tensed a little.

He left her for an instant. She opened her eyes to find him staring down at her.

And now he was naked.

Holy mother of God. She felt at once as if she'd been captured by a satyr in the woods. The naked entirety of this battered, bandaged, bewhiskered man was starkly beautiful and more than a bit frightening and suddenly he seemed almost a stranger. His long, thick cock curved up toward his belly from a nest of curly dark hair. She felt herself in solidarity with every woman throughout history who had waited with a sort of yearning, exultant trepidation to be taken for the first time. For she was a virgin in this regard: she had not occupied her body when Brundage assaulted her. He had used it as a vessel, and for violence.

Hawkes had given her body back to her. She had never been so grateful to be a woman, or so grateful that she had such gifts to give to him in return.

She lay back, naked before him, leaning on her elbows.

"Aurelie . . . your eyes have gone enormous." *His* eyes were feasting.

"I think I am weak from desire."

She immediately felt a right idiot for saying that out loud. It was a truth that had bypassed any filters.

He didn't laugh. Something fierce surged in his expression—his eyes went darker and hotter still and the corner of his mouth tipped into a pleased, piratical smile. She felt weaker still.

"Oh, the best is yet to come," he said.

He lowered himself next to her and took her gently in his arms and this was the best of all, this was so good, his skin against hers at last. She sighed against his lips as they collided again, in searching, carnal kisses. And his hand slid down over the curves he'd earlier claimed, her buttocks, her waist, her belly, to tangle in her damp curls between her legs. Her breath snagged in her throat. Softly, softly, his hand slid between her thighs, urging them wider, and she parted them, allowing him access to where she was wet and aching, and when he stroked, slowly and deliberately, a shocking pleasure bolted through her.

She gasped and arched into his touch. He did it again, and again.

"Is it good?" he murmured.

Her breath shuddered. "So . . . good . . . Christian . . . what is this?"

He didn't speak, and she no longer could. His rhythm was deliberate, teasing; delicate, then harder. Her own hips began to move with him, teaching him the speed she wanted. Somehow she knew.

An astounding pressure was welling against the seams of her being, and at first she didn't know if she was chasing it or running from it when she arched into his touch, but she was moving with it instinctively. It was desire, churned like a sea; she could not contain it. Her hips thrust and undulated with his stroking fingers; her breath was a sobbing roar. She begged him for what she didn't know. She gripped his shoulders and watched him pleadingly, almost accusingly. "Please, Hawkes . . . please . . . I need . . ."

"I have you," he whispered, as though he knew she was about to be launched from her body. "Let go."

She was torn from her body and flung into space, and her head tipped back in a hoarse scream of exultation as she bowed upward from the force of an indescribable, shattering bliss that coursed through her. Shaking her.

The shock of it. The unimaginable glory.

She opened her eyes to find his face gazing down

at her with a sort of burning amazement and awe. So solemn and lustful.

She touched his face. She could not speak her gratitude, but he could read it.

He bridged her with his arms, and she knew what was to happen next.

She saw how his own rough breath moved his shoulders.

"Christian . . . you are trembling . . ." For he was. She drew a hand along his bicep.

"Because you are beautiful and sweet beyond belief and I am moved. I want you so badly, Aurelie. I don't want to hurt you." His voice was hoarse.

"I want you to feel what I felt. You cannot hurt me . . . I know you will not . . . when I want you so . . . I want you so. Please." She arched up.

"Wrap your legs around me," he told her.

He guided his cock into her as she arched up to meet him, savoring the feel of his body joining hers, an act of joyous defiance and reclaiming. *This* man. A man she had chosen for herself.

She rested her hands on his chest as he began to move inside her, slowly at first. Languidly.

She watched in wonder as pleasure and emotion shifted across his splendid face. How his eyes went nearly black and unseeing; how the cords of his neck grew taut; his breath was hot against her lips, coming in gusts. She touched her fingers because she wanted to feel the tension gathering in him. She wanted to savor that nearly unbearable building bliss that he was finding in her body.

And then she could feel her own bliss building again. The marshaling of a shattering release. She gasped in amazement; it tapered into a moan of his name. "Christian . . . I think I am . . . again . . ."

"Move with me, love," he rasped.

They crashed and plunged together like wild things. She whimpered and begged; her breath came in gusts; her fingers dug into his shoulders.

His breath was a ragged roar now. "Aurelie . . . oh God . . . *oh God . . .*"

And she held him fast as she knew he was hurtled from his body as well. She could feel his body racked with pleasure; it made her feel like a conqueror.

Seconds later, her own release nearly blacked her vision.

"Aurelie?" he murmured. "How do you feel?"

"I am not yet in my body. I am up in heaven, I think."

"What a coincidence. So am I. I think I see you there."

She laughed softly. He smiled at her.

They were quiet, their breathing settling still, their senses not altogether recollected.

"It was wonderful. I could never have imagined this. Thank you," she said shyly.

"Oh, well, my pleasure," he murmured. "In fact, greatest pleasure of my life."

It seemed absurd to blush *now*, but she did.

He smiled at her, and it was a somewhat tilted rakish affair. But his eyes were somber and tender and hazed with sleepiness.

And then they drifted closed.

"Oh, God. I shouldn't sleep," he murmured. "We truly cannot tarry here long, Aurelie."

"You must sleep. You need to sleep. Have you a watch?"

"My coat pocket," he murmured.

"I will wake you in . . . two hours. Do you trust me?"

"Very well. Two hours. I trust you," he said. After a moment.

As though he hadn't said those words aloud in ages

and it had taken some time to admit it to himself. Perhaps he had never said them.

She rose and fished about in his coat for his watch. She was aware of his admiring eyes on her, and she was glad. She'd never dreamed she'd ever dare to stroll naked through a vicar's cottage with the eyes of a spy on her.

She returned to bed with the watch. And settled in next to him, arranging their piles of covers over their bodies.

They layered their legs over each other. He looped his arm beneath her.

"I will tell you a story," she said softly.

"Excellent," he murmured happily.

"There once was a man whose body was made of iron and scars. He was as brave as a lion, but underneath his skin, behind the cage of his ribs, his heart was as soft as petals."

"Petals?" he said sleepily, amused and indignant.

"Shhhh," she said. "He was born to be a protector, but he didn't know he needed one of his own, until she arrived. He knew she would cherish the soft petals of his heart. And when he realized this, he discovered that his cage had been unlocked all along."

Then he gave a short, stunned laugh. "Aurelie," he said. As if she had undone him.

Sleep took him under.

SHE WOKE HIM with a kiss.

His eyes fluttered open.

"It *wasn't* a dream," he whispered, quite pleased.

She smiled at him and kissed him again. He laid his hand alongside her cheek and kissed her back. They lost themselves in a series of long, languid, dreamy, kisses that deepened, and grew hungry.

She kissed the base of his throat; then slid her mouth to beneath his ear, where his pulse was quickening. He drew his hand along her hair.

"I may touch you like this? And kiss you like this?"

"You may touch me and kiss me however you please." His voice was hoarse.

"You will tell me how you like to be touched?"

"If you like. Perhaps you'll discover a new way I like to be touched."

She soon found that she didn't need his guidance. She could navigate his pleasure by reading the tensing of his muscles, the pace of his breathing, his sighs, the way his legs shifted restlessly. She set herself free over his body.

Oh, the earthy pleasures of the sweat and the curling hair on his chest and the trail of it that led down to his cock, the salty taste of his skin beneath her tongue, the leathery little bump of his nipples. The little scars, a mole or two—she kissed them—and the tattoo of the dagger beneath his arm. She dragged her finger around its outline, her eyes locked with his. *We understand pain,* she was saying silently, *and we understand how to make it our servant. We conquer it with beauty and pleasure.*

She had never dreamed that she could ever be so shockingly vulnerable while never feeling more powerful and safe. This profound, dangerous, mysterious, remarkable thing—sex—seemed easy with him, because he'd shown her how touching was a language. How sex was a conversation between their bodies and their hearts. That it had movements, like a symphony, rests and crescendos.

She traced the shape of a heart with her fingers over the places his heart bumped against his chest, and then she lightly closed her teeth over his nipple, and she knew, when one hand covered the back of her head, and his fingers curled into the little quilt, that she possessed the magic to drive him to madness, too, and this notion spiked her own desire.

And she saw his cock stir, and swell again.

She wanted to hear him beg her with words, as she'd begged him. And then she wanted to save him from that desperate want by giving him what he needed, just as he'd done for her. She wanted to hear his breath come ragged and short. She wanted to see his eyes go black, black with lust and mindless intent. And then she wanted to be taken again.

He hissed in a breath that ended on a little groan when she dragged her hand over his cock. "Like this?"

"Your fist," he rasped. "Take me in your fist."

She closed her fingers around him gently, and he covered her hand with his and showed her how he wanted to be touched. And she did, and in her fist it swelled and leaped like a living thing, and she felt weak and wild again. She was the magician, this time. He was at her mercy.

"Aurelie . . ." he gasped.

"Do you want me again? Please, I want you, Hawkes."

"Yes. Yes," he said. "Come to me . . ."

She came to him as though he was pulling her from a choppy sea, and stretched out alongside him. He rose up over her and he arched her hips up to take his thrust into her, and locked her legs around his back. She pressed her palms into those lovely indentations in the muscles of his arse that seemed made for that purpose, urging him on, rising up to meet every thrust of his pale hips. Gasping when he dipped to touch his tongue to her nipple.

"Christ," he groaned, gratifyingly.

Every touch, every sigh and moan, every wave of bliss, brought her closer to herself. To wholeness. And drifted her farther away from everything that had ever hurt her.

It ripped her out of herself and she bowed backward with a silent scream, her fingers digging into his shoulders.

"Oh, God . . . Aurelie . . ."

She held him while he shook with it.

He propped himself up on his elbows and looked down at her. And then gently rolled away.

"Sweetheart . . ." he said softly. "Are you weeping?"

She was. Quietly and softly.

He thought his heart would break again. But he also knew the value of tears.

"It's just emotion," she said. "I think perhaps every emotion. So many lovely new ones are arriving, and so many terrible ones dissolving."

He was quiet for some time.

With his thumbs, he gently gathered the tears brimming on her lashes and for a solemn moment they gazed at each other.

"I love you," he said quietly.

That was the secret she'd driven from him with the gift of her body, the way he'd driven a secret from her last night.

His voice was graveled. The words felt strange in his mouth, and he thought it was perhaps because he hadn't said them aloud since . . . perhaps he'd said them as a boy. Suddenly he felt more naked than he already was.

Was it true? Yes. It felt as though it had always been true. It didn't matter how they'd arrived at this love.

Her face was luminous and suddenly his eyes burned, too.

"And I love you," she whispered.

Chapter Twenty-Four

"AURELIE," HE said softly, "I fear we must discuss the inevitable encroachment of reality. We can't abuse Mr. Bellingham's unwitting hospitality forever. I can't make a habit of that sort of thing. Wandering—or staggering—into places, setting up housekeeping. Like that."

"Very well." She propped on her elbows to look down on him.

"I must return to London as soon as possible."

She smiled, but her smile faded as she noted how serious his expression had become. "I will go with you, of course."

It sounded like a question, and his heart squeezed. *Forever and always, you will go with me everywhere,* he wanted to say. Though given the current outrageous uncertainty of his life, he wasn't certain he had the right to assume it. Or to ask it of her.

But he needed to tell her the whole truth. He loathed introducing it into their idyll, but drama, violence, and tragedy were indirectly why they were lying naked in each other's arms at the moment. There was no one without the other, currently. And while she might try to be an optimist, neither one of them were fantasists.

He mustered nerve and considered how to begin.

"Christian?" she said softly, worried now.

"Before you decide to . . . align your fate with mine,

Aurelie . . . I need to tell you something important. Three years ago, I believe Brundage arranged for my arrest and capture because he realized I suspected him of selling secrets to the French and I was close to proving it."

She exhaled in shock. "Oh my God! Was he? Is he? Christian!"

"Yes. I'm afraid he did. I'm certain of it," he said tersely. "But if not for you, Aurelie . . . well, when you ran away, he found himself in quite a bind, because the necklace he gave to you had been loaned to him by a French family who lost most of their fortune in the Revolution—he hadn't yet purchased it. He faced the kind of scandal that could cost him the ambassadorship to France. He must have weighed his options and decided there was nothing I could prove about him now that the war was over. And that perhaps if he paid me enough, I wouldn't bother to try. Or that I'd lost my taste for vengeance, or curiosity, in prison. But he also knew I was the only man who could possibly find you." He smiled faintly. "He was right about one of those things."

She was silent and tense, taking this in warily. She sensed, rightly, that he hadn't yet come to the worst part of the story.

"Thanks to you, Aurelie, and as fate would have it . . . I am, in fact, once again close to proving he committed treason. He learned of this, and so he hired an assassin to attempt to dispatch me with a knife. Which is, of course, how you and I met."

Before his eyes her lovely face went cold and astounded and blackly furious. "How . . . how . . . bloody . . . *dare* . . . he try to kill you."

He could imagine her ancestors ordering beheadings. He gazed upon that expression, impressed and very proud.

"The cheek of him, right?" he said with a certain black irony.

She gave him that fierce expression, and then she covered her face with her hands.

"Oh, no . . . Christian. The necklace . . . did I *steal* it?"

He knew that necklace constituted the whole of her current financial worth.

"We will return it to its owners," he said calmly. "And all will be well."

It was a bold claim. But it wasn't as though he hadn't fought his way out of blind alleys before. If The Grand Palace on the Thames could have a secret smuggler's tunnel, surely so could their lives. He would find it. With Aurelie in his arms, it was easier to believe in miracles, because she was a benediction.

"So here is the thing, Aurelie. Returning to London together may be a bit of a risk, because Brundage managed to get a warrant seeking my arrest for kidnapping you and stealing the necklace. While you were traveling to this cottage, soldiers descended upon The Grand Palace on the Thames looking for me—Captain Hardy helped me escape. I'm certain Hardy made short work of them, and Hardy and Bolt are helping me to prove the case against Brundage. But soldiers may even now be looking for us on roads all over England."

Her eyes went wide and astounded.

She tipped over stiffly and lay on her back again staring up at the ceiling.

He held his breath, praying.

She turned toward him again and propped herself up to look down at him.

"I am just so terribly sorry," she said, "that this bad man has been a part of our story."

He went still. Stunned.

It was perhaps the perfect thing to say. He liked the word "our." He liked the confidence of the past tense: "has been." It allowed for the fact that one day Brundage would be a mere distant memory. He liked the singular of "story." For, somehow, for all of the turmoil, their stories had converged into one, and that was what mattered.

"He is only a chapter, and that chapter is almost over," he said.

She gave him a half smile, sad and wry.

"But Aurelie . . . in order for us to have a future, I cannot let him go free. He needs to pay for what he did to you." His voice was hoarse now. He had ground out the word "pay" a little too viciously. He took a steadying breath. "And for what he did to me. And for what he did to England. And in order to do this . . . I must return to London. And . . . I must confront him."

Aurelie stared at him.

Slowly her gut turned to ice.

He didn't need to tell her how stunningly dangerous this was. A British soldier who thought Hawkes was intent on harming an earl would likely be inclined to shoot him on sight if he saw him anywhere near Brundage.

Don't do it for me. You're all I need. We can cross the ocean and begin again and forget all of this, all of this.

But she already knew he wouldn't be able to live with himself if he didn't do it, and she would never wish that suffering upon him.

Moreover . . .

The largest part of her wanted him to do it.

Her life had been characterized by injustices and violence. *Enough,* she said silently now, to fate. *We've had enough. This is where we win. This is where we fight in the way my parents had been unable to fight, and Hawkes had been unable to fight. This is where our green meadows are cleared of hidden knives. Forever.*

What would become of her if Hawkes was captured or killed?

Grief and fury and frustration at the caprices of fate, at the onslaught of injustices and upheavals in her life . . . they were like the enemy clamoring with torches and pitchforks outside her castle. She couldn't let them get past the drawbridge.

Because he was right. There would be no future until they'd vanquished the past, and he was the only one in the world who could do it.

No matter how else she felt, what he needed was her strength and her faith and her love.

"Of course, you must go and get him, Hawkes," she said softly. "For me, and for you, and for every other person he's harmed or may harm."

She saw in his eyes that he knew what this had cost her.

He lifted her hand and gently, tenderly, lingeringly kissed her wrist. And then he kissed the other. As though he could exorcise the memory of another man shackling them in a single fist. A promise to her that they would soon be free of that man forever.

LUCK WAS THE breeze at their back from the moment they woke before dawn the following morning.

Just past dawn, Hawkes rode into town to deliver his hired mount unto the care of the livery stable in charming Baggleston, and there he learned his favorite thing about Bagglestonians: they were thrifty. Because while the regular stage coach was already jammed full of passengers, every traveler in Baggleston refused to pay the exorbitant prices of the royal mail coach, which would be passing through in just an hour or so. Save one.

With a little assistance from the shrinking cache of bank notes in his pocket, he persuaded one potential royal mail coach passenger to await the next coach so that he and his new wife, Mrs. Mary Gallagher, could have seats together as they traveled to visit his ill, possibly dying, father, in London. Another shilling pressed upon the driver along with a liberal application of charm and supplication persuaded them to stop at Starling Cottage to fetch Aurelie's trunk, as well as Aurelie.

And then the royal mail coach driver cracked the ribbons and they hurtled down the road.

Both Hawkes and Aurelie found themselves craning their heads for one final view of Mr. Bellingham's cottage.

Aurelie's eyes misted over.

She brushed at them with one hand.

Hawkes threaded his fingers through hers and brought her knuckles to his lips.

Mrs. Farquhar—of Mr. and Mrs. Farquhar, their companions on the journey—beamed at them with indulgent curiosity. Her salt-and-pepper curls sprang from beneath a bonnet trimmed with a preponderance of felt cherries. Mr. Farquhar, solidly built, a great handsome English nose jutting from a pleasant face featuring thick, anarchic gray brows, was clearly an old hand at long trips: in moments he'd fallen asleep.

Hawkes and Aurelie smiled back at Mrs. Farquhar.

The six-hour trip to London began.

For five hours, the trip passed in a blur of pretty country and good roads. The stage scarcely did more than pause as the mail was hurled down and more mail hurled up in the towns through which they traveled;

they stopped for all of ten minutes every few hours to change horses and for everyone who needed to leap out and relieve themselves or to buy a few buns from a waiting enterprising vendor.

Mr. Farquhar woke and he and Hawkes somehow wound up talking of cricket, of all things, while Aurelie leaned across to admire Mrs. Farquhar's embroidery, and this was the sort of life she wanted. Easy conversations that contained nothing fraught. Peaceful pastimes.

In the silences Aurelie gazed out the window, enthralled, imagining the life she could lead in each town they passed through. *That would be my church,* she thought, as a spire and a little graveyard passed by, *and that would be my milliner shop, and those ladies I see strolling would be my friends, and Hawkes would know their husbands.* She wanted a life with friends. She liked snug rooms full of laughing people sitting so near each other she could hear the click of knitting needles and the rustling turn of a page.

But what did Hawkes want?

They loved each other. The miracle of this made her feel as though their carriage was a chariot driven across the sky. But it seemed odd not to know his thoughts. His fingers were twined through hers but his face was abstracted and his gaze fixed as he watched the English countryside, likely familiar to him. No doubt he was thinking about what lay ahead, and what he needed to do to help bring Brundage to justice. This morning, he'd told her briefly of his evidence. He perhaps would share more thoughts if they were alone. But she supposed the details of each other they would come to know over time. The essence of each other they already knew.

And surely they would have time? Surely the emotions of their lives would cease crescendoing, and one day be as peaceful as the pond they'd just rolled past?

Would he ask her to marry him? Surely he would do that, too.

And the notion of being asked to spend her life with a man with whom she was so in love—the notion sent a breath-stealing bolt of anticipation through her.

The coach slowed to stop for another change of horses just as Mr. Farquhar, who had retrieved a great shining watch from his pocket, announced, "One hour to London."

All of them tumbled out of the coach to take that brief opportunity to stretch their legs and breathe the air.

And they all froze when they saw the redcoats.

The soldiers—about five of them, mounted—had clearly been watching the road. They were likely more interested in coaches going in the *opposite* direction from London, but one never knew.

Hawkes squeezed her hand gently, leaned, and whispered against Aurelie's ear, "Follow my lead."

And as they casually stretched, the soldiers stiffened when they got a look at Hawkes and Aurelie.

"Hold there, sir. We'd like to have a word."

The driver was having none of it. "I've a schedule, Sergeant, and this is the *royal mail*."

"We know, sir. We've been charged with the apprehension of a possibly dangerous fugitive named Mr. Christian Hawkes, who might be in the company of a Lady Aurelie Capet, and we've a few questions for your passengers."

There was dead silence as the soldiers—five of them—stared at Hawkes and Aurelie.

Hawkes eyed the soldier with mystification.

"This Mr. Hawkes sounds fearsome indeed, sir, but I am Mr. Paul Gallagher, and this is my wife, Mary." He didn't bow. He stood, feet akimbo, staring down at the soldier, unblinking.

"And I am Mr. Edwin Farquhar, and this is my wife, Mrs. Farquhar," said Mr. Farquhar, with equally icy calm.

"I fear, sir," said the officious young sergeant crisply to Hawkes, "that you fit precisely the description of an accused fugitive criminal we've been charged with locating. A tall, dark-haired dissolute man accompanied by a beautiful woman with dark hair and blue eyes."

Hawkes was very, *very* amused at the description, particularly the "dissolute," imagining the relish with which Brundage had delivered the word.

A breeze whipped the ribbons on Aurelie's bonnet and ruffled the cherries on Mrs. Farquhar's. One of the fresh horses, unaccustomed to standing still so long after being harnessed, whickered softly.

Aurelie's hand was still in his, and he could feel her pulse racing.

And then Hawkes took a half step forward, lowered his voice, as if he were discreetly informing the sergeant he'd forgotten to button his trousers after taking a piss, "I say, sir, I truly don't know what you're on about, but we are Mr. and Mrs. Gallagher, traveling from Baggleston to London, and it's not sporting to imply that Mrs. Farquhar here is homely."

The soldier went still. His mouth dropped open. "What on—I didn't—what—"

He nearly squeaked.

Mr. Farquhar slowly drew himself up to his full height and his chest puffed out like a rooster. "How *dare* you, sir. My wife was a *great* beauty in her day." He was incensed. "And she is a great beauty in *our* day. The *insult*, sir! How . . . dare . . . you."

Mrs. Farquhar gazed upon her husband as if he were Sir Galahad.

"Yes. There are clearly *two* beautiful women in this

mail coach," Hawkes said with dignified indignation. "As anyone with eyes in his head could see, and you have eyes in your head, soldier. Forgive me for being abrupt, it's just . . ." He took a breath. "I always assumed our soldiers possessed more grace. And I'm very disappointed and rather embarrassed for you, and for all of England. I fear I must know your name, Sergeant, so I can inform your superior officer."

The sergeant's mouth was still hanging open.

"I . . ." The word he finally uttered produced a dry squawk. He clapped his mouth closed again.

The expressions of the four soldiers behind him reflected that they were variously amused, embarrassed, and deeply uncomfortable.

The sergeant rallied. "I was told that both Mr. Hawkes and Lady Capet had unusual blue eyes," he said stubbornly. "And yours are rather unusual and—" He looked at Aurelie. "Hers . . . hers are . . ." He drifted off, and while Hawkes couldn't blame him because that's what Aurelie's eyes did to him, too, he fixed him with a deadly warning glare.

And then he gestured sardonically and abruptly with both hands to his companions, both of whom, because the fates were on their side, had blue eyes. Mrs. Farquhar's were quite large and round. Mr. Farquhar's were narrowed with outrage.

"Half if not most of England has blue eyes," Mr. Farquhar said in disgust.

Hawkes nodded in indignant agreement.

A fraught silence ensued.

The coach driver stood with his hands on his hips, his expression increasing in outrage with every passing second.

"And Sergeant, sir." Hawkes softened his tone, and then he sighed. "I fear the word 'dissolute' was painful to hear, because I'm certain there's a little truth in it. If I look a bit hard done by it . . ." He swept a hand through his hair, and lowered his voice and stepped toward the soldier. "My wife is *enceinte* . . ." he said delicately. "It's our first child, you see, and we are so very excited . . . but she's been ill all morning. I'm worried. It's been so difficult for her. We haven't slept at all. But she insisted we should go to London to see my father, who is ill . . . before he died because . . ." he turned to smile meltingly at Aurelie ". . . she's brave and very thoughtful and kind."

Aurelie smiled bravely and meltingly back at him.

And everyone at once visibly melted, soldiers included.

"*Awwww*," crooned Mrs. Farquhar, her hands clasped beneath her chin. "How lovely! You know, I thought something like that was afoot! It was like that with my first, too, my dear. I will tell you all about it during our journey."

Mr. Farquhar's blue eyes went wide with alarm.

The driver was the only one who had not melted. He was doing a veritable dance of impatience atop the coach. "THIS IS THE ROYAL MAIL, boys. Can we get on wi' it? They'll tan me 'ide! I've a perfect record with punctuality. This is obviously all bloody nonsense!"

The soldiers backed away. "Our apologies sir, and congratulations and felicitations on your blessing, Mr. Gallagher, Mrs. Gallagher," the sergeant said stiffly. He was a little pink in the cheeks.

Hawkes nodded, curtly as one who is graciously forgiving an egregious affront would nod, and he helped Aurelie back into the coach as if she was made of spun glass.

And the coach tore off again.

Chapter Twenty-Five

As promised, Mrs. Farquhar regaled Aurelie—well, the whole carriage, really—with stories of morning sickness and babies.

Aurelie had seemed unnerved into utter silence for a time for a few minutes after they were rolling again, but Mrs. Farquhar seemed wholly undaunted.

Mr. Farquhar slumped and vanished behind a newspaper, half of which he handed to Hawkes, so that he might do the same.

And after a time, Hawkes saw the tension leave Aurelie, and far from being appalled, frightened, or nauseated, a sort of animated fascination lit her up. She leaned forward and listened and asked questions and Mrs. Farquhar was clearly absolutely in heaven to have such an audience.

Hawkes wasn't entirely certain why this charmed him mercilessly. Her resilient embracing of the new, her willingness to learn and hope . . . It was like breathing clean air after too many years lived in a stifling room. He realized he had been released from a cell, but the cell was still in the process of releasing him.

He imagined what a delight it would be to travel with her, discovering new places.

But raising a family was a new frontier, too.

And the notion that she could, in fact, even now be *enceinte* . . . stole his breath.

So Hawkes pretended to read but he listened, too. Because frankly he rather hoped this extraordinary and ordinary part of life, the charming, disgusting, amusing rearing of children, would be part of their story, too.

Yes, they would suit, he thought, watching her with a sort of possessive wonderment. Neither one of them knew a damn thing about marriage, or even love. But they both confronted challenges resourcefully and resiliently, and they both would cherish the bloody hell out of every moment, knowing how precious and few they truly were. They would make love like animals, and face challenges like warriors.

He didn't feel he had the right to ask her yet to make a promise to him until he'd settled things with Brundage.

But they both understood that promise was already implicit. They were made for each other.

Aurelie was mute with awe for a time after they reboarded the mail coach. The frighteningly swift, skillful way in which Hawkes had seized the upper hand and maneuvered the circumstance in their favor when five soldiers were staring them down was clearly a glimpse of him acting in his professional capacity. It was rather extraordinary. She felt proud and unsettled—and, quite frankly, aroused. She hadn't realized until she'd met Hawkes that competence could be so unutterably thrilling.

He seemed to understand people swiftly and thoroughly, and this underscored for her how very much he knew of the world and how very little she did. And yet he never condescended to her.

He needed what she had to give, and the opposite was true as well. She wanted to bring him peace. She longed to make him happy.

They were the qualities he brought to bear as a lover, too: The ferocity, and insight. And a vulnerability she sensed he'd likely never shown another person. There was, improbably, an innocence in it. They were both new to real love.

She understood, too, how terrifying and implacable an enemy he would be—and how coldly tenacious. And at this she knew another thrill, a colder one at knowing the man who had inflicted such grave harm on both of them would soon be at Hawkes's mercy.

Before they'd boarded the mail coach that morning, he'd told her about the astonishing way in which the two of them were going to return to The Grand Palace on the Thames. He'd arranged this with Captain Hardy before he'd departed.

It apparently all depended on whether a ribbon was tied to the hook upon which the light was hung. And despite everything, she was rather looking forward to it.

A harrowing few moments ensued after they bid a fondish farewell to the Farquhars, who urged them to visit. There was a bit of a wait for a hack, during which Aurelie felt exposed and tensed every time she caught a snatch of the color red out of the corner of her eye, lest more soldiers appear. Hawkes's composure never wavered.

But he'd noticed Aurelie watching, somewhat wistfully, as the Farquhars departed.

"We'll have friends," he told her, quietly. With a sort of wry conviction.

We'll. She smiled up at him. Those three words

vividly conjured a future that lay on the other side of this day.

He smiled back at her, thrust out a hand, and a hack rolled to a halt, and they were away again.

Nearly thirty minutes later, at half past two o'clock in the afternoon, Aurelie and Hawkes emerged from a wardrobe in the room on the first floor of The Grand Palace on the Thames.

Hawkes had instructed the hack driver who had delivered them to the entrance of the livery stables to bring Aurelie's trunk to The Grand Palace on the Thames within the next hour, since it was simply logistically impossible to drop it down a hatch in a horse stall and maneuver through a tunnel that still smelled vaguely of a very singular blend of tobacco.

Hawkes had managed to employ one of the local, usually inebriated men that he had met and bribed earlier to knock on the door of The Grand Palace on the Thames to alert Hardy to his return with a code word he and Hardy had agreed upon earlier—"Gargoyle"—so the floor of the wardrobe was cleared for them.

Aurelie, her heart thundering, had silently followed his lead, as though in a terrifying and exhilarating dream.

And before he turned the knob of the door to emerge into the hallway of The Grand Palace on the Thames, Hawkes pulled Aurelie into his arms and kissed her as hungrily as if it were the first, or last, time.

They held on to each other, and both were imagining a time where they could linger together behind a locked door for hours, if they so chose.

"I'll return in a few hours," he told her gruffly, confidently.

With a certain resolve, he finally turned the doorknob. They emerged into the hallway, where they startled Dot bearing a tray. She stared at them, at first dumbstruck, then puzzled.

And then comprehension set in, along with delight.

"Welcome back!" she said brightly, finally. "Will you be in for dinner?"

THE NEXT PERSON on the scene, almost at once, was Captain Hardy.

"Lady Aurelie," Captain Hardy said gently, "would you be so kind as to join my wife and Mrs. Durand in the sitting room? They will be delighted and relieved to see that you have returned safely. I must speak to Mr. Hawkes on a matter of some urgency."

It was Captain Hardy's gracious way of saying he needed a word alone with Hawkes. Immediately.

Her heart gave a painful thud. She turned to Hawkes.

He nodded subtly, and his eyes were so tender and bracing she thought her heart would simply crack from the simultaneous worry and joy.

"Please be careful," she said, her voice frayed. And what she meant was, "I love you."

"I will," he said. And he meant, "I love you, too."

And she turned swiftly to go down the stairs.

CAPTAIN HARDY PUT Hawkes in the picture straightaway.

"I met with Valkirk, who now has possession of the account books you left with me. You should have seen his face when he looked through them, Hawkes. He understood at once. He spoke with the Alien Office, and they've quietly taken possession of the books at Guthrie's Antiquities. They're now surreptitiously watching the premises, along with Berwick, prepared to apprehend Vasseur when he appears. Brundage, for his matter, has put it about that you confronted him at his home, assaulted him, kidnapped his fiancée, stole a necklace, and that he believes you intend to go back to kill him as soon as you can. I'm not certain they believe him at this point. You can thank me later for that," he said ironically. Hardy had already told him how he'd sent the soldiers with a warrant away instilled with shame and filled with doubts about not only Brundage's veracity.

Hawkes told Hardy about the soldiers they'd encountered on the road, and Hardy's face went grim.

"Well, they aren't precisely guarding Brundage round the clock, but a few soldiers have been rotating in and out of St. James Square for the past several days. I suppose just so they can say they're attending to the earl's adamant concerns, even if those concerns are mad."

Hawkes took all of this in with cool equanimity. Not much of it was a surprise, but there was a good deal here for him to work with.

"They probably don't yet have in possession enough information to arrest Brundage. But they will. I have a plan."

"Valkirk has asked me to send word to him at once when you return," Hardy said.

Hawkes nodded shortly. "I in fact need to get a message somehow to Valkirk for my plan to work. I'm going to Brundage's townhouse now." He paused. "Has The Grand Palace on the Thames considered hiring a footman?"

Captain Hardy gave a short, dark laugh that tapered into a sigh.

"Welcome back, Lady Aurelie. We're so glad to know you are sound," Delilah told her.

Hawkes had departed again through the tunnel, which was still currently the only safe way for him to leave. And Captain Hardy had taken a message from Hawkes to the Duke of Valkirk.

"Thank you very much for your kindness," she said haltingly. Her cheeks ablaze. "I am terribly abashed to have left so abruptly and so mysteriously."

"Please do not apologize. Mr. Hawkes described for us a general sense of your circumstances before he departed to find you. And we are so sorry for your troubles."

"I am sorry to be a bother." Aurelie twisted her hands together. "I am so embarrassed to have caused an uproar after all, when I promised I would not."

Delilah gave a short laugh. "Well, I suppose we are even, Lady Aurelie, since we refrained from telling you that we actually have a good deal of experience with uproar. And we manage just fine."

All the other guests were listening to this with absorption, eyes bright and wide, as if this was a thrilling new story being read aloud in the sitting room.

Aurelie cleared her throat.

"I have heard that soldiers intruded upon the premises. I should like to tell you that I know definitively that Brundage is not a good man. I was once engaged to him, and I was compelled to leave very quickly. Mr. Hawkes was hired to find me. And so he did. I am now . . . with Mr. Hawkes willingly."

And she blushed hotly.

Still, she found she did not care what they surmised about her use of the word "with." Regardless, no eyebrows so much as twitched.

Conclusions had already been drawn, and the proprietresses of The Grand Palace on the Thames did not appear inclined to be shocked, and the guests took their cues from them. Mr. Bellingham, who was never to learn that she'd made wild love in his inherited cottage, looked fascinated and gently sympathetic. He was probably a very good and beloved vicar.

"Thank you for telling us, Lady Aurelie," Delilah said very gently. "We believe you, and we are terribly sorry for your trouble. It is our hope that all will be put to rights for you and for Mr. Hawkes soon."

"Thank you," Aurelie said. Her eyes began to well up. "I should be pleased if you would simply call me Aurelie. I am so terribly sorry to have . . . to have . . . deceived you all before. It just . . . it just seemed necessary."

Dot handed her a handkerchief embroidered with the initials TGPOTT, and Aurelie dabbed her eyes with it.

"Most of us have known a moment or two in our lives when we've needed to pretend we are something we are not," Angelique said gently. "Is there anything we can do for you now?"

"You have already done so much, and I am forever grateful. I want to sit here, and listen to the click of knitting needles, and the turning of pages. I should like to knit a coverlet."

Angelique found a ball of wool dyed blue; Delilah found a pair of knitting needles for her.

Quietly, all of the ladies knit, as if each neat stitch could restore order to the world. As if they were building safety nets for the men like Hawkes, who had already saved her, but whose lot it was to go and fight for justice even years after the war was over.

In the end, a footman was one of the heroes of the story.

Because despite the fact that he'd been told to do otherwise, Pike of course let Hawkes into Brundage's house.

Hawkes had watched the St. James Square townhouse long enough to know that no soldiers stood watch before calling at the door.

As instructed in whispers by Hawkes, Pike had called the earl out of his office on a pretense of concern over whether to dust a particular urn in the sitting room—to the earl's great and audible incredulity.

The earl's day was only going to get worse.

And now Hawkes waited and watched from behind one of the long velvet curtains in Brundage's vast office as the earl, wearing a scowl, settled with a sort of irritated vigor again at his desk, from which Hawkes had already removed a letter opener and hidden it in the windowsill. He'd done a swift search of the desk drawers for other easily accessible potential weapons and found none.

Brundage muttered something as he seized a quill, bent over a sheet of foolscap, and began filling it with words.

Hawkes silently, in minute increments, breath held, slipped from behind the curtain. His footsteps muffled by the gorgeous, thick carpet, he came to a stop right in front of the desk, pistol aimed at Brundage. And stood there.

Three or four seconds elapsed before Brundage paused in writing, sighed.

And glanced up.

His body rocked violently backward as though he'd been lightning struck and a sound emerged—a sort of choked howl of terror. His hand went over his heart.

His mouth was cavernously agape. "H-H-Hawkes . . . h-h-o-w . . ."

He paused to gulp for air.

"Perhaps I'm a ghost," Hawkes suggested pleasantly. "Perhaps it's all been a dream. Perhaps you actually succeeded in having me killed after all, Brundage. But just in case I'm real . . . you don't want to move a single hair, or I'll pull the trigger."

Brundage's complexion was a sickly green-white. He managed to get his mouth mostly closed but he continued to suck air through parted lips in short bursts, like a fish.

"I want you to know what it feels like, you useless, vile secretion," Hawkes continued conversationally. "And I want you to scream—go ahead, do it—with the knowledge that no one will come to help you in time. That no one cares. I'm just going to rest the barrel of this loaded gun against your head, and you are just going to have to take it. And do you know why? Because I want to. Because I can."

He leaned slowly toward him, and he did just that.

Brundage's face glistened with sweat.

His lips trembled. His words emerged as dry, staccato clicks. "Y-you . . . don't . . . want . . . to . . . do . . . this, Hawkes."

"Here is what I want," Hawkes said silkily. "I want you to sit with the feeling that you are helpless to do anything at all to defend yourself right now. I can violate you in any way I please. I can do anything

I want to you right now, and I want you to imagine what those things will be. Go ahead, let your imagination run amuck. I want this feeling to soak into your bones, into your desiccated black soul. This violation of your personhood. This disavowal of everything *you* might want or feel. This negation of you as a person. I have stolen every choice from you. Do you like that feeling, Brundage? Do you know why I'm doing this? Because I want to. Because I can. I have the power right now, over you. Do you know why and in whose name I'm doing this?"

Brundage's chest heaved.

"I asked you a question," Hawkes snapped. "Answer me *loudly* now or so help me God . . ."

"Yes," he croaked. "Aurelie. You're doing it for Aurelie! You're doing it because of what happened with Aurelie."

Hawkes slowly stepped back from Brundage, but kept the gun aimed on him. He lowered himself into the chair across from him.

"Open your eyes," he snapped.

With an enormous struggle, Brundage opened one, then the other.

"Her life is more important than your death," Hawkes said. "And so is mine. And that better be the last time you utter her name."

They stared at each other from across the desk.

"She lies," Brundage said.

Hawkes lunged forward and slapped Brundage across the face so hard his head snapped backward and he fell sideways out of his chair.

With difficulty, Brundage righted himself. His shoulders were moving like bellows now with labored breaths.

Hawkes kept his gun pointed at him. "I knew you were evil. But I didn't think you were. Just. That. Stupid. Test me again, Brundage," he hissed.

Brundage was furious now. His eyes were slits, and so was his mouth. But Hawkes could still all but *smell* his fear.

"L-listen to me, Hawkes. This m-melodrama is unnecessary. I never meant to become . . . so carried away with . . . with her. I *apologized* to her afterward. I gave her a damned emerald. And it ought to have been sufficient. She was to be my wife. It was to be my *right* to take her whenever I wanted, however I wanted. What difference would a few days have made? And she literally *pushed* me."

Hawkes's gut twisted when he realized that what he saw in Brundage's expression was a sort of supplication: he was actually pleading with Hawkes for understanding. He thought his point of view had merit. He wanted some affirmation from Hawkes that he wasn't entirely a monster, and perhaps some sympathy for the fact that he'd been at the mercy of his own inability to endure the anguish of not getting what he wanted, precisely when he wanted it.

And what he'd wanted from the beginning, as he'd told Hawkes, was Aurelie in his bed.

It would have been easier to understand if Brundage had been an actual monster, Hawkes thought. One without a conscience.

Instead, this man had created a hellish trap for himself, despite all of his advantages—and he'd scrambled ruthlessly to save himself again and again at any cost, no matter who needed to suffer. And now he was attempting to justify it in order not to experience a twinge of emotional discomfort.

Hawkes fought back a violent wave of nausea and something primal. Almost fear, of the sort that makes one stamp out poisonous spiders. But nothing quite so merciful as pity.

Hawkes said evenly, "Yes. We all know apologies make everything better. Perhaps you ought to apologize to Valkirk for the losses he suffered in battle when you informed your friend Florian Vasseur of the general's planned troop movements in exchange for five hundred pounds."

Brundage visibly stopped breathing. He was rigid. But Hawkes could almost sense the frantic rush of his thoughts.

"You've been thorough, Hawkes."

"Just thorough enough," Hawkes confirmed, pleasantly.

"All right. We both know you aren't going to shoot me, Hawkes, because that's the sort of man you are." Brundage said this with a tinge of bitter mockery. "So you must want something for your silence. Name your price."

"It's tedious how you think everyone can be bought, just like you, just as an expediency. You sold *me* out to the French, Brundage. I spent three years in prison. You sold your *country* out to the French. You sold Valkirk out. I wonder how many mamas would love to have their sons back. Ask them how much they want for their sons. Ask Valkirk if those losses haunt him."

Brundage was silent. His lips pressed together.

"You see, I know precisely how you did it. I know how you hid the money in the fake charity, the Society for the Relief of English Prisoners of War—the money funneled to you through the antiquities shop that was a front for Cafard's activities, that is. You arranged for me to be captured years ago because you sensed I was already suspicious, and if I'd kept looking, I would have discovered the entire truth. And then just a few short days ago you tried to have me killed because I was closing in on it again. You hadn't counted on *that*. How inconvenient for you."

"You can't *prove* any of this." Brundage was struggling to sound bored.

"Well, yes, I can," Hawkes explained patiently. "I've quite a bit of evidence, actually."

The ensuing silence all but rang in Hawkes's ears. Brundage regarded him through narrowed eyes. His breath came audibly through his nostrils. Sweat beads amassed like a regiment at his hairline and one at a time, poured down his green-white face.

And all the time Hawkes's gun arm never wavered. Brundage's view was still the dark center of his pistol. And he still apparently valued his sorry life, because he made no attempt to move.

"And so. I did what you paid me to do, Brundage. I found Lady Aurelie. She is safe, and will be from now on. She obviously wants naught to do with you. I also found . . ." With his free hand he dipped into his pocket and retrieved the emerald necklace, which he dangled from one finger.

Brundage's eyes flared, then fixed upon it, as if it were a mesmerist's pendulum.

"Since you'll never see your erstwhile fiancée again, which would you choose: The necklace for which you haven't yet paid, and which would lead to an enormous scandal and the loss of the ambassadorship if you don't return it . . . or the account book listing your fake charity, the account books listing the false prices you paid for the vases, or the account book from Guthrie's Antiquities showing how the vases were actually promptly returned for a much higher price. The balance of which was applied to the charity, whereupon, instead of directing the funds to Lloyd's Patriot Fund, you magically made your debt disappear. You can have only one of these things."

The silence was punctuated by a subdued pop from the low-burning fire.

Hawkes could just imagine the black snarl of Brundage's thoughts.

"Are you suggesting a deal?" Brundage said tonelessly. His voice was low, and it trembled a little.

"Which would you take if you could have them?" Hawkes repeated patiently. "Mind you, you can only have *one* of the books. Together they tell the story, so if one is missing, it's rather more difficult to prove your guilt. Decide which one is most incriminating, and I'll give it to you. I imagine you can always find some other way to swindle enough money out of someone to pay for the necklace if you can't do that now."

"You had no right to take those books from Harrigan's," Brundage said, quite superfluously.

"No, I suppose not. Why don't you report me to the authorities? I'll be happy to explain why I did it. You have until the count of five to make a decision. One . . . two . . . three . . ."

"My personal account book." Brundage's voice was a tortured rasp.

"Why is that one the most incriminating?"

"I think you already know why, Hawkes," he said coldly. "I think you know one can't get a Ming vase for five pounds fifty. Why the theatrics?"

Brundage's head jerked up and fixed on the door at the sound of scuffling footsteps, low voices, and a sharply muttered command.

Hawkes didn't turn.

But Brundage's face reflected a cold, ugly triumph and relief.

"Do you hear that, Hawkes? My footman has been instructed to hail the soldiers in St. James Square if you should dare show your face here. He must have heard our voices. It's a shame, but you won't leave here alive. You can go ahead and shoot me now, but if they find you like this, they'll splatter your guts all over my Axminster. It's my word over yours over what's happening here, and you're the one aiming a gun at an earl."

"Brundage," Hawkes said gently. "Who do you think invited me into your house? A man who was once knocked to the floor because he accidentally poured cognac instead of brandy. Cognac which he obtained from Guthrie's Antiquities, owned by one Florian Vasseur, also known as Cafard, who is even now in custody and willing to talk all about your association. A man whose brother, as it so happens . . . was killed at Dos Montañas. In other words, your footman."

Horror slowly flooded into Brundage's expression.

"But yes," Hawkes continued. "You have the right of it. Soldiers have converged upon your house. I believe one in particular would like to speak to you."

Brundage tracked his motions as Hawkes stood. Slowly, slowly. His gun remained trained on the earl as he crossed the Axminster to open the door.

To reveal General James Duncan Blackmore, the Duke of Valkirk, who had been listening all along.

Behind him were a half dozen grim-faced soldiers.

They were efficient, as always. They already had a warrant.

Hawkes's handprint was still faintly visible on

Brundage's cheek when they took him away. Per Hawkes's request, both of his wrists were bound.

Dinner hour came and went, and though Captain Hardy had returned that afternoon after getting a message to the Duke of Valkirk, Hawkes had not.

The meal was devoured by most and picked at by Aurelie. Conversation was desultory.

And now everyone—Delilah and Angelique and Dot, Captain Hardy and Lord Bolt, Mr. Delacorte and Mrs. Pariseau and Mr. Bellingham, had convened in the sitting room, and attempts at discourse seemed to be swallowed in the void of tension, as the clock softly bonged out seven, then eight o'clock.

"Do you want us to see if I can learn anything, Aurelie?" Lord Bolt offered quietly. "I will go to White's in—"

Rap rap rap rap.

A knock sounded at the door.

They all froze. Hearts and breathing and knitting and reading stopped.

"Well, that was a very ordinary knock, wasn't it?" Dot said presently, with cautious cheer. "Which makes it *out* of the ordinary this week. Isn't that rather funny?"

They all knew that Hawkes would only go to the front door if it was now safe for him.

"Funny indeed," Delilah said carefully, noting Aurelie's still hands, her white face. Her voice was taut. "Why don't you go and see who it might be, Dot?"

Every eye tracked Dot to the door.

Aurelie didn't breathe. She closed her eyes and said a silent prayer.

The tiny little latch of the peep hatch echoed like a mausoleum door when Dot swung it open.

"Mr. Hawkes!" she exclaimed happily, and flung open the door.

Aurelie shot to her feet abruptly. Her knitting fell from her lap.

Everyone stared at Mr. Hawkes as his footsteps crossed the foyer. No one breathed.

"They arrested the Earl of Brundage on charges of treason. I am safe and free from all suspicion now. Thank you all so . . . very much for your help. I appreciate it more than I can ever say."

He said this evenly, with the gravity it deserved, as one would deliver a military dispatch.

And his words were addressed to the entire room. But his eyes were only on one person.

And as everyone exhaled with enormous relief and murmured congratulations and welcomes, Aurelie remained frozen in place, her knuckles against her lips, her eyes burning with tears of joy and relief.

Hawkes moved toward her, gently took her other hand in his. Threaded his fingers through it.

And without a word, led her out of the room, across the foyer into the little reception room.

And she went, because she would follow him anywhere.

He closed the door behind the two of them.

She reached for him as he was reaching for her and he buried his face in her neck and breathed her in and exhaled. She stroked his hair and murmured soothing things to him.

"You are unharmed?" she murmured.

"Yes. It's done. I'm well. I'm in fact perfect now. And you are . . . are you . . ."

"Yes. I am well now that you are here." She brushed away tears.

He turned his head and his lips sought hers and she felt his sigh of relief and desire vibrate through her own body.

It was so easy to fall into the world of a kiss with him, and that's where she wanted to be.

But suddenly he loosened his arms and stepped back from her. "I've something I need to say at once," he said. Almost sternly.

He looked so earnest she knew a tinge of worry.

He took a deep breath.

"I had thought and thought about whether I had the right to ask this of you, when my future was still so uncertain. But maybe you've discerned that I'm no bloody martyr, Aurelie. We both know how capricious and fleeting life can be, and how glorious we can make it. And whatever we don't know about each other, I figure we'll learn along the way. I like you . . . *so* much." He gave a short, almost pained laugh. "And the way I love you makes my breath stop. I cannot believe the astounding good fortune I have to be alive at the same time you are. We can have any life you want—cottages, boardinghouses, green meadows, a trip across the ocean—we'll create it together . . ." His voice was hoarse now. "If you'll do me the honor of marrying me."

She drew in a sharp breath as happiness at once flooded her. Or was it peace? Perhaps they were one and the same, after all.

"I would follow you to the ends of the earth, Hawkes," she whispered.

"So . . . yes?" His face had gone as luminous as the man she'd once seen in a ballroom, long ago, from the top of the stairs. Shining like the North Star. Somehow, miraculously, she'd been steering toward him for her entire life.

"Yes, please. I would be honored to be your wife."

He heaved a great sigh and closed his eyes, then opened them. Shook his head wonderingly, lips pressed together, as she nestled into his reaching arms.

"I think you will make a splendid husband," she told him, when she was folded safely there again.

"So do I," he murmured. "I intend to do my very best."

Epilogue

HAPPINESS SEEMED an absorbing, rewarding occupation in and of itself. Sitting next to Hawkes on the pink settee where the king once rested his bum seemed a fine way to spend the rest of her life. Their hands were laced, and she looked down at his long fingers, wondering at the rough palm against her soft one, and thought, almost dizzily, of how familiar his hands would become to her over the years: the feel of them twined with hers or gliding over her body, holding their babies, helping her down from carriages. And she had only just learned his first name. He was a universe. And he was hers.

"I am thinking of something you said, Christian, when you were proposing to me."

"Would you like me to do it again? Did I leave something out? I wouldn't mind doing it over and over, just for the pleasure of hearing the word 'yes' from you again and again."

"Perhaps we can do it once a day, from now on, before breakfast. Or before we go to sleep at night."

He smiled at her.

". . . 'when your life *was* still so uncertain . . .'" she prompted. "That's what you said. Was."

"Ah," he said gravely. "You are magnificently astute. Well, this may come as a disappointment, Aurelie . . ."

She tipped her head. His eyes were glinting suspiciously, so she didn't worry.

". . . but you may never need to learn to haggle."

She put a hand to her heart. "I am devastated," she breathed. "Please explain yourself."

He raised her palm to kiss it. "The reason I was delayed in returning to The Grand Palace on the Thames today, my darling wife-to-be, was that the Duke of Valkirk wanted to tell me that the king has, upon his recommendation, created Letters Patent styling me Viscount Redvers in recognition of service to our country. Attached to the title are lands that previously belonged to the crown. And upon this land is a very fine manor house, surrounded by, as fate would have it . . ." He paused for effect. ". . . green meadows."

She was speechless.

And then all at once he went blurry as tears filled her eyes.

"If you want to stay in England, that is?" he said worriedly.

She knocked the tears from her eyes again. "This is so wonderful and it's only right, they did only the right thing, as you are a hero. It is a dream come true. I want only to be where you are."

"It means I'll have a seat in Parliament. I've also been offered a position at the Alien Office advising on matters of intelligence."

She went still. "Not of the sort that involves guns or knives or kicking or rescuing?"

"No. I am to be a sage now. A grizzled advisor. I will order other talented young men to do all of that and perhaps now and again make terrifyingly important decisions, but I won't need to work very often. And so. We'll have quite a decent income. Resign yourself to ordering servants about, provided we can get good ones."

She considered this thoughtfully. "You won't be bored, Christian?"

"How can I ever be bored? Merely sitting next to you right now is among the most fascinating things I've ever done."

He wasn't lying. When she smiled at him, he felt like a god. What a miracle it seemed that his existence made her happy, and making her happy was to be his job for the rest of his days. He was both exhausted and bliss filled, and the combination was nearly inebriating. Even now Brundage remained on the periphery of his awareness—and on hers, too, no doubt. There would be a trial, Hawkes's presence and testimony would be required, and the outcome, given the damning evidence, could mean that not only would Brundage lose his life, his very title would be eradicated. The historical record of him erased. For such were the consequences of high treason. There would be publicity. Hawkes's name would appear in the newspapers.

He was equal to it. He would see it through no matter what it took. The man would pay. And Aurelie's name would *never* be mentioned in any capacity during that trial. He would use his own influence to see to that and he had friends in high places, indeed.

Aurelie was going to marry a ruthless man.

He supposed this part of him never would change. And he would ruthlessly protect her and their family for the rest of his days.

"We shall find a home in London, too," he told her, more gently. "We will entertain. We will have dinners, and teas—"

"With perhaps singing, and dancing?" she said hopefully.

"Of a certainty. We shall invite Mr. Delacorte and Mr. Bellingham to sing duets."

She laughed.

And he liked the sound of it: For almost the entirety of his previous life, social occasions had been reasons to extract intelligence, or to ingratiate, or to build relationships—so seldom had he been able to lose himself in the lightness of a moment. They would all feel entirely new with her.

"We will go to balls, if you like. And the theater. We will see the sights in London, and have picnics, and make love anytime and anywhere—"

"Anywhere?" she breathed, as if he was telling her a fairy tale.

"—oh, *anywhere*," he assured her. "And any way we want."

"There are other ways?" And now her cheeks had gone very rosy.

"Oh, Aurelie. *So* many ways," he promised huskily.

She ducked her head and went mute and entirely pink, the very picture of a woman overcome.

"The duke also promised to facilitate obtaining a special license from the Archbishop of Canterbury so that we can be married as soon as possible. Perhaps even tomorrow or the day after," he told her softly.

"Christian?" she finally looked up. She sounded so subdued his heart gave a lurch.

"It cannot be soon enough," she said gravely. "I must know all of these other ways to make love immediately."

He nearly stopped breathing.

THEY WERE MARRIED by Mr. Bellingham in the sitting room two days later.

(Having spent two nights—also known as an

eternity—apart in their respective rooms, so as to respect the rules of The Grand Palace on the Thames.)

It was a modest affair, attended by everyone who lived at The Grand Palace on the Thames.

Modest, that was, apart from the tipsy singing, some uproarious laughter, and some sentimental toasts. Everyone was given a commemorative TGPOTT handkerchief, which were liberally employed.

But the new Mr. and Mrs. Hawkes, soon to be Lord and Lady Redvers, went up to his room—their room now—while all of the tipsy singing was still underway.

In tacit agreement, they made a beeline for the bed and sat down, gazing at each other, hearts pounding.

"We have taken a suite in the annex and will stay here for at least three months until we find a London home and we sort out your new title and job," she told him. Gently but firmly.

"We have?" He'd been lost in her eyes.

"Yes. I spoke to Mrs. Hardy and Mrs. Durand about it a few minutes ago. We will move into it tomorrow. You need to rest, Christian, in comfort and quiet, so you will heal and recover all of your strength."

It was true: Galloping on a horse, making vigorous love, and fending off attackers had been more than even Lord Bolt's skillful stitches could withstand. Hawkes lost two of them. And he, alas, needed them.

"A bit like my shirts and waistcoats," Delacorte had said, with a sympathetic wince, when they'd gathered around to fix him up again, "keep the ladies busy here. Ha ha!"

"Mr. Delacorte presents a unique challenge to our mending skills and we relish it," Angelique had agreed diplomatically. "And if you present a unique challenge to our mending skills, we'll see to you, too."

So he'd been repaired again just in time to be married.

"We are happy and comfortable here at The Grand Palace on the Thames, *n'est-ce pas*," Aurelie said, "and there is a smoking room for you and there will be singing and good food and everything we need?"

"*Oui*," he confirmed. "Everything we need." He'd already undone his cravat. And he was now watching, dazed by his outrageous good fortune, as everything he needed unbuttoned his waistcoat.

"And you have very, very beautiful muscles—" The waistcoat was hanging loose now, and her hands had deftly slipped beneath his shirt and were suddenly gliding over his chest.

"Have I?" he said on a rasp, after a bit of a delay. He was feeling light-headed. Not at all minding what appeared to be an abrupt change of subject.

"Every bit of you is very beautiful," she explained patiently, on a hush, as though teaching him a sacred text. "But you are a bit too thin yet . . ." She moved her hands to slide across his belly, below his bandage, dipped her fingers into the fall of his trousers and trailed her fingers across the slightly too-sharp bones of his hips and he drew in a hiss of pleasure. "And so you must eat many of Helga's good meals. And rest." She began, to his great, great delight, unbuttoning his trousers.

"Perhaps the only nourishment I need is kisses," he suggested, his voice a husk, as her hand wandered lower.

She kissed him long and languidly.

"And beef," she whispered against his mouth.

He smiled. "Anything for you," he whispered. "Forever."

Her trust and surrender undid him when they made love; her boldness and sensuality, her innocence and pleasure were gifts he'd never dreamed he'd deserved.

And they both knew that if either of them should ever wake up in the middle of the night, crying out in terror or anger, fighting off the grip of a memory, they would not be alone. They would always be loved. They would always be heard. Forever.

THEN CAME THE business of gathering up and inviting into their circle of happiness the mingled family and friends who would be a part of their shared lives from now on. The people at The Grand Palace on the Thames, naturally, were now among them. And they wrote letters: to her guardian, Jacques Le Clerc, to tell him, succinctly, that Brundage had been arrested and she was now married to a viscount; to her brother Edouard in Boston, who was surely confused and worried by this time; and Hawkes to his sister, Diana, to tell her he'd been married, where he was currently, and that he would love to see her soon, when he was well.

Jacques Le Clerc, returned from his wedding trip and in London on business, called upon them at The Grand Palace on the Thames.

"Aurelie . . . I'm grievously troubled by all that has transpired." They sat across from each other in the reception room, Aurelie and Hawkes on the pink settee, Uncle Jacques opposite them, tea in the middle. "I am so terribly sorry to hear that Brundage is not who I believed him to be, and to know what a near thing it was . . ." He closed his eyes and exhaled. "How close you came to wedding him . . . If I'd known . . . perhaps

I ought to have known. I *never* would have allowed a match. I am grateful to you, Mr. Hawkes, for your persistence in pursuing justice."

Hawkes and Le Clerc were already acquainted. They had respected each other's work for years. Hawkes nodded, once, graciously.

"I don't suppose any of us could have known what the earl was truly like, Uncle Jacques," Aurelie said carefully. "I have learned that we often become so attached to our assumptions about people that we cannot fully see them clearly."

Uncle Jacques nodded, eyebrows up. "Now that I am contemplating becoming a parent, I feel acutely the ways in which I have failed you. I was not equipped, you see, to be a father, nor did I manage well my own grief over the death of your parents. I hope one day you can forgive me for my absences. I should like it if we can be . . . better friends . . . and I should like to learn better how to be . . . how to be a part of a family."

"It is kind of you to say, Uncle Jacques," Aurelie said carefully, gently, "but there is nothing to forgive." She meant it. Life was short and capricious, and resentment could find no foothold in her current contentment. "I am forever truly grateful for all that you did for me and my brothers, and for my mother and father. You are the reason I am able to have everything that I want and need now."

She turned her face up to all she needed and wanted: the man sitting next to her on the settee.

"Thank you, Monsieur Le Clerc, for caring for her, and for taking on three orphan children," Hawkes said. "I shall be forever grateful that she learned to embroider and play pianoforte."

Aurelie pressed her lips together against a temptation to laugh.

"And we are grateful that you are a part of our family," Aurelie added, for the delicious pleasure of using the word "our." For she was an "our" now, and so was Hawkes.

She sensed Uncle Jacques was going to struggle to forgive himself, and to second-guess himself, because he was fundamentally a decent man. With luck, the family he raised with his new wife—they would be her cousins—would benefit from his new sensitivity.

They all sat in a slightly awkward, congenial sort of silence, and then Uncle Jacques gave himself a little shake and reached into his coat and came out with what appeared to be a small bundle of letters.

"These are from relatives in Paris whom you have not yet met," he said. "And they would like to one day meet you and your husband, if you are amenable."

Aurelie stared at the letters.

She glanced shyly sideways, at Hawkes.

And then she reached out and accepted the stack with a thrill of pleasure mingled with wariness. As though they might be a cache of stolen pound notes.

She drew in a long breath.

And suddenly it was almost too much.

"Aurelie and I shall read them together, thank you Monsieur Le Clerc," Hawkes said politely. He sensed she was a little overwhelmed with happiness, and speculation, and trepidation, and newness. Wondering how or if all of these people would fit into their lives. "And we will respond soon. Thank you, Monsieur Le Clerc."

"You are welcome, Lord Redvers. Do call me Jacques."

There was a pause as both Aurelie and Hawkes remembered that *he* was Lord Redvers.

"Hawkes will do among family." And Hawkes smiled at him.

Through diplomatic channels, Hawkes was able to contact the rightful owners of the emerald and diamond necklace, who then traveled to London to discreetly retrieve it from him. Its newly acquired, somewhat dark, glamor—it now was associated with an English traitor and an English hero, after all, as well as French aristocrats who had managed to keep their heads—ensured it promptly fetched a higher price than it would have if Brundage had ever actually purchased it.

"I've learned that one must often take a circuitous route to happy endings," Hawkes told them dryly. "And serendipity lurks in the damnedest places."

One chilly evening after a satisfying meal at The Grand Palace on the Thames, nearly two months after they'd been wed, Hawkes and Aurelie were telling everyone in the crowded, cozy sitting room about the house on Wimpole Street that they were contemplating purchasing, and the big party they planned to have if they did buy it, when there was a rap at the door.

Dot sprang up to see to it.

Through the peep hatch, Dot held a conversation. A bass voice rumbled faintly in response.

Outside, the wind was brisk enough to rattle window frames and rain was slanting down. Everyone in the sitting room waited with sympathy and speculation and a certain trepidation, wondering what circumstance would bring someone out to them, after dinner, and in such weather.

Then Dot said, *"Oohhhhh!"* delightedly and she swung the door open.

In strode a strapping stranger wearing a many-caped greatcoat that dripped onto the foyer floor. He whipped off his hat to reveal hair swept back from a proud, high forehead and impressive dark brows dipped in a scowl of concern. His eyes blazed. Such was his princely bearing that everyone, frankly, gawked at him in silence for a moment.

And then:

"DODO!" Aurelie howled.

Hawkes watched with disbelief as his wife launched from her chair, tore across the foyer, and leaped right into the man's arms.

"Oof!" said the man. "LiLi! Thank God!"

"My brother Edouard," she announced over her shoulder, so her husband wouldn't challenge the man to a duel or faint of shock.

She kissed both her brother's wet cheeks and he kissed hers and swung her about and put her down.

Hawkes did not quite clap his hand over his heart but it was sobering indeed to realize how bloody *relieved* he was. How thoroughly his heart and whole world was entwined with hers now.

And how overjoyed he was by her joy.

Aurelie dragged her brother by both hands into the sitting room. "Come and meet my darling husband and our friends. Dot, will you take Do—Edouard's coat and hat and bring him something warm to drink or perhaps you would like brandy?"

Edouard, who had been indescribably worried by the cryptic letter announcing she was coming to him, then startled and made suspicious by the rhapsodic one announcing her marriage to an erstwhile-spy-now-viscount, had boarded a ship from Boston practically upon receipt of the last one.

Hawkes shook hands with his new brother-in-law and found himself subjected to the kind of burning scrutiny of which only spies and older brothers seemed capable. Edouard's eyes were unnervingly like his sister's.

"It is a funny thing, Mr. Hawkes, but when I told my hack driver I was going to The Grand Palace on the Thames, he said your name immediately, and . . . well, I have never heard anyone's praises sung so thoroughly . . . by a hack driver."

It was said with amusement and challenge.

"Ah, that would be Mr. Berwick," Hawkes said contentedly. "I find it prudent to have friends in all places. Even Boston."

Edouard laughed, and settled into a chair, accepted his brandy, and smiled at the room as if he'd lived there for ages.

"WELL," DELILAH SAID to Angelique and Dot, sinking with weary satisfaction into one of their chairs in their cozy room at the top of the stairs a few nights later, "when we write our memoirs of life at the docks, I think we ought to call this chapter, 'There are easier ways to get a footman.'"

Angelique laughed.

It was tempting to feel like the point of a saga involving a house milling with soldiers, a fleeing Bourbon princess who had adopted an alias, a spymaster, and an evil fallen earl was to bring them the true footman of their—and, perhaps more worrisomely, all the maids'—dreams: Mr. Benjamin Pike.

He was well-spoken, tall enough to reach the sconces, and had proven himself brave and resourceful and able to hold a very righteous grudge—Hawkes had vouched for all of this. He could competently read and write. He *never* wanted to work for an earl again. He liked a bit of a challenge, and he liked sea air.

He possessed a fine wit, a calm presence, years of

excellent experience, his own recipes for silver polish and stain removal, a trust-inspiring deference and clear respect for women, shoulders for miles, very fine gray eyes and a jaw so cleanly hewn one could use it to cut glass. He was regrettably unequivocally handsome, from all angles.

("I'm a little worried all of the maids will be pregnant inside of a month," Angelique whispered to Delilah, after the interview.)

They hired him anyway.

They liked him very much, and one did not look gift horses in their handsome mouths.

(After all, he could reach all the sconces.)

But so far Dot and the other maids were behaving angelically. Almost tiptoeing about, and speaking in hushes, and performing their work with exquisite care. As though they simply could not *believe* their luck, and they thought Mr. Pike might be taken away from them if they put a foot wrong.

And Mr. Pike was somberly, flawlessly polite when he met the household staff, all of whom were women. He did not smile rakishly or twinkle or wink, though of course he might be capable of doing all of those things. One never knew. They would discover soon enough.

Captain Hardy and Lord Bolt were relieved, as well—they had their own work with the Triton Group, and they felt better knowing The Grand Palace on the Thames would have at least one large man on site when they were away. They'd subjected Mr. Pike to their own form of questioning.

"Do you know how to shoot?" Captain Hardy had asked.

Pike didn't blink. "Yes, sir. Quite well, sir."

"Do you know *when* to shoot?" Bolt asked.

Ben Pike gave this some thought. "When physical

force is insufficient to any problem at hand, and a lady is in danger, strikes me as the appropriate circumstance."

Bolt whistled. "Oh, well said."

"I'm satisfied," Captain Hardy said. "Welcome to The Grand Palace on the Thames, Mr. Pike."

"Do you suppose Mr. Pike will be lonely, as he's the only male servant?" Dot asked casually. Perhaps too casually.

"Why, Dot, do you think we ought to get a matched set?" Angelique said this earnestly, with wide, innocent eyes. Delilah bit her lip to restrain a laugh.

Dot froze mid-stitch, breath held, teeth in bottom lip, eyes saucer-sized with hope.

"Perhaps we'll just start with one footman and see how it goes." Delilah shot Angelique a droll, quelling look. "What a relief it will be to have someone to run to and from the annex and about town for us, if necessary, and to answer the . . ."

She stopped herself just in time.

But Dot's head jerked up alertly in alarm.

Answering the door was her favorite thing to do. She thought it was like opening a gift every time.

"But I'll still answer the door?" she pressed, worriedly, into the silence.

They'd in truth always been concerned about Dot's safety when it came to answering the door later at night, just before curfew.

"Perhaps whoever gets there first, between you and Mr. Pike . . ." Angelique mused wickedly, and Delilah bit back a laugh.

They could just imagine the thundering of footsteps from all parts of the house, shoving matches at the door between Dot and Mr. Pike . . .

But Dot, like everyone else, was daily discovering new qualities in herself, and one was a sense of competition.

Suddenly Mr. Pike the footman seemed like more of a rival than a gift.

"I should like to answer the door," she said firmly.

They were proud of her for asserting her preference. Though it presented a bit of a sticky wicket.

"But we're concerned for your safety, Dot, especially at night, and we feel that bringing a gun straight to the door with you might send the wrong message. Why don't we discuss it when Mr. Pike begins his new job?"

Which would be in a week; he'd gone to visit his mother and sister before beginning his new job.

There were still several empty suites in the annex, and a few empty rooms in the main house. Aurelie and Mr. Hawkes would be moving out soon. Mr. Bellingham, who'd had an almost too-marvelous time in London, had stayed nearly two months, and promised to return again soon and invited everyone to visit him at his vicarage. The Grand Palace on the Thames was prospering, but they knew prosperity was like the tides; it ebbed and flowed ceaselessly. And now they needed to feed and house an entire other man, and pay him, to boot.

(Little did they know, that even as they sat there, like a storm forming out at sea preparing to move onshore, events were percolating that would indirectly lead an extraordinary man, and a remarkable woman, right to their door . . .)

While their husbands waited for them in their respective rooms, the ladies reviewed the business of the day and planned for the next.

Contentedly, Delilah fished one of Mr. Delacorte's shirts from the enormous basket of mending, which was in some ways emblematic of all of their blessings: Some ragged, some fine, occasionally tear- or blood-stained, much loved, never ending. There was nothing in that basket that couldn't be repaired, and for that reason they found it one of the most satisfying tasks of all at The Grand Palace on the Thames.

And then suddenly a vigorous knocking sounded at the door.

They all went still, and exchanged glances of amused anticipation and speculation.

"It's not yet eleven o'clock," Dot said hopefully.

Delilah and Angelique's eyes met in a wry, silent consultation.

"Go ahead, Dot," Angelique said.

And while she and Delilah stood to smooth their hair and untie their aprons, Dot sprang from her chair and scrambled down the stairs to discover who their next chapter might be.